DEFIANCE

HELL ON EARTH BOOK 4

IAIN ROB WRIGHT

Gates → #1
Legion → #2
Extinction → #3

IAIN ROB WRIGHT
Fear On Every Page

"Today I choose life."
— **Kevyn Aucoin**

"Be ashamed to die until you have achieved some victory for humanity."
— **Horace Mann**

"We cling to what is gone. Is there anything in this life but grief?"
— **Illyria, Angel (1999 TV Series), The WB**

PART I

1

LUCAS

"Get ready," said Lucas. "The Red Lord is about to grace us with his presence." The Infernal Throne hissed and spat.

Heat filled the chamber, and a million screams erupted from the flames. Something massive emerged and started down the steps towards them. Something wicked.

"Holy shit!" said Vamps. "I'm gunna need a bigger sword."

Daniel and Rick froze in place, staring up at the horror before them.

Vamps stood with Damien and Aymun, each of those men also frozen in shock.

Lucas stood alone.

The Red Lord was a giant, not in stature but in presence. Its form seemed to smother existence itself. Lucas recognised the beast immediately, the mystery of his enemy's identity finally revealed to him.

The Red Lord was kin.

Lucas could barely breathe. "I-It can't be."

"What?" asked Rick, daring to glance back for a split-second. "What is it?"

Lucas shook his head. "The end of everything."

The Red Lord grabbed Daniel while the fallen angel was still stunned. Perhaps he recognised the Red Lord's true identity as well. The Red Lord broke him in his fist and allowed the angel's crushed body to fall to the ground.

Lucas tore the air with his screams, inadvertently hurting his companions with the damaging frequency. The Red Lord was unaffected by the sonorous assault and marched towards his next victim—Aymun.

Lucas threw out a hand and sucked Aymun backwards out of danger, the air swirling around him and lifting him away. Once Aymun was beside him, Lucas grabbed the man's skull and infused him with knowledge. "We can't win this fight. Not here. I'm getting you all out of here. Find each other back on Earth and stay strong. Fight another day."

Aymun was confused, but before the man had a chance to question, a gate appeared behind him and yanked him through it. He was gone in less than a second. Vamps gawped at Lucas, his gold fangs flashing. "What you doing, man? We came here to gank this bitch."

"Not here. Just get through the gate and—Damn it!" Lucas leapt aside as the Red Lord tried to crush him with an almighty fist. The monster struck the ground and the whole of Hell trembled.

Damien appeared and gathered Lucas to his feet. "I never seen you scared before, boss."

"It's been a while since anything gave me cause."

"Who is this geezer? Why won't you fight?"

"Because, our enemy can't be killed. Not here. Maybe not anywhere. We need to leave and regroup. I need time to think."

The Red Lord cackled, an awful sound, but it was broken

by the shrill voice of another. The weaselly politician, Windsor cowered before the terrifying beast and begged for his life. "I-I-I'm on your side," he stammered. "I serve your man, Oscar Baruta. Please, I am not... I am not your enemy. Oh god."

Lucas had to give the fella props for bravery. It took a lot to stand before the universe's wickedest being and try to start a discourse. It was pointless of course, and Lucas winced as he awaited the inevitable outcome.

The Red Lord studied the tiny man before him and then blinked its many glistening black eyes.

Windsor's spine spewed forth from his mouth and clattered on the ground. His formless body crumpled like a bedsheet.

Lucas sighed. "Not the first spineless politician I've met. Idiot."

Vamps swung his flaming sword at the Red Lord, but the instant it struck the leathery flesh of its huge right leg, it exploded into ash. Vamps wheeled backwards, horrified. "She-it!"

"Get away," said Lucas. "All of you get away. We must leave here."

Rick stared down at Daniel's broken body, but then looked up and shook his head. "We leave now and we're back to square one."

"We stay and we die. Through the gate. Now!"

Damien was the first to obey. He would never run from a fight, but he would also never disobey Lucas either. It appeared his obedience outweighed his pugnacity. Good.

Lucas threw out a spark that hit the Red Lord and delayed his approach. It gave him a chance to grab Rick and throw him through the gate.

That left just Lucas and Vamps. Vamps was retreating, no

longer brave or courageous, but terrified and defenceless. "Get to me, lad. I'll get your arse out this fire."

Vamps leant forwards and then broke into a sprint. The Red Lord stomped after him.

"Run, lad!"

"I am, yo!"

The Red Lord kicked out and caught Vamps in the back, sending him flying.

Lucas threw out both arms and closed the gate he'd just opened, then reopened it ten-feet in the air, to catch Vamps. Before Vamps disappeared through the gate though, the Red Lord reached out and snatched him out of the air. But the massive beast could not stop himself quickly enough to avoid going into the gate itself. Both it and Vamps tumbled through together and disappeared.

Lucas found himself alone, standing there in silence, in the centre of the throne room that had once been his. What had just happened? The Red Lord had passed through a gate. What did that mean?

He walked forwards, heading up the bony steps towards the Infernal Throne. Could he reclaim it and regain dominion over Hell? The notion of being tethered to this vile realm once more drove him to despair, but with the throne came great power. Power to control the damned. If he took the mantle of *Infernus* once more, he could close the gates and prevent any more evil spreading to the Earth. It would be a mighty blow to the Red Lord's plans. Now that Lucas knew who his enemy truly was, he could try to find a way to end him. The throne would help him to do that.

There was no choice but to do it. Lucas would have to become Lucifer. He just hoped he could resist the darkness that came along with the name.

Lucas traversed the final steps to his destiny and felt the pull of power. His soul trembled.

His entire being grew hot.

Something was wrong. The throne belonged to him, forged of his own will. Yet what he was experiencing was something hostile and foreboding.

Pain jolted his mind, and he felt himself being pulled apart, his very atoms splitting. What was happening? What had ahold of him?

"No. No!" He reached for the throne, needing to take it and its power. Once sitting in it, nothing would remove him from this place. He would hold dominion over all.

He reached out a hand, but before he could touch the throne, his flesh disintegrated to burnt ash. The more he moved, the more of him that vanished. Agony consumed Lucas, but he couldn't summon a scream. A searing heat exploded inside him and he ceased to exist.

Hell's throne room lay empty.

2

CALIGULA

Blood salted the general's tongue. Once, in his explorative youth, he'd indulged in the greasy flesh of a giraffe bull, but it paled compared to human flesh.

"Imperator," one of his minions trilled. A lowly slave by the name of Rux; the creature cowered, ready to deliver a message.

"What is it, slave? Speak now or lose your tongue."

Rux flinched, trembling as he gave his reply. "T-The human army has scattered, Imperator. Our troops folded their right flank and rolled them inwards just as you commanded. Y-You desired I alert you at battle's end, so you may—"

"Silence! Do not deign to speak of my desires."

"Yes, Imperator!"

"If that is all you wish to say, then begone, slave." The general waved a massive hand to dismiss the Gaul, and he couldn't fight the cruel grin spreading across his skeletal face. It had been unnecessary to lead the assault—his handpicked Germanic Guard were more than capable—but he savoured that moment when an enemy's morale shattered. That rolling wave of despair spreading across an army was ambrosia. A delicious cascade of terror.

The general exited his tent and set eyes upon the battlefield. The human army had entrenched itself at a *car supermarket,* a place—his scouts informed him—where humans had once purchased their motorised litters. Elegant, in some undefinable way, the steel boxes now littered the green and grey landscape as relics of a forgotten kingdom. He saw not their utility. What use had they been to the humans when war had visited them?

The humans had positioned several of those *cars* end-to-end, forming a steel palisade behind which to cower. It served them well for a time. Battle had raged for several days and nights now, with the humans firing their tiny cannons almost endlessly at the beginning—unleashing metal wasps that flew so fast you didn't see them until they were buried in your flesh. The general had to admire the musicality of the slaughter the humans directed at his own troops. Even *he* had been stung several times, but his army took the brunt, falling by their hundreds in the first hours. But eventually, the human cannons fired less and less, and whatever ammunition they consumed ran out.

The humans postponed their fate a while longer after that by employing yet another impressive weapon, this time an innocuously dull metal pipe pointed towards the sky. It summoned fire from the heavens and reduced the general's forces to cinders. It nearly turned the tide in the human's favour, but the general had instilled too much fear in his troops for them to flee. Never would his troops dare rout. Before two hours passed, the heavens ceased their fiery fury, and the human resistance died out. As with the barbarians in Germany, the general had outlasted them.

At his order, a legion of troops clambered over the human's

car-wall and set about them with excitement, tearing open throats and gouging eyeballs. Some humans tried using their empty cannons as batons, but their impudence was swiftly punished. They fell in their hundreds.

A rapturous orgy of death.

A glorious day. May Jupiter himself give gratitude.

As he walked amongst his adoring legions, it reminded him of his triumphal march along the floating bridge between *Baiae and Puteoli,* basking in the adulation of the baying masses. That his glorious mother empire was now a thousand years dead tore at his soul terribly, but a new empire rose in its place. Humanity would tremble before its Red Lord and his loyal generals. Like the Red Lord, Caligula too was divine—a living god.

I have existed from the morning of the world and I shall exist until the last star falls from the night. Although I have taken the form of Gaius Caligula, I am all men as I am no man and therefore I am a god.

Let them hate me so that they may fear me.

Caligula's elite Germanic Guard lined up before him as he crossed the road towards the human fortifications. They were the finest assemblage of battle-hardened warriors—picked only to serve at his side. Their humanity had shorn away long ago, replaced by an oily darkness, yet their loyalty to Caligula was absolute. In life, they had slaughtered the treacherous senate to avenge his assassination. In death, they would murder the world at his bidding.

Each guard now held a human in their grasp, an offering for their Imperator—their dignified and highest leader. Caligula turned to the first human captive, a woman masquerading as a soldier, and scowled. A woman on the battlefield was an insult to Mars. She begged him for mercy, her warrior's clothing now torn away to reveal her bloodied bosom. All manner of fluids glistened upon her naked chest. Caligula reached out and brushed his bony fingertips against her cheek. "Quiet your weeping, child, your suffering is at an end."

"P-Please, just—"

He sank his thumbs into her eyes and left her wailing in agony. Licking his bony fingers, Caligula moved onward. The next human was more defiant, a thick-chested male scowling and spitting curses. A lengthy gash split the man's torso and slowly bled him to death, yet he did not fall to fear nor despair. Caligula held a modicum of respect for this one. "You are dying, human."

"So fucking what? Least I took a dozen of you limp-dick pussies with me. Do your worst; you don't scare me." The Germanic Guard struck the back of the human's shaved skull, but it only drew another stream of defiant curses. This human was tough.

Caligula sneered. "I do not need fear, human. I am fattened by it already. You are a treat to be savoured at my leisure, a mug of *Falernian* wine or fresh snails. Let us take a taste." He tore off the man's ears and stuffed them into his screaming throat, choking away the defiance at once. By the end, the man most certainly *did* fear Caligula.

The general toyed with the other offerings for a while, then approached the single-story building housing the last human holdouts. They fired their cannons from the windows, and occasionally threw exploding rocks, but it was easy to read from their faces that they knew they were beaten.

Caligula's troops surrounded the building waiting for his orders, so he stepped forward and addressed them.

"My blessed legions, today you have earned yourselves great victory. Each of you has distinguished yourself before the gods, including me. The battle was hard fought, yet no enemy can resist the strength and fervour of Roman hearts. We are a new empire rising." The troops cheered, and writhed like unclean beetles, but while he might loathe each of them individually, he adored them as a whole. His mighty legions. "We have spent two seasons in this wretched land," he continued, "amassing our strength while reducing the enemy's. The journey has led us here, to victory. This land's north is wiped clean. Our brothers in the South will have eradicated our enemies there, and therefore this island belongs to us. And soon, the world. The Red Lord shall deliver us our paradise, a home for warriors and gods." He smiled at his troops, admiring the darkness in their hearts. "From different backgrounds you may be—cohorts forged from Hell itself—today you stand as Romans. The chosen people."

The demons cheered again, an exultant cry of a conquering army.

"What would you have us do with the leftovers, Imperator?" asked one of his guards, pointing towards the building and its barricaded windows. There was a sharp *ping* and a nearby demon fell down dead. Caligula knew the humans were aiming for him, for their only victory now would be to take out the enemy's general. Such a thing would not happen though.

"Do we possess fire?" Caligula asked his bodyguard, a badly scarred warrior named Adelgis.

"Yes, Imperator." The guard nodded towards a nearby barrel. "We have the human's *petrol*. We learned how to ignite it. Jupiter himself would marvel."

"Then set the human's fort ablaze and ensure they remain inside as it burns. The day has not yet ended. There is time yet for more screaming."

Adelgis grinned and rushed to carry out his orders. Caligula remained, satisfied, while the last of the humans stared out from their holes in terror. His good mood curdled, however, by the re-emergence of Rux. Just for the sheer joy of it, he struck the demon in the face and sent the creature tumbling to the ground. Caligula stood eight-feet compared to Rux's five, which made it feel like he was striking a bug. "What is it, slave?"

Rux clambered to his feet, flinching as he feared another blow. "Apologies, Imperator, but our messengers have returned from the South. They... They bear horrendous news."

Caligula raised a hand, ready to strike the slave again, but stayed himself a moment. "What news? Victory is ours, surely?"

"No, Imperator!" Rux cowered. "The South is lost. The humans have fortified themselves along the coast and pushed back. Our army there is in ruins, the demon lords have fallen, and several gates have been destroyed. The southern human army is turning north to reclaim the land. Eventually, they shall face us here. We must prepare."

Caligula struck Rux in the mouth and kicked him while he was down. The fury of it sent the small demon tumbling across the road. Several moments passed before the Gaul stirred, but by then Caligula's mind was elsewhere. He turned back to the humans inside the building, now trapped and encircled by the liquid they called 'petrol.' One of his guards struck the pavement with a heavy, metal pipe and sent sparks into the air. The petrol ignited, and a fiery imp grew into the spirit of *Ignis*, spreading out and racing in all directions. Soon the flames encircled the entire building, but the screams from inside were not enough to quiet the probing voices in Caligula's mind. It reminded him of the insecure squabbling of Rome's curia.

How can the South be lost? The bulk of our army is there! The scouts must be mistaken. What a travesty is this? I shall see these scouts disembowelled, Caligula decided, as the inferno took a painfully long time to do its job. In a different moment, he might have enjoyed the prolonged misery, but right now all he wanted was to think in silence. *Had his brothers truly fallen? Mighty Lords of Hell defeated by human insects? What did this mean for the Red Lord's plans? The invasion would fail if humanity was not extinguished.*

No, Caligula chided himself. *The invasion is not a failure. The war is not yet concluded. My duty is done, my obligations fulfilled. As general of northern Britannia, I succeeded. Lord Amon and the others though...*

Damn them.

Damn them back to Hell.

Caligula would continue this war alone if need be, for he was the earthly incarnation of Jupiter himself. These lands were his. If no other lords remained, then so be it. It meant he would be favoured amongst the Red Lord's servants.

Caligula watched with glee as a human threw himself out of a window, fire singeing the flesh from his back. He staggered in agonised confusion, flesh bubbling on his bones, eyes melting in his head. Caligula's troops tore his flesh apart hungrily.

Burnt flesh and *glory*.

3

TED

Ted wiped dirt from the truck's petrol gauge with the cuff of his grimy blue jumper but succeeded only in adding more grime. He needed to find diesel soon, but the prospect made him groan. It was getting harder and harder. The pumps at the petrol stations and supermarkets needed power to run, and the National Grid had kicked the bucket over a month ago now. The last time he'd refuelled, he'd pried open a manhole cover and ferried up the diesel with a bucket on a rope, but most fuel tanks were more secure than that. Easiest way to get diesel these days was to syphon it from other vehicles or scavenge it from garages and sheds, but it was a time-consuming chore. Two petrol cans in his truck's flatbed were the last of his reserves, about another three-hundred miles. That might seem a lot, but when you spent your entire day driving, the road rolled up fast.

Just keep heading north, he told himself. If he lost that purpose….

Just keep heading north.

Ted had started his journey a month ago in Colchester,

and it had been hard going every inch of the way. At first, he'd considered heading south, after hearing rumours of the Army gaining a foothold there, but if there was a fight going on, he wanted no piece of it. So he headed the other way, his only plan to head north until the land fell away to the sea. That was his first and last destination.

But right now, something was attempting to get in his way.

A pack of demons presented itself in the middle of the road a hundred-metres ahead of him. They saw him coming and spread out to block his path. It would be impractical to try to run them down. Ted had seen enough wreckages to know flesh and bone did not yield the way it did in the movies. Windscreens shattered, axles snapped, and tyres punctured. He couldn't hope to drive around them either. The demons were remorseless monsters, but they weren't stupid. Often, if they saw you turning to avoid them, they would throw debris in your path and try to make you veer off the road or into a tree. They didn't fear being run over, they feared their prey getting away.

So Ted never tried to avoid them anymore. He never tried to run the demons over or go around. Not anymore. Not since...

He slowed and came to a stop, switching off the engine. The demons approached cautiously, twenty-feet from the nose of his truck now. His stopping had made them wary, burnt faces betraying their confusion, and when he stared at them defiantly, they became even more puzzled.

Ted climbed out of his truck and stepped out onto the road. The demons hesitated, still confused by what they were seeing. Ted went around to the side of his truck's flatbed and pulled out his 5KG sledgehammer. Blue-handled and copper-headed, the sight of the weapon was enough to incite the demons to launch their attack, but Ted stood his ground and taunted them. Their screeching hurt his ears, made his temples pound with blood, his heart beat faster.

Bring it on.

The bunched-up muscles in his middle-aged back flexed in unison, and he swung the hammer horizontally, striking the nearest demon in the ribs and folding it in half. Then he threw a kick to keep another demon from getting too close while he readied his next swing. The demon tumbled backwards into its pack-mates and gave Ted the space to thrust his hammer. The heavy copper mallet shattered the demon's face. Next, he swung it overhead and crushed another demon's skull flat like a stamped-on Coke can.

More demons threw themselves at Ted, forcing him to stop swinging and use the hammer for defence. He held it with the shaft across his chest and thrust it out laterally, checking any demons in front of him.

They spread out around him.

Ted took several steps backwards towards his truck, trying to keep from being overwhelmed. But while the truck gave him cover, it also made it easier for the enemy to trap him. The more they surrounded him, the harder it was to wield his hammer—or make a run for it.

He just needed to get himself a yard of space.

He swung his hammer in another massive arc, striking the bodies of two demons and knocking them away. Then he took his chance, reaching into the truck's flatbed and retrieving the gas-powered nail gun he kept there. It was his back-up weapon, running on a battery that wouldn't last forever, but when he used it, Christ, did it do the business. Having to move fast, he yanked the trigger and released a stream of 1-inch brad nails into the air at head-height. His jaw locked in a maniacal grin as demon skulls spat blood from dozens of tiny holes opened by the whizzing nails. Demons were resilient creatures though, and not all fell to the sudden onslaught. Some took nails to the eyes and neck and merely hissed in anger.

Ted tried to create more space with his hammer, but found it wrenched away and thrown to the ground. He brought the nail gun around with his other hand and fired off another stream of brads. More blood stained the air as demon faces tore apart, but not enough of them went down. They absorbed the wounds and kept on coming.

They continued closing in on Ted.

Damn it.

A demon slipped inside Ted's defences and grabbed him by the throat, pinning him against his truck. He tried to bring up his nail gun again but couldn't get his arm at the right angle. The demon snarled. Ted closed his eyes and thought of Chloe.

Rat-a-tatta.

Ted spluttered as wet coated his face. He opened his eyes and saw the demon's head reduced to a pulp. Its hand slipped away from Ted's throat and its body slumped to the ground.

The thing was brown bread. *Rat-a-tatta-tat.*

Like a firework display, demon heads erupted one after the other, a bloody mist filling the air. The demon mob dispersed, scrambling to spread out, and desperate to locate whoever was killing them. The unidentified gunman continued firing. Demons continued to fall.

Ted scooped his hammer up off the ground and pounded it into the back of the nearest demon he could find, crushing its spine. Then he set about mopping up the other demons while the mysterious gunman continued laying down fire. Within a minute, more than a dozen demons lay dead in a pile in the centre of the road.

What the bleedin' 'ell just happened?

Ted was uninjured, but out of breath. He was also confused. Scanning the tree line, he searched for his saviour, but it wasn't until they stepped out onto the road he saw them properly.

It wasn't what he expected.

4
___

TED

The young woman appeared to be a soldier, togged in combat fatigues with webbing around her waist. In her arms, she held a combat rifle, but thankfully she pointed it at the ground as she crossed the road towards him. It'd been a while since Ted had last seen another survivor, and the sudden arrival of one now was unsettling. He wanted to get back in his truck and speed away, but he knew he should at least thank the young woman for her help.

"You alright?" The soldier kept the rifle pointed at the road, but glanced warily, obviously ready to raise hell at a moment's notice. Despite her previous lethality, she smiled at Ted warmly like a shop assistant—he didn't return the gesture, wasn't even sure if he could. To smile was so utterly alien now.

"I'm fine," he told her. "Cheers for the help."

"What happened, pet?" Her brown hair was bunched up so tight it failed to move in the breeze. "Did your vehicle break down?"

"No, I stopped."

She frowned. "Why would you stop right next to a pack of demons?"

Ted shrugged. His obligation to chat had expired once he'd given his thanks, and now he just wanted to leave. "Look, I appreciate you wasting bullets at my expense, luv, but you should get back to whatever you were doing."

The soldier rolled her shoulders tiredly, making the rifle bounce on its strap. "I wasn't doing much of anything, mate. Been sticking to the trees to stay hidden, but thought I heard a vehicle." She nodded to his truck. "Good thing, too, because one-second later and those dees would have ripped you apart."

Ted grunted. "I had it covered."

"Aye, well... It's been a while since I came across another person. Were you heading somewhere?"

"North."

"What's north?"

Ted sighed. "The sea."

"You planning to get a boat or something? That might not be a bad idea."

Ted finished talking and turned away. There was no safety in numbers. The bigger the group, the higher chance of demons spotting you, and he couldn't afford to let anything stop him from doing what he needed to do. He shouldered his hammer and tossed the nail gun in the flatbed. "Like I said," he grunted. "Get back to whatever you were doing, luv."

"Hey, no need to be like that, pet. We're all in the same boat, aye? If we can help each other—"

Ted snarled and cut the soldier off, shoving a finger in her bewildered face. "I don't need or want your help, okay? What I want is to get back on the road."

The soldier's brief shock transformed into irritation. "You stay on the road, you're dead. There are dees everywhere. You know those gates opened all over the place, right? There's no safety out in the open like this."

Ted barged past to the front of his truck. "I'll take my chances, luv."

She stumbled out of his way, then glanced around again as if worried the movement would bring unwanted attention. She was like a deer suspecting predators. Maybe that was what had gotten her this far.

The soldier seemed to finally accept his inevitable departure and stepped away from his truck. "Alright, suit yourself. Be careful on the road, okay?"

"Don't worry about me." He swung the door to his truck open and climbed into the driver's seat. Before he slammed the door shut, he gave the soldier one last glance. "Look, thanks again for your help."

"Aye, don't mention it." She patted the truck's bonnet but couldn't disguise her sadness. "Safe travels, pet."

Ted twisted the key to start the engine, but instead of rumbling to life, an unhealthy ticking emanated from beneath the bonnet. The dashboard lights flickered but were unable to claw themselves to life. "Come on, damn it!" He twisted the key back and forth, again and again. All he could summon though was that mocking *tick-tick-tick*. He pounded the dashboard with his fists. "Bastard!"

"Sounds like the battery." The soldier stood at his window, arms resting on top of her rifle. "Pop the hood, and I'll have a nose."

Ted shoved the door open and nearly hit her. "I'll handle it myself."

"What the hell is your problem? I'm only trying to..." She trailed off as something captured her attention. Staring grimly at the front of Ted's truck, she muttered to herself, "Ah shite."

"What? What is it?" Ted bustled his way past and stood in

front of his van. For a moment, he didn't understand what he was seeing, just a ragged puncture in the side of his bonnet. Then he realised. "You shot my bleedin' engine, you daft cow!"

The soldier apologised profusely, but Ted wasn't interested. He shut her up with a stern shove, sending her backwards by several steps. His anger took hold of him, and he had to turn away to keep from losing control. The soldier's reaction took a few seconds. At first, she stood there looking stupefied, but then her face creased in anger. Thankfully, she didn't point her rifle at him. "You've got a screw loose, mate."

"I'm not your mate!"

"Damn right, you ain't. If you're not careful, you'll end up my enemy."

Ted sneered. "And then you'll shoot me, right? Go ahead, luv. I'm passed giving a monkey's."

"What? Of course I won't shoot you. I don't shoot people for being arseholes. You'd have to try a lot harder."

"Whatever," said Ted. "Just bugger off, okay? I don't like company. I just... I just want to be left alone."

The soldier kept her hands at her sides, and the angry expression drained from her face. She seemed to chew on something for a moment, then looked at him with pity. "My name's Hannah, okay? Hannah Weber. I'm sorry about your truck, but when I saw you surrounded by dees, I was more concerned with dropping bodies than picking my shots. At such a short range, my rounds would have gone in and out. Let me look under the bonnet, okay? I might be able to find a workaround."

Ted knew his way around an engine, but other than identifying the obvious, he had no specific skill. As a soldier, this bird—Hannah—might know how to fix what was broken better than him. He laid his hammer across the truck's front seats, then pulled the lever under the steering column. The bonnet hopped two inches and Hannah went over to it, lifting it all the way and propping it open with the shaft. "Here's your battery," she said, pointing.

Ted rolled his eyes. "I know what a battery looks like."

Hannah shook her head and whispered something under her breath which he assumed wasn't a compliment. She undid the terminals on the battery and removed the contacts, then lifted the cell out of its housing. It was clearly beyond saving. The bullet had entered the left side but hadn't come out the right—lodged somewhere in the unit's gooey centre. A thin, clear liquid leaked from the hole, and an acrid odour irritated Ted's eyes as he leant over the engine. He stepped back and grunted a litany of obscenities.

Hannah turned to him, a pained look on her face. "I'm really sorry, mate."

"Ted," he said, sighing as his curse words ran dry and left him utterly deflated.

"Huh?"

"My name is Ted. Look, I'm sorry I shoved you. My temper, it's.... It's not what it used to be." He ran his hands through his thinning brown barnet and looked up at the darkening sky. Night approached. "Sodding 'ell!"

Hannah warily offered her hand. "Nice to meet you, Ted. Wish it were under cannier circumstances. Tell you the truth, I was wondering if I'd ever see another person."

"There's still a handful about if you search enough, but there's less and less every day. I ain't seen a soul in a couple days now, not since some family in a clapped-out camper van heading south on the highway. They were moving at a fair old nick, so I don't think they were leaving anything good behind them."

"Do you know if there's anywhere people are heading? Any camps, safe places?"

Ted frowned. "*You're* the squaddie. Shouldn't you know better than me?"

"You're right, but it never hurts to ask. There's nowhere safe I know of. I'm sorry."

"Sorry for what? I ain't searching for safety."

Hannah rubbed at her forehead, perplexed. "Then where are you...?"

Ted sighed. He'd lowered his guard more than he'd intended to already. This Hannah seemed a decent enough sort, but he still wanted to get back on the road, alone and moving. "It don't matter," he said. "Nothing matters anymore."

Tellingly, the soldier didn't argue. She stared at the floor and breathed out slowly. Both knew the hopelessness of their situation. The demons had invaded the world from several thousand locations at once, making any attempts at an organised defence impossible. Ted was no military strategist, but before the televisions had stopped working, he'd garnered enough to know the enemy had obliterated humanity before it even realised it was under attack. The demons hadn't come for war, they'd come to behead mankind with one swoop of a sword.

Ted reached into his truck and pulled something out of the glove compartment. He thought about shoving it into the small rucksack he kept on the passenger seat but slid it into his jeans instead to keep it close. He slung the rucksack over his shoulder and gathered up his hammer before starting up the road. The breeze seemed to whisper threats, but he ignored them.

Hannah called after him. "Where are you going?"

"North."

5

DR KAMIYO

For the first time in his life, Dr Christopher Kamiyo had no idea where he was going. As a child, he'd accounted for every minute of every day far into the future. He'd known which college he'd attend by the age of ten, and which university by the age of twelve. Informed decision-making was the crux of his existence. That was what his parents had demanded of him.

Now, Kamiyo was sitting at the side of the road in mismatched shoes while bleeding from his left ankle—a prize for climbing over a barbed-wire fence. He fingered a glob of super-glue taken from his rucksack into the two-inch gash and hissed at the resulting sting. Fixing himself up was becoming a regular occurrence, and he envisioned a future where he casually popped his eyeballs back in his skull or stitched up his own intestines. The world had become a jagged place, and every corner waited to cut you.

His travels had taken him north, almost as far as Scotland. He'd spent so long keeping to the fields and side-roads it was hard to know for sure where he was, but he had at least zeroed it down to the county of Northumberland. In the early days of the demon invasion, he'd hidden out in the apartment building where he lived with several other junior doctors and staff. A safe place, inhabited by colleagues and familiar faces, but when the riots began, the building gradually bled its inhabitants. A pair of residents went out for supplies and never returned, a group of nurses packed bags and made a dash for safer climes, while a newly qualified anaesthetist hanged herself from the stairwell with IV tubing. Things only got more desperate after that.

Kamiyo's parents lived in London, which was part of the reason he'd taken a position in Manchester two-hundred miles away. Both cardiologists, his parents had been absent and overbearing in equal measure, yet he missed them now. He knew he'd never see them again. London might as well be Timbuktu. Or Mars. His mother hadn't hugged him since childhood, but he would give anything to collapse into her arms again someday.

Did I make them proud before everything went sideways? Or will I never get the chance?

When the invasion began—hordes of demons spilling out from those bizarre gates—trains skidded to a halt and planes stalled beside runways. Motorways became snarled war zones. The country disintegrated in a matter of days, and everybody found themselves locked-in place and surrounded by chaos. There was nowhere to run, and no way to get there. The invasion spread and spread, and soon Kamiyo's apartment building stopped being a sanctuary and started resembling a tomb.

Twelve had remained inside when the demons first arrived. The monsters swarmed the streets like locusts, picking clean the flesh of anything living. Kamiyo and the other survivors watched in horror from a third-floor window while people were dragged from shop fronts and other hiding places. A mother with a baby locked herself inside the boot of an old Volvo but was promptly discovered and torn apart. The demons tossed her baby into the gutter like old fish and chip paper. As a maternity doctor, Kamiyo had seen dead babies before, but that image had replayed itself in his mind every night since. Even as he thought about it now, it placed him right back into the nightmare of that day.

No one had escaped the killing. A man in an unravelling turban had made it as far as a Ford Ranger, and nearly got away after mowing down half-a-dozen demons in his path, but then he had careened into a laundrette's plate-glass window and slumped against the steering wheel. A monster covered in burns dragged the man out and snapped his neck.

"Come on!" Sonja had urged Kamiyo during that time they'd watched the horror from the windows. Sonja was a pretty nurse from Oncology who lived in the building, and Kamiyo had often wondered if there was a spark between them. Now he'd never find out.

"We have to run," Sonja had begged him, "before they find us."

Kamiyo had agreed, but a registrar from Plastics argued against, making it clear he would take his chances staying put. A nurse and a senior administrator vowed to remain as well. That left nine people willing to make a run for it, and of those nine, only Kamiyo ever made it farther than a single block. Sonja had called out to him as demons peeled strips of flesh from her body, but he hadn't turned back to help her.

That Kamiyo was still alive now, weeks later, astonished him, but it left tomorrow a blur, like coming up from his parent's swimming pool with chlorine in his eyes.

There appeared to be three main types of demon. There were what he thought of as the '*burn victims*', who seemed to make up the bulk of the demon army—walking and moving like human beings, but so mortally wounded they couldn't possibly be alive. They attacked without pause.

Secondly, there were the apes. He called them that because they loped about on all-fours, leaping and bouncing like chimpanzees. They were the least human-looking and attacked with terrifying ferocity.

Finally, were the zombies—the most human-looking, but rotting like the horror film staple to which he compared them. Unlike the other two types of demon, the zombies were—ironically—the smartest. They could talk and think and often acted with intent. They did not attack without pause, and appeared to be the ones who called the shots.

He avoided all three types.

Kamiyo heard rumours of other types of monstrosities back in the days before the internet had fallen and people had still gathered to share news and supplies. The last time he'd seen another person now was four days ago—a hairy biker riding an American-style chopper with a crossbow on his back. The man slowed down to eye Kamiyo, but decided the introduction wasn't worth it and sped on by, his dirty hair flapping in the wind and a pair of angel wings on his dirty denim jacket. *Where are the angels now?* Kamiyo had asked himself at the time.

He'd never been a religious man—both parents were atheists—but he feared he may have been wrong about the whole thing. Hell had invaded Earth, and that proved there was more to existence than Science understood. Did that mean Kamiyo had devoted his life to a fallacy? Was Science a false path?

No, I devoted my life to healing people. That isn't a waste.

In the pulpy science fiction novels he'd secretly binged on as a teenager, doctors had always been a part of the hero's group. Healers were the good guys. Yet, since the demons came, Kamiyo had not helped a single soul. Instead, he'd watched people die by the thousands with no hope of medical intervention. You couldn't staunch blood from a torn-up abdomen with no operating room or team of surgeons. Out here, medicine was impotent. That deadbeat on the chopper was more capable in this new reality than Kamiyo. Part of him wondered if he should have died outside his apartment building with the others instead of running. His cowardice had got eight other people killed regardless of whether or not he had meant it. Pushing Sonja aside to shield himself had not been an intentional act. It had been instinctual. But it still made him a murderer. He would always be a murderer—and a coward.

When the demons had spotted them leaving the apartment building, a sudden jolt of abject fear had seized Kamiyo's higher functions and left a caveman in charge. When an ape-like monster leapt at him from behind a Volkswagen, he had shoved Sonja into its path without thinking. His survival instincts kicked in and protected him, even at the expense of someone else's life. The memory of it sickened him.

And yet, he was still alive when everybody else was dead.

Kamiyo gathered his rucksack and started walking, and it wasn't long before he spotted something in the distance he valued—a large home. One might assume petrol stations and supermarkets the jewels in the apocalyptic desert, but most were looted early on. You'd be lucky nowadays to find a tube of toothpaste or unused toilet paper. No, Kamiyo had stayed alive these last few weeks by raiding rich people's homes.

Well-defended and secure, the owners had typically stayed put during the early days of the invasion. Furthermore, the largest homes were rurally situated. It meant they'd avoided any damage from the mass riots and arson of the towns and cities. Despite all that, the wealthy only held out so long before running out of food or being exterminated by roving gangs of demons. Now the big houses were empty—mansions and cottages ripe for the picking. A house last week even had power, drawn from solar panels on the roof. He'd spent the night kicking back, playing *Fable* on a dusty old Xbox. It had seemed like Heaven, and he only left because the place was empty of food and water. You had to keep moving to keep living.

Kamiyo approached this latest house with a near-swagger, so used to the apocalyptic-procedure by now he had little to fear. He would enter through a back door, out of view of the road, and re-supply himself with whatever he found inside, perhaps staying a while if it suited him. The house was a modern dwelling, probably custom-built for some businessman or other. While it possessed brick foundations like a majority of UK houses, it also featured a great amount of wood, making it more akin to an American farmhouse, or the New England colonial property his parents had owned in Maine. Whitewashed wood panelling covered the brickwork beneath a large triangular roof, and a balcony jutted out beneath a pair of elevated French doors.

In the rear garden, Kamiyo discovered a cavernous workshop and a large shed, both unlocked. A chainsaw hung inside the workshop on a large hook and Kamiyo grabbed that first. In his previous life as a registrar on a maternity ward, he never would have dreamed of firing up a chainsaw like Ash from the *Evil Dead* or something, but nowadays, power tools were the first thing he sought. Like a pro, he fired up this chainsaw now with confidence, and he carried it towards the house. When he got there, he sank the spinning blade into the back door, cutting around the hinges in two neat semi-circles. The door was still snug in the frame, so he had to yank it three times before it came free.

Open sesame.

A familiar stench met him.

That Kamiyo found the home owner dead in the kitchen was not a shock—it was to be expected more often than not— yet this particular scene took him by surprise. The deceased gentleman lay sprawled face down on the kitchen tiles. There was no blood. Kamiyo presumed an overdose, and again that wasn't an anomaly, but what *was* out of the ordinary were the two Alsatians rolled up beside him, and the fluffy white cat next to his head. All three animals were uninjured too, yet also dead awhile. The home owner had presumably dosed his pets so they would die alongside him. A kind gesture—or selfish? Who was to say? Kamiyo had not seen the demons show much interest in animals, so the owner might have released them into the wild to fend for themselves. They might have been fine. Or they might not have.

As a child, Kamiyo had begged for a puppy, especially when it had become clear he would not get a sibling. The response had always been a firm, decisive no. Two working parents, and a host of after-school clubs for Kamiyo, meant no one at home to care for a hound, which were filthy animals anyway, said his father. Childhood had been the loneliest time, and a dog might have changed that. A loving lick to send him to sleep each night might have filled his head with pleasant dreams instead of mundane nightmares of school-work and piano lessons. What kind of man would he have been if his parents had given him a dog in his formative years? Did such things change a person? He wondered what the grizzly scene in the kitchen would look like if the home owner didn't have pets.

Kamiyo moved on through the hallway and into the lounge, feet sinking into its plush carpet. A granite fireplace dominated the room, and an enormous television hung above its mantlepiece, an obsidian slate reflecting the room like a dark mirror. What Kamiyo wouldn't give to sprawl on the room's sumptuous sofa and spend an evening in front of Netflix. He'd much prefer watching an apocalyptic drama than living through one. If he'd known civilisation was due to end a year before his thirtieth birthday, he wouldn't have spent so much time building a career. He'd put off living— travelling, romance, drugs and alcohol—for the promise of a better tomorrow. But now there was no tomorrow, and there'd never be a chance to experience any of what he'd missed.

I'll never find out how Game of Thrones *ends.*

In the house's front reception, Kamiyo located a spacious cloakroom, and scrounged a thick, padded coat and scarf. The weather was turning chilly, Summer at an end, so his current black denim jacket was fast becoming inadequate. He also took some woollen gloves, which he placed inside his rucksack. Finally, knowing no other choice existed, he took himself back into the kitchen. The sight of the homeowner and pets was still heartrending, even upon second viewing, but he needed to search for food. He had remained well-fed so far, but increasingly he was finding food spoiled or pilfered by animals. Before long, he feared he would have to learn how to hunt—if he lived long enough that is.

A glossy, slab-door larder cabinet filled one side of the kitchen, and inside he found a vast array of tins and dried packets, all assembled on pull-out wire shelves. Kamiyo stuffed his rucksack full of dried rice and tinned fruit until there was no room left, then filled his coat pockets with several tubes of tomato puree—high in calories and useful for moistening anything too dry to eat. Overall, it set him up for a good few days. If he could find medical supplies in the bathroom, he would call today a massive win. He'd had enough of fixing himself up with super-glue.

Kamiyo smiled, but the expression felt odd. Could it be

that he was actually good at this survivor-man existence? Or had he been lucky so far? *No, there's no such thing as luck anymore. Not the good kind anyway.*

He gathered as much food as he could carry, then shoved the wire trays back into the larder cabinet. As he went to close the door, he fumbled a can of peaches. It dented against the tiled floor, and in the silence of his solitary existence, the sound was jarring and made him flinch.

"Kelsey Grammer!" he garbled in fright. An odd habit he had picked up to avoid swearing on the ward. He clutched his chest and chuckled to himself, then knelt to pick the can up. He placed it back on the shelf and closed the larder door the rest of the way. Time to leave.

A demon glared at Kamiyo.

Kamiyo leapt back in fright, tripping over the dead home-owner and landing on his butt. The demon was one of the burnt kind, the smell of charred flesh intoxicating. How had he not noticed the stench earlier? Had the demon been hiding in the house this whole time?

The abomination clumsily stalked him—left leg seared to the ankle bone. Kamiyo scrambled to his feet and made for the door, but the demon closed the distance and wrapped its blackened hands around his throat. His lungs seized up, unable to draw breath. He gagged. If he didn't get free, he might have as little as two minutes before he lost consciousness.

Was this it? Was this his death?

His borrowed time was due to be paid back.

No, I'm not ready.

Kamiyo threw his arms out, blindly groping along the granite work surface at his back. His hands found various objects—fingers slipping inside the crumby slots of a toaster one second and the handle of a coffee maker the next. When he yanked the appliances, they refused to come to him, plug and flex tethering them to the wall.

His vision swirled, pressure forcing the capillaries in his eyes to haemorrhage. Light-headedness set in, brain already deprived of oxygen. Time was running out. Fast.

He fumbled frantically along the counter, cajoling his attacker at his front. The demon's eyes were soulless, two lumps of coal inside a blackened skull. Hatred poured off it in fumes. A flap of pink and black skin hung from its chin— rancid kebab meat.

Kamiyo's hands finally found something hanging on the wall behind him. He knocked the thing loose. It made a loud clatter, something heavy, and thankfully it didn't fall far from his reach. He closed his fingers around whatever it was and wasted no time in swinging it against the demon's head.

Air rushed into Kamiyo's lungs as the pipeline in his throat re-opened. He gasped and wheezed. Stars swirled in his vision. He was alive, but barely.

The demon stumbled backwards, the side of its head caved in like a dog-bitten football. Despite already being burnt to a crisp, its body smouldered. Kamiyo had struck it as hard as he could, yet it made little sense it would be so gravely injured. He looked down at his hands and found himself holding a cast-iron skillet. Bits of congealed flesh clung to its rim, sizzling like barbecue. He tossed the skillet down in disgust.

The demon slumped to the ground, coming to rest on top of one of the dead Alsatians. Kamiyo took it as his cue to leave, so he snatched up his rucksack and headed for the door.

Back out in the garden, he realised he was no longer alone —a dozen demons waited for him on the lawn, burnt faces sneering. All at once, they shrieked like devils.

Kamiyo fled.

6

DR KAMIYO

This was not the first time Kamiyo had run for his life—
he'd been doing it regularly for months now—and the
truth was he'd gotten rather sprightly. A slender individual
before the fall of mankind, after surviving on the road for
weeks, he was now all sinew and muscle. He bolted from the
house, a thoroughbred horse, and made it back onto the road
before the demons even entered a jog. That they were the
burnt variety meant he had a hope of getting away, for they
were clumsy and damaged, not at all like their hulking, ape-
like cousins.

Kamiyo got himself a decent head-start, but was running
down the middle of the road with a laden rucksack. Eventually, he would tire, and then the question would be whether
the demons got tired too. If they didn't, they would wear him
down like a fox.

His only chance was to shake them off.

The demons hissed at his back, and when he glanced over
his shoulder, he saw them reaching out their hands like
Frankenstein's monster, yet it was that lack of coordination
which allowed him to pull even farther ahead.

How had they snuck up on him? Had they been nearby when he'd fired up the chainsaw? Why was this group out here alone? Were they another of the death squads he'd seen cleansing the streets outside his apartment building? Had they done such a thorough job that only the countryside remained? Soon, there would be nowhere left to hide.

Nothing lay on the horizon, the road seeming to go on forever. Fields lay to his left, too exposed to lose a pursuer, and on the other side of the road were thick trees and tangled bushes. He could break his neck running through there, but what other choice did he have?

I have to lose them.

Kamiyo bolted to his right, leaping over a roadside ditch and entering the first row of trees. The branches fought him, thorns whipping at his face and slicing his cheeks. The demons followed. He could hear them crunching and snapping through the undergrowth behind him. He felt more than ever like a hunted fox. His lungs burned, and his throat ached from having been strangled. *I'm not out of the woods yet.*

Laughing at his own joke, Kamiyo wondered if he was crazy or if it was just the adrenaline in his system playing havoc with his emotions. He leapt over a fallen tree trunk and ducked under a willow canopy before zigzagging between other trees he couldn't name. Desperately, he fought to disappear into the thick foliage. The noise of his pursuers seemed to fade. The distance between them was growing.

Kamiyo locked his jaws and powered forward. The ground fell away beneath his boots as he bounded over a dried-out stream, and the split-second of air made him feel like a leaping stag. The more the sounds of his pursuers faded, the more elated he became. While most of the world was dead, he was alive and defying the odds. The demons couldn't kill him, no matter how many times they tried. He wouldn't let them. It made him feel powerful, denying the universe control over him like that. An alien sentiment, to answer only to himself. No parents, no superiors. No plan. Only survival.

He wanted to slow down and catch his breath, but he couldn't. Even though the demons had lost sight of him, they would keep on coming. He needed to ensure he moved completely out of their path before he allowed himself to stop.

The woods were vast, and he considered he might have reached Kielder Forest Park in Northumberland, a vast swath of nature marking one of England's last surviving wildernesses. He'd planned to visit it a year ago, to relax and connect with nature, but studies and work had got in the way. How idiotic that felt now.

Heading ever deeper into the forest, Kamiyo entered a world without signs or pathways. The vast tangle of nature contrasted with the perverse monstrosities chasing him. This was a place of solitude and peace, and as much as the forest unsettled him, it also offered safety.

Kamiyo kept on running for another twenty minutes or so, and when he stopped, it was because his knees buckled. Flopping against the mud, his fingers slipped into a thatch of weeds, twigs, and brambles. This deep in the forest, the floor was a carpet, and it made it even harder to resist just lying there and taking a nap, but it was only late afternoon. Incredible, how adrenaline could burn out a body so rapidly.

He allowed himself a few minutes, tempting death by enjoying the sway of the trees overhead—the first movement in weeks that hadn't immediately panicked him into hiding. The forest embraced him, hid him, and made him feel protected. He couldn't help but cling to it for a few moments more.

Once he'd caught his breath, Kamiyo got up and continued, but this time he kept to a walk. The demons were clumsy enough that he would hear them if they got close, and he was fairly confident he'd dodged out of their path. They could be two miles in the other direction by now, as lost as he was. Not that it was possible to be lost when there was no place to go.

For now, walking through the vast forest was as far ahead as Kamiyo wanted to think. Perhaps he would stay here and learn to hunt as planned. Squirrels and birds zipped about everywhere between these branches, and if he could just figure out a way to snare them... He could even fell trees and make himself a cabin. Find a stream to fish in. Maybe survive until he was an old man. Was this the place? Could he survive here? *Ha, I'll be half mad within the year. Solitude is not good for emotional health.*

But it sure as heck beats dying.

He increased his pace, catching the last of his breath. A slight stitch needled his ribs, but he was in good shape overall—uninjured, and with a rucksack laden with supplies. Although, as he inspected his pack now, he saw it had torn at the bottom. It must have caught on a branch. A large bag of rice had split open inside and now contained barely a dozen grains, the rest spilled on the ground behind him in a meandering line. Not a disaster, for there was still plenty of food left in his rucksack, so he tossed the empty packet to the ground and headed up the slight incline ahead.

Then, as he started down the other side, he saw an end to the forest. The trees thinned out abruptly in an ordered line, and he could make out some kind of structure beyond. It caused him to stop and think.

Part of him was excited, as it always was when he encountered a possible source of supplies or aid, but there was also that sickening trepidation that there might be demons around —or unhinged survivors. After barely fleeing with his life intact once already today, did he want to risk exposing himself again? How much longer could his luck hold up?

He should just skirt around the clearing—follow the trees until they reformed on the other side—but what if he missed out on even greater sanctuary? Whatever lay ahead was hidden in the depths of the forest, and perhaps it would remain hidden. A ready-made roof over his head was better than having to fell trees and build one. Or going back out on the road.

With no choice at all, Kamiyo's curious nature ordered him to at least take a peep at what lay nestled beyond the trees. Perhaps it would be curiosity that killed him in the end, but the thought of acting against his own nature was a death in itself.

Staying low, he traipsed the remaining fifty-metres of woodland and headed for the clearing. The bushes snagged his jeans, and it was difficult to get an unobstructed view of the structure, but once he managed it, there was little doubt of what he saw.

A stone gatehouse marked the bottom of a long elevation leading up to a crumbling castle on a hill. The gatehouse adjoined a single-storey ruin that sat in front of a ten-foot stone wall, thick and old like plaque-hardened teeth. The only part of the fortification not to stand the test of time was the gate itself. Cast from iron, it lay flat in a patch of long grass.

The castle drew his attention, and he floated towards it in a daydream. He had travelled back in time and could imagine colourful knights on horses trotting down the hill to meet him. But in reality, the castle and its courtyards stood deserted. Unlike the lower gatehouse, the large iron portcullis of the upper gatehouse still hung in the recesses of the castle's front aspect, locked in place by a pair of modern steel cuffs on either side. A bronze plaque adorned the wall on the left side of the gate and read: *'Portcullis' derives from a French word meaning 'sliding door.' This iron grate can be lowered in an instant if the castle is under attack and has been functional for over four hundred years. It is raised by a pair of interlocking chains housed inside a small room above the gate.*

Was this castle a tourist attraction? It made sense, for it was more than a ruin. In fact, it appeared almost whole, and as he passed beneath the portcullis, he briefly feared it might drop like a guillotine and slice him in two. The castle itself wasn't huge, a large manor house rather than a feudal fortress like Stirling or Edinburgh, but it stood stout and proud. Three-stories high, it was almost square, but slightly wider than it was tall, with a central tower breaking up the uniformity by jutting out in a hexagonal shape. The crenellated roof was the only broken part of the castle. Its right side had fallen away, replaced by thick swaths of ivy that trailed all the way to the ground. Timber frames and glass made up the windows and would not have been part of the original structure, but they didn't take away from the castle's antiquity. Defensive walls looped around the castle on every side, the portcullis punctuating the front approach. A small, but very real castle. And it was his!

At least that was what he thought until he felt a poke between his shoulder blades. "Dow yow move!" came a gruff voice in his ear.

Kamiyo was pretty sure it wasn't a chivalrous knight.

7

TED

Ted groaned when he heard Hannah's footsteps behind him. He'd expected nothing else, but a slim chance had existed that she might walk the other way. "We should keep to the side of the road," she warned. "The forest will give us cover if we need it."

"You know the area?" asked Ted without looking back at her. If he didn't look at her, she might go away.

"Not really. I was based out of Stafford with 16 Signals but I'm from Durham originally. Only been in the service two years, just made Lance-Corporal. What a time to enlist, huh?"

"Least you had a gun when all this started. You had a better chance than most."

She was silent for a moment, the only sound their boots on the tarmac. When she spoke again, her voice was pained. "Believe me, guns didn't make a whole lot of difference."

Ted huffed. "No kidding. A lot of use you lot turned out to be."

Hannah surprised Ted then by grabbing his shoulder and whirling him around to face her in the middle of the road. She might have been a tiny bird, but she was stronger than she looked. "Fuck you, pal! You have no idea how hard we fought. I watched hundreds of good men and women run straight into certain death because they knew their duty. We did everything we could.... We... You have no fucking idea, okay?"

Ted was angry at being manhandled, but the fragile fury on Hannah's face was enough to make him seek peace. He shrugged her off but apologised. "You're right. I've seen enough to know there's nothing anyone could have done. It wouldn't have mattered how hard the Army fought. I'm sorry, okay?"

Hannah relaxed her shoulders and stared down the road vacantly. "We were slaughtered."

"What you talking about?"

"The Army," she said, looking back at him. "It's gone. Wiped out. We made our last stand on the outskirts of Derby. Command set up at the Rolls Royce plant there. We had tanks, helicopters, even a few light aircraft scrounged from civilian airstrips and equipped with various armaments. We assembled two-thousand servicemen, and twice as many civilians, the most organised we'd been since the shit first hit the fan. We were taking the fight to the enemy."

Ted couldn't believe such a thing had happened without him knowing—a massive battle involving thousands of people. The world was a different place without daily news, phones, or internet. Used to be a shot fired in Glasgow echoed in London thirty-seconds later. Now the world could explode, and you'd have no way of knowing until you were staring into the blast wave. It reminded Ted of those Japanese snipers still guarding their rural outposts years after the war had ended. He'd always assumed those types of stories were urban legends, but now he could see how easily they could become a reality.

"I had no idea," Ted admitted. "I thought the fight was over before it got started. Most of our forces were abroad, I assumed."

Hannah nodded. "A majority, but not all. There were soldiers on leave, reserves, and the token forces left to provide security on our stockpiles and camps. We had police officers with us too. Not a massive army, but enough to make a go of things—or so we thought.

At first, things went well. We found the dees gathered near one of their gates in Nottingham, like they were trying to assemble an army of their own or something. We rolled in our tanks and sent them into a panic, blasting them to pieces with flechette rounds and anti-personnel rockets. Then our two choppers battered them with Hellfires while our planes surveyed the area. It looked like a sure thing. We moved in our troops to clean up, tearing the dees apart with small arms fire. We must have dropped a thousand in less than an hour. Hit 'em harder than anything's ever been hit."

"So what happened?" Ted couldn't see how this tale could turn bloody.

"It was a trap." Her jaw tightened, upper lip curling. "The dees we found were just cannon fodder to draw us in. We had pushed through into a cramped industrial estate, full of long factory buildings and chain-link fencing. We assumed it was an enemy base camp, but really, it was a container for our army. The tanks got wedged in alleyways, and our troops bunched together so much that the choppers couldn't recognise us from them. The second wave of dees came from behind, spilling out of a supermarket depot at the front of the estate. A thousand of 'em right at our backs. We opened fire, but we were so squashed together that we shot as many of our own as we did the dees. A few hundred of us retreated to a car lot, taking cover behind the vehicles and trying to build a barrier between us and them. But there was no chance of us coming out of that fight alive. The dees were everywhere, and we were running low on ammo. We held out for a whole day, but when I saw the enemy general coming, I knew our time was up."

"The demons have generals?" Ted had assumed they were more swarming wasps than organised invasion force. It was their sheer, mindless ferocity that had given them such swift victory.

Hannah nodded, her eyes haunted by the things she was sharing. "We never found out fully, but the demons have some sort of hierarchy. You saw the videos of the giants, right?"

Ted nodded. The massive beings stomping around London on the news had been one of the last things he'd witnessed before the broadcasts ceased. It hadn't seemed real then, and hearing about it now didn't completely register either. Giants? Bollocks, surely?

Hannah continued. "The giants are at the top of the demon food chain, but there are other leaders too. The one that turned up that day to finish us wasn't a giant compared to the ones in London, but it was eight feet tall at least, and more skeleton than it was man. If I ever doubted the dees came straight from Hell, this creature confirmed it for me. Watching it approach put a fear in me I thought would stop my heart." She pinched the bridge of her nose and sniffed. "I ran. Made it out through a back door and hopped a fence. There were dees everywhere, but somehow, they didn't spot me, too focused on their leader coming down the hill. They aren't just monsters, you know? They had respect for this thing. It was like they were standing at attention or something."

Ted commented on another part of the story. "You made it out of there in one piece though? What about the others with you? You said there were hundreds."

Hannah swallowed and looked away, glancing towards the

trees. She gave no answer to the question, which left Ted picturing her running away while her colleagues stayed to fight. Did that make her a coward, or just smart? If she hadn't run, she would have just died with everybody else. And the dead didn't care about loyalty or courage. In the grand scheme of things, it probably didn't matter. If you counted the death toll in the United Kingdom alone, you were looking at tens of millions. A couple hundred soldiers was insignificant when you thought of it that way.

With no more words spoken, they carried on along the road in silence. Hannah bowed her head solemnly like she hoped Ted might offer words of advice or solace. That wasn't his duty. Let the soldier make peace with herself.

The road widened ahead, with a listing burger van parked in a lay-by off to the left. Ted was parched from the walk, and the near-death experience he had just had at the hands of the demons—or dees, apparently, in military speak—so he quickened his pace and made a beeline for the van.

"Don't be so hasty," warned Hannah.

"It's a burger van, not an unexploded bomb. How have you been surviving?"

"Hunting mostly. I took down a deer a few days ago and camped out by a stream. Learnt a bit of bushcraft during a training tour in Belize, like."

Ted made it over to the van and opened the back door. "Sounds nice, you should've stayed—" He covered his nose with his arm and gagged. "Bleedin' 'ell!"

"What is it?" Hannah hurried to catch up, raising her rifle.

"It's nothing." He stepped up into the van while keeping his face covered. "Think I'd be used to the stench by now."

The corpse was an insect-ridden puddle on the floor, with ghastly cheeks hanging from a browning skull. Its eyeballs were yellow and massive, skin drawn back around them. The tongue also seemed overly large, jutting from between exposed jawbones. It was unclear how the person had died, but the fact they were in one piece suggested they had taken their own lives.

"Get out of there," said Hannah. "You'll catch... I dunno, something."

"Just a sec." Ted clambered towards the back of the van where a fridge stood. No power, of course, but inside were three-dozen cans of pop and several bottles of water. He searched beneath the counter until he found a bunch of plastic bags, then filled them with the drinks. The cans were warm, but it didn't matter. The time of chilled drinks and fresh sandwiches had passed.

Ted gathered the carrier bags along his arm and climbed out the van. Hannah saw what he had and licked her lips, which were notably dry and pasty. "You gonna share?"

"You're the one with a gun, do I have much choice?"

"It's a rifle."

"Huh?"

"You keep calling it a gun. It bugs me. It's a rifle."

Ted pulled out a can of cherry cola, a flavour he hated, and handed it to her. "It shoots bullets don't it? That's a gun as far as I'm concerned, luv."

Hannah took the can of pop and sighed. "Yeah, I suppose so. It's just an Army thing. A gun is something you'd find on a Navy boat. A rifle is what this is, pet."

"SA-80, right? I still remember the big hoo-hah when they introduced it. Weapon of the future and all that."

Hannah patted her rifle like a pet. "Aye. I think the original left a lot to be desired, but they improved it over time. I've been carrying it so long now it feels like a part of me." She pulled the tab on her can and took a swig.

"How many bullets you got left?" Ted asked.

"Rounds."

"Huh?"

"It fires bullets, but it's loaded with rounds. The round is the casing that houses the bullet. To answer your question, I have one magazine of ammunition left after saving your arse. Plus a few rounds left in this one." She tapped the magazine hanging out the bottom of the rifle. It rattled and sounded hollow. "When we made our last stand in Derby, we knew we'd be up against a large force, so each of us had about a dozen mags of ammo. It still wasn't enough. I was down to my last two by the time I made a run for it."

"How long have you been on the road?"

"Nine days, like."

Ted blanched. "Nine days? I assumed you were talking about things that happened right at the start. You're telling me the Army was still around as recently as nine days ago?"

Hannah nodded. "I might be the last soldier left. Sorry."

Ted nodded. Was she really the last soldier left? The final witness of mankind's pitiful last stand? It wasn't for definite. If the Army in these parts had still been around nine days ago, perhaps there were other groups fighting back. The world was cut off from itself. No telling who was alive and where. Strangely, it sparked a slither of hope inside of him, and he had to push the feeling away before it wrecked him. He uncapped a bottle of water to take a sip. As he tilted his head back, he spotted something at the side of the road fifty-metres ahead. "Hey, there's a bus over there."

"Yeah, I see it," said Hannah following his gaze. "You think we can get her going again?"

"Was thinking more I could try the battery in my truck and get back on my way."

"Heading north?"

"North and *alone*."

Hannah grunted. "Were you this sociable in your former life?"

Ted started up the road, unwilling to comment on his *former* life—couldn't even *think* about it. Hannah, followed him like a stray dog, nipping at his heels the whole way until they reached the bus—although it turned out to be a coach when they got there. Rather than being parked off to the side of the road, it was actually set in a small parking area, big enough only for five or six vehicles. The nearby forest was so thick it had hidden the spot from the road. A large wooden noticeboard stood beside the beginnings of an overgrown path, and a bronze plaque fixed along its top read: KIELDER FOREST PARK OUTDOOR ACTIVITY CENTRE.

Hannah nodded to the sign. "Ever been?"

Ted shook his head. "I'm from Essex. This might be the furthest I've ever been north."

"Yeah, I imagine Scotland's not far away."

"I might already be there if you hadn't shot my bloody engine."

"I said I'm sorry. Look, I'll help you get back on your way, like, but wouldn't it be better to stick together?"

"No." Ted went around to the bus's door and yanked on it. It didn't move until Hannah arrived next to him and pushed a red button that released it manually. "My dad was a bus driver most his life. How about yours?"

"My old man was a professional piss head. Laid a brick from time to time, and taught me how to do it, but most the time, you could find him down whatever boozer hadn't barred him yet."

"You're a brick layer then?"

"Builder. Ran my own firm for twenty years. Call me a brick layer again and we'll have a problem."

Hannah put her hands up, letting her rifle hang free on its

strap. "Long as you stop calling my weapon a *gun,* we have a deal."

Ted stepped up into the coach's interior and started down the carpeted aisle. It was clean and empty, with only the odd crisp packet to show that anyone had been there.

"What you looking for?" Hannah enquired, climbing into the aisle behind him.

"I dunno yet. One thing I've learned these last couple months is you never know what you'll find where. One time, I found a dildo in a washing machine. Still haven't figured out how the bloody thing got there."

Hannah cackled with laughter.

Ted cursed in a mixture of fright and irritation. "Soddin' 'ell!"

Hannah covered her mouth. "Sorry!"

"Just try to remember this is the end of the world, yeah, luv'?"

"It's been a while since I heard anything funny. I wasn't ready for it."

"Glad I amuse you." Ted flipped over a magazine he had found on one of the seats. It was some kind of teen magazine coloured pink and emblazoned with pictures of girls in snazzy, plastic jewellery. On the next seat, he found a half-eaten apple.

"Hey," Hannah called from near the front. There's something stashed in the seat pocket here." She pulled it out and examined it. "Looks like a roster full of names." She squinted and started reading out loud. "*D of E pupil list...* Is that the name of a school, you think?"

"Duke of Edinburgh. It's a youth reward scheme. Hiking, archery, stuff like that." He pulled out the photograph he kept in his jeans pocket and peeked at it before sliding it back.

Hannah shook her head, embarrassed. "Yeah, our regiment was always taking those kids out on weekends. How did you twig what it was so quickly?"

"My daughter was working to get her award." As soon as the words left his mouth, he felt the tears behind his eyes. He looked away, biting his lip until it hurt, punishing himself for talking.

"You had a daughter. Shit, I'm—"

"A lot of people had daughters," he grunted. "Things are a bit beyond sympathy, don't you reckon?" Hannah kept quiet and stayed where she was at the front of the bus. "There's nothing here we can use," he said. "Let's get the battery and go."

"All right." Hannah climbed out of the coach, and Ted was right behind her.

"Where d'you think they went?" asked Hannah as she continued studying the roster sheet in her hand. "The kids, I mean."

Ted shrugged and gave no answer. Why torment himself by thinking about a bunch of dead kids? He headed for the front of the coach, wanting to get back on the road more than ever. He'd never opened up a coach before, so he was hoping Hannah's knowledge went further than the emergency door release. Soon, he might actually be rid of the yappy squaddie.

She was still chatting away, even now. "They must have been here visiting the activity centre," she said. "You don't think they could still be alive, do you?"

"No. Help me get the bonnet open."

Hannah laughed. "You're more likely to find the engine at the *back* of a model like this. The battery might even be at the side. Search for a compartment. You take the far side and I'll take the—shit!"

Ted barked irritably as Hannah grabbed him by the

shoulder and shoved him into the ditch at the edge of the car park. "The hell you doing, you bleedin' idiot?"

Hannah shushed him, her rifle aimed down the road ahead. "Look!"

Ted followed the aim of her rifle until he saw the pack of demons a hundred metres down the road. They were spread out in a line, scouring the landscape. They bounded like playful children, hopping and rolling. Luckily, the trees hid Hannah and Ted from their sight.

"They'll be on us any minute," said Hannah, sinking lower into the bushes.

"So shoot 'em."

"No. It's the bloody apes! When we fought them back in Derby, we wasted half our ammo trying to hit them. They never move in a straight line, and once they spot you they move like the clappers. I fire a single shot and they'll rip us apart before I can take a second one. We have to get out of here. And now!"

"Where? There's nowhere to go. Maybe we can hide on the bus?"

Hannah looked at him like he was a moron. "No way! They're looking for survivors. These small groups are all over the place, like Nazi death squads. They'll check the coach just like we did. Come on, we have to head into the forest."

Ted stared into the dark mass of trees and hesitated. "I-I'm really more of a city person."

"Fine, then stay here and be a dead person. I thought you knew what you were doing out here!"

"Damn it! Okay, I'm coming."

He allowed her to drag him into the forest, and within a few seconds, he had never felt so lost. So much for heading north.

8

DR KAMIYO

"Dow yow move!"

The sight of the castle still had Kamiyo's mind reeling about a world of knights and squires, and that the weapon digging into his back was a lance or sword. He had to remind himself that this was reality, and that death lurked around every corner.

In a calm, non-threatening voice, Kamiyo addressed the man holding him hostage. "I'm sorry. I didn't know anybody lived here."

A derisory chuckle sounded in his ear. "It's an 11th Century castle. Nobody lives here, idiot."

The stranger possessed an accent that sounded local to the Midlands, a slightly-ridiculous sounding drawl. Kamiyo wasn't about to state that opinion out loud though. "My mistake," he said. "If you let me turn around, I'm sure we can sort the matter out. There's no need for trouble."

"Well, aren't yow the polite gentleman!" The pressure between his shoulder blades increased. "What am yow doing 'ere? How'd yow find us?"

"I didn't know this place existed! I'm just trying to stay alive. Please, let me turn around. Please!"

"How 'bout I kill yow right 'ere instead?"

"Leave him alone, Frank!" came another voice. It shared the same Black Country accent but was female and not as thick.

The man with the weapon argued with the mystery woman. "We dow know where he came from, or who he's with."

The woman spoke again. "Settle down, Frank. Let's not assume he's an evil monster until we at least get his name."

"My name is Christopher," said Kamiyo quickly. "Chris."

"Yow dow look much like a Christopher," said the man who was apparently 'Frank'.

Kamiyo groaned. "Seriously? My father is Japanese. My mother is English. Or, I suppose, they *were*. Either way, they named me Chris."

"Let him go, Frank!" The woman was demanding it now.

"Bloody 'ell, fine! On yow 'ed be it, Jackie!" The pressure removed itself from Kamiyo's back. "Any sudden moves, pal, and I'll stick yow like a pig."

Kamiyo kept his hands in the air and turned around to face his captor, imagining some ruffian with a scar across his eyebrow and a broken tooth. Instead, he stared down past a thatch of messy brown hair to see the pudgy face of a little man glaring up at him. 'Frank' snarled at him like a bulldog and wielded a large stick. "Um, hello, it's, um, good to meet you."

A woman appeared from behind a crumbling outbuilding that was little more than an archway and a single wall. "Sorry about the greeting," she announced while approaching at a brisk pace. "You're the first person we've seen in, well, forever.

We've been worried about someone finding us and making trouble."

Kamiyo glanced around but couldn't make sense of what she was saying. "I'm sorry for trespassing. I just stumbled upon this place, I swear!"

"No way did yow," said Frank, shaking his stick like a little caveman. "We're a mile inside a forest the size of a city. Nobody just stumbles here."

"Well, I dow know..." Kamiyo cleared his throat and started again. "Well, I *don't* understand what you want me to say."

Frank continued to glower at him. He absolutely did resemble a bulldog; except bulldogs were friendly.

"My name is Jackie," said the woman, placing her hands on her bony hips. "Before the demons came, I was an overweight office manager. Now I'm an apocalyptic survivor living off the land." She laughed a little too fraughtly. "I imagine you have a similar story of your own, Chris."

"I was a doctor at St Thomas's Hospital in Manchester," he explained. "Maternity. I've been travelling alone for... however long it's been. Months?"

"Time has certainly lost its significance, hasn't it? If you're really a doctor, you couldn't have come at a better time."

"He ain't no doctor," said Frank, rolling his eyes in dramatic fashion.

Kamiyo sighed, took a moment to study the dumpy man, then decided upon a gambit to earn his trust. "You have PSS, right? Proportional Short Stature? What was it, a thyroid problem? Childhood sickness?"

Frank tried to maintain his glare, but his eyebrows quivered. "I-I had a tumour as a babby. It were on me-"

"Pituitary gland?" Kamiyo queried.

"Yes!" Frank lowered his stick for a second, then realised

and thrust it out again. He squinted one eye at Kamiyo. "How could you know that?"

Kamiyo focused on Jackie, the more diplomatic of the two. "You see? I *am* a doctor. Not saying I'm Gregory House, but I have a medical degree, at least."

Jackie frowned. "Who's Gregory House?"

"It doesn't matter. So, is it just you two here, living at this castle?"

Frank tutted. "I already told yow that no one lives here."

"Then where?"

Frank grew tight-lipped again, but Jackie seemed happy to give an answer. "Kothal Castle sits on a hill, and at the bottom of that hill is a lake and an activity centre. That's where we've been camping out this whole time."

Kamiyo frowned. "You keep saying *we*. There are more people here?"

"Dow tell 'im, Jackie!"

Jackie gave Kamiyo a wry smile and rolled her eyes. "Follow me, Doctor. Frank, will you kindly go back on guard duty? Eric shall relieve you later."

Frank mumbled but headed back to the wall surrounding the castle's front approach. Despite his mildly buffoonish air, the man had done his duty well—Kamiyo had never seen the guy coming—and he certainly took the job seriously.

Jackie led Kamiyo deeper into the courtyard. Against a side-wall stood a wooden snack bar, but instead of being stocked with packets and cans, it was piled with sharp sticks and other weapons.

"Nice bow and arrows," Kamiyo said as they passed by an old stone well.

"We've been trying to learn how to hunt. Some of the kids have gotten rather good at it. We fish, too, of course."

"Of course..." Kamiyo struggled to understand. The

woman talked as though she were part of some medieval settlement, but where was it?

They approached the castle's rear courtyard, and then veered towards a small rear exit on the furthest wall. A 'sally port,' the trivia-loving part of his brain whispered to him. A small door where troops and villagers could come and go without opening the main gate and leaving the castle vulnerable. This sally port comprised a thick oak door with iron hinges. It opened easily when Jackie pulled on it, as if it was brand-new and not some ancient relic.

"Step on through," she said warmly, waving her arm. "Welcome to our home."

Kamiyo felt uneasy, wondering what exactly he was heading in to. For the last several weeks, he had faced danger and death at every turn, and other than the odd lonely survivor, he'd encountered no one in weeks. The last time he'd been around a group numbering more than three was back at his apartment building. That was months ago and had ended badly. With no other plan, Kamiyo took a deep breath and stepped through the sally port into a patch of overgrown grass that fell away rapidly into a steep, almost vertical slope.

"It's a bugger to climb," said Jackie, "but I suppose that's the point, to stop marauding armies marching up it. There's a pathway nearby that's a little less treacherous, but you might make part of the trip on your bottom."

Kamiyo's jaw fell open, and he had to prod himself to get his lungs working again. He crept to the edge of the slope and stared at a massive, shimmering lake below. Dusk was only minutes away, which left the sinking sun to cast its silver rays across the shimmering surface, turning the water into a giant mirror. But as breath-taking as the lake might be, it was not what had stolen his breath. It was the several-dozen bodies buzzing around industriously below, casting fishing nets into the water and bustling along with various other tasks. An immense log cabin balanced on stilts against the edge of the thick forest, and for a moment, Kamiyo felt like he was in rural Montana rather than northern England.

"Quite a sight, huh?" said Jackie proudly.

Kamiyo's mouth went dry, and he had to rub his throat to find his voice. "H-How long have you all been here?"

"Like I said, since the gates first opened. We were here on an activity weekend." She looked down the hill, eyes flickering as though a movie played that only she could see. She went on, "When the invasion started, we watched it on the televisions in the cabin, and on our phones—the place had WiFi back then. We watched the world die, but it felt like a soap opera. Not real, you know? This place has kept us safe the entire time. We've encountered none of the horror firsthand. In fact, you're the first soul we've seen. If we had been anywhere else, I dare not think of what would have happened to the children."

"Children? What do you mean?"

Jackie pointed down the hill at the human ant farm beside the lake. "There are forty-seven of us in total. Forty of which are children and teenagers. It was a Duke of Edinburgh awards weekend for the older children, but we also had younger children along as part of a junior adventure scheme some of the parents and I ran." She let out another fraught chuckle. "It's all very middle-class."

Kamiyo stepped towards the edge and almost tumbled down the slope. He stopped himself just in time by digging in his heels. "I-I'm really the first person you've seen? No demons. None at all?"

Jackie smiled. "I'm not saying it's been easy. We've lost our families, our friends, and we live in fear every day, but no, we have seen none of those... things. Only on the news."

Kamiyo couldn't take his eyes off the scene below. The group had butts for collecting rainwater, racks for drying fish, and even boats out on the water. "It's unbelievable. You've had everything you've needed this whole time."

Jackie moved up beside him and spoke earnestly. "Not everything. We haven't had a doctor or any medicine, which is why you're a gift from the gods. Some of us are sick. Last night, one of the children died."

Kamiyo sighed. "How old?"

"Thirteen. His name was James."

These people might have found themselves a sanctuary, but you couldn't hide from disease. "I suppose some things never change," he said. "Let me see your patients."

9

DR KAMIYO

The slope was so long and treacherous that it was dusk by the time Kamiyo reached the bottom. Immediately upon his arrival with Jackie, the entire camp froze and stared at him. A few younger children cried, and the smattering of adults had to work to comfort them. The concern was obvious, and Kamiyo realised he truly was the first person this group had seen since the gates first opened.

Astounding.

"Don't be alarmed!" Jackie spoke in a voice louder than any noise Kamiyo had dared make in weeks. What must it be like not to fear demons finding you? "This is Christopher," she said. "He's a doctor who stumbled upon us through blind luck —*our* luck! We're still hidden from the outside world, and Frank has everything under control. Nobody else knows we're here."

"How did *he* get here then?" someone in the crowd demanded.

"How do we know he isn't dangerous?" asked another.

"He's too young to be a doctor."

"I don't trust him. He's not one of us."

Jackie leaned in to Kamiyo. "Sorry. This is a massive shock to them."

Kamiyo understood—it was a massive shock to him too. They all looked at him like wounded barn owls, wide-eyed and skittish. The tension in the air was so thick he worried they might suddenly decide to lynch him. It worried him enough to speak out in his own defence. "Before the gates opened, I was a junior-registrar on a maternity ward. I'm not a hugely experienced doctor, but if I can help anyone here, I will. This place is amazing. The reality out there, beyond the forest, is... well, it's horrific, which is why I've been travelling alone for over a month now. The roads are dangerous, so I've been keeping to the fields and trees. That's how I stumbled upon the castle. I'm sorry if me being here upsets anyone, but I promise I'm not dangerous. I'm just trying to stay alive."

"Bullshit," someone shouted, and Kamiyo was sure it came from a child. More people shouted similar sentiments.

But then the mood changed.

"Thank God we're not the only ones."

"You're welcome here, kidda. We're glad to have you."

"The lad's a doctor? Bostin!"

"My son is poorly. Will you help him, please?"

Kamiyo homed in on the last speaker and spotted an ashen-faced gentleman wearing a bedraggled polo neck with a muddy designer logo on the breast. One lens of his thin-profile spectacles had cracked, and his brown hair was over-grown and greying at the temples. He looked at Kamiyo imploringly.

Kamiyo nodded at the man. "That is what I want to do! If you allow me to stay, I'll do everything I can to look after your sick and injured. I can't work miracles without medicine or equipment, but I'll do what I can."

The bedraggled man stepped forward and lunged at Kamiyo. Kamiyo nearly yelped in terror, but the man only grabbed his hand so he could shake it enthusiastically. "Thank you," he gushed in Kamiyo's face. "Thank you. Heaven must have sent you."

"Let's not get ahead of ourselves, but I would like very much to see your son. What's his name?"

"Bray. His name is Bray. He grew sick three days ago. Just the sniffles at first, but last night he got a terribly high fever. He hasn't come out of it—doesn't even know where he is. We already lost James last night... If my boy..." The man struggled to contain himself.

It sounded serious, and Kamiyo tried not to show concern. In the old world, the world that existed just three or four months ago, a fever was not the end of the world—most could be managed with cool baths and paracetamol—but now, and especially with delirium-level fever, there might be a battle to contain it. Kamiyo eyed the lake and its frigid waters. "Take me to your son."

Sensing the sudden authority in his voice, Jackie stepped away and took his arm. She, along with the worried father, led Kamiyo up a series of wooden steps into the large log cabin that was deceptively framed in steel and only adorned with timber. It was a sturdy, impressive building.

Their footsteps thudded as they headed across a deck and between two large glass doors which lay open, inviting them into the warm reception area. Kamiyo took it all in quietly, not wanting to miss anything. A canoe hung from the rafters, and fishing nets lined all four walls. A wooden reception desk stood to one side, with a muscular swordfish mounted on a chestnut shield behind it. Topping things off was a quaint brass bell on top of the counter. Kamiyo had to resist tapping it.

The worried father was right behind Kamiyo and hurried to the front now. "My boy is in here." He moved in front of a door with a plaque reading: FIRST AID.

Jackie opened the door for them.

The stench of sweat and sickness wafted out like a slap to the face. The air inside the small room was stifling and muggy. The smells oddly comforted Kamiyo, reminding him of the hospital and his days of being a simple doctor. Two children and a grown woman lay asleep on cot beds. All three of them were clearly unwell, and heat radiated off their bodies. In the flicker of nearby candles, their skin appeared grey and lifeless. "We should move them outside," Kamiyo urged. "This room is too small. There's no ventilation. It's a petri-dish for whatever we're dealing with."

Jackie appeared disturbed by that, and she stepped back into the doorway. "Are we in danger?"

"I don't know, but the weather's mild at the moment so we should move the sick outside to help keep them cool." He wiped his forehead with his forearm. "Can't you feel how hot it is in here?"

The father didn't seem to have been listening. He pointed at the young boy on the left, a kid just into his teens. "This is my son. This is Bray."

Kamiyo nodded. "Any diarrhoea? Sickness?"

"No, the opposite. Just fever."

"Same with Michael and Carol." Jackie spoke from the doorway. "Except Carol has a rash."

Kamiyo frowned. "Show me."

Jackie fidgeted with herself like she didn't want to come inside, but she summoned the courage and shuffled over to the grown woman on the right, lifting up her t-shirt. The woman was half-awake but didn't seem to notice being interfered with. She murmured to herself and stared up at the ceiling. The rose red rash covered her entire trunk. Jackie stepped back and folded her arms. "She had a cough as well, but that's died down."

"A cough?"

Jackie nodded. "Before her fever got bad, Carol was hacking and coughing constantly. Had to sleep in a tent on her own to keep from waking everyone up."

Kamiyo groaned without realising and saw the concern it caused the others.

"Oh god," said the father, clutching at his unruly brown and grey hair. Behind his broken spectacles, his eyes were panicked. "You know what it is, don't you?"

"I can't be certain," said Kamiyo, trying to keep his tone even and calm. "It could be several things, but there's a chance it's Typhoid Fever."

"Oh god."

"Now, don't panic." Kamiyo put a hand on the man's arm. "Sir, can you tell me your name?"

"Philip."

"Okay, Philip. Typhoid Fever more often than not clears up on its own. It sometimes affects adults worse, which is why Carol has more symptoms. We need to keep Bray and the others cool, so I suggest we take them outside as soon as possible. There's a nice breeze tonight."

"Is that all?" Jackie asked. "They'll get better? Doesn't Typhoid kill people? We lost James last night. He had the same symptoms as Carol."

"In a few cases, yes, Typhoid can be fatal. It's easily treatable with antibiotics, but I'm guessing nobody is in possession of any?" They shook their heads at him. "Okay, then we'll have to manage them through their fevers and wait for them to fight it off on their own. In the meantime, we need to isolate them from the rest of the camp. Typhoid is bacterial in nature, and highly contagious."

"How did my boy get it in the first place?" Philip was on the verge of tears as he spoke.

Kamiyo shrugged and sighed. "Contaminated food or dirty water, perhaps. Typhoid is uncommon in the UK, but the country has taken a step back recently in terms of health and sanitation. You need to boil any water before you drink it, even rain water, but especially if it comes from the lake."

Jackie groaned. "In the first couple of weeks, we were a disorganised mess, as I'm sure you can imagine. Some of us wanted to leave and find our families. Others argued about who was in charge. It was a while before we reached a consensus about keeping the children safe here and staying put. While all this arguing was going on, the kids were drinking straight from the lake. Once we realised, we started collecting rainwater. Every night we build a fire and boil the water."

"Good. What about food? What are you all eating?"

"You saw the fish drying, I assume? We've been catching whatever we need from the lake, drying it in the sun and smoking it over the fire at night. We also hunt birds and rabbits with our bows and arrows. Steve in our group is a butcher. He guts and skins them for us. They get eaten the same day. There are acorns and things too that we gather. There's a poster we've been using to identify what we can eat."

Kamiyo examined the three patients for a moment while he considered. "Someone may have caught it before all this started, during a trip abroad most likely. They could have been asymptomatic and passed the bacteria on accidentally. It's probably the water though, so no more drinking from the lake. Anyone with a fever or a cough needs to be isolated right away. They can stay together, but not around healthy people. What have you done with... James, was it?"

"We buried him this morning at the edge of the forest."

"Good. You should quarantine anyone who handled his body."

"Right, yes, okay." Jackie turned toward the doorway, heels clicking on the wooden floorboards. "I'll go, um, spread the word."

"I need to get Bray outside," said Philip. "I need someone to help me lift him."

Kamiyo placed a hand on the father's back. "I'll help. Let's lift the cot."

The cot bed was a canvas spread across a small trellis, so it wasn't difficult to lift between them. Kamiyo held the head end while Philip took his son's legs, and together they sidled out of the first aid room and into the larger reception area. Night was only minutes away, and the cabin was cast in a featureless grey. Shadows danced near the entrance, aroused by the glow of a fire outside. Kamiyo hadn't acknowledged it when he arrived, but there was a large pit in front of the cabin, piled high with logs and branches. An adult was lighting the whole thing with a bundle of flaming twigs. Did the group sing *Kumbaya* every night while roasting marshmallows? It was astounding, and Kamiyo couldn't help but stare as he shimmied past.

"There's a spot over here," said Philip once they'd trekked down to the lake. "It's a nice shady area."

"Okay," said Kamiyo, wheeling around with the sick teenager. "You sure it's wise building such a big fire like that? What if the demons see the smoke?"

Philip huffed.

"Did I say something funny?"

"Demons. I saw them on the news, but I'm still not sure I

believe it. We haven't seen a single one. Whole thing could be a hoax for all I know."

"I take it you were one of the ones who wanted to leave early on?"

Philip nodded, a bead of sweat appearing on his brow as he heaved his son. "Yes. I'm not prepared to spend the rest of my days hiding in the forest. We have no idea what's going on in the rest of the world."

Kamiyo couldn't believe what he was hearing. "I do! There's nothing left out there, I assure you. The demons have won. If it wasn't for this place, you would all be..." He sighed. "You've been very lucky, trust me."

Philip grunted. "*You're* still alive. You can't be the only one."

"I'm not. There are others, but very few. Soon, there might not be anyone. You all need to stay here."

To Philip's credit, he seemed to think about it. "Perhaps," he muttered, looking down at his son and seeming to put a pin in the matter. "Here, set Bray down beneath these trees."

Kamiyo looked up at the trailing canopy of a willow tree and agreed it was a nice cool patch. He bent his knees and eased the boy onto the ground. "We need to set up ground cover and a tarp overhead. Can't risk bird faeces landing on the patients."

"I'll see what I can find. Thank you, doctor. I appreciate this."

Kamiyo smiled, then looked out over the moonlit lake. Several ducks and a bevy of swans idled on the water. Their presence worried him. In fact, the entire lake shimmered with movement. "Someone needs to watch over the sick at all times. There's too much wildlife here. Once we have Carol and Michael situated, I'll take the first shift."

Philip nodded. "I understand. I'll keep watch on my boy until then."

Kamiyo glanced back at the shimmering lake, unsettled by it. It seemed alive, almost apprehensive, like Mother Nature herself was trying to call out a warning. Then Kamiyo turned to watch the growing campfire outside the log cabin. Plumes of black smoke and glowing embers rose into the sky.

Could this place really remain hidden?

10

TED

"I think we're okay." Hannah scanned the trees with her rifle. As chatty as she was, she'd been utterly silent for the last hour. In fact, her unwavering focus unnerved Ted. She straightened up from a crouch and looked at him. Her hair was still wound tight as steel. "They were sticking to the road when we last saw them. Hopefully, that's where they'll stay."

"They'll start checking out places like this eventually," said Ted, sweeping aside a thorny bush with his hammer. "They've already moved out from the towns and cities, spreading out like a net, and we're the fish."

Hannah turned a circle, studying the ground and then peering up at the canopy. "They'll have a hard time finding us in this forest. I didn't know places like this still existed."

"You didn't think forests existed?"

She chuckled. "Well, yeah, I knew they *existed*. I just thought they were elsewhere, in places like Norway and... Narnia. I thought England got paved over long ago."

"Don't swallow everything the media feeds you, luv. There's plenty of land left, but they drip-feed it to keep the house prices and rents high."

Hannah frowned. "Why would anybody do that?"

"Because half the MPs in Westminster own digs. Landlords and developers, the lot of 'em. Every law that passes through Parliament benefits some Tory muppet or another."

"Wow, are you one of those conspiracy nuts?"

He shot her a dirty look. Why were the young so blind to what was piled in front of them? Maybe because they spent their entire lives staring at their phones. No point trying to educate her now. In fact, he should be using the past tense. "Guess, it don't matter anymore. The politicians are all dead. One of the few good things to come out of this soddin' mess."

Hannah winced. "Shit, Ted. That's cold."

Ted used his hammer to push back a branch as he stepped through some brambles. Hannah followed him, as always, yet somehow she managed to do so without making a sound, while he sounded like a bowling ball rolling through cornflakes. "Morbid jokes are the only jokes I have left," he told her. "You don't have to laugh."

"I know what you're saying," she said. "Being alone has a way of making you numb. Most days, my head is full of empty static."

"Really? Because it seems like you never go on bloody standby."

"It's my anxiety. I get pretty jittery and talking gets out my nervous energy. My sergeant used to say it was a wonder I could shoot straight with my shaky hands."

Ted climbed up and over a fallen log, landing on a rock that sent a jolt up his heel. The pain quickly subsided, and he oddly missed it once it was gone. "Seems to me," he muttered, "that you have steady enough hands when the shit hits the fan."

"Thanks. I can't believe you took on a group of demons

with nothing but a hammer and a nail gun. That was pretty badass."

"Pretty stupid, you mean?"

"Yeah, actually. That is what I meant. Were you trying to get yourself killed?"

Ted didn't answer that. It would reveal too much of himself. He didn't want to be friends. He didn't want company.

"I tried to kill myself once," Hannah said bluntly, as if she were sharing something no more intimate than her favourite colour. Ted glanced back at her, surprised by the candour, but she gave him a shrug and carried on speaking. "It wasn't recently," she said. "Not since, you know, all of *this*. It was when I was a teenager. Suppose that was when I first got my anxiety. Normal teenage problems, mostly—boys, booze, bitch fights. My grandfather was a Nazi."

Ted stumbled and had to use his hammer as a crutch to keep from falling. He opened his mouth to speak, but no words came out. He tried again. "H-Huh?"

Hannah chuckled. "Yeah, Grandpa Weber was a fully carded Nazi. Had an iron cross and everything. He was as brave as he was racist."

"And you're what? Proud?"

"Fuck no! It was finding out that made me suicidal, or at least pushed me over the edge. Dad was ashamed of where we came from, but he still loved Grandpa—kept all his old things in a box in the garage. I was rooting around one day and found it all. Dad got angry at me for snooping around and refused to tell me anything about it. He got so furious, like he'd caught me with a needle in my arm or something. I was so confused. Didn't know who I was, like, or who my family was. I took an overdose a few weeks later. Dad hadn't spoken to me once in that time. I just..." She swallowed a lump in her throat. "I just felt alone."

Ted realised then how young Hannah was. Not in years, for she was mid-twenties at least, but in spirit. She wore her heart on her sleeve like a child did, and as annoying as it was, it was hard to hate someone so honest. "I'm sorry," he said, having to force the words out. "That must have been tough."

"To a mixed-up girl coming to terms with being a lesbian, yeah, it was a shit time in my life. Dad found me in my bed, barely alive. The neighbours heard his screams. After I recovered in hospital, he broke down and told me the truth about Grandpa. The old Nazi killed himself a day after Germany surrendered. My dad had just turned sixteen, and he left the country in shame. Moved to England as a kind of penance, met my mum and tried to put the past behind him. He told me the best way to make up for the past was to protect the future. That's why I joined the forces, not to fight Islamist extremists or topple foreign regimes. No, I wanted to show that I stood for what this country is about. I wanted to do what my grandpa did, but for the right side. Huh, maybe it was a way of reorienting my family's identity."

"Why are you telling me all this?" Ted decided that over-sharing was as awkward now as it had ever been.

"Because I'm hoping that if you get to know me, you won't ditch me first chance you get. Besides, who you gunna tell?"

Ted stopped walking and turned to her. "Do you have daddy issues or something, luv? You've been like a stray mutt since the moment I met you, licking at my elbows and begging for scraps."

"I think I explained that, yeah, I have major daddy issues, but that's just one item on a long list, pet. Truthfully, I don't want to be alone again. I've been alone since the battle in Derby—like, *really* fucking alone. For all I know, you might be the last *other person* alive. Means I'm a little reluctant to let you go wandering off on your own."

Ted took his hammer from over his shoulder and thumped it against the ground and leant on it. Somehow, in their retreat, they'd lost sight of the narrow access road, and had entered the energy-sapping undergrowth. "Being alone is better, trust me."

Hannah had stopped too. "Being alone is scary. The type of scary that tears at your soul. I know I'm being clingy, but I don't think I can go back to that. Please, Ted, just... give me a chance to grow on you, okay?"

"The only thing that grows on me, luv, is athlete's foot. I don't want a pet."

"Okay, that's disgusting, but point taken. Just give me the night then. We can figure out a plan in the morning."

Ted looked around at the trees, which grew increasingly ominous as night set in. "I usually sleep in my truck. How the hell am I supposed to sleep out here in the stix?"

"You grab a load of weeds and moss to make a mattress. It's a cool night, we should be okay in just our clothes. We could even start a wee fire. I have a lighter in one of my pockets somewhere."

"I ain't sleeping in the mud. There's still a little light. Let's head back to the road. The demons will have gone."

"I really think we'll be safer here, Ted. Besides, do you even remember which way the road is? I don't even see the road anymore."

Ted pointed. "We came from that direction. So, let's..." He trailed off, squinting and sniffing. "Huh? Do you smell burning?"

Hannah took a moment, tipping her head back and breathing in deeply. Then she looked at Ted. "Do you think it's a forest fire?"

Ted pulled a face. "We're not in California."

"There used to be fires every day when the fighting started."

"But not anymore. There's no one left to start one."

Hannah shrugged. "What then?"

"I don't know. Maybe the demons are up to something. Maybe..."

"Maybe what?"

"Maybe there's someone out here in the woods. You mentioned starting a camp fire."

"You think the burning smell is coming from a camp?" Hannah appeared incredulous at first, but then Ted saw hope creep onto her face. "Let's go. Let's go see!"

"Hold your horses!" He waved a hand, keeping her from sprinting off like a Labrador. "We don't know what it is. I'd say a burning smell is bad more often than it's good."

"Well, I can't walk away without checking." She moved past him, too eager now to stop. "Stay here if you want."

Ted sighed, and for the first time today, he was the one following *her*.

11

DR KAMIYO

Kamiyo could barely believe it when the group did indeed start singing around the campfire. It wasn't *Kumbaya*, but one adult did strum away on an acoustic guitar.

"That's Eric," Jackie informed him as she handed him an honest-to-god cup of tea and pointed to a short, black fellow. "He's a music teacher and a local volunteer here at the activity centre. He was the only member of staff that stayed behind with us. Next to him is Carrie-Anne, she's a caterer. That's Steven, a butcher. Frank and Philip, you already know. That's all of the adults, along with Carol. She's a florist."

Kamiyo found it odd how Jackie introduced people by what they *are* instead of what they *were*, but he accepted it and tried to enjoy the good fortune he was receiving. The sound of children singing was beautiful, but also haunting, and he couldn't ignore the distant glaze in each of their eyes, or the hollow way they smiled at one another. As settled as they appeared, they must have swum through a torrent of misery to get here. With so few adults, the children would be grieving the loss of their parents, and siblings too. Amazing that they were alive, but was the pain worth it? The *suffering?*

Is this life? Or just a crude imitation?

Kamiyo left the campfire to check on his three patients, weighing up the numbers in his head. Left untreated, Typhoid Fever killed one-in-five. With James dead before Kamiyo had even got there, it meant all three of his patients should pull through, and when he checked their temperatures, they seemed stable. If there *was* a fatality, he expected it to be Carol. Her condition was worse, and the children, being young, had a far better chance of recovery. What made Kamiyo angry though, was that there shouldn't even be the probability of *anyone* dying. Simple antibiotics or bactericides wiped Typhoid off its feet in days. Instead, Carol and both of the children slipped in and out of consciousness, burning up in front of him.

The camp had isolated another five children at his request, and they now sat on the far side of the campfire, ready to retire to a pair of large tents that Jackie had allocated them. If they had Typhoid Fever, the odds predicted one of them might die—or suffer severe after-effects at the very least. For centuries, mankind had striven to lessen the odds against its survival, to make death's job harder, but now the medical breakthroughs were meaningless. You were more likely to die trying to retrieve medicines from a hospital than you were from whatever you hoped to treat. And this wouldn't be the end of things either. This camp, without medicine, electricity, fresh water... More people were going to get ill. In this new world, a simple infection could be deadly. A toothache could be deadly. Christ, even asthma could be deadly. They were back to the old days when kings died of syphilis and the elderly froze to death every winter. Living beside a body of standing water was a risky proposition too.

The shimmering lake still possessed that unsettling aura of consciousness, hidden secrets beneath its surface. Kamiyo scanned the shadows of the distant reeds. As much as the world had changed, for the ducks and swans, it was business as usual. Crickets trilled almost as loud as the children sang.

Movement to his left captured Kamiyo's attention, and he saw Jackie coming towards him with something in her hands. When he saw it was a paper plate full of food, his mouth watered.

"You trotted off without dinner," she said as she handed over what looked like dried fish and a handful of nuts and berries. "It's all safe. Part of the activity weekend here was foraging, so we have plenty of guides about what's good and what's not. We've been eating the stuff for weeks."

"Thank you. I've been eating out of tins and packets so long I've forgotten what fresh food tastes like. Never make me eat peaches again, alright?"

Jackie chuckled. She sat on the grass and prompted him to do the same. "I can only imagine. What is it like out there? Is anyone left at all?"

He answered her question with a sigh. "I'm sorry. It might be different elsewhere, but there's nothing left outside this forest that I saw."

Jackie stared at her hands for a moment, then shook her head and looked at him. "I don't believe that. There has to be other people out there because there's *us*."

"People used the same logic about finding intelligent life in the universe, but did you ever meet an alien?"

"I never met a man from Peru, but I know they exist."

Kamiyo considered that might no longer be true, but he didn't voice his thoughts. "I just think you're better off not worrying about the world beyond this forest. What you have here is all that matters. You need to survive."

"That's what we've been doing all this time!" She leant

over and pinched a nut from his plate and chewed on it. "We've done a fine job of it too, if I say so myself."

Kamiyo took a nibble of the dried fish. It was largely taste-less, which was nice. The tinned peaches and cold baked beans he'd been living off were at times hard to swallow. It was nice to get something down with little effort. "Where does everyone sleep at night?" he asked.

"Upstairs in the cabin mainly. There's a conference room where we all bed down together. There are the tents outside too, which you will have seen. Some of us sleep in those during the hotter nights, but it's getting chillier now. So yes, we all bed down together in the cabin. Rather cosy to tell you the truth."

"That needs to stop. People shouldn't share enclosed spaces wherever possible. Spread out into separate rooms and set up more tents. Sleeping in groups is unhealthy in these conditions. You're already getting sick."

Jackie smiled, but it seemed strained. "If you think that's best, doctor. The younger children were all supposed to sleep inside the cabin during the original camping weekend so that's what we came prepared for." She sighed. "Only the teenagers brought tents. We'll figure something out. Any other suggestions?"

"Not at the moment. The biggest threat to this camp, aside from the demons, is infection. Maybe I can cultivate some penicillin, I'd need to look at your supplies first. We need to keep sterilised water at hand, boil bed linens once a week, set up a latrine far away from camp. Maybe up in the castle?"

"We already set one up when the toilets in the cabin stopped working. It's an area at the edge of the woods."

"Good. Look, I'm not saying I'm an expert, Jackie. Far from it. But this might be last piece of civilisation left on earth. We have to protect it."

"It's not going to matter though, is it? The demons will find us. Perhaps not today, but eventually. What chance do these children have of growing old?"

"Probably none." Kamiyo hated to admit it, but pleasantries were dangerous. It was better to face the dangers of the world with a lucid mind. "The only thing to do now is make what life they have left as comfortable as possible. It might be years before the demons find this place."

Another person approached and Kamiyo looked up to see Philip. "How's Bray doing?" he asked. "I only stepped away for a minute to get some foo-"

"He's good, Philip. His fever has come down a little since we brought him outside. A couple days and he might be on the mend."

Philip deflated like an old balloon. "Thank heavens. What about Carol and Michael?"

Kamiyo glanced at the other boy and the woman. Carol didn't look good. "I have the same prognosis. We just have to keep them settled and cool. Fingers crossed, the infection will burn itself out soon. I'm sorry I can't do more."

"Poor Carol," said Jackie. "She devoted her life to these kids. Couldn't have any of her own, bless her. She's our mother hen."

Kamiyo watched the sleeping woman and once again feared she would fall victim to the odds. Death might find her too weak to resist its bony grasp.

"So how did you end up here again, doctor?" Philip chose not to sit and instead hovered over them. His greying hair was still as dishevelled as ever, and his broken specs hung slanted from his ears.

Kamiyo didn't want to admit he'd been fleeing demons only mere hours ago, and it felt absurd to be in this place now, sat beside a picturesque lake beneath a castle on the hill. All notions of demons and monsters now seemed ethereal and unreal. These people didn't need to know demons had come so close to their sanctuary, so he decided not to tell them.

"I was just trying to keep out of sight," he said with a shrug. "I've been travelling alone, and it's safer to keep to the countryside. Tell you the truth, I entered the forest and got lost. I found this place totally by accident. It's still hard to believe that you're all here. I never thought I'd ever see children again."

Philip didn't seem to accept fully what he heard, and his eyes narrowed behind his specs. "Seems a tad unwise to wander into the largest forest in the UK. You might have died out here if you hadn't found us."

"I had no idea the forest was so big. I'm not from around here originally."

"Neither are we," said Jackie in a lighter tone. "We travelled from Smethwick. Philip here owns fifty sandwich shops throughout Staffordshire."

Philip rolled his eyes. "I own four, Jackie."

Kamiyo smiled. "Still impressive. I'd give everything I have for a Ploughmans with mustard."

"Ha! You help Bray get better and I'll give you a lifetime's supply when things get better."

Kamiyo smiled. Did this man truly believe there was a 'better' ahead? These people were dangerously sheltered. How would they react if demons attacked? Would they stand around kidding themselves that the monsters weren't real?

Jackie seemed to sense his doubt because she looked away sheepishly. Kamiyo was about to tell them to wise up, to understand that they weren't on a camping holiday, and that this was the end of the world. He was about to tell them that, but something else happened first.

An almighty bell pealed from atop the hill. It sent the

whole camp into high-alert, and the adults sprang to their feet, hustling the children into the cabin. Jackie leapt to her feet too, staring at Kamiyo like he might suddenly take charge. He just stared at her blankly.

The whole time the bell continued to ring. *Clang-clang-clang.*

Kamiyo grabbed Jackie as she went to dash off. "What's happening?"

"It's Frank," she cried. "He's never rung the castle's bell before."

"What does it mean?"

"It means the demons have found us! It means they're here."

Kamiyo released the woman and allowed her to race off to join the others. He tried to see the castle up on the hill, but the night cloaked the land in shadow.

What horrors had spilled out of the forest? What had Frank seen?

12

TED

The bell rang out from nowhere.

Hannah raised her rifle. "What the hell is that? A goddamn bell?"

"A church maybe?" Ted looked around. Whatever it was, it didn't give him a good feeling.

"A church? In the middle of the forest?"

"What else could it be? We might be closer to the edge of the forest than we thought. I still smell smoke. It must be coming from the same place. It can't be anything good. That amount of noise..."

"Yeah," agreed Hannah. "Any survivors would have to be insane to ring a bell like that. Unless..."

"Unless what?"

"Maybe it's some kind of alarm. Maybe there's a camp in this forest somewhere, and it's under attack. It could be the Army."

"I thought the Army was finished."

"The Army I served is," Hannah scanned the trees. "but Command splintered early on. There were other units out there on their own, doing their own thing."

"Well, Army or not, you don't ring a soddin' bell nowadays for any good reason."

"Whoever they are, we have to find them."

Ted shouldered his hammer and grunted. "No way!"

Hannah looked at him, eyebrows dropping into a V. She didn't use words to convey what she thought, but the disgusted shake of her head said enough. After a moment more of judging, she turned and pushed off into the trees. Within seconds she had gone, only the sound of her footsteps crunching on distant twigs proving she existed.

Ted stood there in the middle of a vast forest. Just when he'd thought he was getting to grips with things, he found himself in the wilderness haunted by a disembodied bell. "I must be round the bend," he said to himself before taking off in a run.

He found Hannah twenty-yards ahead, pushing her way through a tangle of bushes. When she sensed him coming she turned and smiled, clearly pleased that he had decided to come along.

She'd gone back into silent commando mode and moved in crouches and crawls. This was *her* ballgame now, so Ted stayed behind and followed her lead. Once again, her focus was unnerving, and she moved through the undergrowth like a ferret, flicking her gaze left and right and not missing a single leaf. Whatever anxiety she claimed to have, this was her cure. Action was this girl's emotional salve.

The smokey stench increased, but the ringing bell still seemed distant. Were the two things connected, or separate?

Hannah threw a hand signal that Ted guessed meant come closer, or possibly to stay low, so he did both just to be safe. "There's something ahead," she whispered. "People are crying out. Do you hear them?"

He did hear them and wondered why he hadn't sooner.

Then his ears homed in on something even more horrifying. "Those are children screaming."

Hannah nodded grimly. "I know. Stay on me. We'll check it out."

"Fuck that! Those kids are in danger." Ted rose out of his crouch and surged forward. He exited the forest within a hundred steps and was half-blinded by a roaring campfire. At first, it seemed the ground was a giant mirror, reflecting the stars in the night sky. Then his eyes adjusted and he saw a massive lake and reflected in it was a dozen screaming children.

Ted saw a woman crawling in the grass, clutching her neck and bleeding from her throat. A demon stalked her, grinning at the sight of its wounded prey. Ted's vision turned red. His head seemed to narrow at the temples and blood pounded the back of his eyes. He hoisted his hammer and bellowed at the top of his lungs. "CHLOE!"

He brought his hammer down on the demon's head, obliterating it. He spotted another creature rounding on a group of screaming children. They were backed up against the steps of a huge log cabin, unable to escape. The demon had one of the children by the arm, and the sight of the terrorised youngster sent Ted deeper into his rage. Crossing the space between himself and the demon, he swung his hammer so hard that the demon's entire torso folded in half like a paper plate. An enraged warrior, Ted somehow sensed rather than saw the next demon, and as it moved behind him, his hammer came around like a meteor and sent it sprawling across the grass.

Gunshots lit up the night at the edge of the forest. Hannah crept out from the trees, picking her shots with that grim determination of hers. Ted sought his next target and blinked in disbelief when his gaze fell upon a castle on a hill. What the hell was this place?

Something brushed his shoulder, and he lunged, yelling at the top of his lungs. "DIE!"

A young woman melted in front of him, hands out and mouth wide in a scream. "Please!"

Ted stopped himself from caving in the woman's skull just in time, twisting his wrists and sinking the hammer's head into the mud. He tried to say something, but his heart leapt into his mouth and choked him. His arteries threatened to burst. All he felt was the need to smash and destroy. To kill. Or die.

More gunshots snapped the air. Hannah fired and moved, fired and moved, until she reached the campfire. She scanned the tree line with her rifle, the calmest, most even-headed person there. "I think we got them all," she shouted. "The dees are down."

Strangers huddled together around a large campfire, and they stared at Ted and Hannah like they were aliens. Ted clutched his hammer, panting and snarling, desperate for another target, but there were none. Dark shadows lay scattered in the grass, but it was impossible tell demon from human. The woman he'd nearly brained stepped in front of him and startled him. Then she shocked him even more by throwing her arms around his neck and kissing his stubbly cheek. "You saved us!" she cried. "You saved us!"

Hannah was grinning, but all Ted could do was groan.

13

DR KAMIYO

The bell stopped ringing, but the chaos remained in full swing. Kamiyo knew he couldn't stand by and do nothing. For months, he'd avoided the demons at all costs. But this was different. He was the only person there with any idea of what they faced, the only person in the entire camp who'd encountered demons before, a veteran among civilians. Only a coward could stand by and do nothing. Yet, that was what he did for an entire minute, hoping somehow that this gathering of people would take care of things, that they possessed a contingency plan for this situation. Clearly, they did not. They had only planned as far as ringing a bell.

The children screamed and sobbed while adults fought not to do the same. Only a few had a mind to pick up weapons, or to try to corral the children into cover. Jackie was one of them, shouting at the other adults to calm down and stick together. She looked terrified but was a doer not a spectator. Fear didn't control her.

Kamiyo knew demons could be killed, had witnessed people fight them in the early days and score victories. From his third-floor apartment, he witnessed a guy in a white shirt and red tie hold his own against a mob of demons with only a cricket bat. Then there had been a lone police officer who fled a corner shop by shooting his way back to his squad car. He eventually drove away unscathed, three dead demons in his wake. Kamiyo himself had killed a demon this very afternoon with only a frying pan. Now he wished he hadn't left the weapon behind.

Kamiyo turned to Philip and told the man to go find himself a weapon, but Philip froze in terror. "M-My boy. Bray?"

"You can't help Bray if we're all dead. Arm yourself and defend this place. Now!"

Philip nodded and sprinted off.

Kamiyo tried to get his bearings. The danger seemed to originate from the castle. It was hard to see in the dark, for the blazing campfire confused his eyesight, but Kamiyo counted less than a dozen demons coming down the slope towards the camp.

"Fight back!" he yelled as he ran from the lake towards the cabin. Unarmed, he gravitated towards Jackie, now handing out broom handles, shovels, oars, and an all manner of other long, stiff objects. Kamiyo put out both hands. "Give me something. There's enough of us here to fight back."

Jackie's face contorted. "There are less than ten adults. We have to get the children out of here."

"We protect the children by fighting back," said Kamiyo. "How have you not prepared for this?"

"We have! Why do you think I'm handing out weapons?" She thrust a fishing spear into his hands that must have been a prop from the cabin, for it was blunt and hollow.

Kamiyo gave the woman a steely look which she returned in full force. It wasn't that these people were unprepared to defend themselves, it was that they weren't battle-tested. Their resolve shattered the instant that bell had rung, and they needed help growing back their spines. If Kamiyo took down a demon, they would see the monsters were just flesh and bones. Not bogeymen.

But he was a doctor, not a fighter. A healer not a killer. Could he really take on demons with nothing more than luck to rely on?

No choice anymore. It's time to stop running.

Kamiyo clenched the spear in his hands and hurried toward the campfire. He homed in on the screams to know where he was needed; first the terrified cries of children, and then the agonised wails of adults. Soon, he fought against a tide of bodies—panicked men, women, and children striking him from all angles as they tried to find safety. Kamiyo was the only one heading *towards* the demons, adrift in a no-man's-land between safety and danger.

A pair of shimmering eyes spotted Kamiyo, and a demon launched itself in his direction. His terrified mind froze, but his body reacted well. He swung the spear and struck the demon in the jaw. The impact jolted his wrists, a sudden flare of pain that sent him stumbling backwards. When he attempted to swing again, he realised the spear had broken. It really was just a prop.

The demon collided with him, and he grappled with the demon just in time to keep it from slicing open his face. The stench of burnt flesh made his eyes water as he came nose-to-nose with the monster. The odour of its breath made him gag.

Kamiyo fought with all he had. This was the moment he lived or died, and with both arms busy, it left him with only one option. He aimed a head butt. Awkward and ineffective, it succeeded only in making the demon roar. The creature raised a jagged claw and prepared to open Kamiyo's throat.

Kamiyo cried out, anticipating pain followed by death.

A gunshot fired. The demon hit the dirt, bleeding out from a massive hole in its forehead. Kamiyo glanced around, wondering what on earth was happening.

More gunshots rang out and more demons fell. Something moved through the camp, a bulky shadow jerking violently. It looked... It looked like a man swinging a hammer—a viking berserker brought up from Valhalla. The man took down demons left and right, like he was fighting infants. Kamiyo could barely believe his eyes. A soldier appeared out of the tree line, popping off shots as he moved towards the campfire. Where had these people come from? A soldier and a viking.

Within minutes, the demons had all been dealt with. The threat was over.

The dust settled. People crept out of their hiding places. Jackie ran to meet their saviours while everyone else stood agog. The whole crisis played out in scant minutes, but they hadn't come through it unscathed. Carrie-Anne, a woman he'd not even got to say hello to, leaned up against a tree, clutching a gushing neck wound. Nearby, a child lay face-down, motionless.

Somebody cried out behind Kamiyo. Distant. He turned towards the lake and saw someone flailing in the water. They waved their arms madly and yelled for help.

The lake was glowing.

In the chaos, nobody else noticed the drowning man, or the amber glow pulsing beneath the water. Kamiyo needed to figure out what was happening, but he would have to do so later—*after* he helped the drowning man. He raced towards the lake, praying the pulsing glow beneath the water wasn't a leviathan waiting to devour him or an alien craft about to take off. Both were crazy notions, but once so had been demons invading the earth.

Dashing into the water, Kamiyo pinwheeled his arms to keep his balance. The drowning man was ten-metres out, too far to wade to, and he tried to remember the last time he'd swum, deciding it was childhood. He threw himself forwards into a breast stroke and hoped it all came back to him. The water was oddly warm, and the glow beneath the surface hurt his eyes when he tried to look at it. So he focused on the flailing stranger in front of him. How had they got out here? Had they taken to the lake to escape the demons? It made sense on an instinctual level—like how people threw themselves from burning buildings four floors up.

The stranger continued panicking, unaware Kamiyo was trying to save him. If the man didn't calm down, he'd grab ahold of Kamiyo and drag him under.

Kamiyo concentrated on his breathing, frightened he'd be too tired to make it back to shore, or fight off the stranger if they struggled. He turned into a side paddle and called out. "Hey! Hey, I'm coming to get you. Try to stay calm, okay?"

The stranger spotted Kamiyo, and his eyes flashed like torch beams. Then his mouth opened wide—too wide—and from within came the most awful of sounds. An inhuman screech.

Kamiyo realised he'd swum into a trap—a demon trick. The stranger reached out and grabbed him by the shoulders, pushing him beneath the lake, trying to drown him. The world went dark. Sounds swirled together in an aural blur. Kamiyo fought back, kicking and thrashing until he got his head back above water. Disorientated, he tried to keep an eye on his attacker, but when he looked now all he saw was a man —a drowning, desperate man.

"Help me!" the stranger cried. "Please, help me!"

Kamiyo was seeing things, stress and fear messing with his mind. Reality was a strange beast, and one to be wary of these

days, but there was, without a doubt, an ordinary man
drowning in front of him. Kamiyo kicked his legs and reached
out with both hands, grabbing the exhausted stranger and
pulling him towards the shore. He hoped he had enough
stamina left to get them there.

14

DR KAMIYO

By the time Kamiyo got to shore, the drowning stranger had lost consciousness. Kamiyo's training kicked in and he began chest compressions at once. Within ten beats, the young man coughed up a lungful of lake water and breathed on his own. *Thank God! Or whoever the Hell is in charge up there.*

The next threat was hypothermia. Kamiyo touched the back of his patient's neck and found it chilly, so he peeled off the young man's t-shirt and rubbed at his body brusquely with both hands. After a while, he spotted Jackie and called for her help. "I need to go check on anybody else who might be injured," he told her. "I dragged this young man out of the lake. He's stable, but he's cold."

Jackie studied the half-naked young man uneasily. When Kamiyo asked what was the matter, she told him. "I've never seen this man before. What is he doing here?"

"I don't know."

"I have a bad feeling, doctor. We've been hidden in this forest for months without seeing a soul. Now we've got strangers coming out of our ears. First you, now him—in addition to our two action heroes over there."

Kamiyo looked towards the campfire, locating the soldier and the unknown man who'd intervened during the attack. The man with the hammer was large in a burly, beer-gut kind of way—all strength and no stamina. The soldier—who was not a man but a woman—carried herself like a cobra, coiled and ready to strike. Whoever they were, the people here owed them a debt—including Kamiyo. That demon had been about to eat his face when the soldier had taken its head off.

Kamiyo put a hand on Jackie's shoulder. "It's been a crazy evening, but it isn't over yet. Can you get this young man indoors for me, please?"

She nodded. "I'll go get some help carrying him. You go check on everybody else."

Kamiyo scrambled off the ground and hurried over to the campfire. Most of the survivors gathered there, no doubt feeling safer in the light of its flames. Beyond the fire lay several inert shadows, featureless mounds representing bodies. How many of them were human and how many were demon? He dared not think.

The screaming died down and turned to anguished sobbing. The few adults were spread thin but tried their best to comfort the several dozen children and teenagers.

Kamiyo's first destination was the spot where he'd seen Carrie-Anne bleeding from her neck. She was still lying up against the same tree, but now she was dead. Two blonde boys leant over her body and sobbed quietly. Kamiyo stayed back rather than interrupt their grief.

The unforgiving part of himself flared and tried to place blame for not helping the woman earlier, but the rational part of him knew the woman had never stood a chance—not without immediate modern medical intervention. He had known it earlier, which was why he chose to help the young man flailing in the water. After four years in a hospital, triage became an innate skill, and most doctors knew within a single second who to save and who to let die. You helped whoever possessed the most chance of surviving, which sounded counter-intuitive, but the reality was if you tried to help the person closest to death, you only wasted time better spent on someone else with more time to spare. Carrie-Anne had provided the death in exchange for the drowning man's life.

There were still other people who needed his help. Kamiyo knew this because he could hear their plaintive cries. People crammed the clearing around the campfire, rushing around while paying little attention to what was in front of them. It made searching out the injured difficult. Five minutes passed before he spotted a child in need of help.

The young lad was sitting on the wooden planks leading up to the cabin. He wasn't crying out in pain, but the angle of his lower arm was grotesque. Despite the hideous injury, the boy stared off into the distance as if lost in a daydream.

Or a nightmare full of demons.

"Hey," said Kamiyo, approaching the boy carefully. "I'm Dr Kamiyo. You're hurt, and I want to help."

The boy gave no response, but his eyes flicked to the side, watching Kamiyo's arrival.

Kamiyo put both hands up in peace. "A terrible thing has happened, but it's over now. You're safe. I think your wrist is broken though, so I'd like to take a look at it." The boy sighed but sat back to let Kamiyo look at his arm. It was as if he had no interest at all. Unsettling, because a broken wrist should be immensely painful. "Does it hurt?" Kamiyo probed the wrist lightly. Without the luxury of an x-ray machine, it was hard to be sure, but it felt like the ulna had snapped. The bone hadn't broken the skin, which was a blessing because the resulting infection might have been deadly in these conditions. "I have to say, you are one very brave boy. What's your name?"

"Nathan."

"How old are you, Nathan?"

"Fourteen."

"You want to talk about what happened to your arm?"

"Monsters," he said, still staring off at the lake. "One of them grabbed me. I tried to get away, but my arm twisted. Then that man came with his hammer and smashed the thing to pieces."

Kamiyo glanced at the man with the hammer, sitting down now and staring into the fire. His heavy hammer lay on the grass beside him. Kamiyo looked back at Nathan. "One of the bones in your wrist is broken, but we'll get you sorted out, okay? What we need to do is find something we can use as a splint to keep the broken bones in place while they heal. Good thing is, bones grow back even stronger after they've broken."

Nathan blinked languidly, possibly in shock. Unsurprising, as everyone was likely suffering various levels of psychological trauma.

"Nathan, you wait right here, okay? I'll find something I can use for the splint." Kamiyo headed away but didn't need to go far. His eyes fell upon the pile of weapons Jackie had been handing out during the fight. It lay depleted now, but he found a perfectly sized wooden stake right near the top. At first, his mind conjured images of vampires in the forest, but when he found two more matching stakes, he realised it was a set of cricket stumps. He left the two spares and took the other to Nathan. The remaining problem was how to secure it to the boy's arm, but he resolved the issue quickly by using the child's boot laces. "We need your arm to heal more than we need your boots to stay on," he said with a smile. Nathan nodded blankly, not even reacting to the sound of a young girl shrieking nearby.

A few minutes later and the splint was held firmly in place.

As long as the boy kept his wrist out of harm's way, he had a good chance of healing well. "Do you want me to get anybody, Nathan?"

He shook his head.

"Okay, well, you stay here and rest. I'll go see if anybody else needs my help." He stepped away from the boy, still unsettled by the lack of emotion. Was it a psychotic break? Tonight, Nathan had learned that monsters were real.

Kamiyo sought more people in need, but again it was hard to see past the rushing bodies. He spotted Jackie and made eye-contact with her as she followed Steven and Eric into the cabin, carrying the young man from the lake. They shared a brief nod, but Kamiyo left them to their business.

"Help me! What's happening?"

Kamiyo turned to see a woman rushing towards him; although truthfully, he was just in her way. He reached out and caught her in his arms, then held her until she stopped struggling. "It's okay. It's okay. I'm a doctor. Do you need help?"

"I... Who? What is happening?"

"Demons attacked the camp, but it's okay. They've been dealt with, you're safe."

"W-We were attacked?" The woman calmed herself a little, loosening enough that Kamiyo dared release her. She didn't run off, or try to fight him, but she seemed disorientated. He recognised her.

"Is... Is your name Carol?"

The woman nodded. "Yes, who are you?"

"My name is Christopher. I just arrived here. You've been very unwell, Carol,"—He touched her forehead with the back of his hand—"but I think you're on the mend."

She nodded, as if suddenly remembering herself how ill she had been. "I remember being hot," she muttered. "What's wrong with me?"

"You have Typhoid Fever, but your temperature has come down a lot. Your body has fought it off, but you'll need lots of rest to avoid complications. Come with me, away from all this pandemonium."

She allowed him to take her by arm and guide her towards the steps of the cabin. He sat her down next to Nathan, and the two said hello. They obviously knew one another, but Nathan showed no surprise at Carol suddenly being back on her feet. He promptly resumed staring across the lake.

Kamiyo turned to help the next person, but before he made it two steps, Carol called after him. "Did Bray have Typhoid Fever too?"

Kamiyo turned back, frowning. "Yes, why?"

Carol swallowed, and it seemed like an effort. She took a moment to get her mouth moving again. "When I woke up on the grass, Michael and Bray were lying next to me. Bray was dead. Philip must be devastated."

Kamiyo jolted. "What?"

"Bray is dead."

Kamiyo turned and ran.

At the shaded area next to the lake, a trembling silhouette hunched over an inert shadow—Philip sobbing over his son's body. Kamiyo knelt beside the father, checking Bray for a pulse. There was none. The boy's body already cooled.

"What happened?" Philip demanded through his tears.

Kamiyo put a hand on his back. "I'm sorry. Bray must have gone into convulsions due to his fever."

"You said he would get better!"

"I hoped he would. These conditions... Nothing is certain, Philip. I'm so sorry."

Philip turned to face Kamiyo. Snot and tears caked his face. "I wasn't here with him when he died. The demons attacked and I..." He broke into sobs.

"We had a fight on our hands."

"If the demons hadn't come, you might have done something. You could have saved him."

Kamiyo doubted it. He had hoped bringing the boy outside would have been enough, but perhaps he should've submerged Bray in the lake. "I don't know if I could have done anything. He needed medicine—antibiotics."

Philip sobbed into his hands. "We're all going to die in this godforsaken forest. I didn't think the demons were real, but they are, aren't they? They're going to kill us all."

Kamiyo wished he could offer words of comfort, but the man likely had the truth of it. So he checked on Michael instead—the last remaining patient. The boy's temperature had dropped just like Carol's. He, too, had fought off the infection.

Bray was an unlucky statistic.

15

CALIGULA

Caligula sat on a pile of bodies assembled from a small group of humans his troops had plucked from a farmhouse. The foolish worms had been raising chickens and growing crops, naïve enough to think they had a future. His troops had tortured them for hours before finally slaughtering them, starting with the youngest so that the adults could watch.

Now his troops were resting. He released his psychic grip on their freewill for a while so he might clear his mind and recuperate. Even the damned needed respite, for it was only the brief moments of tranquillity that made damnation so complete.

And it was during these brief moments of rest that Caligula revelled in his past glories and basked in the anticipation of future glories ahead. His would be the Earth's final, lasting empire. The southern human army may have crushed the Fallen, but they would not crush the mighty god Caligula. When the humans from the south travelled north to reclaim their lands, they would dash themselves against the most terrifying army in the history. With Caligula as its triumphant general. The Red Lord would have no choice but to consider him an equal.

Rux shambled towards him now, eyes pointed at the ground. As always, the sight of the pathetic Gaul caused anger, and Caligula had to fight the urge to pummell the wretched creature into dust. "What is it, slave?"

Rux dared make eye-contact. "The Germanic Guard have carried out your orders, Imperator. Several cohorts have been sent to retrieve the splinters of our broken southern legions. Their numbers shall be added to our own. Your scouts report that many scattered when the Fallen were defeated."

Caligula snarled. "You do not speak of the Fallen, slave. They are exalted even in death."

"Yes, yes, Imperator! I prostrate myself before you."

Caligula kicked the slave, but there was little passion in the act. "Begone!"

"Yes, Imperator, but..."

Caligula roared. "What is it?"

"The troops suffer confusion. They hear the voice of the Red Lord no more. Hell echoes empty. We... fear. We fear, Imperator."

Caligula struck Rux across the face, denting his cheek. "The Red Lord's will is not your concern. You follow only my command. The wishes of the Red Lord are for my understanding alone."

"Yes, Imperator, it is just..."

Caligula struck the demon again, sending it rolling in the dirt. "Silence, before I crush your eyes into sludge."

"The brother's *feel*!" Rux cried out insolently, almost in anger. How dare this wretched slave shout at him, a god on earth? But what the demon said gave Caligula pause. Sensing he wasn't about to be struck again, Rux regained his feet. "We *feel*, Imperator. The Red Lord has abandoned our thoughts, and instead we... we have maggots in our brains, worms in our minds. What is it we see? What is it we... *feel?*"

Caligula rubbed a lump in his emaciated and ulcerated throat. "What do you speak of, slave?"

Rux trembled and clutched his head. "It hurts, master. Make it stop!"

"I am not your *master*. I am your *Imperator*. Your god. You feel nothing, slave. You are flesh and obedience, and nothing else." Caligula pounced on Rux, his eight-foot frame crushing the five-foot slave against the ground. He beat the lowly creature for an hour until there was barely anything left. Then he rose up and looked upon his troops. The fear in their eyes was palpable. His legions were afraid. And somewhere, deep down, Caligula was too.

Red Lord, where are you?

16

HANNAH

Hannah couldn't believe what was going on around her. For the last two hours, she'd been warming herself beside a campfire while watching people rush around like headless chickens. It was as though she'd made a wish, and it'd come true. She'd been alone for almost two weeks, her sanity cracking, and unsure if she would ever see another human being again. Then she had bumped into Ted and found this place. It was like stumbling upon a ruby in the desert.

The chaos had settled, and now she and Ted were receiving suspicious glances from the strangers whose camp they'd invaded. Did they suspect she and Ted had something to do with the dees attacking?

They should be thanking us. If me and Ted had arrived any later, there'd be nothing left but bodies. We saved these people's arses.

Ted had been an animal during the battle, rushing from the trees with that hammer of his like a balding action hero with a beer gut. Something had come over the guy, the kind of bloodlust she'd heard stories about from guys who'd fought in

Afghanistan. It happened to a person when all that remained was rage. Even now, while Ted sat staring into the fire, he wasn't right. His shoulders rode too high beneath his ears, and he went minutes at a time without blinking. "You okay?" she asked him cautiously.

Ted half-glanced in her direction. "Just another day in paradise."

"This place *is* paradise, Ted. Aren't you glad to catch your breath?"

"You don't know what I've been through," he said evenly. "Or what I deem to be paradise."

Hannah sighed. "Fair enough, but still... can you believe this place? They must have been hiding here the whole time, surviving off the land. They have fishing poles and nets. There's even a castle up there on the hill. A freaking castle!"

"Pity it ain't filled with an army of swordsmen." He picked up a clump of grass and threw it into the fire, watching it burn. "These idiots have been making camp while the world was ending. If we didn't get here when we did they'd be demon food. They weren't even fighting back."

Hannah had witnessed the same thing. The people here had been screaming in terror instead of trying to defend themselves. It reminded her of the very first days of the invasion. People had given into panic back then, too, falling back on their faith that somehow things would be okay—that reality would suddenly tilt back into place and the powers that be would save them. There was no such thing as monsters, they had told themselves as monsters devoured their families. Those days of denial soon ended as people learned you either fought back with everything you had, or you died. "These must be the Duke of Edinburgh kids from the coach," she said. "You reckon those dees on the road found the coach and guessed people would be out here?"

Ted huffed. "No. Demons don't investigate or plan. They move in straight lines, eating up the world piece by piece."

"Then how did they find this place?"

"Because I led them here," said a voice from behind them. Hannah looked up and saw a slender young man with thick black hair and mildly East-Asian features. He smiled at them but looked weighed down by invisible anchors. "I think the demons followed me from the road."

"You what?" Another man emerged from the shadows and approached the fire. He was older, with wild greying hair. Tears streaked his cheeks behind broken spectacles as he glared at the other man. "Y-You led those monsters here?"

The doctor became anxious. "I-I... Yes, I think I might have. They chased me from a house I was searching. I escaped into the forest. They must have followed me. I'm so sorry, Philip."

The older man looked shocked. He kept moving his lips, but it took a while for him to get his words out. "My boy," he uttered. "Bray died alone because of you!"

The younger man didn't see the punch coming, and it clocked him right in the jaw. His lights went out, and he belly-flopped to the ground. His left arm landed right inside the campfire, and if it wasn't for Ted dragging him back and smothering the flames with his sleeve, he might have gone up like a match.

Hannah leapt to her feet and put her hands out to the violent man. "Back off, mate!"

"Who are you people?" he demanded. "We were fine here. We were fine until all of you turned up!"

Hannah kept her hand in his face. One thing she hated was a bully, and this man had just sucker-punched someone. "Just calm down. Philip, right? No one needs to get hurt here, okay?"

Philip glared at the man he'd punched and shook his head. "Too late."

A woman appeared and ushered Philip away before he could do more damage. Hannah joined Ted on the ground and tried to stir the unconscious man whose eyes fluttered open and shut. "I'm sorry," he muttered.

Hannah frowned. "Sorry for what? You're the one who got punched, pet."

He sat up gingerly, rubbing his chin and groaning. "I deserved it."

"No, you didn't." She patted his back. "I'm Hannah. This is Ted."

"Christopher Kamiyo. Doctor." He pulled up his charred sleeve and checked his arm. The skin there was unharmed, but it could have easily been different. His hand, however, was red and sore.

"You're a doctor?" Hannah raised her eyebrows. "Wow."

He sighed. "I *was* a doctor, with modern medicine and equipment. Not sure what I am now. I couldn't help Philip's son. He had Typhoid."

Ted blanched. "Typhoid? How on earth did he catch that?"

"Drinking from the lake, or maybe someone was carrying the illness when things all started. Illness will increasingly become a problem. Even if these people let me stay here, there isn't much I can do without medicine and proper sanitation."

"Why *wouldn't* they let you stay?" asked Hannah. "You're a doctor. Even without equipment, these people need you."

Kamiyo rubbed his jaw again and flexed it left and right. He winced. "I'd imagine they need someone like you more. You saved my life earlier, you know? A demon was about to eat my face, and you took its head off with that rifle of yours."

Hannah smiled and patted her weapon. "Don't get too used to it. She's running out of food."

"What happened to the rest of the Army—if you don't mind me asking?"

"She's *it*," said Ted morosely.

Hannah rolled her eyes at him before looking back at Kamiyo. "My regiment and others, we... we lost a big battle a couple of weeks ago. No one got out except for me."

Kamiyo appeared crestfallen but nodded his head as if he'd known the truth all along. "Well, I'm sure these people will be glad to have you. One soldier is better than none."

"I hope so," she said. "This place is amazing. What d'you reckon, Ted? Will they let us stay?"

Ted shrugged. "Don't know, don't care. I'm leaving in the morning. If these people want to give me supplies in thanks for pulling their arseholes off the stove, they're welcome, but last thing I plan on doing is sticking around with a bunch of lambs waiting to be slaughtered."

Kamiyo grimaced as if the notion of anyone leaving this place was sickening to him. "What? Where else would you go?"

"North," said Hannah, knowing what Ted's answer would be before he gave it.

"Yeah," said Ted, side-eying her. "North."

Kamiyo frowned. "Why North?"

"My business. All I know is that these people are living on borrowed time. The only way to survive in this world is to keep on moving."

Hannah couldn't have disagreed more, and she told him so. "The best way to survive when you're outnumbered is to bed-in. History is filled with small, entrenched armies repelling three-times their number. Sparta was more than a movie, mate, it happened. Huh, you know, if these people had any sense at all, they'd make camp inside the castle up on that hill, not down here in the open."

Kamiyo chuckled. "It's quite a place up there. I passed through it when I stumbled out of the forest. The walls are in good shape and the gate house is still standing. I almost expected Lord Stark to come down and meet me. Suppose these people made camp down by the lake to fish and live inside the cabin."

Something appeared to run through Ted's mind, so Hannah waited to let him speak. Eventually, he said, "You know, that might not be the stupidest idea in the world. They built castles to keep enemies out. Modern weaponry made them obsolete, but this isn't a modern world anymore. The demons ain't stupid, but I can't see them rolling up in tanks. The castle is protected by a steep drop on at least two sides that I see. If the walls are standing on the other two, then maybe these people could defend themselves."

"The walls are standing," said Kamiyo. "All of them. The original gate is still in place too. It's clamped open, but with some tools someone could get it down."

"Someone like *you*, Ted!" Hannah grinned at him and gained a small amount of pleasure from his obvious discomfort of the idea. "You're a builder."

"*Was* a builder."

Hannah sighed. The guy never got any easier to talk to, but at least he'd lost that look of wanting to kill someone. "My point," she said, eyeballing him, "is that you can help these people, Ted. We can all help each other. These people haven't seen the enemy like we have. They don't understand what they're up against. We can organise this place to defend itself, move everyone up the hill and help make it as hard as possible for anything nasty to get at them. And the canny doctor here can patch up anyone who needs it."

Ted threw a twig onto the fire. "These people ain't my problem. I was only thinking out loud."

"Come on!" said Kamiyo, as incredulous at Ted's attitude as Hannah had been upon meeting the stubborn mule of a man. "This camp might be all that's left. We have to-"

"Dr Kamiyo?" A woman came hurrying down the cabin's steps. "Doctor?"

Kamiyo turned from the fire. "Jackie? What is it?"

"It's the young man you pulled from the lake. He's awake."

Kamiyo got up and hurried after the woman, leaving Hannah and Ted sat beside the fire. Hannah frowned at Ted and asked, "What young man?"

Ted just shrugged.

17

DR KAMIYO

Kamiyo followed Jackie into the stuffy cabin which was now littered with exhausted teenagers and shell-shocked children. Dozens of long candles lit the interior as well as a small log-fire at the rear. Several younger children were asleep on sofas. Shock had switched off their little minds.

A man Kamiyo thought was called Steven stood over by the reception desk and gave Jackie a reassuring look. He said, "He's still in there, Jac. Hasn't caused any fuss, but do we have reason to be worried?"

"I don't know, Steven. We should all be very careful whatever transpires."

Kamiyo nodded hello to the man but received only a suspicious frown in return. He could barely blame the man.

Jackie showed Kamiyo to a small room behind the reception desk, and when he entered, he found the young man from the lake sat up on a wood-framed couch. He appeared confused and ill, dark-skin ashen and his coarse hair somehow singed as if he'd been pulled from a fire and not a lake.

Kamiyo approached the young man. "I'm glad you're awake! My name is Dr Kamiyo, and I was the one who pulled you from the water. May I ask your name?"

The young man palmed his forehead for a moment, seeming in pain, but gradually his hands fell back into his lap. His bleary eyes settled on Kamiyo. "Name's Vamps. Not my real name, just a street name, innit? Only thing left now is the streets."

"Oh marvellous," said Jackie. "We have ourselves a thug."

Vamps shot her a glance. "You got a problem with the colour of my skin, sweetheart?"

"What? No, of course not! But I have little time for louts and layabouts."

"Fair enough. Whose digs is these, anyway? Where am I?"

Jackie huffed. "You're in Kielder Forest Park."

The young man stared at her blankly. "Come again, sweetheart?"

"We're in Northumberland," said Kamiyo. "Just south of the Scottish border. You sound like you're from London."

"Innit! Brixton boy, born and bred. Furthest north I ever been is Birmingham—got a cuz in Sutton-Coldfield. How's the fight going up here?"

Kamiyo folded his arms. "What fight?"

"The Army, bruv. Are they taking it to the demons? General Wickstaff got things tied down in Portsmouth, but no one knows what's happening elsewhere. Communications are whacked out."

"Who's General Wickstaff?"

"Leader of Portsmouth. Bitch is like Braveheart, 'cept with tits and shit."

"What are you talking about?" Jackie demanded. "How did you find us here?"

"I went through Hell, luv."

"I think we can all empathise with you there." Kamiyo wanted to keep things from getting argumentative, and Jackie had obviously taken a disliking to the young man. "Vamps, can you follow my finger, please?"

"Yeah, no bov, bruv." Vamps did as asked and followed his finger. His pupils were of an equal size, responsive and alert. In fact, Kamiyo was sure the young man only needed rest. Even now, he was smiling like everything was fine. A pair of gold fangs glinted briefly in the candlelight, and the young man's nickname made sense. "So how am I looking, Doc?"

"I think you'll be just fine. A few more questions and I'll let you get your rest. I still don't understand how you ended up in the lake." *Or how you seemed to turn into a demon when I first reached you.* "Can you tell me how you got there?"

"I went through Hell, bruv."

Kamiyo squinted in confusion. "That's the second time you've said that. What do you mean exactly?"

"I mean I went through Hell to get here, bruv. Like, *literally.*"

Jackie groaned. "What are you on about?"

Vamps shook his head at her and chuckled. "We turned things around in Portsmouth cus we learned how to close the gates."

Kamiyo's eyes widened. "You know how to close the gates?"

"Just walk right through 'em, innit? Soon as something living passes through a gate, it explodes like a nuclear bomb. Best thing is that the shockwave takes out every demon in a five-mile radius but leaves everything else sound. Makes the giants weak too. We took 'em all down in the South. Then we decided to take the fight to the demons at their source. A gate popped up right in the middle of our base in Portsmouth. We had to close it, and I made up my mind to go through. Don't remember much of what happened afterwards. Next thing I know, I open my eyes underwater not knowing up from down. Thought I was finished. Nuff respect for saving me, Doc."

Kamiyo studied the young man, searching for signs of delirium, but while the patient spoke madness, his words were fluent and articulate. He seemed wholly sane on the surface of things. "So, how did you end up in the lake, Vamps? You almost drowned the both of us."

"Must have got spat out of a gate underwater. Only way in or out of Hell I know is through the gates. Shit is trippy, like going through a carwash stoned."

Jackie sneered from the doorway. "Are you saying there's one of those gates at the bottom of our lake, and that you came out of it?"

"Yeah, sweetheart, that's what I'm telling you. For real and shit."

"Rubbish!"

"It's the truth," said Kamiyo, surprising them both. Jackie glared at him like he was insane, but he didn't care. He couldn't shake the image of that glowing light beneath the lake. "When I leapt into the water, I saw something beneath the surface. Something bright. It could've been a gate."

Jackie waved her arms theatrically. "You think we wouldn't have known there was a gate beneath our lake all this time? We've been here for months."

"Must have been inactive," said Vamps. "The gates are all linked to the seals that bind Hell and Earth together. God placed 'em here at the dawn of time, innit? The landmasses were different back then though—Pangaea and shit. Guess some seals ended up under water after the continents shifted. The demons probably don't activate ones in unsuitable places."

Jackie was smiling, but it wasn't because she was having

fun. It was a mocking smirk. "So why did it open tonight, huh?"

Vamps shrugged. "I must have opened it from the other side. Don't remember what went down in Hell exactly, but I know it turned sour." He rubbed at his head again and exhaled wearily. "Look, I don't mean to abuse your hospitality, but I need to get back in the ruck. If I can't get to Portsmouth, then I need to know whose end I'm in so I can help out here. I didn't get a look at this place. How many soldiers you got? Any coppers?"

"One soldier," said Kamiyo. "And according to her, she's the last—around these parts, anyway. Whatever fight happened up north, the demons won. There's nothing left."

Vamps appeared to grow tired suddenly, his shoulders slumping. "She-it. So, what is this place? Police? Militia?"

"It's a Duke of Edinburgh Awards scheme," said Jackie. "We're at a camp in the middle of the forest. Until tonight we'd never encountered demons or other survivors. Now you're all crawling out of the woodwork like lice. Doesn't fill me with confidence."

Vamps stared at Jackie, still weary, but vital enough to show genuine surprise. "For real? We're hidden in the middle of a big-ass forest? Damn, you niggas won the apocalypse lottery. So how 'bout you—" He grabbed his head again, groaning.

"Are you okay?" Kamiyo moved forward and eased the young man backwards into the couch. "You should lie down and rest. We've talked enough for one night." He turned to Jackie. "Can you fetch Vamps a glass of water, please? And a blanket."

Jackie nodded, disgruntled but still obliging. "I'll be right back. We need to have a chat later, doctor. Philip has told me some rather upsetting things."

Kamiyo waved her off, unwilling to discuss her concerns right now. He got Vamps settled on his back and checked the young man's pulse, then his temperature. His forehead was hot. Much hotter than a drowning victim's should be. He hoped it wasn't another fever. "Close your eyes and try to relax, Vamps. Your body has... been through Hell, apparently."

Vamps deflated onto the sofa, tiredness coming off him in waves. "Thanks, Doc."

Kamiyo needed to let the young man rest, but he couldn't help himself from asking another question. Somehow, he believed that Vamps possessed answers to some very big questions. "I'm so sorry," he said, "but before I leave you in peace, can I just ask you... What is Hell like?"

Vamps gave no answer. His eyes were closed, and he was breathing rhythmically. Kamiyo sighed and crept over to the doorway to await Jackie's return. Tomorrow would provide time for more questions. He just hoped the answers were comforting.

"Glorious."

Kamiyo turned to face the room. Vamps once again perched on the edge of the couch. As tired and weary as the young man had looked only moments ago, he'd now degenerated further. His face was *decayed*, eyelids dark and baggy, cheeks sagging. His gold fangs twisted forwards out of his mouth. The room turned cloying, heat from the candles seeming to increase.

"I-I'm sorry? What did you say?"

Vamps stood up, jerking into position like a puppet on strings. "Hell. Is. Glorious."

Inhuman eyes glared at Kamiyo. A change had come over Vamps, one that made the flames on the candles retreat.

Kaiyo tried to swallow, but his throat was sandpaper dry. "Vamps? Y-You really should rest."

"The worm is gone. Its soul screams in agony. I hear it singing."

Kamiyo backed up against the wall. "W-Who are you?"

"I am God. Bow, and your death shall be quick and brutal."

The candles snuffed out, and the room went pitch-black. Kamiyo howled in terror without realising it, his fear acting quicker than his mind. Something primal—something ancient—stalked him in the dark. He fumbled in the dark for the door handle, but a blow struck his kidney and dropped him to the ground in agony. A reptilian laugh shook the room.

Kamiyo tried to climb, but a second blow struck his ribs and sent him rolling across the ground. He tried to cry out again, but his lungs had twisted in his chest. The darkness closed around him. This was how he died. Alone in the dark. Hell had taken over the earth and only oblivion waited.

But a slice of Heaven entered the room suddenly, a radiant knife cutting through the shadows. The darkness retreated. Kamiyo instinctively reached towards the light and saw the door was open. Jackie stood in the rectangle of light. "Dr Kamiyo?"

"Jackie! Jackie, please, you have to—"

Something surged out of the darkness and seized Jackie, dragging her by her hair into the dark corner of the room. Her screams felt far away, but perhaps they were smothered by Kamiyo's own wails of terror.

The door slammed shut, and the light withdrew. Once again, darkness was all that remained. That, and the reptilian laughter of a beast.

18

HANNAH

Hannah was still sitting with Ted when she heard the scream inside the cabin—the soft din of someone calling out for help. Ted heard it too, and he glanced at her with something between indifference and mild interest.

Hannah grabbed her rifle. "The hell is that?"

"I dunno. Leave 'em to it."

"What? No, we should go check it out. Someone might need help."

She got up, expecting him to go with her, but he didn't. In fact, he seemed irritated by her insistence. "At what point did you decide we were an apocalyptic duo? You're the soldier. Go save the day."

"You're a real arsehole, you know that, Ted?" She didn't wait for a rebuttal. It was possible she was done with Ted and his abrasive attitude.

She raced up the wooden steps into the cabin alone. People were huddled inside, staring towards a door behind a reception desk. The woman who'd summoned Dr Kamiyo was rushing towards it with a blanket and a glass of water, and when she saw Hannah approaching with her rifle, she gave a strained smile. "Everything is under control. Dr Kamiyo is struggling with a patient. I'll help him handle it."

Hannah's jog faltered, and she stood still, awkward now like running for a bus she'd missed. The woman dismissed her so snippily that Hannah's ingrained obedience to authority kicked in and made her stand to attention. Another adult stood in the room, watching over a group of teenagers, and he glared at Hannah like she was a stinking rodent.

She waved a hand. "Hi!"

The man gave a mistrustful nod, but no reply.

"I'm Hannah."

"Steven."

"Great place you have here, Steven. Did you pick the decor yourself?"

The man turned his back on her and resumed tending to the teenagers.

Jackie opened the door behind the reception desk. The room inside was pitch-dark, so she stood there looking confused for a moment, peering inside. "Dr Kamiyo?" she enquired.

Then, in a flash, her body lurched forwards, an invisible rope yanking her by the neck into the darkness of the room. The door slammed shut behind her. From inside, she screamed.

The teenagers screamed too.

Hannah stood frozen. What the hell just happened? What was going on in that room? A dark room full of screams.

After a couple of seconds, it became clear that nobody was going to act. The teenagers pressed up against the walls in fear. The man watching over them did the same. Hannah decided she would have to be the one to do something, so she sprinted behind the reception desk and kicked open the door. Enough candlelight flickered on the reception desk that she could make out grey shapes and flickering shadows inside the room. People crawled along the floor. Something large and upright stalked them.

Hannah raised her rifle to the gasps of those in the cabin behind her, but she couldn't take a shot. There was no way to know what she would be hitting. One of the shapes on the ground scuttled towards her. It slipped out of the darkness and into the small pool of light bleeding inside the doorway.

"Get me out of here!" Dr Kamiyo cried out from on his belly. Hannah reached down and grabbed his blood-slick hand and dragged him out of the room. He was shaking like a leaf, and bled from a wound buried beneath his thick, black hair.

Hannah left the doctor behind the reception desk and hurried back to help Jackie. But before she was able to rescue the woman, something swiped at her from the shadows. The blow knocked her sideways, and she bounced off the door-frame before tripping over an obstacle on floor. Something grabbed her, and she realised it was Jackie. "Help me!" the woman cried. "Get me out of here!"

Hannah was tangled in her rifle's strap, but she managed to grab Jackie and shove her up onto her hands and knees. The two of them hurried towards the doorway, and Hannah got Jackie out into the light. Before she could reach safety herself though, the shadowy presence still in the room grabbed her belt and yanked her backwards. She threw out her hands and grabbed the doorframe and then screamed as the door slammed shut on her hands. She kicked her legs, trying to shake off her attacker, but the pain in her hands dizzied her, and made her weak. Those inside the main cabin howled in fear, but no one came to help her. Only a sliver of light existed in the room. If she let go of the frame, the darkness would consume her.

A laugh broke out in the shadows, turning her blood to ice. The evil let go of her belt and grabbed her ankles. The darkness was going to devour her. "H-Help me! Please... somebody!"

The laughter in the darkness mocked her.

She tried pulling herself through the doorway, but it was no use. The door cut into her fingers, and the force pulling her back was too strong. Her wrists would give out any second. Her fingers began to tremble. And slip.

The darkness retreated.

Hannah found herself being pulled into the light.

The laughter behind her stopped, and a frustrated snarl. A dog losing its bone.

Ted gathered Hannah into his thick arms and dragged her away from danger. He didn't put her down until she was well out from behind the reception desk. "You have a talent for finding trouble, luv."

"You're the one who jumps in with nothing but a hammer and a bad attitude," she shot back.

"This makes us even, deal?"

The candles on the reception desk blinked out. Dr Kamiyo shot to his feet and pointed frantically. "That's how it started! The candles snuffed out and I was attacked. The thing inside that room is evil."

Hannah flexed her hands, wincing in pain. She felt confident they were unbroken, so she got a grip on her rifle and pointed it at the open doorway.

"What is it, Doctor? A dee?"

"What the hell is a dee?"

"A demon."

Kamiyo shook his head. "No, it's not a demon. It's just... it's just a young man I pulled from the lake. He's behaving like he's possessed. Maybe he is."

"Take the sod down," said Ted. "We don't need this aggro."

Hannah glanced at Jackie. A bloody wound dissected her cheek, making it clear that whatever had attacked her in that room wasn't a man. "Come out or I'll blow your goddamn head off," she yelled at the darkness. "I don't want to kill you, but you've got a lot of people out here scared."

Silence. The people in the cabin pressed together like spooked cattle, children in the middle, adults at the front. They all fixated on the rectangle of darkness coming from the open doorway.

Whatever was inside did not come out. Hannah cursed beneath her breath. For the first time since she'd been a recruit, her finger trembled over the trigger guard. Something was wrong about this. The presence in the room had been more than just a dee, but it wasn't some deranged guy either. She sensed something unnatural, something that turned her stomach and sent feverish quivers across her skin.

"Okay, whoever is in there, you have three-seconds to come out. Fail to do so and I will fire and kill you. A shot from this range will cause your internal organs to rupture even if I hit you in the shoulder. It is important you understand that. Okay, I'm going to start counting. This is your last chance. Come out or I will shoot you dead."

Candles deeper in the room blinked out, one by one, leaving the frightened spectators in near-darkness. Hannah exchanged a glance with Ted, who was the only one in the cabin who didn't look terrified. In fact, he looked irritated. He had his hammer raised, ready for action, and was the only one in the room she would count on helping if a fight broke out. She decided being grumpy was better than being a coward.

Hannah started her count. "Okay. Three... two..." She slipped an aching finger inside the trigger guard. "One!"

"Don't shoot! Please!" A young black man appeared in the

doorway with his hands on top of his head. Sweat and grime covered his entire body, and flesh hung from his skull like it was unattached. He looked utterly afraid.

Hannah lowered her aim, but only by five-degrees. "Who are you?"

"My name is Vamps. Don't shoot me, yeah? I'm one of the good guys."

Dr Kamiyo moved beside Hannah and whispered to her. "Vamps is who I was talking to, before he... changed."

Ted overheard and huffed out a laugh. "Before he changed? People don't turn into monsters."

Kamiyo glanced at him sternly. "I don't think any of us know what's possible anymore. I believe whoever this man is, he has answers that could help us. He's not in full control of himself. There's something wrong with him."

"No shit!"

"I'm not a monster," said Vamps. He looked at them desperately, a man before a firing squad. "I blacked out. I don't understand what's happening. Please don't take me out, yo."

"It's a trick," said Jackie. "He's wicked."

"He's ill," Kamiyo argued. "I don't know why I'm so sure of it, but I am. We can't kill him, he's innocent."

"He's dangerous," said Jackie, her bloodied face adding impetus to her words.

"Does he need putting down or not?" Hannah asked testily. "Because I can't be doing this all night long. We need to make a decision."

Vamps still had his hands held up, but he dared step out of the room and into the open. "I honestly don't know what happened. I-I was talking to the doctor and I just... I just closed my eyes for a moment. This is the next thing I know, innit? Please, don't shoot me, yeah?"

Hannah lowered her rifle. "Okay, okay, just keep things nice and slow, yeah?"

"He's a monster," Jackie yelled. She pointed her finger accusingly at the sickly young man and marched towards him. "You're a monster!"

Dr Kamiyo hurried after her. "Jackie get back! It's not his fault."

She snarled at the doctor. "You really think that? This thug isn't possessed, he's a psychopath!"

The young man who called himself 'Vamps stood there calmly, even as Jackie stormed towards him with an obvious intent to do him harm. Then he started to laugh. His eyes turned black.

"Watch out!" Hannah aimed her rifle, but the damned woman got in her way.

Jackie tried to dodge out of the way, but she was too late. Vamps grabbed her forcefully.

"Let her go!" Ted bellowed.

Hannah continued to try to take the shot, but Dr Kamiyo lunged at her and shoved her barrel towards the floor. "No! You'll hit Jackie. Something is going on that we don't understa-"

"He needs putting down. Move out of the way!" She stepped closer to her target, but she still couldn't get the shot. Jackie persisted in getting in the way, squirming to escape Vamps' grip as he sniggered in her face. He held onto her playfully, toying with her like a cat.

But the game ended.

Vamps wrapped a hand around Jackie's throat and squeezed. She turned bright purple, the need for Hannah to take a shot becoming even more urgent. Every time she thought she had it, Vamps would wheel around and shove Jackie in the way. She was a human shield.

Jackie made no noise, suffocating quietly.

"Damn it!" Hannah knew it was now or never. Her hands shook, fingers bruised from being crushed in the door. She had to make her shot count. If she missed, Jackie was dead.

Just do it. Pull the trigger.

Clack!

Everyone in the room yelped with fright. Vamps stumbled backwards on his heels, clutching his ribs and roaring in pain. Jackie collapsed to the ground, liberated but gagging and choking. She'd been rescued from death's claws right at the last moment.

Hannah peered through her rifle sights, wondering if she'd pulled the trigger without realising it. But her finger still hovered in place.

Ted grabbed Jackie and hustled her out of harm's way. Then he raised his hammer and swung it at Vamps for a second time. This time its heavy copper head struck Vamps on top of the shoulder and dropped him to the ground like a lead weight. He finished the young man off with a boot to the face. "Arsehole."

Everyone in the room had been holding their breath, but they released it now in unison. Dr Kamiyo hurried over to Jackie and checked her over. Hannah lowered her rifle.

Crisis averted.

Ted propped his hammer over his shoulder and turned a circle, taking in the whole room with a look of fury and disgust. "Do you people ever do anything to help yourselves? No one is going to save you except yourselves, so stop standing around like a bunch of spare pricks."

Everyone's mouths fell open, but nobody in the room said a thing. The adults were possibly even more afraid than the children.

Ted stormed out of the cabin, cursing out loud.

Hannah pointed a throbbing finger at Vamps, unconscious on the floor. "Tie him up. Looks like we caught ourselves an enemy combatant."

Wondering if it was hope or dread she felt, she marched out of the cabin to join Ted.

He had been right; these people were useless.

19

TED

Ted spent the night in a small boat shed beside the lake. Specifically, he bedded down inside a half-painted kayak with the number 3 on it. Sleep never came fully, dashing away whenever he was about to get ahold of it. He was glad for the silence if nothing else. He usually kipped in the flatbed of his truck, so sleeping rough was not an ordeal, but when the sun rose, and brought the merry chirping of birds, he realised how exhausted he was. Yesterday had been a shit show from the moment he'd stepped out of his truck. If he'd never encountered those dees—or Hannah—he would still be on his way north. Now he'd have to make the rest of his journey on foot. With zero supplies.

Ted meant what he had said to Hannah about expecting supplies from these people before he went on his way, but now he decided he would outright demand them. Not only had he helped save the camp from a demon attack, last night he'd also put down a crazed lunatic. What was that lad's deal anyhow? Had a demon really got inside of him?

Hannah had followed him out of the cabin last night when he'd stormed off, but he had yelled at her to leave him alone.

While he admired her ability, he held no desire to stay acquainted. All that talk last night about making camp up on the hill, living in a castle...

Jesus wept!

Hannah needed to wake up and accept that nothing made a difference. Their lives were cigarettes smoked down to the nub. Ted was prepared to die, but not until he finished his business. He couldn't afford to waste any more time here. These people were not his responsibility. His responsibilities were all dead. The only thing he needed was his hammer, and that was propped over his shoulder.

No one had seen Ted enter the small boathouse in the dark, so he didn't expect company when he exited, but as he headed for the cabin, a young lad stepped out from behind a rack of fibreglass canoes. "Hi," he said. "I'm Nathan."

"Oh, um, hello." Ted was unsettled by the lad's sudden appearance. Nathan was thin, with an arm splinted and tied against his body. His eyes were a dark—almost black—brown that seemed to look right past Ted rather than at him. Ted realised he'd grabbed his hammer in defence, so he lowered it now and nodded to the lad. "What are you doing out here by the water?"

"You don't feel fear, do you?" The boy's dark eyes swirled excitedly. "You fight the monsters because you enjoy it."

"I don't enjoy it, lad. It's a necessary thing."

Nathan nodded as if he'd just heard something monumentally enlightening. "The monsters will be back, won't they?"

"Yes."

"They're going to kill everybody?"

Ted sighed. "Look, I'm sure you'll all be fine. Good luck to the lot of you."

Nathan showed a little emotion, his face falling into a

frown. "Aren't you staying? We need you. The other adults, they don't get it. They don't know how to fight."

"They'll learn, trust me."

"If you're leaving, I want to come with you then."

Ted closed his eyes and pinched the bridge of his nose. He teetered forever on the edge of a headache. Why did people want to keep following him? He just wanted to be alone—was that a crime?

He studied the odd child and tried to keep his voice on the right side of compassionate. "Look, lad, the last thing you want to do is leave this forest. You've been safe here—and may be for a while longer. The monsters will come again, but they can be dealt with. If you fight, you'll have a chance."

Nathan shook his head and sighed. "The adults are too afraid, and the other kids are idiots. I'll get to watch them all die."

Ted frowned, wondering why the lad spoke so wistfully about such horrid things. "Nathan, you should go join the others. Leave the worrying to those older." Before the boy could argue, Ted cut him off. "Skiddaddle!"

The lad hurried off, and Ted experienced a pang of guilt for wanting to leave. Nathan was obviously a mixed-up child, but who could blame him after living through the end of mankind? The lad had been right about one thing though, the adults here didn't get it.

A rumble in Ted's stomach got him moving again. He'd not eaten in over a day, his meagre supplies abandoned with his truck. If these people didn't resupply him, he'd have a tough time on the road. They owed him.

As he approached the campfire, he saw the woman from last night. Jackie, he thought her name was. She was piling up primitive weapons beside the cabin steps. When she turned to look at him, her left cheek was purple and swollen with a thick gash running down its centre. "Stone me," he said. "That bloody animal."

She gave him a grim smile. "It wasn't his fault, apparently. Dr Kamiyo contends the young man has been possessed by something monstrous, something with no qualms about hitting a lady. Honestly, I don't know what to think. When I was cornered in that dark room... It was like being stalked by the Devil itself." She became teary, holding her cheek. "Not sure how I'm supposed to carry on after that."

Ted studied the woman for a moment, torn between staying silent and speaking. It was difficult to comment on such things. "I don't know you people, but it's clear you're the only one switched on here. When the demons attacked, you were trying to take charge and help instead of running around like a headless chicken."

Jackie nodded and looked down at the ground. "I fear we were terribly under-prepared. We had no idea what was out there, what you and your friend have been going through for months."

"Hannah's not my friend. We met yesterday. I know her about as well as I know you. Jackie, isn't it?"

"Yes, and you're Ted? We owe you our lives. If you hadn't come with that stupidly manly hammer of yours..." Her tears ceased, and she chuckled. "Thank you. I failed the children here, but you gave me a second chance."

"You've kept them going this long. Trust me, Jackie, you've done a good job." He looked past the campfire to where a group of adults were heaving bodies through the grass. Most of them were demon, but not all.

"How many did you lose?"

"Two children, Reece and Alexia, and one adult, Carrie-Ann. I think we're all still in shock."

"I'm sorry."

"It would have been much worse without you. We're lucky you found us."

Here came the awkwardness, the part of dealing with people he hated. The expectation, the obligation, the responsibility. "I'm not the answer to your problems, Jackie. You need to prepare yourselves to fight. Those demons won't be the last, and when the next group comes along, you need to be ready. Cut down some of these trees and make spike walls. Better yet, get your arses up that hill and behind those stone walls. You have a bloody castle up there and you make camp outside of it."

Jackie's unwounded cheek blushed, so much that it matched the purple bruising on her other one. "The castle is cold and uncomfortable. We need the lake and the forest for food."

Ted sighed. "Fine, you do things how you want, but I'm telling you—that the castle is the place you want to be."

"Okay, I'll discuss it with the others. I'm sure they'll be interested to hear your suggestions."

Ted shook his head. "Talk to Hannah. She's the one who wants to stay here and help. I have to get back on the road."

"Oh!" Jackie turned back to the pile of weapons and resumed her work. With her back to him, she said, "You'll probably laugh, but I feel much safer with you here. Last night you didn't show an ounce of fear. It's been a while since I've been around a man who knows how to look after himself."

"There are other men here."

"Ha! Philip might know his way around a sandwich knife, and Steven can butcher a rabbit, but none of us here has any experience when it comes to fighting."

"And you need a little bit of rough like me around the place to help you sleep at night, huh?"

Jackie didn't allow his offence to penetrate her. Instead,

she smirked. "I suppose you could say something like that. Perhaps you might just stay a while and help us get set up."

Ted grimaced. "I really have to—"

"Just spend one more night before you go and make any silly decisions, Ted. You don't know us yet. Allow people to at least give you their thanks. If you still want to leave tomorrow morning, I'll pack a bag full of supplies and see you on your way. Deal?"

Ted was still grimacing. Yet, as he wilted under the woman's pleading stare, he found himself nodding. Sighing in defeat, he said, "Fine, I'll spend one more night here, so I can at least help you people learn your arses from your elbows. After that, I'm back on the road and you people are on your own."

Jackie offered out her hand. "Thank you, Ted."

Ted shook the woman's hand reluctantly. He had a bad feeling things were turning south.

20

TED

Ted was amazed by the workshop he found. A single story, flat-roofed building made of green-painted steel siding, it was located directly behind the log cabin. The smell in the area was foul, and he realised the camp's latrine was also nearby. Pulling his shirt over his nose, he stepped inside the workshop. He found a workbench and all manner of tools. A petrol-powered ride-on lawn mower sat in the corner, and a pair of chainsaws hung on hooks. Best of all, he found a set of wood axes and a two-man saw. While the chainsaws would have been the easiest way to bring down trees, they would attract too much attention—and were of better use as weapons. Therefore, the two-man saw and the wood axes were the tools about which he was most excited. He took them out of the workshop in a wheelbarrow.

"Oi! Where yow think yow going with that stuff?"

Ted stopped and lowered the wheelbarrow to the ground. Before him stood a short, stocky man with a pudgy face. Ted was taken aback. "I-I was hoping to get some of the older kids cutting down trees."

"Why?"

Ted cleared his throat and tried to stand tall before this strange fellow who unnerved him so. "Well, for one thing, we could build a fishing weir, which would prevent the need to spend all day casting lines over the lake. You could move up behind the castle walls and come down each morning to check the traps. Cut down enough trees and you could even fashion a pike wall and booby traps to protect the perimeter. Skies the limit. Wood is a marvellous thing."

"How yow know all that?

"I was a builder. And I read an SAS survival guide once that I guess must have stayed with me."

The other man squinted like it hurt him to think. Everything about him was suspecting and accusatory. "Where did yow and that soldier come from last night? How did yow find us?"

"We were hiding in the forest and smelt smoke. Then we heard a bell ringing, so we came to help."

The combative little man folded his arms and looked cross. The words out of his mouth were begrudging. "We would 'ave been stuck in the mud without yow, I admit it. These are good people, but they've been living in cloud cuckoo land. I dread ta think what woulda 'appened if yow hadn't saved us."

"Oh," said Ted, surprised to hear sense, and what almost sounded like a thank you. "Well, yeah, you're welcome. I told Jackie I would stay a day to help make this place more defensible, but then I'm heading off. I'm Ted."

"I'm Frank. Was me what rang the castle bell last night. I didn't see the ugly blighters until they were right on top of me. It was dark, and the grass is long. Hey, yow know what would make sense? Cutting back the trees outside the castle walls so we have a better view."

"I agree," said Ted, finding himself nodding in absolute

agreement. "You should do that, Frank. Move the camp into the castle and entrench yourselves behind those walls. Next time the demons attack, they'll have to get past three-feet of stone to get at you."

Frank let his cynical expression drop and allowed himself to smile. It made such a difference to the man's face that he transformed into a warm and friendly person. "Ted, yow am a man after me own heart. No bleeder listens to me though. Until last night, I don't even think they believed what had happened to the rest of the world."

"They'll listen now," said Ted. "You *need* to make them listen, Frank. You're the first person I've spoken to that understands—"

Frank cut him off. "That we're at war. And that the best place to be during a war is inside a blinkin' castle."

Ted nodded. "The workshop is full of tools. There's plenty that could be done to make this place a tough nut to crack."

"I know it. We've raided the workshop already for shovels and weapons. In fact, the shovels are in use right now. We're burying our dead." He folded his arms and tapped his foot angrily. "Two kids and poor Carrie-Anne, can yow believe it? If only we'd been better prepared..." He shook his head and sighed. "Anyway, I was trying to scrounge up some petrol. There are other bodies which won't be getting a burial."

"Demons?" Ted had never seen enough of them dead to require petrol.

"I could use yow help, if yow don't mind. It's a grim task."

Frank was straightforward, which was a trait Ted admired, but agreeing to help the man would feel too... familiar. But how could he refuse? The man was asking for help to bury dead children. "I'll bring the petrol," said Ted. "I'll meet you round front in a few minutes."

"Bostin! Thank yow, Ted. It's really great to have yow here.

I'll admit, I was concerned by all yow newcomers, but I suppose I was wrong. We should stick together."

Ted nodded. "I'll catch you up."

He watched Frank disappear around the front of the cabin which, with the man's short legs, took a while. Ted leant back against the side of the cabin and took a moment to think. The more he stayed in this place, the more he felt tugged in a dozen different directions.

But there was only one direction in which he wanted to go.

Ted revisited the workshop and scavenged a canister of petrol, adding it to his wheelbarrow. He rolled the whole lot around to the front of the cabin where he spotted an assembly of people in the clearing beside the lake. Frank was now talking to Jackie, while the other adults stabbed at the ground with shovels. At the edge of the activity, several children watched in solemn silence. The younger ones were weeping.

A little girl with blonde curls sat away from it all, sobbing into her lap by herself. Ted tried to walk right by her on his way to the main group, but her whimpers jabbed at his heart. He had to stop and ask if she was okay.

She'd been so lost in her grief that she hadn't seen him arrive. A yelp escaped her lips, then she looked up at him. Her eyes and cheeks glistened. "I'm okay," she said softly. "Sorry."

Ted knelt so he wasn't looking down on her. "Sorry for what, sweetheart?"

"For crying. Reece said only cry-babies cry."

"Who's Reece?" Ted felt the name was vaguely familiar.

The girl pointed off at the assembly of adults. "My brother. The monsters hurt him last night. We have to bury him now."

"Oh..." Ted didn't know what to say. His mouth turned dry. How could you console a child who witnessed a monster eating her sibling? Every day, this world made him hate it more. "What's your name, sweetheart?"

"Milly."

"I'm sorry about Reece, Milly, but it's okay to cry. Crying shows Reece how much you care about him."

She looked up at him, wet eyes hopeful. "He can see me?"

"Sure he can. He'll know everything you do, and he'll see how brave you are."

"I'm not brave. I'm scared."

"You have to be scared to be brave. It's okay, I get scared too."

"Really? You don't look scared to me."

He ruffled her soft, blonde hair and smiled. "That's because you don't know my secret."

"What secret?"

"Wasps terrify the pants off me. Seriously, I leap ten-feet in the air and scream my lungs out every time I hear buzzing. I was at a supermarket once and I fell right over a Pot Noodle display. They went all over the floor."

Milly erupted in giggles. She wiped the tears from her eyes and gave him a warm smile that struck him hard in the guts. "You're funny," she said. "Wasps won't sting you if you stay perfectly still, don't you know that?"

"Wow, thanks for the tip, Milly. I'll try that next time. You going to be okay?"

"I'm scared of the monsters."

"I know you are, sweetheart. Things will be okay though. The adults are going to put a plan together and keep everyone safe."

"You promise?"

Ted hesitated, but not long enough to alarm the girl. "I promise."

He left Milly to her thoughts, but took his time reaching the others. He wasn't relishing being around so many emotional people at once. It was all for nothing because Jackie saw him and came rushing over immediately. "Ted! I see you've already got stuck in helping us. Thank you so much."

Ted's eyes fell upon a dead woman lying on the ground, and then three dead children. Dried blood covered only two of them. "I thought you said there were two children that..."

Jackie knew what he was asking, and in a quiet voice she said, "We lost Bray to sickness last night. That's his father, Philip, over there."

Ted recognised the man with greying hair as the one who'd struck the doctor last night. His cold, empty stare was familiar to Ted, a consuming grief he knew all too well. There would be little of Philip left by the time his pain was done.

Ted searched for Dr Kamiyo but couldn't find the man. Doctor or not, he obviously chose not to surround himself with death. Perhaps he was avoiding Philip.

Frank came and shook Ted's hand like they hadn't just been talking five minutes ago. "There am two crews," he explained. "Which one yow want to join?"

Ted studied the two huddles of people, one larger than the other. The larger group tended to the three dead children and adult, digging a line of neat graves. The smaller group, a short black man and two teenagers, were gathering demon corpses into a pile. It was the worse job, but one which was being done in grim silence. Ted cleared his throat. "I'll help burn the monsters."

Frank nodded solemnly. "Not afraid to get your hands dirty, am yow?"

"My hands are beyond washing."

"Yeah, I imagine they might be. Thanks for helping us, Ted.

Jackie placed a hand on Ted's shoulder, a gesture he found at once repulsive and electrifying. He shuddered and stepped back, but she behaved as if she didn't notice and smiled at him. "Dr Kamiyo said we need to burn the bodies in case they make us sick. Sooner the better."

"I'll get to it then." Ted grabbed a shovel from Frank and trudged over to the demon disposal crew. Rather than touch the monstrous corpses, the workers were using their shovels to roll them into a pile. The adult male nodded at Ted, but the teenaged boys didn't even make eye-contact. Ted recognised one as Nathan. Had the boy volunteered for corpse duty?

Ted shoved his shovel underneath a demon with a hole in its forehead—Hannah's aim was impressive—and rolled it towards the pile. Some of the demons were in worse shape, victims of his hammer rather than Hannah's precise rifle shots. He looked back now to check his hammer was still in the wheelbarrow where he'd left it. He felt dismembered without it. His unease was multiplied when he saw Hannah heading towards him. She waved a hand. "Hey, Ted. You sleep okay down there in the boat shed?"

"I've had worse nights." He remembered how tired he was and let out a yawn. "Not many though."

Hannah grabbed a shovel and got to work beside him, rolling over that same corpse with a bullet wound in its forehead. "I remember this one," she said. "It was attacking the doctor."

"You remember it from a bullet wound?"

She smirked. "Believe me, you don't forget a perfect headshot. I hit the other three in the chest."

"You took out four all together?"

She nodded. "What about you? How many did you take out?"

"He took out three," chirped a voice. It was Nathan's. He pointed at the line of bodies. "You can tell because they're all mashed up. That hammer is so brutal."

Hannah huffed. "Shit, kid! You sound like his biggest fan."

Ted nudged her. "Don't encourage him."

"Nathan's a weirdo," said the other teenaged boy. He pulled a face and sneered at Nathan. "He's always been into sick shit. No one ever went near him at school. A mate of mine found him in the toilets, masturbating over animal porn."

Nathan growled. "That was a bunch of bullshit, and you know it!"

The adult looking after the boys barked at them to get back to work, then approached Ted and Hannah. He looked embarrassed. "Sorry. There's not a lot to entertain kids nowadays. This has all been a bit too much excitement for them."

"We understand," said Hannah. "I'm Hannah, and this is Ted."

"I'm Eric." They all shook hands. "It's nice to have some new faces around here, if only to show us we're not alone. Thank you for helping last night."

"You're welcome. You, um, don't have the same accent as the others."

Eric gave a titter. "No, I'm not blessed with their Black Country twang. I'm from a village about ten miles from here. I used to volunteer at the activity centre. My colleagues left to find their families when everything started, but I... well, I never had anyone to get home to. I wanted to stay here with the kids."

Ted wondered what choices a middle-aged man had to make not to have anyone calling him back home. "You never had kids of your own?"

He shook his head with enough sadness to show it was a regret. "I probably spent too much of my time stuck in the past to ever interest a woman. I volunteered here for fourteen years, when I should have been getting a social life." He stopped to have a little smile to himself. "Even with all of the horror that's gone on, I still love it here—the nature, the memories, the sense of history. That empty castle up there reminds me that things never stay the same. I hope that one day what we're going through will be just another chapter in mankind's history." Ted frowned, which caused Eric to laugh. "What, you never met a black historian before?"

"Not an optimistic one."

Eric looked at the demon corpses scattered at their feet. "I suppose I was always a nerd. Ask me anything about Kothal castle, and I can tell you."

"Um, yeah, okay, how old is it?"

Eric grinned. "The castle was built by Stanley Godlaw in 1045, and it saw extensive use during the Norman conquest of England. Godlaw died in the castle during a siege in 1068, leaving the castle to his nephew, William Fulford. William went on to—"

"We should probably get on with this important work," said Ted, motioning with his shovel.

Eric gave another small titter. "Now do you see why I never found a woman willing to marry me? Thanks for the chat—it actually distracted me from all this misery for a moment."

Ted couldn't help but smile at the man's self-desecration, but he hoped it wasn't cruel to do so. To move things along, he planted his shovel under the demon corpse and got back to work. But moving the corpse that way was cumbersome, so he quickly decided to just sod it and use his hands. He heard the others gasp, but Nathan watched him the entire time with interest.

"Wow, you're not a squeamish one, are you?" Eric winced, and crow's feet crept from the corners of his eyes.

"They're just flesh and bone." He dragged the corpse over to the pile and tossed it on top. "Doesn't six of their corpses prove that to you?"

"I suppose so," said Eric with an awkward shrug.

Hannah marched over to the corpse pile and kicked at it. "Wait! What?"

Eric looked worried. "Something the matter?"

"Yeah! Ted just said *six* corpses, but that can't be right. I shot four and Ted *hammered* three—that's seven. Where is the seventh corpse?"

Ted inspected the corpse pile. Three demons with their head bashed in and three more with red, ragged gunshot wounds. He then turned to Hannah. "You're sure you shot four of them?"

"Positive. One headshot, three body. I watched every one of them drop."

Eric had his arms folded. "So, what does that mean?"

Ted scanned the tree line, wishing he had his hammer already in his hands.

"It means one of 'em got away."

PART II

21

DEMON

The demon was named David. After centuries burning in Hell, that was the only thing he remembered. Every flap of skin had seared from his bones long ago, his soul torn to pieces until all he felt was pain, but he still had a name. The agony only stopped when he served his masters. The current orders imprinted on his mind were clear: *Kill and devour. Tear flesh. Rip muscle. Crush bone. Mutilate humanity in all its forms.*

But those orders were not always possible. The humans in the forest had fought back, killing his infernal brothers and wounding David—the female with the loud shouty stick had shot fire into his chest. He clawed at the wound now and pulled out a piece of shiny, nasty metal. He threw it into the dirt with a hiss. The humans fought back too hard. The one they'd followed from the road had tricked them, led them into an ambush they were too weak to repel.

Some ancient part of David, some fragment of fear remaining, had caused him to dash into the safety of the trees. Weak, oily memories flowed through his broken mind and made him feel somehow at home amongst these many trees. Had there been a time when running through the woods had made him feel free and... *happy*? The thick scabs on his mind fell away. He pictured a small boy that might once have been him.

No, must think not on things. Must only obey. Obey masters. David must kill.

Killing was good but dying was bad. David did not want to go back to the burning place. This place was better. This place had trees. But he would not go back and face the human with the big hammer or the female with the loud shouty stick.

No, David would find more of his brothers and come back. Yes, that would be to serve. His masters needed to know there were secret humans in the forest. Secret humans in the trees.

David knows. David knows their secret. Must tell. Will tell.

Humans in the forest.

22

DR KAMIYO

Dr Kamiyo was happy with his infirmary, given it had only been a day since he'd arrived at the camp. Jackie had agreed to disperse people throughout the log cabin, and have them sleep in tents where possible, but she also allocated three rooms on the third floor to be used for treatment. One was a conference room with enough space for five or six people. The other two rooms were small, and ideal for anyone infectious. Each room had windows that could be opened to allow ventilation. At the moment, he had a group of six in the conference room—one adult and five children. They each had fevers, possibly more Typhoid. Carol and Michael were amongst the patients, resting out their recovery. Of the other two smaller rooms, one was empty and one was occupied by a single occupant. It was with that occupant that Kamiyo remained now.

Vamps had been unconscious since Ted struck him with that savage hammer of his. The young man's collarbone had been obliterated, and his shoulder badly dislocated. Kamiyo had managed to reset it that morning. Despite severe injuries, it was odd the patient had not yet awoken. Vamps had fallen unconscious from trauma, yes, but not from a head wound. That he was still asleep was a troubling sign.

Kamiyo had carried Vamps upstairs last night with the help of Eric—and Philip who had glared at Kamiyo the entire time. The grieving father was a concern, for he truly blamed Bray's death on Kamiyo. Grief could be a dangerous thing, and the world was already dangerous enough.

It had been Eric's idea to tie Vamps to the radiator with rope, and Kamiyo had agreed. The room already had a bed, so they slid it beneath the window to secure Vamps to the radiator. It made it awkward to check on the young man, but Kamiyo wasn't ignorant to the danger Vamps posed.

Vamps had said he'd come from Hell and taken part in a triumphant battle against the demons in Portsmouth. Could that be true? It was only the slim possibility that Vamps was a good person in need of help that had allowed Kamiyo to convince the camp to give the young man a stay of execution.

Despite his failure to awake, Vamps' vital signs were healthy, and he had lost much of his sickly pallor. In an ideal world, Kamiyo would have placed him on a hydrating drip, but as it was, he was forced to dribble small amounts of water into the young man's mouth every half hour, along with packets of salt and sugar from the cabin's small café. A crude way to give sustenance, but better than nothing. If Vamps didn't awake soon, he might not ever.

Come on, just wake up and talk. Give me those answers I'm praying you have. Like, what is the meaning to all this?

As if his thoughts were magic, Vamps opened his eyes and sat bolt upright in the bed gasping. Kamiyo yelped at the unexpectedness. "Boris Johnson!"

"The Red Lord," the young man said. "He's here."

Kamiyo placed a hand on Vamps' chest to calm him, but

when he realised he was bound, he panicked and started yanking at his ropes. The radiator rattled.

"Hey!" Kamiyo shouted in his face. "Hey, Vamps, calm down. You're safe, okay? It's me, Doctor Kamiyo."

Vamps stared blankly like he didn't recognise Kamiyo, but gradually he settled. "D-Doc? Doc, I'm in trouble, bruv."

"What do you mean?"

"The Red Lord. He's here."

Here we go again, thought Kamiyo, but then reminded himself that he somehow believed the craziness this young man spouted. "Who is the Red Lord, Vamps?"

Vamps puckered his mouth, like he was trying to bring forth saliva. Kamiyo got him a glass of water, and after taking a sip, he spoke. "The Red Lord is Darth Vader, bruv. He's the one behind the end of the universe, you get me?"

"You mean the world?"

"Nah, I mean the universe, bruv. God made bare amounts of worlds and filled 'em with people, innit? The Red Lord has been attacking all the Earths and wiping out humanity on each one as he goes. Now he's here to finish off this one."

"What? You're saying there are multiple worlds? Other dimensions? String theory, that kind of thing?"

"Bruv, I dunno what that is, but yeah I think you get me."

"What does the Red Lord want?"

"To spank God's ass and take his place. If he destroys the last remaining worlds, he'll get a shot at the big man. That's why we have to fight to survive, bruv. The Red Lord can't win."

Kamiyo leant forward, making sure what he was hearing was coming from a lucid mouth and not an addled mind. "Where is the Red Lord?"

"Here!" Vamps shook his head and looked as though he might go back to sleep, but then he beat his chest like a gorilla. "He's in *me*, bruv. I remember it all. The fight in Hell went hella bad. Lucas—he's the ex-Devil—got me out of there, but the Red Lord... Fucker hitched a ride, innit? Now he's right where he wants to be."

"Sorry, did you just say the Devil helped you?"

"*Ex*-Devil. Turns out the guy ain't so bad once you get to know him. Look, Doc, the whole point of this demon invasion is to bring the Red Lord to Earth and allow him to consume the souls of the living—shit is like Big Macs to him or summin. He's already taken the souls of Hell, but it's the living what give God his strength. That's why—"

Kamiyo stood up straight and placed a hand to his forehead. "Okay, please stop." He took a deep breath and looked out the window. Outside, the other campmates dealt with last night's fatalities. There was a lot of sobbing going on, a lot of heartache, and it made him glad he wasn't out there. He kept his back to Vamps as he asked his questions. "Were you really possessed last night? This 'Red Lord' truly took ahold of you?"

"And will again," said Vamps. "I'm sorry. You need to kill me, Doc."

Kamiyo turned around. "What? I shall do no such thing!"

"Did you not hear me about the Darth Vader thing? The Red Lord is bad news, bruv. The worst."

"Darth Vader fell to ruin," said Kamiyo, feeling a sudden pang of sadness that there would never be a new Star Wars film. An odd thing to grieve, so he moved on. "Perhaps you're to be Luke Skywalker. You're still in there too, aren't you?"

"Not for long, bruv. I remember hurting you last night, and that woman."

"Jackie. She's... okay. I explained it wasn't you."

Vamps shook his head. "It was like being trapped in a bath full of scolding water. I kept trying to come up and get my breath, but someone kept holding me down. I don't know why the Red Lord is gone, but I can still feel him in me. He'll be back."

"You're restrained. I won't let you harm anybody, Vamps."

"That won't matter, bruv. Take me out. Cut my throat or summin'. Just make it quick. And tell everyone I said something gangster at the end."

Kamiyo shook his head firmly. "No! That's not what I do. You are my patient. My duty is to heal you. Twice now, I have spoken with you lucidly. There's a reason this Red Lord has retreated, and I shall find out what it is. Then I shall keep him at bay permanently. Vamps, if you're one of the good guys, I'm not giving up on you. Twenty-four hours ago, I wondered if I'd ever see another person again—then I found this place. Perhaps I'm supposed to be here to help you. Christ, just give me something I can do to make myself feel useful again, okay? Let me try to help you, please."

"Why do you even care so much, Doc? I'm just one guy."

Kamiyo looked out of the window and stared off at the lake. It seemed to reflect his own memories back at him. "There are things I need to make right. Saving your life is a good start."

Vamps pulled at his ropes, clunking the radiator. "I can't spend the rest of my life tied to the wall. Sooner or later, I'm gunna need to take a slash, innit?"

"You can go in a bucket. For now, just relax, Vamps. Everything will be okay. You're safe."

"Yeah, maybe," he said. "But I'm worried *you people* ain't."

Kamiyo folded his arms and held his ground. "I suppose time will tell."

23

TED

News of a wounded demon on the loose spread throughout the camp like wildfire. Eric had suggested they keep a lid on it, but Nathan had spilled the beans less than an hour later, telling the other teenagers in the camp with a gleeful sneer. Once it got back to Jackie, she swiftly summoned everyone into the cabin's main space. Ted didn't appreciate being summoned anywhere, but he was too weary to argue.

Jackie stared at Ted now like he was the only one in the room. "What is this I'm hearing about a demon on the loose?"

Ted shrugged. "There's a demon on the loose."

"Could you elaborate, please?"

"There's a *wounded* demon on the loose."

Jackie scowled at him. "Is this a game to you, Ted?"

"No."

"One demon isn't a threat," Hannah chimed in. "The wound I gave it might not have been immediately fatal, but it probably ran off into the woods and bled to death."

"Or it's gone off to tell its dirty little friends," said Frank, hands on his hips. "We have no way of knowing."

"The demons don't operate like that," said Ted. "They're mindless animals that don't know how to do anything but attack."

Hannah nodded, but then argued. "Exactly, Ted. When have you ever seen one run away? They don't show fear, they just keep attacking until either they're dead or you are."

"Then perhaps you're mistaken about the body count," said Eric hopefully.

"I'm not mistaken. I shot four."

Jackie put both her hands against her temples and looked like she might scream. "Then what does this mean? You say those monsters don't retreat, but one of them has. Why?"

"It's gunna bring more," said Frank, sticking to an apparent philosophy that things would always turn out in the worst way possible. Even Ted thought the guy could do with lightening up. "It won't be lung before we're attacked again, I promise yow."

Philip moved up beside Jackie and glared at Dr Kamiyo who was standing next to Hannah. "We were fine here until you people came. You brought the monsters. Our children are dead because of you!"

Jackie put a hand on his arm. "Philip, that isn't helping. We need to focus on today, not yesterday."

"No," said Ted. "You need to focus on tomorrow. It's nothing but dumb luck that's gotten you people this far, and that luck has run out. You all need to be ready."

Eric rubbed at his forearms nervously. "How?"

"By moving into the castle," said Hannah. "By preparing to fight."

"And by building defences," said Ted. "You have all you need to make it a job for any demons to get at you."

"You mean like the ones you brought last night?" Philip yelled.

"He saved us," argued Nathan, who was sitting alone on the reception desk while the other teenagers and children stood on the opposite side of the cabin.

"He endangered us," said Philip. "He and his friends led the demons right to us. I heard Kamiyo say so himself."

Ted shrugged. "Maybe we did bring the demons. Maybe we didn't. Tough shit either way, ain't it? You gunna do something about it or what? Because I promise, pissing and whining ain't gunna help."

Philip stepped up to Ted. "How about I start by sending you back the way you came?"

"Suits me fine," said Ted, and he turned around and headed for the exit. In no way did he need this shit.

A little girl rushed to block his way. It was Milly, the grieving child he had spoken with earlier. "No, please," she begged. "Don't go out there!"

He frowned. "Why not?"

"Because you fought the monsters last night. I watched them get Reece, and no one came to help,"—she glared at the others in the room—"until you did. You killed the monsters before they hurt anyone else. If you leave, who will be here next time?" She put her hands on her hips and tried to look stern, but she ruined it a moment later by saying, "There are no wasps here, I promise."

Ted knelt in front of her and then pointed a finger at Hannah. "That young lady right there is ten times more dangerous than any demon. Stick close to her, and you'll be fine."

Hannah waved at the little girl and smiled.

"But I don't want to stick close to *her*. I want to stick close to *you*!"

Ted swallowed, a sudden thickness in his throat. He studied the three-dozen children packed into the room—all were terrified. *Terrorised*. Then he looked at the adults, who seemed little better. If they couldn't get their act together by the time the demons next came, they would all be slaughtered.

Forty children dead.

Could he walk away from that?

Ted moved away from the doors, and released a long, drawn-out sigh. Then he clonked his hammer down on the floorboards. It got everyone's full attention. "When all this started," he began, "I was a builder. The very day it started, when the monsters spilled out of those gates, I was building a block of toilets for a primary school. Nobody had any clue what was happening, of course. People just knew they needed to panic. Cars started piling up in the road, people looted, and then the monsters came and started eating people. The teachers at the school were some of the bravest individuals I ever saw. They moved the children into safety and contacted the parents—but most of the parents never arrived. Instead, the demons came and waited them out. I saw a hundred kids get eaten alive while everyone stood around in shock, telling themselves it wasn't happening. Me and the five guys on my crew wanted to stay and help, but we were terrified—no different to all of you last night. We ran, leaving those children and teachers to their fate.

A month later, the guys on my crew beat off a dozen demons without a single loss on our side. Only thing that changed was we knew we had no choice but to fight back. There was no point in running or screaming. No one was going to save us but us. That's the learning curve of survival, people. You need to learn it fast."

Frank flapped his arms. "How? How do we get experience without facing the monsters? Dunno, if yow noticed, but I ain't exactly built to battle demons. Unlike Lord of the Rings,

Dwarfs aren't all that handy in a fight. If you have anything useful to share, I'm open to suggestions, kidda."

Ted sighed, wondering if he was being unfair to these people. They were just doing their best, and it wasn't their fault whether or not it was good enough. "You all need to listen. Not just to me, but to Hannah and the good doctor here. We know how to survive. Listen to what we tell you and you might have a chance."

Frank crossed his arms, grumpy yet obliging. "Fine by me."

Philip shook his head in disgust and disappeared into a side room. A few of the older teens followed him. Eric appeared in two minds but stayed put.

Jackie stepped forward so that she was right in front of Ted. She stared at him hard, drilling into him with her eyes. "Okay. You three can call the shots, so long as you stay here and help us."

Ted could barely believe what he was agreeing to, but he knew there was no turning back now. "First thing we do is move up into that castle. The camping trip is over, people. Time to embrace the Dark Age."

Hannah glanced at him with a smirk on her face. He didn't know why, but he got the impression she thought she had won.

Ted took his hammer and went outside. There was work to do.

24

DR KAMIYO

D r Kamiyo looked out the window at the wooden palisade erected at the bottom of the cabin's steps. The sharpened spikes were only four-feet high, but he'd like to see a demon try to get over them without being careful. Ted had done a fine job in the last two weeks, working tirelessly with both the children and adults to first move the camp up onto the hill and behind the castle walls, and then make it an absolute nightmare to attack. He'd also fortified the cabin by the lake, so Kamiyo could continue to use it as an infirmary, and as a place for everyone to work during the day.

The cabin constantly reeked of fish now, for Steve, the camp's butcher, gutted the daily hauls from the lake. With the weir Ted had built, they were now more than able to keep themselves fed calorie-wise, if not nutrition-wise.

Life was okay. The demons hadn't arrived as they'd feared, and behind the thick castle walls everyone slept quite soundly. Frank ran a squad that spent each day thinning out nearby trees to make it easier to spot approaching threats, and they deposited the timber in the castle's courtyard where Ted's team would then make use of it. In the late afternoon, Hannah taught hand-to-hand fighting techniques that the teenagers in particular loved learning. The group was toughening up, in more ways than one.

But there were problems too. Problems like the fact Kamiyo was peering down at another dead child. Emily was only twelve-years old, but she'd never reach thirteen. Her cause of death had been an innocuous nail jutting out of one of the canoes in the shed. A careless accident, but one which had taken her life in the space of six days. Nothing Kamiyo had done to keep the three-inch gash clean of infection had worked, and within forty-eight hours the gash was oozing pus, and the redness and swelling had crept up her entire arm. In the end, sepsis killed Emily.

Kamiyo also had a patient with suspected Lyme disease, and a child with a broken finger. The Typhoid had burnt itself out days ago, taking no other victims, but it had left the sufferers weak and depressed. When you counted the dead, sickness had taken more than the demons had during their dreadful attack two weeks ago.

And great stone walls couldn't keep out sickness.

"You need help with her, Doc?" Vamps nodded to Emily. The young man had not turned violent since the night he'd attacked Kamiyo and Jackie in that darkened room. It appeared that, whoever the Red Lord was, he had gone for now—perhaps forever. Every day, the relief on Vamps' face grew increasingly obvious, and eventually he had asked to have his bonds removed. Kamiyo reluctantly agreed, despite arguments from others in the camp, and the two of them had gone on to become friends of a sort. Despite being shunned by everyone at the camp, Vamps worked tirelessly to help wherever he was needed.

"We should tell the others," said Kamiyo, patting Emily's

damp hair so it was neat. "They will want to bury her with the others."

Vamps sucked at his teeth and shook his head sadly. "She was a good kid. Wanted to play violin in an orchestra, she told me. She must have had a different upbringing than I did, bruv."

"But she ended up in the same place anyway," said Kamiyo. "We all did."

"Yeah, Doc, I guess you're right."

Kamiyo asked Vamps to keep watch on the patients while he reported Emily's death to the others. He went downstairs, and the first person he bumped into was Philip. The man still hated him after losing his son and had been very vocal about it in the last two weeks.

"Christopher," said Philip curtly, refusing to call him 'Doctor' like everybody else did.

"Philip. How are you?"

"Wonderful, thank you for asking. It's almost like my son hadn't died two weeks ago."

Kamiyo rolled his eyes. While he appreciated that the man was in pain, he was losing patience with the endless derision. "I'm afraid Emily has just passed away. Could you get word to Jackie for me, please?"

Philip shook his head in disgust. "You killed another kid? Go tell her yourself. Don't get me involved."

"Infection killed her Philip, not me. As for getting involved, we're all in this together. If a child dies, it's on all of us."

"You're the only doctor here. Not a very good one, admittedly."

"Yes, I'm a doctor," Kamiyo shot back. "Not a miracle worker. I have no medicines to administer. No equipment. No staff. I do whatever I can, so get off my fucking back, Philip."

"Do not swear at me, or I promise you I'll—"

"You'll what, Philip? You want to throw another punch? Do it!"

Philip stood for a moment, lip curling, hands clenching and unclenching at his sides. "I'll pass your message along to Jackie," he said. "Tell her you've failed again."

Kamiyo waited for him to leave, then stepped out into the fresh air to take a breather and calm down. He'd never been a violent man in his past, but it took a lot not to strike Philip. A man could only take so much.

Steven was nearby, carrying a large fish that Kamiyo had no idea the identity of. He nodded to Kamiyo and smiled, reminding him that others welcomed his presence despite Philip's misgivings.

"Morning, Doc."

"Morning, Steven. How was the catch today?"

"Not bad. We're getting two or three bigguns each morning, so can't complain. Look at this Barbel, she's a stonker."

"Good, good." Kamiyo thought of telling Steven about Emily but decided he'd prefer the news come from Jackie. She was better at making announcements.

The sky was overcast, and the breeze from the lake chilly. Kamiyo wondered how everyone would fare once winter arrived. The castle's stone was frigid, but there was room for a campfire right outside and several hearths inside. The bedding had been relocated from the cabin and placed into the castle's upper rooms, but few in the group possessed coats suitable for winter. How much sickness would the camp be dealing with then?

Kamiyo spotted Nathan sitting by the lake and gave an involuntary shudder. The glowing light beneath the water hadn't returned since the night he'd seen it while saving Vamps. Jackie had asked him not to share the theory of there being a gate beneath the lake with anyone else unless they were certain it was the case. They didn't have proof, nor could they do anything to address the potentiality. Even so, it worried Kamiyo to see Nathan so close to the water. He went over to check on the boy. His wrist had been healing well, but Emily had taught him that things could spiral downwards quickly. "Hello, Nathan, what are you doing?"

Nathan looked up from what he was doing, revealing a pile of blood and guts. "Just preparing a fish," he said.

Kamiyo was not averse to blood—two years in a maternity ward thrashed any squeamishness from a person—but what he saw now disturbed him. Nathan wasn't so much gutting the large carp as cruelly eviscerating it, slicing at its organs and innards instead of merely removing them.

"Um, didn't Steve collect all the fish this morning, Nathan?"

"He's training me. I want to be a butcher like him. Next time we catch another rabbit, he's going to show me how to skin it."

"Oh, well, it's good you're acquiring new skills. How's the wrist?"

Nathan held it up in its sling bandage, which was stained with fish blood. "It hurts when I move it, but not as much as it did."

"Great. Make sure you wash your hands in clean water when you're done here."

"Will the blood make me sick?"

"Not necessarily. But it *will* make you stink."

"Is Emily dead yet?"

Kamiyo frowned. "Um, yes, she passed this morning, but why would you assume that?"

He shrugged. "It was obvious. She kept getting worse. Could you have helped her with medicine?"

"Yes, probably quite easily."

"Shame." Nathan said it without emotion.

"Were you friends with Emily, Nathan?"

"Nobody is my friend here."

Kamiyo folded his arms and waited a moment before speaking again. He felt like the conversation was nearing a sensitive issue. "I've noticed you don't interact with the other kids, Nathan. Do you feel alone here?"

"We're all alone here, Doctor."

"That's not correct, Nathan. We have each other."

Nathan prodded the dead carp with his knife. "You're wrong. People only care about themselves. The only loyalty in this world is blood, but there are no more families left. Survivors only care about surviving."

Kamiyo had suspected it for a while—Nathan was suffering from some kind of dissociative disorder. Whether it was the trauma of recent events, or something deeper, was unclear, but he was certain the child had a clinical lack of empathy. The question was whether it was reversible or permanent. "Do you miss your family, Nathan?"

Nathan frowned as if he didn't understand the question, but he did give a nod after a moment's thought. "I miss my little sister sometimes. Her name was Sophie. I miss the sound of her laugh."

"You were close with Sophie?"

He shrugged. "I used to look after her. She was mine."

"Yours?"

He nodded and showed emotion, a faint glimmer of a wistful smile. "I had no friends at school, and mum was never around. She put me in after-school clubs for as long as she could, so she could work. Sophie was the only person who was ever happy to see me. When I got home at night, she would always smile and give me a great big hug. When she had nightmares, she would climb into my bed. She was happier when I was around. Only time I ever felt like I mattered was when I was looking after Sophie. She cried the morning I caught the coach to come here. She wanted me to stay home. If I had, I'd be dead. I wish I knew what happened to her though."

"She might have made it somewhere safe. *You* did, Nathan."

He shook his head. "No, she's gone. I hope it was quick, but I don't think it was. I think she was screaming my name when the monsters ate her."

"You shouldn't think about things like that, Nathan. It's not good for you."

"What else should I think about?" He held up his bloody knife, wafting the stench of fish guts. "When the demons come, I'll be ready. Will everyone else be?"

Kamiyo looked up at the castle, to where people were milling about with various tasks. They were more ready than they had ever been, but it still might not be enough. As cold and disconnected as Nathan so clearly was, he might actually be the most suitable person to survive in this new reality. He did not shy away from the horror. Instead, he embraced it.

"Everybody is ready, Nathan, because they all know that sticking together is the only way to stay safe."

Nathan stared at him blankly. "Lot of good it did Emily."

"We need medicine," said Kamiyo, nearing anger at the thought of the dead girl. "If we had some basic supplies, I think we could ride things out here long into the future. Without them though..."

"So, go get some. You survived outside the forest. Go find what we need. Save us, Doctor Kamiyo."

It was a terrifying suggestion, but something fast

becoming necessary. "You might be right, Nathan. It's something I need to think about."

"Not really. We can't hide in the forest forever, can we? When you go out to find supplies, take me with you."

"What? Nathan, no! You and the other children need to stay here."

"I'm fourteen."

"It's too dangerous."

"Exactly! I need to know what's out there, so I can survive it. You can show me how to make it outside the forest, how to fight."

Kamiyo shook his head. "You survive by *avoiding* fighting."

"But you can't avoid it forever. I want to live, Doctor, that's all. Hiding here won't make any of us stronger. If the demons ever take this place, I want to know how to cope on my own."

Everything the kid was saying made perfect sense, yet it still felt wrong to willingly expose a child to the horrors of this world. Yet, there might come a day when the children needed to survive on their own—a time for the young to learn how to face the monsters underneath their beds.

"I'll think about it, Nathan, okay? I'll think about it." Kamiyo turned back towards the cabin, ending this tense conversation that had caused his palms to sweat. Why did Nathan frighten him almost as much as the demons?

25

TED

Ted strolled the ramparts with a canister of petrol in hand. During the last few hours, he'd had the teenagers wrapping arrows in cloth. If the demons tried coming up the front approach, they would rain fire on them. Next on his list was to restore the gate inside the lower guardhouse and shore up the outer wall in several places. With enough time, Ted also intended to dig trenches and place spikes. Anything to make life harder for the demons.

He wanted to see the lot of 'em dead.

The more time Ted spent at the castle, the more he thought it might actually be possible to make a stand. The walls, if anything, had only strengthened over the centuries, compacted by their own massive weight. It would take a hell-fire missile to knock them down, and he couldn't imagine the demons turning up in Apache helicopters. Leaving would be easier once he knew the people here were safe. Another week, maybe two, and he would've done more than enough to walk away with a clean conscience.

With the petrol placed strategically along the castle's walls, he now headed into the castle's courtyard. The area had been filled with tents, and a campfire was fed daily and lit nightly. Inside the castle, hearths burned constantly, and cot beds were set up throughout the upper floors. All in all, there was plenty of space for the group to live their lives. There was even a dungeon if such a thing ever became necessary.

The group spent most evenings eating together in the main hall which was a wide, cavernous room in the centre of the castle's ground floor. It had the largest hearth, several windows, and a collection of ancient tables cut from solid, dark wood. With the modern chairs they had requisitioned from the cabin, the castle's cavernous interior became an odd mixture of ancient and new—much like a renovated church. It was a warm, fortified space, and its embrace lifted people's spirit's after a hard day's work.

Ted went into the main hall now but continued until he entered a small chapel on its east side. No one in the group claimed to be overtly religious, and even those who identified as Christian did not require a space to pray, so the chapel was put to use as a pantry. Small and chilly, it was the closest thing they had to a refrigerator.

Jackie noticed Ted in the pantry and came to talk to him. "Ted, is there anything I can help you with today? I must say, I feel a lot safer since you braced the front gate."

Ted had managed to drop the large portcullis last night and had braced it with two thick pine logs. "A tank would struggle to make it through now," he said. "I 'm planning on building a palisade too. If we position them right, we can force the demons into a huddle and torch the bastards with fire. We'll warm ourselves on their corpses."

Jackie grimaced. The healing slash on her cheek opened and closed like a ghoulish mouth. "Oh my."

Ted blushed. "Sorry! I've, um, lost a lot of my filters after spending so much time alone."

"It's okay. I need to toughen up. I'm glad you're here, Ted, unfiltered or not." She put a hand on his arm. The touch filled him with guilt, but he endured it. Part of him stirred at the human contact, but he fought it away. Jackie may have sensed his conflict because she pulled her hand away from his arm. "Hannah told me how the two of you met," she said. "That you were driving on your own. For how long?"

Ted turned his back to check the food supplies on the shelves. He started with the crab apples collected from the forest floor. "I lost track," he muttered. "More than a month, less than two. I started out from Colchester."

"Why did you leave?"

He scooped the crab apples together into a pile and moved on to counting bundles of dried fish. "Because I had no reason to stay."

"Hannah said you were travelling north. How far north?"

"As far as north goes."

"Why?"

He stopped counting and leant his weight against the racking. The furious imp that lived inside him was begging to get out. "Because I made a promise I intend to keep."

"A promise to whom?"

He wanted to turn and yell in her face, to shove her away and tell her to mind her own fucking business. "A promise to my daughter."

Jackie gasped. "Oh, I'm sorry. I shouldn't have pried."

He turned to look at her, glad the tears remained behind his eyes and not on his hairy cheeks. "It's okay." He wondered if he might implode by continuing to speak. The memories he tried so hard to suppress were now right at the surface. "We've all lost people, Jackie. Did you... did you have any children of your own?"

Jackie smiled, which wasn't the expression he'd expected. "I have a son somewhere. All grown up. A fire fighter."

"You believe he's alive?"

"I do." She smiled again, and the pride showed in her eyes. "He's out there somewhere, helping people, being brave. I know it."

Ted returned her smile, unable not to feel at least some of her hope. It radiated off her, and in the presence of that emotion, Ted did something that surprised him—he took the photograph of his daughter out of his pocket and handed it to Jackie. A kindly stranger had taken it for Ted while he cuddled Chloe at the zoo. Chloe was beaming beside him while an Emu stuck its head into the space between them.

"Chloe was only eight," Ted explained, watching Jackie while she took in the sight of the most precious thing in his life. The thing he'd let die. "I rescued her from her school across town when things went bad. Her mother and I had separated two years before, but I tried to get to her too. No matter where I looked though, I couldn't find her. Eventually, it was too dangerous to keep trying, so I took Chloe and left with the men on my crew. Most of them had their families with them, and together we made a go of it for more than a month. We hid at a new housing site one of the lads knew about. The whole area was ringed with barbed-wire fencing, and several houses were nearly finished. It kept us safe for a while. Just for a while."

Jackie handed him back his photograph. "She's beautiful, Ted. I'm so sorry."

Ted struggled to fight his tears. He felt them amassing beneath his eyes. "She was destined to do great things." He looked at the picture for himself and smiled, trying not to let the image of Chloe's smiling face destroy him. "Look, Jackie, I hate to share bad news, but we don't have enough food."

"What?" She looked past him to the food arrayed on the shelves. "We have plenty."

He nodded. "For now, yeah, but fish and the occasional rabbit ain't gunna cut it, luv. The kids need vegetables, fruit... stuff beside meat and fish."

"We have apples."

"Crab apples. And we've only found one tree. If you want to make a go of things here, you need to plant food, crops, or whatever. Fishing and hunting are too unreliable, and impossible if you're ever put under siege. I think I need to leave the forest and try to find a garden centre. I'll search for seeds—tomato plants, mint, lettuce, that kind of thing. I'm not green-fingered in the slightest, but it won't be too hard a job to grab whatever I see."

"You can't go out there, Ted. You need to stay here."

"Who else is gunna go?"

"I don't know. Just not you. We need you here. You're getting so much done. The children have come out of their shells with you around. They see you as this mighty guardian from the forest, come to save them."

Ted chuckled. "They just enjoy having something to do. Put the kids to work and they don't have time to worry."

"Well, whatever the reason, you need to stay here, Ted. You're too important."

"Then who?"

"I'll go," said Hannah, startling them both by coming up behind them. Steven was by her side with a small pile of dried fish to add to the stockpile. He kept quiet while Hannah spoke. "I love this place too much to see it fail," she said. "If we need supplies, I'll go get them."

"Are you sure?" Jackie didn't sound as though she intended to argue. "Your hands?"

Hannah linked her fingers together and cracked her

knuckles. "My hands have been fine for days, and I can survive out there better than anyone. I'll find what we need. We need medicine too. I just heard from Philip that Emily died this morning."

Steven groaned at that. He was a quiet man, always in the background, but he worked constantly to provide them food and was often amongst the children playing nanny. Ted liked the man from the little he knew of him, and it was painful to see him so devastated. "She was a sweet girl," he muttered.

Hannah nodded. "Yeah, she was."

Steven handed Ted the dried fish. "Sorry," he said, rubbing at his glistening eyes. "I'll get out of your hair."

Hannah patted the man on the back as he departed, then gave Ted a hard stare. "I won't let another child die because of lack of medicine. I'll go and get what we need."

"I'm coming with you," said Ted. "You can't take the risk all by yourself."

"No, Ted! Jackie's right. The changes you've made these last two weeks... Everyone will be rudderless if you leave."

"We'll make you a list, Hannah," said Jackie. "And if things get too dangerous, you come right back to us, you hear? You're too valuable to lose."

Hannah appeared touched by that, and she snapped off a playful salute. "Understood. It will be a good opportunity to scout the area for threats. I'd rather know where the trouble is before it finds us."

Ted nodded. Someone needed to go out, and Hannah was the obvious choice. She moved through the wilderness like a silk-slippered ocelot, and she could kill a dozen demons with her rifle before having to make a run for it. While Ted wasn't afraid to go, he knew he was a lumbering bull. He looked at Jackie. "Could I have a minute alone with Hannah, please?"

"Oh, um, yes, of course. I'll, um, go start on that list." She gave Hannah an affectionate smile and trotted out of the room and into the Great Hall.

Hannah studied Ted expectantly. "What's up, boss?"

"Don't call me that!"

"Sorry. What's up, Teddy?"

"Don't call me that either! Look, are you sure you want to go out there? Two weeks ago, you were desperate never to be alone again. Why do you want to leave suddenly?"

"I don't *want* to leave, Ted. I want to be of use. You have the whole master builder thing going on, and Kamiyo is a doctor. Steven's a butcher. Frank is... well, Frank is Frank, but this is how I can help. This place needs to survive, and unfortunately, I'm the soldier in the group. It kinda feels like my gig."

"You'll be on your own again."

She nodded. "But now I know I've got people to get back to. It's different."

"I suppose it is." He reached out and touched her shoulder. "You make sure you *do* come back."

She gasped. "Ted, are you showing concern for me? What happened? Are you ill? It's hemorroides, isn't it?" She put on a fake crying face. "You never think it will happen to someone you love."

Ted shrugged her away with a grumble. "Get outta it, you daft mare."

She chuckled with glee, but then grew serious. "I'll be back, Ted, I promise. And when I return, this place better be a god-damn fortress."

"Then you better come back with enough supplies to feed a nation."

Hannah put out her hand. "Deal."

With the slightest of smiles, Ted shook his friend's hand.

26

HANNAH

Hannah waited until the following morning to depart, and it left her time to ruminate on the undertaking. As a result, she had slept little, but her anxiety was enough to leave her buzzing with energy. It was just past dawn, and the sun remained hidden behind dark clouds—a bad omen.

Kamiyo approached her in front of the castle's portcullis. He handed her a list. "I'm not expecting miracles," he said, "but any of the items on this list will really help. Failing that, grab anything you can find."

Hannah scanned the list and looked up. "Okay, Doc, got it."

"I should go with you," he said. "There are hundreds of medicines, and I'm the only one who can identify what most of them do."

She hefted the large rucksack on her back and smirked. "I see a pharmacy and it's all coming back with me. You can sort the wart medicine from the antibiotics afterwards. These kids can't be without their doctor."

He nodded but didn't seem happy about it. "You bring back antibiotics and you'll be saving lives."

"I know. That's why I'll get what we need. I promise."

"Don't promise. Just come back."

Ted came to see her next, looking even grumpier than usual. "I passed a small village before I stopped to fight those demons," he told her. "If you come across my truck, head down the road behind it, and you might find something. Also, look in the back of my flatbed. There's something in the lock box you can have. Combination: 2-0-0-6." He grunted and walked away, leaving her to memorise the number.

Frank appeared and surprised her by handing her a sword. She had to blink and do a double-take. "I nabbed this for meself early on," he told her with a smug grin on his face. "It's 16th Century. Set above the mantle in the Great Hall, it was. Maybe it was owned by a lord. Or a king."

Hannah patted her rifle. "I have this, Frank. You keep your sword."

He thrust it at her pommel first. "Take it. Guns have a nasty way of running out of bullets."

"Rifle," she said.

Frank frowned. "What's that now, kidda?"

Hannah took the sword and sighed. "Thank you, Frank."

Jackie was standing with Philip in front of the portcullis while Eric and Steven occupied the small winch-room above. "Thank you again for doing this, Hannah," said Jackie. "None of us are ignorant to the danger you're putting yourself in."

Hannah shrugged. "I'll be fine. I was out there on my own for weeks."

Jackie hugged her. "Thank you."

"Oh, um, you're welcome." She turned and gave everyone a wave, tussled the hair of the youngest children, and then took a deep breath to steel herself. Her tummy turned somersaults as she peered towards the tree line at the bottom of the hill. Usually, when she went out on a mission, she was focused and determined, the perfect version of herself. It was how she imagined maestro piano players must have felt when they played Beethoven—it was what they were built for. Today though, she felt nervous and unsure. Afraid. Like stepping towards the edge of a cliff with black, rushing waters below.

She waited for the portcullis to rise and ducked beneath it. Everyone shouted good luck to her, but she didn't look back. It was like saying goodbye to family, best done quickly. Two weeks, and they already felt like family.

And she was their provider.

Still not looking back, she descended the hill and passed the lower guard house still absent its portcullis. The first two rows of trees had been felled, leaving behind a minefield of stumps. Beyond that, the forest grew thick rapidly, and it swallowed her up in seconds. She looked towards the castle but could no longer see it.

She was alone again.

But no longer homeless.

A compass attached to her belt would ensure she kept a straight line out of the forest, and she would mark her exit, so she knew where to enter again later. Last thing she needed was to lose her way home. It felt good to need a compass.

Despite keeping to a straight line, in a direction she assumed would lead her to the road, an hour passed by without the forest ending. Her empty rucksack swayed on her back and holding both a rifle and sword was difficult. Despite those burdens, she felt good. Energised. She moved through the undergrowth swiftly, in tune with her surroundings. That determined focus came back to her, and she thrived. Her anxiety and fears melted away. She was a huntress.

She'd never seen true combat in the Army, having joined at the tail end of the Middle-Eastern hostilities. Iraq and Afghanistan were winding down and only a token force remained in either country. She'd been to Belize, Germany, and Canada, but only on training exercises. When the demons invaded, she'd been forced to put her training straight to the test. It had surprised her how well she'd taken to killing. How little it bothered her.

Could she kill a human the same way she so readily killed demons?

It would be a lie if she claimed her lack of remorse didn't worry her. It did. Like Ted, something took over her in battle that she wasn't in control of, but it wasn't the same maddened fury that set Ted on the warpath like an enraged bull. No, it was something more akin to a tiger stalking its prey, a singular focus on making the thing in front of her dead. She didn't know where that part of herself came from, or where it ended exactly, but she knew it was a significant piece of her core. Hannah had an innate talent for murder.

That innate part of herself spoke up now, whispering to her. Warning her.

Leaves crunched.

Something was near.

Hannah crouched in a tangle of weeds, allowing her muddy combat fatigues to blend into the foliage. Twenty-metres ahead, the forest shuddered as twigs snapped and branches swayed. She raised her rifle and closed one eye. Her heart beat hard in her chest, keeping time and breaking down every second for her appraisal.

The movement got closer. Something dark flashed through the gaps in the trees. Time passed in slow motion. Hannah drew into herself, viewing the world only through the scope of her rifle.

A bush burst apart, and a bounding shape leapt into view.

Followed by several others.

Hannah didn't pull the trigger. She didn't pull the trigger

because she didn't want to kill a pack of hungry dogs. Instead, she stood up and put her hands out. "Hey! Hey boy! It's okay."

The leader of the pack was some kind of leggy mongrel, black and brown. The other dogs were smaller breeds, two cocker spaniels and a Staffordshire bull terrier, each of them lithe and bony, yet not emaciated. They looked like their wild ancestors.

The pack leader growled, yellowing teeth unsheathed. Behind it, the other dogs followed suit and did the same. Hannah was still in no mind to shoot a bunch of dogs, and if she could shoo them off, she would. "It's okay. It's okay. Just... stay calm."

The mongrel snarled and took a step closer, lowering its head. The black and brown fur on its neck ruffled. Hannah held her hand out farther, close to its snout. She continued making soothing sounds and saying words the animal might once have known. Words like "good boy" and "heel."

"Are you hungry, huh? Okay, let's see what I have here." She un-shouldered her rucksack and dropped it on the ground. She put down her sword and unzipped it, searching for some dried fish.

The snarling mongrel pounced. Hannah reacted just in time to keep its jaws from snatching at her face, but the impact of its bony shoulders knocked her backwards. Instinctively, she kicked out her legs and kept it from mounting her, so its sharp jaws clamped around her ankle instead. Burning hot spikes pierced her flesh. She cried out, then stifled herself to keep from attracting more attention, or stoking the prey drive of the other animals. The mongrel thrashed and growled—her ankle rolling in its jaws. Her tender bones might snap at any moment, but she couldn't pull herself free.

The other three dogs closed in, too timid to attack yet, but it was only a matter of time before they worked up the courage. Hunger was a fierce motivator. Even for the weak.

Hannah scrabbled around in the mud, trying to keep from being rolled over onto her belly. Her rifle was strapped to her shoulder, but the way she'd fallen had trapped it beneath her. She tried to pull it around and get a shot off, but the strap was too tangled.

Then she saw the sword.

It glinted in a shaft of sunlight spilling through the trees. She reached it with her fingertips. "Thank yow, Frank!"

The mongrel yanked at her ankle, trying to tear it off. A wave of sickness spread through her and she gagged. As the mongrel pulled her along the ground, she lost her grip on the sword. She kicked her free-leg into the ground to shift herself back towards the sword. Inch-by-inch, her fingers curled around the sword's handle.

One of the other dogs leapt into view—one of the cocker spaniels—overgrown and matted. It bit down on her outstretched hand just as she was about to retrieve the sword. It dug its front paws into the mud and shook her. More pain flared through Hannah's body. She was going to die here, an hour's walk from camp. And not at the hands of any demon, but a pack of stray dogs. She wasn't the warrior she thought she was, and the people at the castle would never know what had happened to her, or how awfully she'd failed them.

No! No one else is dying on my watch. I need to complete my mission. This is what I trained for, and why I've been fighting to survive. This is my chance to make a difference.

Despite it causing her even more agony, Hannah pulled her arm inwards, dragging the cocker spaniel. Its claws ploughed lines in the mud, dragging the sword underneath it. Hannah heaved with all her might, even as the dog chewed her arm like a squeaky toy. It snarled right over her face and could remove its jaws from her wrist at any moment to clamp down on her throat.

Hannah acted fast. She lifted her head and bit down on one of the cocker spaniel's floppy ears. She tasted matted fur, then greasy flesh. Finally, she felt gristle and veins give way to blood. It filled her mouth, viscous and metallic. The dog yowled, and she allowed it to pull away, opening her mouth and yanking her wrist free from its jaws—a trade of limbs. Her whole lower arm throbbed and burned, but she flexed her hand and found it moving. She threw out her arm and finally retrieved the sword, lifting it towards the sun and praying she didn't drop it pommel first onto her face.

She brought the blade down on top of the mongrel's thick skull.

There was a loud *clonk*, as the blunt sword acted more like a bludgeon than a blade, yet it was enough to stun the animal into releasing her ankle. It reared up and shook its head.

Hannah struck like lightning, sitting up and thrusting the sword out in front of her. The sharp point pierced the mongrel's chest easily. It yelped, but the thrust must have struck its heart because it fell down dead with no further fuss.

The wounded cocker spaniel leapt again but retreated when it realised its pack leader was dead. It backed away, eyes wide, then turned and bolted back into the bushes. Its less courageous pack mates hurried to join it.

Hopefully, they wouldn't wander anywhere near the camp and the children.

Hannah rolled onto her side and freed her rifle, then pointed it at the bushes, ready to fire if the mutts came back for another round. Her compassion for their plight had evaporated, but at least she had felt compassion to start with. She wasn't a monster. After a while, she decided she was in the clear. Just as well, she couldn't afford to bury her little remaining ammunition into someone's former pets.

As her heart rate lowered, and the adrenaline left her system, it lumbered her with a great deal of pain. Her ankle was a mess, not broken, but ripped wide open. Her wrist wasn't as bloody, but it felt sprained. She needed to get back to camp so Dr Kamiyo could patch her up.

But what if she ended up like Emily? The wounds on her ankle might already have been infected by the mongrel's bacteria-laced jaws. She might be dead in a week if her wounds turned like Emily's had.

Can't think about that now. Focus on what I can control. Find medicine and infection won't be an issue.

Biting her lip, Hannah crawled over to an old oak tree and used it to climb to her feet. She tested her ankle and found that, while it hurt terribly, she could just about walk on it. She tried a few tentative steps, and bit down hard on her lip. It was gut-wrenchingly painful, but her focus and determination were enough to get her moving again.

She headed for the road.

27

HANNAH

Hannah discovered the overgrown access road cutting through the forest. When she and Ted had first entered the forest two weeks ago, they'd been trying to evade the demons and hadn't stuck to the designated route. Now the path was a godsend, showing her precisely how to get back to the road. With her sword now threaded through a hole she'd made in the top of her rucksack, walking got a little easier, and before long she was back at the coach, reminiscing about the last time she'd been there.

Ted's bag full of soft drinks still rested on the ground where he'd dropped them. She grabbed herself an orangeade and swigged the whole thing down in one go, not having realised how thirsty she was. Next, she limped over to the coach, and for a few minutes she took a breather on the bottom step, enjoying the peace and quiet. There was no sign of any demons, which was beyond a relief.

Once she'd caught her breath, she limped down the road toward Ted's truck. He had told her to check in the back for something. That intrigued her now.

The truck came into view after a few minutes of limping

along the side of the road. On the ground, beside the rear tyre, she found Ted's nail gun. It had been an effective weapon when he'd used it and would also be useful for building work back at camp. She placed it inside her rucksack, pleased that her ordeal had at last started to bear fruit. She then leant over the flatbed and searched for the lockbox Ted had spoken about. It was welded against the rear of the driver's cabin, a small, metal compartment with a padlock threaded through its latch. What was the code again? She searched her mind.

2-0-0-6

She rolled the padlock and snapped it open. Inside was a small nylon bundle that she took out and unwrapped. "Holy mother!"

The Ka-Bar was beautiful, a perfectly weighted military knife, perfect for both close-quarter killing and bushcraft. She had no idea how Ted had got the blade—a Ka-Bar was favoured by the US Navy and Marines—but it overjoyed her to receive it as a gift. Maybe Ted wasn't heartless after all. He certainly knew how to put a smile on her face.

The euphoria wore off, and she got back on task. Now she had to focus on the larger task of finding supplies—medicine at the very least. Which direction should she go? Ted had told her to head past his truck, and that she would find a village.

So she set off in that direction, pain jolting her ankle with every step. Tomorrow, she'd be unable to walk on it, so she needed to grab whatever she could today and head back soon. It wasn't ideal, but she was sure she could find something and head back into the forest by nightfall. Longer sorties could come later. They only needed a band-aid to buy them some time.

Heading down the road, she thought about what Vamps had told the group in recent weeks while he'd been working amongst them—that there was a massive human army in the

South that would one day reclaim the country. It felt like a lie. She had seen an entire army massacred in Derby and found it impossible to imagine any other outcome. Yet, Vamps seemed to know way more than everybody else did about what was going on

Her mind turned down dark alleyways, ones where humanity was ashes blowing on the wind, and she, along with the people at the camp, were dangling over a flame and becoming ashes themselves. Was anybody else out here? Anyone at all? She tried with all her might to believe there was, and that salvation might truly lie in Portsmouth.

She heard moaning.

The noise came from the long grass at the side of the road, and it reminded her of a zombie. The smell of burning clung to the air, but she saw no fire. After what had happened with the dogs, she was ready to shoot first and ask questions later, so she raised her rifle and stepped away from the road and into the grass.

A tractor sat parked in the field, but there was no one behind the wheel. The driver's door was ajar and a vast network of cobwebs filled the opening. A trailer sat behind it, full of rotten, damp hay.

"*Salam alekum*," muttered a man slumped up against one of the tractor's giant tyres. He had a light-brown complexion and dressed in Middle-Eastern clothing. Hannah wanted to describe him as *Arabic* but was unsure whether it was an appropriate way to label someone—he could just as easily be Indian or Turkish or Tunisian. Then she realised such things probably didn't matter anymore.

She pointed her rifle at the man's face. "Who are you?"

"My name..." The man took a breath, visibly exhausted. "My name is Aymun, and I am looking for my friend."

"Who?"

"He is a young man who goes by the name of Vamps. Not his true name, but the only one of which I know."

Hannah tried not to show any recognition at the name. She didn't know this man from Adam and wouldn't share information freely until she got a read on him. "Stupid name. What is this Vamps guy to you?"

"As I say, he is just a friend." The man shifted position and winced in pain. "He is in much trouble and I am hoping to help him."

"Well, not sure I can be of help to you there. Do you need aid? I have water."

The man sighed and looked down at the grass. "No, thank you. My challenges are great it seems. I travelled many miles, and yet nothing do I find. Are you alone, kind soldier?"

"Haven't seen another person in weeks, pet." She worried she might have lied a little too eagerly.

"A dire reality in which we find ourselves, indeed." The strange man grunted and pushed himself to his feet, using the giant tyre at his back.

Hannah shook her rifle at him. "Easy there!"

Aymun smiled, subtle amusement in his eyes. "Surely, you would not shoot a man for getting to his feet? Now, I do not know you, woman, for you have not shown me the politeness of sharing your name. Yet, I know you are not alone in this world. Your pack is empty. If you are a lone traveller, as you say, then where is your blanket? Where are your food supplies? No, your pack is empty because you are looking for resources to bring back to your camp."

"Yes, but the camp is just me."

"No. A camp of one is not a camp. You are clean, fed, and your eyes lack the desperation of a lonely traveller. You are not alone."

She moved her rifle's muzzle closer to his face. "If I shoot you in the face, I'll be alone again. We don't know each other, so dial back the familiarity."

"Have you seen my friend? That is all I ask."

"What do you want with this Vamps guy, anyway? You said he's in trouble?"

"He is. Great danger surrounds him."

"What danger?"

Aymun smiled and placed his hands out in a gesture of defeat. "Alas, you claim not to know this man, so I shall share no more."

"Then I wish you the best of luck, pet. Hope you find him." She stepped back, keeping her rifle raised so he couldn't get a jump on her. She didn't trust this man with the strange accent and odd clothes, but she hoped it wasn't old prejudices making her feel that way. The world had moved on, for better or worse. No, she just got a bad feeling, that was all.

"What is it you seek, woman? What supplies does your camp need?"

Hannah stopped retreating and shoved her muzzle closer to the man's face again. "Call me *woman* one more time. I dare you."

Aymun chuckled. Then he moved like a whipped vine, grabbing her rifle strap and twisting it around her neck until it was squeezing her throat shut. Before she could fight back, he kicked her legs out from under her and put her on her back. The pommel of her stowed sword butted the base of her skull and sent stars through her vision.

Aymun grabbed her rifle and twisted it, tightening the strap around her neck. The more he twisted, the more the strap tightened. He glared into her face, long nose touching hers. "I call you *woman* because you continue to show rudeness by refusing to offer your name. Now you have a choice. Unclip your rifle, and the strap around your throat will loosen.

Or continue to fight and strangulate to death. Fight or think. Up to you, *woman*."

Hannah gritted her teeth and tried to throw the man off her, tried to force her rifle around to shoot him. She could do neither. Reluctantly, and angrily, she reached for the clips on the rifle straps and thumbed them open. A solider giving up her weapon was no soldier. Her second failure of the day.

Aymun snatched the rifle and pointed it at her chest. "You may stand."

Hannah did so gingerly, brushing dirt off her butt and rubbing at her sore throat. Yet another wound to add to the list. As she stood, her damaged ankle buckled and reminded her that this was not her first failure of the day. "What do you want?" she demanded, glaring at the son-of-a-bitch. "I knew you were bad news."

"I only wish to hear your name."

"Hannah." She growled. "My name is Hannah, okay?"

"You are a rude woman, Hannah." He glared at her a moment, then altered his expression and smiled. "But I am most happy to meet you. Forgive my direct way of doing things. I have had a most difficult journey, and it has been many months since I saw my homeland. I miss it greatly."

"And where is that exactly?"

"I am from Syria. Damascus. A most ancient and illustrious city. It was in ruins even before the damned got there. I fear for it greatly now."

"Syria? How did you get here?"

"I went through Hell."

She rolled her eyes. Had this guy and Vamps worked on a story together or something? "Look, just let me go or shoot me. I'm sorry I took a hard line with you, but I've had a pretty miserable journey too."

He pointed back across the fields behind him. There is a

post office in the village beyond this farmland, you see? Behind those distant hedges. I came from that direction." He shocked her then by handing her back her rifle. "So long as you do not point this at me, I shall allow you to keep it."

She snatched it back and almost pointed it right back at him again. *Allow* her to keep it? That was rich. Yet, she didn't tempt fate. The man could have shot her, but he had given her weapon back. That had earned him a little trust at least. "You saw food?" she asked. "Medicine?"

"I saw a post office sign and a large window. I did not search inside. My priority is to find my friend before I expire."

Hannah frowned. "What do you mean, *expire*?"

The man lifted his flowing cotton shirt and showed her a bloody bandage. "I had hoped to find safety before danger, but danger found me first. A pack of fiends fell upon me. I barely made it out with my life. They were not so fortunate."

"You fought them off bare handed?"

"I am not as defenceless as I appear, Hannah. However, I lost all my supplies and most of my breath. I sat down to rest here and... It may have been some time."

"That wound looks a couple days old, but if we can clean it up, you should be okay. It doesn't seem infected."

He nodded as if he understood all this. "You truly do not have a camp? Someone who might offer me aid?"

Hannah took a breath and held it before letting it out and answering. She almost told the truth, but still couldn't quite trust the man. Not yet. "No, I'm sorry, it's just me—but if I find anything to dress your wound in the village, I'll bring it back for you, I promise. Just stay here."

"No," he said. "I shall search with you."

Hannah was about to argue, but then considered it might be useful to try to find out more about Vamps, and why exactly this odd Middle-Eastern man was looking for him, so bringing him along might not be a bad idea. "Fine, but once we find something to help you with that wound, we go our separate ways."

"As you wish. Although, have you considered our separate ways may lead to the same place?"

Hannah shouldered her rifle and started walking. "I'm going this way, pet."

28

HANNAH

annah breathed a sigh of relief when she reached the edge of the field and spotted a row of cottages beyond. Sure enough, the last building in the row featured a red and yellow 'Royal Mail' sign, and it peeked at her through the trees. No one else seemed to be around, and her fear of ambush slowly bled away. While Aymun was an oddball, he had told the truth about this.

She hobbled through a gap in the hedges while Aymun stayed close behind her. A wooden bus shelter with a bench stood at the side of the road, and she took a moment to rest her ankle there.

"It appears bad," said Aymun, peering at her wound. "How did this happen?"

"Dogs," she said ruefully. "Might be man's best friend, but not mine, apparently."

Aymun folded his arms and hid his hands inside his sleeves. "It is not just humankind affected by this calamity. If the Red Lord succeeds in scouring the earth, even the smallest of insects shall plummet into the abyss."

"The Red Lord?" Hannah enquired as if she had never heard the name before.

Aymun shrugged. "A creature I cannot fully comprehend. A destroyer of worlds. A great Evil. The Red Lord erases all so that he may one day create. He is God's adversary."

"Isn't that the Devil?"

Aymun chuckled. "One would think so, but no. I spent my entire life studying the Quran, and the knowledge contained within was a mere thimble-full of water taken from an ocean."

"I was an atheist, so it's always been a load of rubbish to me." She pulled a face. "Guess I was wrong."

"We were all wrong," said Aymun. "Shall I search the Post Office while you rest, Hannah?"

She hopped up from the bench. "No, I'm good. Let's see what we can find."

They crossed the road and mounted the opposite pavement. Good fortune had left the Post Office's heavy glass door unlocked, and Hannah shouldered it open easily before stepping inside. The place had been ransacked, but not emptied, and many goods still littered the shelves. Her boots crunched on bags of crisps, and she kicked aside sprouting potatoes.

"A cornucopia," said Aymun. "Is this what you required?"

She turned to Aymun and nodded. "It's a good start. Thank you."

"A joy to be of service. What is it you need precisely?"

"We need seeds to grow..." She stopped herself from continuing. *Damn it!*

Aymun smiled knowingly. "We?"

Hannah grumbled. She kicked her way through the debris and leant on the Post Office counter. Perhaps she could just ignore the fact she'd dropped her pants and given up Intel.

"I am no threat," said Aymun. He remained standing where

he was, over by the door. "You wish for seeds to grow crops, yes? That means there are many of you, and that you are safe. I am glad. There is safety in Portsmouth too, but our fight is not yet over. I must find my friend. Vamps is not only in danger. He *is* a danger to those around him." Hannah couldn't help but betray her emotions now. This man seemed so earnest. Her bottom lip quivered, and Aymun saw it right away because he titled his head and sighed. "Please, trust me, Hannah."

She looked at him, wavering back and forth, both physically and mentally. It was hard to stand on her ankle, so she continued to lean against the counter. "I *might* know something about this Vamps guy you're after."

"I am no threat," Aymun repeated. "Vamps and I, along with many others have been fighting to ensure mankind's survival. Every human life is precious, more than you can ever understand. My only hope is to see the threat to God's garden extinguished."

"Yeah... Right, okay, well, um just help me find what I need and maybe we can trade info. Later. Maybe."

Aymun sighed, unhappy at the prospect, but seeming to understand that this was a negotiation. "Time is not something I have a lot of."

"Then you better get a move on and start searching, pet."

He sighed and began sulkily piling dried noodles into a blue shopping basket. Hannah went behind the counter to a display behind the tills. The cigarettes and booze were all gone, but she found other prizes. She waved a fist in the air and declared, "Back of the net!"

"You have found what you need?" asked Aymun.

She grabbed the bottle of TCP and held it up like a trophy. Antiseptic might not reverse an infection, but it was perfect for preventing one in the first place. It was what she needed for her ankle, and what Dr Kamiyo would need in the days ahead. "Like I said earlier, it's a good start."

Along with the TCP, she also found bandages, plasters, painkillers, cold medicines, and a shit-tonne more antiseptic. It wasn't what they desperately needed, but it was better than what they had. Along with some food, matches, and sanitary towels, it might be enough to make life easier for a while. She was hurt, and every step made it worse, but this supply run had been successful enough to call a win. She would heal up and then go out again. Maybe by that time, the fabled Portsmouth Army would have arrived to save the day.

Hannah looked at Aymun. "There's really a push-back going on in Portsmouth?"

He had picked up a pack of sanitary towels and was examining them curiously but put them down now and looked at her. "Yes, General Wickstaff, a great woman, led many men to victory. They closed the gates and killed the Fallen."

"The Fallen?"

"Fallen angels. Those of God's chosen who turned away to serve the Red Lord. They attacked London and the surrounding areas. There will be many more to face in the days ahead, but we know they can be vanquished."

"You're talking about the giants? You killed some of them?" It was exactly what Vamps had claimed. Was this some elaborate confidence trick, or the crazy, impossible truth?

Aymun seemed to sense her cynicism because he moved a little closer. "When one who is living passes through a gate, it weakens the damned greatly. I did such a thing myself in Syria and exited in London. I did so again in Portsmouth, and this time came out of a gate many miles from here. I seek my friend. The friend who I believe you have met, no? His name is Vamps."

Hannah studied Aymun and considered it possible that he

was one of the good guys. Just being human made it more likely than not. Was she being hard on him? On the road after Derby, she'd been ready to embrace the first stranger she met, but now she had people depending on her. People she needed to protect.

She sighed. It was time to take a chance. "Yes, I've met Vamps. He was hurt, but our doctor brought him back to health. For a while, he was... I dunno, possessed or something. He attacked some of us, and we had to restrain him." She nodded at her rifle, which she held onto more tightly since having it taken off her once. "He almost got a bullet in the skull."

Aymun nodded but grew weary. He had to steady himself against a fridge filled with spoiled ice cream. "He is indeed possessed, as you put it. The Red Lord resides within him, an unwanted passenger."

Hannah shook her head. "Vamps is fine now though. This Red Lord or whatever, went away. He's been helping us back at the camp for weeks."

Aymun's eyes widened, and it looked like he might topple over. "He... He is..." He crumpled to the floor, wheezing. Hannah yanked him into a sitting position against the fridge and tried to keep him from passing out. Blood stained his shirt, and when she lifted it, his bandage was soaked through. "Shit. You're bleeding."

"I think, perhaps, that I was not done resting."

A sound outside startled them both. Hannah looked out through the door's glass panels and saw something that shocked her—a demon staring right back at her. Unlike the others she'd encountered, this one did not attack. In fact, it seemed alarmed and confused. A healing wound glistened on its horrendously burned chest right beneath its collarbone.

A gunshot wound.

This was the one that had got away.

I knew I shot four of you ugly bastards.

Hannah gripped her rifle and sprang to her feet. The demon's alarm turned to full-blown terror, and it bolted. She'd never seen a demon leg it, and it gave her the confidence to give chase. But Aymun grabbed her leg and kept her from leaving. "Vamps..." he said in a rasping voice. "He-He is deceiving you. He is not who he says he is. Your friends are in terrible danger."

Hannah looked down at him, not quite comprehending his words—her heart beat too loud in her temples. "I... I need to get that demon before it reaches its friends. It's seen our camp. It'll bring an army."

Aymun shook his head, groaning in pain. "You must return to your camp now. Before it's too late."

Hannah kicked him away and threw open the door. She aimed her rifle at the fleeing demon and fired. The demon stopped dead in its tracks, then turned around with its hands on its head like a bank hostage. The rifle shook in her hands, and she stared into its eyes. The demon seemed too... human. It was terrified. "David!" the creature said in a pained and hopeless voice. "David run!"

Hannah pulled the trigger by instinct, but she'd missed her chance. A cottage window shattered behind the demon, and it dashed into a side alley that led to the property's rear gardens.

"Damn it!" She went to take off after it, but Aymun shouted at her from the Post Office. "Your friends," he pleaded. "They are in danger. The Red Lord will kill them all."

Hannah didn't know what to do.

29

DR KAMIYO

K amiyo entered the room he now considered the 'main ward' and found Vamps sitting on a chair with his head slumped. His breathing was unsteady. Kamiyo took a quick visual account of the sleeping patients in the room, then hurried to check on him. "Vamps, are you okay?"

He looked up at Kamiyo, making it clear he wasn't okay at all. His face gleamed with sweat, and his eyes were puffy and red. Fever. "You shouldn't have let Hannah leave the camp," he said in a voice like crisp leaves underfoot. "She'll come back to find you all dead."

Kamiyo frowned at the oddness of the statement. "Everyone here is ready to fight, Vamps. The castle will keep us safe. We have plenty of weapons."

Vamps shook his head and spoke from vocal cords that sounded covered in mucous. "Sticks and stones. You have no hope of defending yourselves."

"Against whom?"

Vamps leapt out of the chair and seized Kamiyo by the jaw. "Against me!"

Kamiyo ducked and escaped Vamps' grab before it was

fully locked in. He suspected his escape might be because the young man allowed it. The way Vamps stalked Kamiyo now, swaying side to side, and humming a merry tune, made it seem like he intended to toy with him.

Vamps' eyes turned black, revealing a horrid realm beyond.

Kamiyo tried to run, but his attacker rushed in front of him and kicked his legs out from under him. He crashed onto his face and struck his chin on the floorboards. Spencer, the boy suffering from Lyme disease, woke at the noise and started calling for help. It woke the others, and they all joined in.

But no one came to help. Kamiyo feared the cabin was empty but for the sickened children. He tried to get to his feet, but Vamps stamped on his hand. He felt at least one delicate bone splinter. Maybe more. He cried out in agony.

"I am trapped inside this festering bag of flesh," said Vamps in a wet, clicking voice, "but it allows me to saviour mankind's suffering firsthand. I shall stalk this earth, slicing your throats one by one, watching you bleed out. Soon, I shall grow fat on your suffering and consume existence itself."

"Vamps!" Kamiyo yelled as loud as he could, clutching his broken hand against his chest. "Vamps, wake up. It's me, Dr Kamiyo."

"Vamps hangs above the inferno from hooks in his eyeballs. Soon, you shall join him."

Kamiyo placed his uninjured hand on the floor and tried to push himself up. Vamps stomped on it, and he screamed again. Now, he had two broken hands, and was forced to shuffle along on his side like a slug.

Vamps resumed his merry humming.

In the corner of his eye, Kamiyo spotted Spencer and the other sick children running for the door. They made it and slipped out of sight. Once again, Kamiyo was alone with this vile, ancient creature, defenceless and at its mercy.

Kamiyo cowered. "You are the Red Lord?"

"I am existence itself. An existence painted red. Worship me mortal and earn your damnation."

Kamiyo shuffled onto his butt and nodded enthusiastically. "I do worship you, Lord. Please, let me go. I shall worship you."

"Only in death may you worship me. To live is to serve Him."

"Please! Let me go." Kamiyo tried to get up and reach the doorway.

Vamps blocked his path, but then began to writhe and contort. The blackness drained from his eyes, and they widened in confusion. "D-Doc? Is that you?"

Kamiyo gasped. "Vamps, is that you? Are you in there?"

"Doc, I... I don't feel right. I... I feel like I want to see you... *bleed*."

Kamiyo groaned. "W-What?"

Vamps shrieked with delight. His eyes turned black once more and his outstretched fingers lengthened into claws, bloody nail beds erupting. His lower jaw distended like a serpent's. The monster became even more monstrous. And it was done playing games.

Twang! Zip!

An arrow struck Vamps in the leg, embedding itself in his thigh. The impact sent him tumbling backwards. Kamiyo scurried away on his butt, unsure what was happening but using the opportunity to escape.

Eric appeared and grabbed Kamiyo beneath the arms. Nathan stood in the doorway, notching a second arrow into a bow.

"No!" Kamiyo shook his head at the lad. "We need to get out of here."

Nathan didn't seem happy to comply, but Eric grabbed his bow and pulled him along. Together, the three of them raced out onto the cabin's upper landing, then hurried down the stairs. Jackie and Philip waited anxiously in the reception area below.

"Outside!" Kamiyo roared at them. The pain in his broken hands added fury to his words. "Outside now! Don't let it corner you."

Jackie shook her head. "What is it? We heard screams."

"Vamps has gone bad again. The monster has taken over."

"He's gone full-on Vlad the Impaler," Eric shouted hysterically.

Jackie blew air out of her cheeks and groaned. "Oh no."

"I knew this would happen," said Philip.

Kamiyo heard no footsteps pursuing them, but somehow that was more frightening. The monster was not rash or impulsive, not a wild animal. It was a monster that took its time—that broke hands when it could just as easily have broken a skull.

Kamiyo made it outside, greeted by the dusk. There was no longer a campfire beside the lake, so it was difficult to see, objects already losing their detail in favour of shadow. The pain in his hands further added to his disorientation. But he could see Spencer and the other sick children racing up the hill to the castle. At least they were safe.

"What do we do now?" asked Jackie, her voice quivering.

Nathan notched another arrow. "We kill him."

"I don't think it's a *him*," said Kamiyo. "It's a *what*."

"Yeah," said Eric. "That thing was not human."

"We kill *it* then," Nathan rephrased.

Jackie touched the lad's shoulder. "You need to get back to the castle with the other children, Nathan."

"No way! I already hit the target once. You need me."

Eric tried to help Jackie. "Nathan. This isn't a game. Get up in that castle where it's safe."

"No fucking way!"

"Nathan!" Jackie snapped.

Kamiyo sighed. "Just let him stay. Everyone, grab whatever you can."

"Why isn't it coming out?" Eric was trembling. "I don't like that at all."

"It's coming," said Kamiyo, knowing it to be true. "Just be ready."

Philip stomped over to the weapons pile beside the stairs and picked up a sharpened stick. He gripped it in both hands and glared at Kamiyo. "We should've put this guy down the moment he attacked Jackie."

"He attacked me too," said Kamiyo, then held up his mangled hands. "Twice now."

"Then you need to stand back and let us handle this, because you clearly can't."

Eric put a hand on Kamiyo's chest and eased him back. "He's right. You're hurt, Doctor. Let us take care of this."

The rest of the adults grabbed weapons while Nathan stood with his bow drawn. The only sound was the swaying branches of the forest. Kamiyo eyed the tree line, fearing a thousand demons would suddenly burst forth and consume them.

They waited.

And waited.

"He isn't coming out," said Eric, his dark skin turning pale. "I'm gunna piss myself if it don't come out soon. Freaking me the hell out."

Jackie was licking her lips. "S-Should we go in?"

Kamiyo barked a warning. "No! Anything but that. Our best chance is out in the open."

"Wait!" Philip held his homemade spear in front of him while he cocked his head to listen. "I hear something."

Kamiyo did too. The *clod-clod-clod* of heavy footsteps on wood. There was also a low, whistling sound. A twisted melody. A dirge that weakened Kamiyo's bladder just hearing it.

Vamps appeared at the top of the cabin's steps and surveyed them all like he was about to give an address. But it wasn't really Vamps. Stood before them was an abomination.

Nathan loosed another arrow, and once again the boy's aim was uncanny. The shaft buried itself in Vamps' stomach, a wound that should kill a man, yet he yanked the arrow out and threw it to the ground like a crushed mosquito. He resumed whistling that dreadful tune.

Nathan notched and released another arrow. This time, Vamps caught the shaft in mid-air and snapped it in his fist. All the while, he carried on whistling. Whistling a tune of damnation—an ode to Hell.

Kamiyo felt terror rising in his chest, and he wanted more than anything to run into the safety of the forest. They were all going to die here, but his sense of duty made him stay. A doctor did not flee people in need of help.

Vamps leapt the steps and landed in the grass before them. He hissed at them, tongue tearing free from his throat and lashing at the air.

"Oh, hell no!" Eric had a shovel, and he swung it at Vamps. Vamps stepped aside so quickly he became a blur. He trapped the shovel in his armpit and yanked Eric towards him. Eric abandoned his grip on the shovel and tried to grab Vamps in a headlock.

Kamiyo yelled out in horror. "No! Get away from him, Eric."

Vamps embraced Eric like an old friend, but then he shoved the man hard enough to launch him into the air. Eric's guts unravelled as he flew backwards, held in place by Vamps' outstretched fist. He hit the ground, dead, a massive hole in his torso. Vamps held up his bloody hand, clumps of intestine sloughing off it, and carried on whistling his tune. He tossed Eric's guts into the grass.

Philip teetered on the spot, eyes rolling grimly in his head. Kamiyo thought he might pass out or make a run for it, but instead, Philip flung his sharpened stake at Vamps like a javelin.

Vamps knocked the spear aside and strode towards Philip, whistling louder in a high-pitched screech that caused them all to cover their ears. Jackie sobbed, her typical resolve evaporating. "We have to get to the children. I need to protect them."

"We let him get away and we're all dead." Kamiyo stared her hard in the eye, trying to keep her mind present and focused. "Even if he doesn't get inside the castle, he'll bring other demons. he knows we're here, and he won't stop until we're dead."

"He's right," said Nathan. "We have to take this prick down."

"We can't," cried Jackie.

"We stay and fight," said Kamiyo.

Philip shoved Kamiyo towards Vamps. "You stay and fight. I'm not ending up like Eric."

Nathan fired another arrow, and it struck Vamps in the shoulder. He pulled it out like all the others and threw it to the ground. It was useless. There was no way to hurt this thing. The Red Lord was invincible.

"He won't die," said Nathan, backing off towards the lake while notching another arrow.

Philip and Jackie backed away too. Kamiyo tried not to flee quite so readily, but he had two busted hands and no idea how to help. Vamps stopped his whistling and sneered at each of them in turn. "None of you shall live to see another sunrise."

Kamiyo shoved Nathan with his elbow. "Run, kid!"

Everyone bolted, but Vamps moved like a leaf in a gale and was in front of them before they even realised he moved. Nathan stumbled right into his outstretched claws.

"Nathan!" Kamiyo barged the boy out of the way, which meant Vamps grabbed him instead. Kamiyo bellowed in pain as razor-sharp claws hoisted him off the ground by his shoulders.

"A noble sacrifice." Vamps snarled in his face. "One you will regret."

A shot fired, and Vamps released Kamiyo to the ground. He turned around slowly, blood spurting from his neck. Three figures emerged from the darkness. Hannah was one, flanked by Frank and another man Kamiyo didn't recognise.

Frank shouted. "We're here, kidda. We're here!"

Hannah knelt behind her rifle and let off another shot. It struck Vamps in the throat, sending him spiralling onto his knees. Blood spurted into the air and he clutched at his throat like he was trying to keep it from falling apart. He sputtered and gurgled, trying to curse at them through the blood.

Nathan notched another arrow and aimed, but Kamiyo shook his head at the boy. There was no need, Hannah had it handled. She hurried over to them now, with Frank brandishing a sword and struggling to keep up with her. The other man, the stranger, stood where he was, seemingly mortified as he stared at Vamps.

Kamiyo faced Hannah. "You're back! Why?"

"Long story, but I knew you were in danger. Is everyone okay?"

Jackie wailed, as all of her emotions gushed out at once. She pointed at Eric's eviscerated corpse. Frank shook his head and swore.

Kamiyo let his head drop. "Not everyone."

Hannah ground her teeth. "Damn it! I was too late."

"It would have been worse without you."

Without reply, she pointed her rifle at Vamps who remained on his knees, still fighting to keep the blood in his neck. "I should have put a bullet in you two weeks ago. I don't care whatever big-shot demon you think you are, you picked on the wrong group of people."

Vamps glared at her, trembling as blood continued pumping from his neck. Gradually, his breathing came to a stop, and he teetered back and forth on his knees like he was about to fall flat on his grave. Hannah pointed her rifle at his head, ready to deliver the mercy shot.

Nathan yelled. "Do it!"

"Let the bastard 'ave it!" Frank cried.

Vamps removed his hands from his neck and held them out to his sides like Christ. Blood dripped from his fingertips onto the grass and gushed down the front of his shirt. "Deliver yourselves from evil," he said mockingly.

Hannah sneered—"Amen!"—and pulled the trigger.

Vamps rose to his feet, arms still held out like Christ. "I am the red thunder, the flame of consumption, the spark of creation. Behold, and I shall make things anew."

Hannah fired again. The shot tore through Vamps' chest, but he sold no injury. He snatched Hannah's rifle, breaking the strap around her neck, and flung it high into the darkening sky.

As if in reply, it started to rain.

Hannah had the presence of mind to launch herself into an evasive roll before Vamps could grab her, and she joined the others. No one moved, stunned into inaction by what they were seeing. This monster couldn't be killed. Not with fists, spears, or bullets.

There was no hope.

The strange man Hannah had brought along now stepped forwards. Twilight made his features appear grey and featureless, but Kamiyo thought the man was Middle-Eastern. He muttered something in a strange language and held out an arm to Vamps. His wide, hanging cuffs made him look like a wizard. Vamps placed all his attention on the stranger, snarling like a wolf. He took a swipe, but the small man dodged aside, still speaking his foreign tongue.

Kamiyo leant against Hannah, for comfort more than anything else. "Who is that guy?"

"His name is Aymun. He knows Vamps, and about what's going on."

"Makes one of us," said Frank, waving the sword that Hannah had returned to him.

Aymun continued dodging, putting himself in danger by further enraging The Red Lord. Whatever he said was getting a passionate reaction.

"We have to get out of here," said Philip. "We have to gather everyone and leave the forest."

"No," said Hannah. "This place is ours."

Philip shook his head. "We can't win this."

Aymun tripped in the dark, falling down on one knee. Hannah yelled at him to get out of the way. Kamiyo groaned, realising this strange man would not be their saviour either, just as powerless as the rest of them—and about to die.

Vamps swiped a lethal claw through the air, aiming for Aymun's exposed neck.

Aymun sprung aside and thumped Vamps in the ribs, then rolled away quickly. A long blade jutted out of Vamp's chest, left there by Amun. "Now!" He yelled at them all. "The beast is wounded. Attack him."

Kamiyo didn't know what he could do with two broken hands, so he got involved by roaring at the others to attack. Frank struck Vamps in the back of the head so hard with his sword staff that it bent. Nathan buried another arrow in Vamp's chest. Jackie and Philip stabbed at his mid-section with sharp sticks. Vamps leaked blood from a dozen places. He thrashed and grew weaker.

The heavens opened, and the rain came down in buckets.

Frank leapt into the air and walloped the bent sword into the back of Vamps' neck. "Boing boing, you shit-faced dingle."

Vamps fell forward onto his hands. Aymun stepped forward and pulled the knife out of his side, holding it to the monster's throat. "Vamps, my friend, if you are in there... my soul weeps for you. You were a warrior until the end. May God shelter you for eternity."

Vamps leapt up and seized the knife before it had the chance to cut his throat. He twisted it until Aymun had no choice but to let go or see his arm broken. He gasped, taken by surprise, and this time he lost his footing for real, tumbling backwards nearly onto his back. Vamps gnashed his filthy, crooked teeth, and raised the blade in his trembling, blood-soaked hand. Everyone stopped what they were doing, too fearful to move, waiting for what the beast would do next.

Vamps tossed the blade into the wet grass and fled into the forest. Frank gave chase, but was too slow, so he resigned himself to shouting obscenities at the trees.

Aymun clambered to his feet. He brushed off his clothes. "We must prepare. The Red Lord will return, and not alone. He has taken my friend's body and will use it to assemble an army. An army designed to wipe out whatever people are still alive in this world. That cannot be allowed to happen."

Frank put his hands on his waist. "Yow don't 'afta tell me twice, kidda."

"I'm sorry," said Aymun. "I didn't catch that."

"I said yow am right, kidda."

Aymun frowned.

Kamiyo's heart was beating so fast he worried he might pass out, but he couldn't take his eyes of the stranger. "H-How did you manage to injure him? Everything we tried before you came…"

"He is bound by my friend's human body. While the Red Lord is immensely powerful, he is still a prisoner to the flesh. Injure his vessel's brain or heart and it will take him longer to recover. I thought we had him, but he is resilient."

"Who is he?" asked Kamiyo. "I know he's The Red Lord— whatever that is—but what the Hell are we up against here?"

Aymun watched the tree line for a moment, then seemed confident enough to address them further. "The Red Lord is a being so powerful that God imprisoned him mere moments after he was formed. The Red Lord's true name is Crimolok. He is the 3rd angel, created after Michael and Lucifer. Crimolok was God's first and only mistake; a perversion of everything he intended to create."

Philip put a hand against his forehead and pushed back his rain-soaked hair. "Why can't the end of the world just be simple? Airborne Ebola virus, a meteor… something like that."

Aymun didn't seem to understand Philip's words, so he continued with his own. "Of the First Three, Michael was good and pure, created to serve and obey. Lucifer was strong and proud, created to honour and lead. Crimolok, however, was impulsive and emotional, created to create. He was supposed to tend to God's creations, as infinitely wise and as vastly knowing as God himself. But one god can never willingly serve another, so Crimolok sought to destroy his creator so he might become the new maker of worlds. He believes his own Garden of Eden would be superior and will not stop until he sees it born."

"So, he's a dangerous shite then?" said Frank glumly. The rain pouring down his face made him look utterly miserable. "Jesus wept."

"And still does to this day," said Aymun. "Tonight, we faced not just our enemy, but the enemy of all existence. These are the end of days, my friends. The Red Lord shall return. And soon."

Kamiyo looked at Hannah and sighed. "Cheery fellow you brought us."

Hannah seemed worried. "It's not just the Red Lord we have to worry about though," she told them. "When I learned you all might be in danger, I had to make a choice. I let a demon escape. The one I wounded in the attack two weeks ago. It's still on the loose. It still might lead others here."

"So, this is it." Philip was shaking his head. "We're doomed."

"Not yet," said Aymun. "But probably very soon."

30

CALIGULA

It had been several days since Caligula tasted human flesh. This air was dry, filled only with the stench of his own damned troops. A vast army had assembled with no enemy to fight. His scouts had come up empty-handed every time they'd set out to find human survivors. It appeared he had done too good a job of scouring these lands. His glory had peaked and was now in decline.

Rome is only Rome when it conquers.

Two-thousand demons formed ranks in the fields where they had made their camp, set to the task of building earth-works and fortifications, if only to have something to do—a Roman camp built by monsters. Monsters who were acting too human for Caligula's liking. Now and then, he caught them staring into space, mouths moving as they tried to form words. Some demons could talk well, but most did not attempt it. Until recently. He had even found one of his creatures fumbling with a pile of red and black cards, trying to shuffle them into random order. What was happening to them? Why was the stink of humanity upon his troops?

He needed to give them something to kill. A reason to be monsters.

"Rux!" he bellowed. "Present yourself at once!"

The battered slave hobbled before Caligula, broken bones grinding with every agonised step. He had almost killed the pathetic Gaul during the last beating but was glad he had not gone so far. Having a pet to kick around pleased him.

"I-Imperator, how may I serve?"

"By telling me we have found humans to slaughter."

Rux trembled and failed to make eye-contact. "I-I fear it is not so, Imperator. The scouts have all returned without news. It is possible that no humans remain in these lands, such is the completeness of your conquest."

Enraged to hear news he did not want, Caligula raised his fist, but before he could strike Rux, he was interrupted. One of his Germanic guards raced towards him with a bedraggled demon trotting behind. "Imperator," he shouted. "I bring you auspicious news."

"What is it? Speak quickly!"

"A casualty returns to us, wounded during a recent battle with humans."

Caligula felt his sinewy eyelids rise of their own accord. He studied the burnt husk of a creature standing behind the guard. "You know the location of humans? Where?"

The demon nodded, drool hanging from his charred lips that were trying their best to form a smile. "Yes, yes, David knows. David knows. Humans live like bears. Bears in woods."

Caligula snarled. This creature had named itself David, suffering the same ill-effects of whatever was happening to his troops. "Speak plainly or lose your tongue, creature."

The demon cowered, a festering wound on its upper chest opening and closing. "David apologises. I..." He stopped to concentrate on what he said next. "David see many humans in woods. In forest. Many. The forest is near. People within. Near. Many. David knows."

Caligula couldn't help but grin. This was the Intel he'd been starving for. "So, there's a camp somewhere in the forest? Most excellent. Guard! Take our dutiful messenger to get cleaned up. Tomorrow, he leads us to new glorious battles. Tell the troops they shall feast on human flesh once again."

The guard placed a fist over his chest in respect and then raced to carry out his general's orders.

Caligula smiled. Tomorrow would bring blood. Finally.

31

DR KAMIYO

They retreated to the castle under the starry night sky, barricading the sally port and posting teenage guards on the wall. Panic erupted when people learned Vamps, or the creature wearing him, was somewhere in the forest, and that the wounded demon had fled to a nearby village.

Kamiyo sat on the brick surrounds of an ancient well and hung his head in despair. The rain fell heavy, matching his mood. The hope of saving this place slipped away, and he now felt the same thrumming dread he used to feel on the road— only this was worse. Instead of fearing his own death, he now feared the death of three-dozen children.

With Eric's death, the number of familiar adults dwindled, which caused the children obvious distress. They huddled together around the remaining grown-ups, but kept their distance from Aymun. Nobody knew the man enough to trust him.

This is my fault. I should never have been so careless with Vamps. My eagerness to actually heal *someone blinded me to the danger. I thought Vamps was better. He seemed fine.*

Kamiyo had risked the entire camp.

Hannah shuffled over to him, stepping out of the light of the campfire and entering the rain-soaked shadows. "Hey, Doc. I brought something for your wounds."

Kamiyo almost asked what she meant, then remembered Vamps had crushed his hands. The pain was so constant it had become the new baseline of how he felt. Agony was normal now. "You found supplies out there on the road?"

She handed him a packet of pills. "Ibuprofen was the strongest I could find, but we have plenty of antiseptics and dressings."

"Thank you. It should help. I'm not sure how bad the damage is yet; my hands have swelled too much to assess."

Hannah took his hands and examined them gently. "Wow! Regan really did a number on you."

"Regan?"

She smiled. "Yeah, you know, the girl from the Exorcist. She was possessed by a demon too."

Kamiyo chuckled. "You're a film geek?"

"Not much to do on a base in peacetime but watch movies."

"Well, the demon in the Exorcist was named *Pazuzu*. Regan was the innocent girl, so your analogy doesn't work."

"Well, whatever, you were lucky to survive."

"It was toying me." Kamiyo thought back. "Whatever's inside Vamps is smarter than the other demons."

"The big bad from what I've heard. The Red Lord."

Kamiyo nodded. Every time he had been alone with the Red Lord, he'd felt a soul-consuming fear. The Red Lord was a creature no human was ever supposed to encounter, one of the universe's vile secrets. "It wants us all dead. It'll be back."

Hannah lay Kamiyo's hands palm-up on his knees and wrapped them in fresh bandages. She had a surprisingly delicate touch for a soldier. "We'll face what comes when it comes," she said. "What else can we do but that?"

"You lost your rifle."

"I know. I could cry. That bastard threw it into the sky like a frisbee. I might try to find it in the daylight, but it was running low on ammo, anyway. Time I learned to rely on something else."

"Plenty of bow and arrows."

"Yeah. Suppose I could be a little less GI Jane and a bit more Lara Croft."

"I can see you pulling that off." Kamiyo grinned a little leeringly and hoped it didn't offend. His social manners were a little rusty.

Hannah laughed, but didn't seem to mind his leer. "Don't get too excited, I bat for the other side."

"Oh!"

She laughed again. "Yeah, well, maybe I'll have to change my preferences, because Jackie is the only other woman in the world as far as I know, and I think she might have a thing for Ted."

Kamiyo cackled, forgetting his pain for a moment. "You're kidding me?"

"Nope. She lights up around him. I think I saw him crack a smile the other day too, which is saying something."

"Wow, I suppose love never dies. Anyway, Jackie isn't the only woman. There's Carol. She's stopped coughing up phlegm now by the looks of things."

Hannah pulled a face and whispered. "She's a bit too old. Plus, I don't think there's a lot going on upstairs."

"Beggars can't be choosers."

"I ain't begging yet, Doc. I have to believe that, somehow, out there in the world, is another lesbian. One day, I'll go out there and find her."

"That's beautiful," said Kamiyo, beaming. "And one day I'm going to find an Amazon warehouse and rip open every box I find until I have all the fun stuff."

Hannah frowned. "Like what?"

He shrugged. "I dunno. Drones? Comic books? Figurines."

"Wow, you're still a wee ben, ain't you?"

Kamiyo blushed. "I never got to be a child when I was actually supposed to be one. I'd just like to try it on for size, and forget all the horror, you know? I had strict parents, and they decided I would be a doctor before I was even born."

Hannah had finished wrapping his hands, so she took a seat on the well beside him. "It's not what you would have chosen for yourself?"

"I don't know. Maybe if it wasn't thrust upon me, I might have been more passionate about medicine. When I was a kid, I remember wanting to be a comic book artist. I wanted to create superheroes and monsters." He laughed to himself. "I suppose at the time I was trying to create friends and family to keep me company. I used to draw myself alongside all the crime fighting giants. My parents used to think I was doing homework, but I would hide my pad behind a textbook."

"Sounds sad, pet."

Kamiyo nodded, then pointed up at a pair of teenagers standing on the castle's rear wall. "I still had it better than these kids do."

Hannah glanced at the shifting shadows of the children. "Puts things into perspective, don't it? Maybe one day, you'll get to draw your comics again for these kids to enjoy. Hell, I enjoy a bit of Wonder Woman myself. You seen the jugs on that chick?"

Kamiyo smiled. "Can't say I have, but I'll keep an eye out next time I'm in a book shop. Thanks, Hannah. For looking after my hands and chatting."

"Don't mention it. You might have grown up a lonely kid, but you're surrounded by family now. We're all in this together."

That thought filled him with dread. "Things are going to turn nasty."

"Survival always does. These kids will get through it though. Kids have been enduring horrors since the moment mankind chucked its first spear. We need to show them that horror isn't all there is. The monsters will come, and we'll fight them, but it's what we teach them afterwards that will matter most."

"You're right. I... need to be more than just a doctor. I used to be a person."

"You still are. You're the same comic book loving geek you've always been. Now try to get some sleep. Nothing more we can do tonight."

Kamiyo got up from the well and ached his back. He felt a hundred years old. "Let's hope our enemy sleeps too. If not, we're in for a tiring fight."

"You're a real downer, you know that?"

"Yes. Yes, I do. Goodnight, Hannah."

"Good night, Doc."

32

TED

Ted slept poorly, and sometime before the sun rose, he gave up trying and left his tent to start work. As much as he still felt the pull of leaving, he had to admit that putting his skills to use was the most content he'd felt since the world ended. He was a simple builder again, starting at dawn and finishing when his body ached too much to go on. It was the first thing that made sense in a long time.

Today, he planned to begin his most ambitious project yet. Something that might help them when the enemy came to their gates. He had everything he needed, the thick trunk of an ash tree Frank's team had felled, and a collection of recurve bows that had once been used to teach archery by the lake. The idea in his head was fuzzy, but he hoped it would clear up as he got to work. Once the others in the camp awoke, he would set them to digging a trench in front of the main gate, then shaping pikes to place along the main approach.

He worked in solitude for around an hour, fighting off the dewy morning chill with physical exertion. The world was silent and peaceful, the only sounds, other than fitful snores from the tents, came from the birds nestled in the forest. Their dawn arias were unchanged, the world no different for them than it had ever been. Whoever won the war between humanity and demons was of no import. Or perhaps they would welcome the end to the animal that had raped and stolen the land for so many thousands of years.

Once the snoring within the tents changed to the clearing of throats, Ted knew his solitude was at an end. The camp would soon erupt into life.

No longer needing to be quiet, Ted set about sawing the ash trunk into sections. He would need to find a way to plane them down into long poles once he was done, and it would be an arduous task whatever method he decided on.

Frank awoke first, scrambling out of his tent like a zombie. He nodded to Ted and exchanged a few words, then headed into the castle like he did every morning. The hearth would need lighting, and as Frank was not a morning person, he enjoyed getting right to work instead of chatting.

Others awoke within the following ten minutes, with the teenagers naturally being the ones refusing to rise until the last possible minute.

Jackie slept in the castle with most of the children, and she approached Ted now with a cup of tea. "We're running out of tea bags," she said. "So enjoy it."

Ted nodded. A hot cuppa each morning was one of the few pleasures left in life, but everyone knew the cabin's small canteen had possessed a finite supply. They'd already begun rotating green tea and earl grey in with the breakfast tea, and that swill was as disgusting as it had ever been.

Jackie scrutinised the thick ash tree half dissected by his saw. "What are you working on?"

"An idea," he said. "Might not pan out, but he who dares..."

"You sound like Del Boy."

Ted chuckled. "Let's pretend I was quoting the SAS and not Fools and Horses. Thanks for the tea, you didn't have to."

"Nonsense. All the sweat you've given us..." She sighed and looked at him for a slightly disconcerting amount of time before speaking again. "You remind me a lot of my husband, you know?"

Ted didn't know why it hadn't occurred to him that Jackie might be married, especially after admitting she had a son, but it was a surprise, and he didn't know how to respond. "Oh, I'm sorry; I didn't realise. Did he, um...?"

"Get eaten by demons? No, cancer was the beast that ate my dear George. Ten years ago now. Colon cancer. Just bad luck really. He put off going to the doctors for far too long. He was thirty-nine."

"That's some shit luck. I'm sorry."

"It was the worst time in my life. Perhaps it was a blessing though, my George not having to face this."

"Maybe your husband dying is what made you so tough. You're a survivor, Jackie."

She blushed and had to glance at the ground. "Anyway, I was saying that you reminded me of my George. He was a glazier, had a small factory that produced windows and doors. Not a glamorous job, but he worked hard at it. The thing I loved about him most was his commitment. He believed there was no point doing anything unless you did it to the best of your ability. I can see you were both cut from the same cloth."

Ted sipped his tea, disguising the fact he didn't know what to say. He liked Jackie even if he wasn't sure why. She wore her heart on her sleeve—the complete opposite of himself—but it made her easy to talk to—no second-guessing or ambiguity about what she was thinking.

She looked at him now and smiled. "I'm glad I met you, Ted. You've kept me sane these last two weeks, do you know that? I think Frank would have driven me quite mad if you hadn't arrived."

"Ha! Yeah, that geezer's an odd one, ain't he? His heart is in the right place though."

Jackie nodded. "It is. It's his heart that led to him being with us in the first place."

"What d'you mean?"

"It was Frank's coach that brought us here. The company we hired let us down at the last minute. With those black stones freaking everyone out, most of their drivers had called in sick. Frank worked for the same company and gave up his day off rather than let the kid's weekend get cancelled. None of us had ever met him before all this started."

"You're joking? He's certainly one of the family now. When I first met Eric, he told me he wasn't one of you either at the start, that he used to work here as a volunteer."

"Yes. When we arrived here, there were lots of staff—cleaners, groundsmen, et cetera. Soon, as the news hit about the attacks, they left to be with their families. They all lived local, but we were a lot farther from home, so it wasn't so easy for us to flee. Eric was the only original member of staff who stayed. He was divorced, no kids."

Ted laced his fingers together and look at the ground. "I was divorced too. I was a bad husband. Spent my nights down the pub and my days working. My dad brought me up thinking women were there to look after a man while he made the money. I never challenged that opinion until Chloe was born. The older she got, the more I couldn't bear the thought of a man treating her the way I treated her mum. By then it was too late, my marriage was already loveless."

Jackie grasped his forearm and looked at him. "That's sad, but at least you changed, even if it was too late. I think where we end up as people is more important than where we start."

He nodded. "Yeah, well, my ex-wife and I got on better after the divorce than we ever did married. Was all for the best."

"I think if there's any good to come of this, it's that we can all let go of the past."

Ted sipped his tea, an excuse to move his arm out of her grasp. He offered the mug to Jackie a moment later. "We should share if it's running low."

She smiled and accepted the drink. After a moment, she turned to him and asked a question. "Are you still planning on leaving?"

"What?" He tried to look like he didn't know what she was talking about.

"Oh, come now, Ted, don't play games. You spend every minute working, barely talking to a soul. It feels like you're trying to finish the job as quickly as you can without getting to know anybody."

"The demons could be here any day. I'm working as hard as I can to make us safe."

She nodded. "True, but I can tell you're still planning to go. There's a far-away look in your eyes, and I know you're thinking of someplace else. But sometimes I think I catch you feeling sad at the thought of leaving us. You're starting to like this place, aren't you?"

"I..." He sighed. "Yes, it's been... easier here than it has been in a long time."

"You think we're doomed?"

He wanted to say no, but he couldn't bring himself to lie. "I do, yes."

"So, you're going to leave us to our fates? You don't want to be here when it happens."

It didn't seem like she was berating him, more just trying to get the facts straight. "I'm doing all I can to ensure you have a fighting chance. I've done more for this place than anyone has—"

She put a hand up and halted him. "You have, without question. If you want to leave, no one has any right to chastise you. I just worry about whether you could live with yourself afterwards."

The statement drew a derisory snort from Ted. "Don't worry about my conscience, Jackie. I'll be okay."

She pointed towards the castle. In front of its main entrance, Philip corralled the camp's dozen preteens. In the last few days, the man had started telling a story each morning. He particularly had a flair for his retelling of *The Gruffalo*. Ted assumed it was a way for him to work through his grief after losing his son, Bray.

Jackie looked at Ted, but kept her arm pointed towards the group of children. "These children need every adult they can cling to. We need to protect them, Ted. We owe it to whatever future might be left."

"The only child I owe anything to is my dead daughter," he snapped, growing angry. His aggressive impulses had lessened recently, but he realised now how close to the surface they remained.

"I understand that, Ted, but what would Chloe want you to do? Ask yourself. Wouldn't she want you to give these children the chance she never got?"

"Be careful, Jackie."

But she didn't heed his warning. Instead, she kept on at him. "Chloe's memory shouldn't be a dagger in your heart, Ted. She should be the smile on your lips. Keep her with you as a strength, not a weakness. These children need you now, and I think you need them too. Whatever promises you made Chloe aren't as important as keeping these children alive. She wouldn't want her daddy to run away. She'd want you to be a hero."

Ted snarled and feared he might lash out. If he hurt Jackie, it would be the end of him. It would mean he truly had lost control. "Y-You have no right," he said. "I..." He felt a tear slip onto his cheek and nestle in his stubble. He clenched his fists in fury. How dare this woman play with his emotions. How dare she speak about his daughter. Yet, the rage sizzled into his fingertips, pushed to his extremities by the warming in his chest. More tears fell.

Jackie leant forward and held him. She rubbed his back, which drew massive sobs. "It's okay, Ted. One day, when this is all over, I want to hear everything there is to know about Chloe. She will never be gone, I promise you."

"She was my little girl, and those fucking monsters took her away from me."

"Too right, they fucking did. So, stay with us and help us fight back. Everyone keeps telling me we're doomed, but I refuse to accept it. I'm not interested in just surviving. I want to show those shitting monsters that they picked the wrong fight. Fuck them!"

Ted reared back, stunned. "Jackie, you keep swearing like that and I'll make you my foreman."

She let out a hoot. "Just don't tell anyone. I'll lose my air of sophistication."

Ted laughed hysterically, tears drenching his cheeks. All of this emotion was wretched, turning him inside out, but it felt good too. It was like coming up for air. "You really think Chloe is still with me?"

Jackie stopped laughing and grew serious. "Can either of us be sure she isn't? Everything we thought we knew about the universe is wrong. There are places beyond this one, we know that now for sure. Perhaps you should stop thinking about promises you made Chloe in the past and make her some new ones. Who knows, she might be watching. Isn't that enough?"

The thought that his daughter might still exist in some form sent a shiver down Ted's spine. It rocked the very core of him and filled him with something he thought he'd lost forever—hope. He looked over at the children huddled in front of Philip and saw they still had it too. As long as there were children, there was hope.

"I'll stay," he said, feeling a massive relief to know his journey had come to an end and that he was home. "I'll stay here and fight."

33

DR KAMIYO

Two days passed without drama, but tension there was in spades. Kamiyo imagined what patients used to go through waiting for the results of a biopsy. That endless, runaway worry about an oddly shaped mole or slight lump in the breast. Waiting for a death sentence was torture. Waiting for demons to attack was no better. Apprehension was a lingering wound.

Speaking of lingering wounds, Kamiyo's hands slowly returned to their original size. They were a sickly purple now, and every slight movement was sickeningly painful, but all of his fingers moved, and he thought he might get close to full use of them back. The main thing was that his hands worked well enough to leave the forest in search of supplies. Injured or not, it had to happen.

"I'm leaving," he announced over the chitchat in the castle's great hall. He stood before the crackling hearth which felt like the appropriate place to give a public address. His statement went unnoticed, absorbed into the evening's background din, so he cleared his throat and spoke again louder. "I said, I'm leaving!"

This time he got a reaction. Those who were eating stopped chewing and looked at him. Slowly, all heads turned his way. Hannah was the one to give the first objection. "The heck you talking about, Doc?"

"I'm talking about the fact we're still low on supplies."

"We're fine. The stuff I carried back from the Post Office bought us some time. Once I'm rested up, I'll head out again."

She was referring to the dog bite on her shin. It had been a deep and painful wound, which Kamiyo was sure would have killed her if not for the antiseptic she herself had found. Kamiyo looked at her now, knowing that getting her onboard would be key. "Any day now we expect to be attacked. That means we might not get another chance to head out and get what we need. Ted here is doing an excellent job of barricading us inside, but the point of a siege isn't to break down the walls."

"What do you mean?" Carol asked. "I don't understand."

Ted groaned. "He means if the demons come in force, they can just wait us out until we starve. How the Hell didn't that dawn on me sooner?"

"We can't survive a siege with nothing in the pantry," Kamiyo explained. "We'll be cut off from the lake, the forest. Once again, it turns to our need for crops, long-term rations, and medicine. We need to plant within the castle's walls and scavenge the nearby village for dried food and water. One summer without rain and we'll die of dehydration in a week. We're living hand to mouth, and that doesn't work with an enemy at our walls."

Hannah frowned. "Okay, Doc, point taken. But why you? Why do you want to be the one to leave?"

"Because we need medicine as much as we do food, and if we're only going to get one shot at this, we'll need to be thrifty with what we bring back. There's no point filling a rucksack with beta blockers and statins when what we need is antibiotics, blood thinners, anti-coagulants, strong painkillers, et cetera. I am the only one who can find a pharmacy and fill a rucksack only with what we need. If there's only time for one trip, there will only be room to carry so much. If you want another argument, then I would point out that Hannah has an injured leg, and Ted is too busy making this place safe. Who else is there?"

Hannah nodded and gave no further comment.

"You're injured too," said Jackie. "Your hands..."

"Are a mess," he admitted. "I won't be writing any letters for a while, but I can hold a weapon and scoop supplies into a bag. There's nothing useful I can do here, but I know how to survive out there."

"You don't have to do this," said Jackie. Her voice tremored, her resolve was fading. She knew it had to happen too.

Kamiyo sighed. The fire at his back was making him sweat, but he used the discomfort to steel himself to push forward with his intentions. "I have to do this. The reason the demons found this place is because my pack ripped open when I was running through the forest. I lead them here."

"You don't know that," said Jackie. "And it was only a matter of time before they found us, anyway."

"If there's even a slim chance I brought the demons, I need to make it right. Everyone is doing their part, but it will all amount to nothing if we don't have supplies enough to last us. This isn't even a decision to be made, it's necessary, and I've decided. I'll head out first thing in the morning."

There was a moment's silence, almost like he'd just announced he was terminally ill. They expected him to die. He expected it too.

"I'm coming with you."

Kamiyo studied the crowd, wondering who had spoken.

When Philip stood up, he repeated himself. "I'm coming with you."

Carol gasped. "Philip, no!"

Philip tutted. "Calm down, Carol."

Kamiyo was confused. Of all the people to volunteer to help him, Philip was the last he expected. What was the man's agenda? "Philip, why do you want to come with me?"

"Because this isn't your burden to take on alone. This place belongs to us all."

"Philip, sit down," said Jackie. "You have no idea how to survive out there."

Philip nodded as if he agreed with her. "Then the doctor will have to do his best to keep me from getting killed. If I go with him, we'll be able to bring twice as much back. Like he said, we might only get one shot at this."

"You can't come with me, Philip." Kamiyo tried to speak with all the authority he could muster.

Philip folded his arms. "Not that I need your permission, but why?"

"Because I don't trust you. You blame me for your son's death."

Philip flinched. He looked down at the floor for a moment like he was trying not to lose control of his emotions. He cleared his throat and looked up again. "I don't know what I feel anymore," he said. "But Bray is gone. Eric is gone. Lots of people are gone. But the rest of us are still here. Whatever you are or are not responsible for, I can see you're trying to do the right thing. I'd like the chance to do the same."

Kamiyo studied the man, disliking him still, but knowing he couldn't live here with an enemy any longer. If this was the risk he needed to take to make peace with Philip, he had to take it.

Someone else shouted out.

"I shall also attend your journey." It was Aymun, speaking from the shadows at the back of the room. The man had made little attempt to integrate with the group, as though he expected to be leaving soon. He spent most of his time on the castle walls, staring off into the distance. "If you two men have trust issues, then I shall be the salve for any tempers that arise.

Kamiyo and Philip exchanged glances, and then a shrug. "Okay," said Kamiyo. "More the merrier, I suppose."

"Then I'm coming too," said Nathan. "You promised to let me come."

Kamiyo located the boy in the crowd and groaned. "No, I didn't Nathan."

Nathan shot up out of his seat. "Yes, you did! You said I could come, and that you'd teach me to make it out there."

"Sit down, Nathan," Jackie demanded. "You're not leaving the camp."

"Fuck you, Jackie. No one here has the right to tell me what I can and can't do. My mum is dead. Everyone is dead. And you're all next."

Jackie's mouth fell open in a huge gasp. Ted, who stood beside her, eased her back down into her seat. He faced down the defiant teenager, looking like he might throw a punch. "Nathan, be a good lad and listen to your elders. There might be a time when you can leave this forest, but it ain't now. If you're looking for things to do, I'm sure there's plenty I can-"

"This is bullshit! If I don't learn how to survive out there, then I'm as good as dead. I want to learn how to fight."

"Sit down, dickhead," one of the other teenagers called out. Nathan shot back a look but kept his focus on Ted.

Ted stepped over to the lad, towering over him. Nathan didn't flinch, even as Ted stared him hard in the eye. "You want to know what's out there, kid? A world where every single child has been ripped to shreds. A world where corpses stink up every street, turning to liquid on the pavement. Outside this forest is a wasteland of horrors that even your warped mind can't imagine. You might think you want to know what's out there, but you don't. In fact, you'd piss your pants."

Kamiyo groaned at the hardline approach. *Nathan isn't the type of kid you can just yell at to behave.*

The teenagers in the room howled with laughter, and Nathan's plain expression cracked. His dark eyebrows lowered into a scowl and glanced back at his peers and cursed at them, using language so foul it was impressive. Once he'd run out of steam, he shook his head in defeat. "You're all dead," he muttered. "Every one of you."

Carol was shaking her head and looking like she might start sobbing. "Nathan, please just calm down."

Nathan kicked a chair. Then he fled, racing out of the hall and into the night.

Jackie stood up and sighed. "I'll go after him."

"Be careful," said Kamiyo. "Nathan is..." He shrugged. "Well, I guess he's just a kid. Don't push him too hard."

"I won't," said Jackie, leaving the room.

Kamiyo put his hands on his hips and looked at Philip who had continued standing there during Nathan's tirade. He seemed perplexed by what he had seen, and Kamiyo had to nod to the man to regain his attention. "So... we'll leave at first light?"

Philip nodded. "Or sooner."

34

HANNAH

It had been twenty-minutes since Kamiyo announced he intended to leave in the morning. Hannah needed to get some air after hearing it. She felt guilty. If she hadn't made such a shambles of getting supplies, Kamiyo wouldn't need to risk leaving the forest. The doctor had plenty of survival experience, but she still felt like it was her responsibility to go out. It had been taken away from her because she'd got wounded —because she failed. Some nights, she heard dogs barking in the forest as if to mock her. Was it the same ones that attacked her?

Tonight, she didn't hear dogs barking. She heard a gunshot. Others heard it too because they came spilling out of the castle. Ted shuffled through the crowd until he was right next to Hannah. He grabbed her by the shoulders. "Was that a gunshot?"

"I don't know." Although she did know. She knew what a gunshot sounded like. "It came from down by the lake.

Ted turned a circle, craning his neck to see through the crowd. "Where's Jackie?"

"I haven't seen her since she left to find Nathan."

Ted panicked, and he suddenly seemed much older and frail. "Damn it. I have to find her, Hannah."

Hannah grabbed his meaty wrist and squeezed it. "We'll both go."

They started towards the sally port, Hannah hobbling on her bad ankle and trying to keep up. Others followed too, in a loose tangle. Everyone was worried, but also solidified in their intent. Whatever was happening, they would face it together.

"Maybe it was a flair or a firework." Hannah looked up at the sky, hoping to see such a thing. "Maybe there are survivors out there somewhere signalling for help."

Ted didn't reply. He marched through the sally port like a man possessed, and when he started down the hill, she worried several times that he might stumble. She worried about doing the same herself. Her ankle nagged at her.

They soon reached the bottom of the hill, but nothing except silence and shadow met them. A glimmer of movement came from the lake, but all else was lifeless. There had been no more gunshots since the first.

Hannah realised they had acted poorly as a group. At least a dozen of them had clambered down the hill to investigate, but there was no reason for them to all be out in the open like this. The only saving grace was that everyone had armed themselves, some with bows, several with spears.

The cabin was no longer lit with candles by night as Kamiyo's infirmary was empty. The building stood empty and unlit. Kamiyo walked with them and seemed deeply concerned like he might know something no one else did. Hannah would have stopped to ask him about it if she wasn't so concerned with Ted.

The man was several paces ahead now, and without his

hammer. If an attack came from the forest, he would be defenceless. It made little sense, but she felt protective over him more than anyone else in the camp. They'd arrived here together, shoved together by circumstance. It felt like they were supposed to have each other's backs.

A single shape shifted in the shadows ahead, and Ted picked up speed, moving even farther ahead of the group. Hannah gritted her teeth to endure the pain in her ankle and hurried after him. "Ted, slow down. Stay with the group."

Ted stopped short and froze stiff. Hannah quickly closed twelve-feet and reached his side. The shadowy shape turned out to be Nathan, standing alone in the darkness. He held something in his arms. Hannah's rifle.

"Where did you find that?" she demanded, marching to retrieve it, but Ted threw out an arm and stopped her. She skidded to a halt, just in time to avoid tripping over a mound at her feet. At first, she couldn't tell what it was, but then she realised.

It was Jackie. Blood covered her chest, silvery in the moonlight.

Ted remained frozen stiff, but he managed to move his mouth enough to speak. "Nathan? What did you do?"

Nathan pointed the rifle at the ground and was emotionless as he spoke. "It was an accident. I was going to run away, but I found the gun at the edge of the forest. It was just lying there. I was going to bring it back and—"

"You're lying!" Ted snarled, a fury coming over him all of a sudden like a match being lit.

"I'm not!" A flash of defiance lit Nathan's face. "I swear, I was bringing the gun back and Jackie just... she startled me. I don't know why she was out here."

"She came to make sure you were okay!" Ted shocked

them all by leaping forwards and punching the child in the face. It was a brutal blow, and it knocked Nathan to the ground. Kamiyo and two older teenagers hurried to grab Ted and hold him back.

Nathan rolled on the ground, clutching his bleeding nose and sobbing. He wasn't so defiant anymore.

Hannah ran and retrieved her rifle and immediately pointed it at the injured child. Her actions horrified her—Nathan was just a child—but in the edge of her vision, Jackie's blood-covered body urged her to move her finger over the trigger.

No one spoke in Nathan's defence. Ted broke free and loomed over the child, looking ready to pummell him into a wet patch. Were they all really about to do this? Was this what they had become?

Jackie is dead.

Hannah put a hand on Ted's shoulder. If he killed Nathan, she feared what it might do to him. "I'll do it, Ted. Let me."

Ted looked at her, unbridled fury ready to unleash in cannon-fire. But he didn't unleash it. Instead of beating Nathan to death, he shook his head and sighed. "I promised Jackie I would protect these children. Which includes this piece of shit. Get him up."

Hannah shook with a mixture of pain and relief as she pulled the lad to his feet instead of pulling her trigger. The emotion of the scene was too much, and she felt ready to double-over and spew her guts. She could fight monsters all day long, but she'd been about to shoot a kid. She had really been prepared to do it.

Nathan didn't struggle, but Dr Kamiyo came over to help Hannah keep him restrained just in case he tried anything. They used her nylon belt to bind the boy's wrists behind his back, and then they shoved him down onto his knees. A pair of teenagers stood close by, holding spears. Nathan sobbed.

Kamiyo moved Hannah aside and pointed to her rifle. "As a doctor, I hate to say such things, but I think you would have been doing the boy a kindness. I don't think this was an accident."

Hannah sighed. "I don't either. You don't accidentally discharge a combat rifle like this. It's not an antique pistol. You need to get a firm hold to make it bark."

Still in a whisper, Kamiyo went on. "I've had concerns about Nathan for a while. I'm not sure if his dissociation issues were caused by the trauma of the last few months, or if he's always been this way, but he's been sending up several warning flags—fascination with death and killing, playing with animal carcasses, lack of empathy. It's all very theoretical, and I'm no psychiatrist—"

"What are you saying?" Hannah asked.

Dr Kamiyo folded his arms and looked over at Nathan. "I'm just saying I don't think this was an accident, and there aren't facilities anymore to care for someone like Nathan. I still plan on heading out tomorrow, but I'd feel better knowing someone is keeping a close eye on him."

"You think he might try to hurt someone else?"

"I don't know, but he worries me enough to say it's a more than plausible risk."

Hannah nodded, and when she glanced at Nathan, she saw the same things Kamiyo did. Nathan was disturbed. "I won't let him out of my sight," she said. "You get what we need, come back, and then we can decide what to do with Nathan."

"I think we might already know," he pointed to her rifle again. "Don't hesitate if he tries to hurt anyone else, okay?

When I get back, I will try to help him, but in the meantime just do what you need to do to keep everyone safe."

Hannah agreed, then turned to check on Ted who was kneeling beside Jackie. He didn't touch her, as though he dared not to. Instead, he peered down at her with his hands on his knees. Tears stained both his hairy cheeks, and she realised that the man was different now to how he'd been in the rest of the time she'd known him. He had shown compassion to Nathan instead of fury, and now he was showing grief. Whatever emotional barriers Ted had been holding onto were gone. That meant he was in pain.

Hannah knelt beside him, saddened by the sight of Jackie's expressionless face, and by the broken expression of her friend.

Jackie's hair was all bunched at the back of her head, and it made it look like she was lying on a dark pillow.

Everyone was silent, and the only thing Hannah could hear was Ted's gentle breathing. "Are you okay, Ted?"

"Jackie taught me something today about not giving up on people. All the people who cared about us, all the people who are gone... they still matter. What we do still matters. Jackie is dead, but I'm not sure I know what that means anymore."

Hannah placed a hand on his back and rubbed. For once, he didn't flinch at the contact. "I know you two were close," she said. "I'm sorry. She was a good chick."

"We weren't close," said Ted, "but we might have been one day. What the hell happened here, Hannah?"

"I wish I knew, pet. This is partly my fault. Nathan used my rifle. I searched for it, but I assumed it was gone. Didn't see much use in worrying about it. If I'd known..."

Ted reached out and squeezed her knee. "None of this fucked up world is our fault, Hannah. The only ones responsible are the demons that came through those gates to kill us all. I don't know how long we can keep surviving, but I will kill every last demon I see until the day of my death."

"And I'll be right at your side, Ted. I promise."

Ted looked at her and smiled. "I'm glad I met you, Hannah."

Hannah wiped the tears on his cheeks and smiled back at him. "I'm glad too."

35

TED

At sunrise, Ted was already down at the cabin to check on Nathan. For the time being, the group decided to keep the boy imprisoned in the cabin's First Aid room away from the camp. It was a small space with no windows, but there was a bed. Ted had fashioned a thick wooden crossbar across the door, held in place by a pair of steel brackets scavenged from the workshop. It wasn't an inescapable cell, but if Nathan managed to get out, he wouldn't be able to enter the castle without being seen, anyway. The worst that could happen was that the kid could flee into the forest never to be seen again. That wouldn't be the worst thing. It would beat having to execute Nathan somewhere down the line.

Every second spent with Nathan put the thought more in Ted's head. The remorseless monster had killed Jackie, a woman devoted to the welfare of others—including Nathan himself. If she hadn't cared enough about Nathan to go after him, she'd still be alive. Her empathy had been the death of her.

Ted opened the First Aid room and found Nathan sitting on the bed. He couldn't look at the boy, so he left some dried pasta and a cup of water on the nearby table and went to exit again.

"It was an accident," Nathan protested. He did the same thing each morning.

Ted stopped in the doorway but didn't face the boy. "I'm not sure I believe that."

"Then why didn't you let Hannah shoot me?"

"Because Jackie cared about you, lad. Killing you isn't what she would have wanted."

"I liked her," said Nathan, which angered Ted enough to turn around finally, but when he saw Nathan's teary eyes, he refrained from further action. "I liked her," he said again. "I wish she were still here."

"But she's not. You shot her dead, Nathan."

"Kill me."

Ted frowned. "What?"

"Kill me, please. I don't want to keep doing this. I don't want to keep being me. You should have killed me, so do it now."

"I won't kill you, Nathan." *Not yet.*

Nathan stood from the bed. "Then I'll hurt someone else. First chance I get, I'll kill someone. Just like I killed Jackie."

Ted felt his hands ball into fists. He bit his lip and forced his rage back down into his guts. "If you don't like who you are, Nathan, then be somebody else. Keep your mouth shut and stay put until we decide what to do with you. Maybe you'll get your wish."

Ted stormed out of the room and barred it from the other side, ignoring the sound of Nathan's fists beating against the wood. Was the kid truly suicidal, or just murderous and insane? He decided it wasn't something he had an answer to right that minute, so he went back up the hill to the castle.

Dr Kamiyo was preparing to leave this morning.

Ted found Kamiyo, like Hannah days earlier, standing at the portcullis. Philip and Aymun stood with him, and all three men had large camping rucksacks on their back. Philip carried a spear while Kamiyo had an old iron poker taken from one of the castle's hearths. Aymun was unarmed.

Frank was there too, shaking hands with the men and wishing them well. Hannah and Steve were in the winch room overhead, waiting to raise the gate. Both shouted 'good luck.' As usual, the children and teenagers huddled in their respective cliques. Milly stood alone as she so often did. Ted went up to her, and when she saw him she smiled.

"Is Nathan okay?" she asked.

Ted nodded. "Yes, are you?" She nodded but didn't look like she was okay. She looked sad in the way only a young child could. Ted patted her head.

"You're upset about Jackie?"

Milly nodded silently.

Ted knelt down, putting a hand on her shoulder. "She's not really gone, you know? There's a place we all go when we die. A better place. She's up there watching us right now. Whenever you miss Jackie, just look up at the sky and smile. She'll smile right back at you."

"She's in Heaven?" Milly said the word tentatively, like she thought she might get told off for speaking the words. "Heaven isn't real."

"Who told you that?"

"Reece."

Ted laughed. "Well, that's funny because Reece is in Heaven too. You see, no one knew for sure back before the monsters came, but now we do. The monsters came from a bad place, but there's a good place we all go that is safe and peaceful. Jackie and Reece, and everyone else, are there."

"Then I want to go there too."

"You will one day, Milly, but not until you're old and grey. I know it's scary here, but you can't go to the good place until it's your time. Until then, you have to be brave and strong so that those already in the good place can be proud of you. Okay?"

Milly nodded.

Ted straightened up and left her. He felt a little fraudulent speaking to a child about Heaven, but he believed his own logic. If demons came from Hell, then there had to be a Heaven. There just had to be.

Either that or there's just one Hell after another.

There were some things Ted wanted for the camp, and he wanted to go tell Kamiyo before he left. Nothing exotic, just things like sealant, hinges, and other small items that would come in handy. None of it was vital, but he gave Kamiyo a list anyway.

Kamiyo took it with a smile. "I'll get whatever I can find."

"Where are you planning to go?" Ted asked.

"We'll follow the main roads until we find a supermarket. If it has a pharmacy, we can get food and medicine in one place. You going to be okay here in the meantime?" Kamiyo looked at Ted with concern. It seemed like everyone was worried how he would react after Jackie's death. They kept waiting for him to explode.

Ted shrugged. "I have Steven and Hannah to help hold down the fort. Carol and Frank are looking after the kids. We'll be fine. Before we know it, the teenagers will be running things without us."

"Ha, yeah, I think you're right. Let's hope they don't put us out to pasture."

"Good luck out there, Doc. And be careful." Ted side-eyed Aymun and Philip. He had obvious reasons for not trusting Aymun, but he also worried about Philip too. The grieving father was emotional and angry, and he made no secret of his hatred for Kamiyo. "There's more than demons that can hurt you."

Kamiyo gave a subtle enough nod to let Ted know he understood. "You're right, I know, but I still have to believe the best in people. We'll be back, safe and sound, I promise."

"Then bring back some whiskey, and we'll have a drink." They shook hands, and the portcullis rose. There was a good chance no one would see Philip, Aymun, or Kamiyo again.

36

DR KAMIYO

Kamiyo and his companions had walked for an hour through the forest and anticipated another thirty minutes more until they found its end. It made Kamiyo wonder how people used to put up with the walk to the activity centre back in the days when few people enjoyed walking farther than the end of their driveway. He supposed he had answered his own question, though, and that the people who would visit an outdoor activity centre were the people who would enjoy the ninety-minute walk to get there. Kamiyo looked forward to the days when people would have the luxury of being lazy again because laziness went hand-in-hand with safety.

"Watch out for any dogs," said Philip. "Last thing we want is to end up like Hannah."

"She was lucky," explained Kamiyo. "A dog's jaws are filthy, and her wounds were deep. If the antiseptic she brought had not been enough..."

"That's why we're out here," said Philip. "We'll find what we need."

"The world is a garden," said Aymun. "It shall provide."

Kamiyo climbed up onto the thick roots of an oak tree and hopped over a tangle of bushes. When he landed, he turned back and waited for Philip and Aymun to do the same. Philip didn't do it with the same grace, and his awkwardness betrayed his lack of agility, but Aymun seemed almost to float over the obstacle.

"Thanks for coming with me, guys. It took guts."

Philip shrugged. "It doesn't feel like that."

"What do you mean?"

He stumbled a little through some weeds, but then made it up beside Kamiyo. "When I saw the demons on TV, it terrified me. Bray was with me, but my wife was at home. I tried calling, but she wouldn't answer. I didn't know whether to stay or leave, and both options scared the hell out of me. After a while, I knew my wife was dead, and some of that fear left me, but then..." He swallowed, visibly struggling. "When Bray died, the last of my fear went away. All that's left now is this," he gripped his stomach, "nothingness. It's like I don't care anymore. I know what's right and what's wrong, but... I don't know. It's not bravery that brought me here."

"Depression," said Kamiyo. "It's a normal stage of grief, Philip, I promise. The good news is that it usually comes before acceptance. I am so sorry about Bray. I wish I had done something more; that I was a better doctor."

Philip nodded, but gave no indication of how he felt. "If I make it back to the castle in one piece, perhaps I'll eventually feel different. But if I die out here, I don't care."

"To die is not something of which to be ashamed," said Aymun, "so long as it is not done so willingly. You must fight to live, Philip."

Kamiyo stared hard at Philip. "I won't let you give up. Bray might be gone, but there're three dozen kids behind us that need you. There aren't many adults left, and without us, those kids will grow up with none of the things we need to teach them. You were a businessman before all this happened, Philip, and it's obvious you were a good father. The kids need to learn from you. Heck, maybe I do too."

Philip sighed and then looked away with an awkward grunt. "Thank you for saying that. And... thank you for trying to help my son."

It didn't feel right to say, 'You're welcome,' so Kamiyo just left it at that.

They walked in silence for another hour until they found the road. It was still early, so the sun was bright and blinding. After several days of dreary, cloud-covered days, the weather was pleasant.

They exited by the coach Hannah had told them to look out for, then headed along the road. They kept to the ditch, ready to dash back into the trees at the first sign of trouble. The good thing about being a wasteland survivor in the UK was that it never took long before a road took you somewhere. What nightmare must it have been in rural America or mainland China? There you could walk a hundred miles and still find nothing. Both were countries Kamiyo had one day hoped to visit, but was there anyone left who could fly a plane?

Maybe in Portsmouth?

Would rescue ever come? It felt impossible.

Just focus on the now. And the now is an imminent castle siege by a horde of demons. Today's Netflix special...

"Bray would have loved this," said Philip after a while of walking. "He was breaking his neck to get out of the forest. Adventure was his middle name."

Kamiyo chuckled. "I was always stuck indoors reading as a kid. Looking back, I think Bray had the right idea. Life is for the living. I wish I'd done a bit more adventuring in my younger days."

"You're still young," Philip commented, "but I understand what you're saying. I worked so hard to make a fortune, to make a life for my family, but all I did was end up being away from them. If I'd known things would end up like this..."

"That's how I feel," said Kamiyo. "I spent my life studying for a future that no longer exists. All that hard work was supposed to pay off later, but now there is no later."

"I spent my life fighting for a lost cause," said Aymun. "I could have devoted myself to peace and love, but I convinced myself I was put on Earth to fight my enemies. It appears we all three spent our lives unwisely."

They walked for perhaps another couple of miles, the road going by fast. Philip was running out of breath, not as seasoned as Kamiyo or Aymun. For Kamiyo, there was a comforting familiarity about being lost on the road again. You never knew what bounty you would find next. Or what danger. The unknown could excite, even if it terrified.

The outskirts of a town formed, and they passed a row of terraced cottages. Next, they passed a builder's yard and a church. Ten minutes after that, they spotted a supermarket—and then two more right behind it. The three glass and brick buildings clustered together, competing via their giant signs and posters.

"Wow," said Philip. "That actually turned out to be pretty easy. I thought we'd get ripped apart by demons the moment we stepped out of the forest, but we haven't seen a single one."

Kamiyo nodded. "They move in packs. Sometimes you can go days without seeing any if you avoid the towns and cities. Stay on your toes though. You never know when they'll suddenly leap out and try to eat you."

Philip nodded, and it pleased Kamiyo that the man had forgiven him enough to accept advice.

Kamiyo stepped over to a line of hedges and crouched behind them. "Come on," he whispered. "Quick and careful."

Philip and Aymun did as Kamiyo asked, and the three of them hurried towards the first of the supermarkets. It wasn't a brand he often frequented before the fall of civilisation—too expensive to please the thrifty buying-habits of his parents. Now money was no object, so he prepared to fill his boots with whatever he could find.

The automatic glass doors obviously didn't open as they approached, and when Kamiyo tried to open them with his hands, they didn't budge. "Damn it."

"We'll have to smash our way in," said Philip.

"That might bring attention." Aymun looked left and right. "If the damned dwell nearby, they will hear."

Philip scanned the car parks on both sides of the main road. "It looks clear. I don't see what other choice we have."

Kamiyo explored a short distance. "We should try around back. The loading bay. Staff doors. Windows even."

Philip shrugged. "Yeah, that's not a bad idea. Want me to check?"

"We should all go. Stick together."

The others held no objection, so they followed the building around to the back. They passed a massive collection of trolleys, and a row of giant wheelie bins.

Kamiyo couldn't quite understand it, but something wasn't right. He told Philip and Aymun to keep their eyes open.

A large gate barred access to a side road leading to the supermarket's loading bay, but a small access hatch was unlocked. They passed through it into a litter-strewn area with a single parked lorry. All the litter lay in piles around the perimeter.

They climbed a set of cement steps up onto the loading bay and looked around. Philip tried to lift one of the large square shutters, but it was locked and rattled defiantly. "Looks like we might have to go back to the smashing the doors open plan," he said.

Kamiyo sighed. "I don't think they'll shatter easily. Those things are thick."

"Then how about we try to kick in one of these back shutters?"

Aymun spoke up. "Just as noisy. We need to think about this."

Kamiyo studied the iron poker in his hands. "Maybe we don't need to get the shutters open. Maybe we can just... make room."

Philip didn't understand, but he knew enough to stand back from the shutter and wait to find out. Kamiyo stepped up and rammed his poker into the gap between the shutter and the track it ran in. The poker was too blunt for stabbing, but it was narrow enough to shove into the gap and lever back and forth. Grunting like a mule and trying to ignore the pain in his damaged hands, he worked the poker in every direction until he popped a section of the shutter out of its track. It created a slim opening, wide enough to pass an arm through.

"Wow," said Philip. "You'd think supermarkets would have tougher security."

"Most were staffed 24-hours a day, with security alarms and cameras too. There was no need for them to have six-inch steel doors."

"You think you can work it any wider?" Philip patted his tummy. "I've lost a few pounds recently, but not that many."

Kamiyo locked his knees. He wrenched and levered higher up the track, trying to unseat more of the shutter. Every inch widened the gap further, and after a while, Philip and Aymun pulled at the shutter while Kamiyo worked at it. Eventually, the shutter was flapping about like a towel in the wind. It was still locked in place at the bottom, and attached to the roller mechanism at the top, but there was enough slack for Kamiyo to yank open a gap just wide enough for Philip to pass through. It wasn't the most delicate of entries, but he made it to the other side with some effort.

"Okay, I'm in," he said from inside the supermarket. "You think you can get through as well?"

"I think so." Kamiyo pulled the shutter aside and forced his right leg through. As he moved his weight from one side to the other, the shutter pushed back against him, causing him a mild amount of agony, but with his mangled hands, pain was something he was used to by now. He forced his way through the gap like a struggling cat, face pulling back on his skull as he forced it through. Just when he thought he might get stuck, the thickest part of his chest and skull made it inside the supermarket and he slipped through the rest of the way easily.

He found himself in darkness. Aymun was already halfway through behind him, so he grabbed the man's arm and helped him through. "Thank you, my friend."

"You're welcome. Hey, Philip, what are you doing over there?"

Philip gave no answer. His eyes were wide and there was nothing visible in the darkness of the shadows where he stood. Kamiyo took a step towards him, but before he could take another, something pressed against his head and clicked. "Drop yer weapon. One wee step, pal, an' I'll blow ye fooking' 'ed off."

Kamiyo put his hands up, remembering clearly the day he had first met Frank. *Why does this keep happening to me?*

37

DR KAMIYO

"Okay, okay, just take it easy!" Kamiyo was more annoyed by the gun to his head than afraid. If they were going to shoot him then what could he do about it? He was human, and they were human, which meant they should be on the same side. He told himself to have faith that things would pan out okay.

"Who are ye?" the man at his back demanded, which reinforced Kamiyo's faith that this was a simple case of frayed nerves.

"My name is Dr Christopher Kamiyo. My friend's names are Philip and Aymun. We're just looking for food and medicine. We didn't know anyone was here."

"Well, there is, and ye fooked up, pal."

"Why don't you guys take a minute to calm down and act like gentlemen?" said Philip quite reasonably, but then had to add, "instead of a bunch of neanderthals?"

Kamiyo heard Philip grunt and realised someone had struck him in the back of the head. He tried to turn back to get a look, but the man behind him poked the gun into his back. "Keep moving."

"We are men of peace," said Aymun.

"Ye'll be men in pieces if ye dinna shut up."

They moved through a well-ordered warehouse filled with pallets of food, drinks, and... beer! Christ, they had pallets and pallets of beer, wine, and spirits. Kamiyo almost drooled before they pushed him out of a set of open double doors and into the dimly lit aisles of the supermarket. He wasn't even a big imbiber but getting rat-arsed sounded quite splendid after so long without an emotional release.

The shelves of the supermarket were only half-full, and after a moment's inspection, it became clear that all the perishables had been removed. Everything else had been organised fastidiously. These people were efficient and care-ful. That was why the outside was so neat and tidy. It hadn't added up earlier, but now it did. Most places Kamiyo had ransacked on the road were scenes of riots and demon attacks. Few places remained in order like this. The people here had taken care of the place. It was their home.

There were about two-dozen people, grizzled strangers with faces like battered shoe leather. These people were survivors like Kamiyo and Aymun, not fortunate bystanders like those back at the castle.

"Wow," said Philip. "Look at this place."

Kamiyo scanned the crowd, trying to find a friendly face. "How many of you are here?"

His captor kicked the back of his knees and sent him to the ground. "Shut it! Any questions will be coming out of my mouth, not yours."

Philip and Aymun were forced to the ground as well. Kamiyo did what he was told and said nothing. He did, however, try to take in as much detail as he could. The first thing he noticed was the smell of bleach on the hard-wearing floor.

Then he took in the survivors. They were a mixed bunch —men and women both, and a few infants, but there were no teens or preteens. They all wore clean clothes and were visibly healthy and well-fed. The supermarket had obviously provided well for them. Despite their easy living, however, there was a weariness to each of them that betrayed past ordeals. They glared at Kamiyo with an undertone of violence. Tribalism. He wasn't one of them, and people who were not one of them were a threat to what they had. They were Iraq sitting on a stockpile of oil, and he was America.

The man who'd been holding a gun to Kamiyo's head stepped out in front of him now. He was handsome and strong, with forearms covered in tattoos. His head was shaven, but he wore a thick beard.

"Where did ye three come from?"

"Nowhere," said Philip. "Why are you doing this?"

Philip's indignation wouldn't get them anywhere. Kamiyo took a quick scan of the group, counting numbers and weapons before taking a calculated risk. "We came from a camp in the forest. There are sixty of us." A calculated exaggeration.

"Don't tell them anything!" Philip shouted.

"It's okay," Kamiyo gave the strangers a subtle smile. He noticed one of them was heavily pregnant. "These are good people, like us."

"You dinna know shit about us," said the man with the gun. "So, where's this wee camp I'm supposed to believe ye have?"

Philip grunted. "Dr Kamiyo. Don't!"

"Kielder Forest Park, right near here. It's at the activity centre."

"I know the place," said the gunman, taken aback. He ran a thick palm over his bald skull. "There are really people there?"

"Yes! Good people. We're all staying at the cabin by the lake." Kamiyo saw Philip's expression change as he realised he wasn't giving entirely accurate facts. He seemed to settle and go along with things after that.

"Well, we might be neighbours, but this stuff is ours." The gunman turned to some others standing behind him. "Tie em up and lock 'em in the offices. If there's another group, it might come in handy having some of their people as prisoners."

Philip leapt to his feet. "No way. We need to get back. There's going to be an atta-"

The bald gunman head butted Philip and sent him to the ground bleeding and moaning. At the sight of his companion being hurt, Aymun leapt up and tackled the gunman, knocking him backwards on his heels. Not willing to stand by, Kamiyo got involved too. He launched from sitting, and took the gunman around the thighs, lifting him up and sending him crashing onto his back. Kamiyo landed on top and smashed the man in the face with his elbow. Quickly, he was able to snatch the pistol out of the man's hands.

"No one fucking move!" Kamiyo bellowed, turning the gun and pointing it in the bald man's bleeding face. All in all, he was pretty proud of himself.

No one moved. Aymun helped Philip off the ground.

The elbows to his face had rattled the bald man, but slowly his eyes stopped rolling about in his head, and he was able to focus again. Then he cracked a smile and broke into laughter.

Kamiyo didn't understand. He shook the pistol in the man's face to show this was no laughing matter, but then he realised something was off. The weapon was light, not heavy like he would expect a chunk of metal parts to be. It felt hollow, and as he stared at the barrel, he saw it was not jet black like it first appeared to be, but streaky with flecks of orange showing through from underneath. The gun had been painted black.

"A wee toy," said the bald man, still lying underneath Kamiyo. "A wee squirter."

Kamiyo raised his fist to hit the man in the face, but arms wrapped around him from behind and dragged him away. The man on the ground climbed back to his feet and snarled. He stepped up to Kamiyo, no longer laughing. "Me gun might be fake, but me fists are real, pal."

He smashed Kamiyo in the middle of his face.

The lights went out.

38

TED

Ted was fairly pleased with the rope swing. The lengths of thick climbing rope he'd employed were springy yet tough, and the children bounced vigorously as they swung back and forth. The large wooden crossbeam Ted had attached the swing to had another, more important purpose, but today it worked just fine as a swing.

Moods at the castle were down since Kamiyo and Philip failed to return after two whole days. While there had always been the chance they might remain on the road for a while, the hope had been that they'd return the night of the day they'd left. Ted knew what it was like out there, which was why he was probably most worried of all. That was why he'd set himself to a task, to occupy himself, but he didn't work on any more defences. No, the camp needed to focus on something other than merely surviving. Just for today.

So, he had erected a rope swing from karabiners and climbing rope. The kids were ecstatic. It might not be a Play-Station, but it was the first time they'd had fun since monsters had eaten their world. Watching the children now, smiling and giggling, made Jackie's absence all the more painful. She would've been overjoyed.

Ted needed to go check on things down at the cabin. He did so every morning, to check Nathan was still locked up, and to see if Steven needed help collecting whatever fish had made it into the traps. There were wooden snares too, but they were yet to catch any rabbits. Ted would have to find a way to improve them.

He took his hammer and passed through the sally port, starting down the hill in a diagonal line to keep from tumbling headfirst. Steven remained at the castle, but he knew the man would come down in the next hour. Until then, Ted would have peace and quiet, both things he still very much appreciated. Knowing the kids were happy was enough to lift his mood, even without watching the joy firsthand.

At the bottom of the slope, he started towards the cabin. This morning was the coldest in a while, and dew hung from the tips of the overgrown grass. The wooden planking over the cabin's exterior was damp, as though the building had been sweating.

He continued walking beyond the cabin to a nearby clearing. All the graves there had markers, but the most recent marker had been put there by Ted. It was a sturdy cross made from the thick limbs of an oak tree. A strong, no-fuss marker for a strong, no-fuss woman. He hoped Jackie was some place safe. Some place she would be happy.

"I let Nathan live," he said, as if not murdering a child would somehow impress her. "But I still don't know what to make of him. I wish you could tell me whether he shot you on purpose. Everyone is certain he did. Think I am too. The kid is weird." He blew air out of his cheeks and looked up at the grey sky. "I have to believe it was an accident. If Nathan is a killer... I suppose it would make me question a lot of things. Things that would make me wonder if things would be better if mankind just finished. You would probably argue with me about that." He ran a hand over the loose dirt and imagined her body down there. "I hope you found your George up there, Jackie. Tell him I say hello."

After his one-sided conversation ended, Ted got up and headed back to the cabin, planning to go check on Nathan. He hadn't expected to see Vamps standing there.

Ted raised his hammer.

"Chill!" Vamps put his hands out. "It's me, not... the bad guy."

Ted started up the steps. "You're going down, fucker. Eric was a good bloke, and you gutted him."

Vamps didn't move. "The attack will come tonight while you're sleeping. They'll come right to your front gate and smash their way through any way they can."

Ted stopped in his tracks, only making it up the first step. "What? How do you know that?"

"Because the Red Lord knows, innit? He can sense all the other demons nearby. He knows there's a large group getting closer. They will wait until the middle of the night and then come at you while you're in your beds. It's gunna be bad, yo."

Ted took another two steps up, close enough now to take a swing at Eric's killer. "Like I'm going to trust any word that comes out of your mouth. You're just another monster."

"No, man, I ain't. I get these brief sessions where The Red Lord goes away. I don't know why. But I came to warn you all. Get ready because tonight is the night. They're coming."

Ted ran scenarios through his mind, trying to pre-empt any angle the Red Lord might be working here. Warning Ted to be on his guard didn't seem like something that could hurt him though. Maybe this really was just Vamps trying to do them a favour. The young man had worked amongst them for weeks without causing harm, and as a human he had skin in the game by default. Did he truly have periods of time where he was himself? What happened to the Red Lord then?

Ted decided he couldn't be sure, which meant it wouldn't be acceptable to kill this man who might be innocent. "Okay, I'll have everyone be ready."

Vamps nodded but didn't seem done. "Ted, can I ask you to do me a favour?"

"Now you're pushing it. What do you want?"

"For you to take me out."

Ted didn't understand immediately. "You... want me to kill you?" He looked at the hammer in his hands, wondering if he could do it. He was pretty sure he could. "Are you playing games?"

"No, man. My fight is over. I've done my bit, and now I'm a danger to everyone trying to do theirs. The Red Lord will be back soon, and he won't stop until he wipes every last one of us off the face of the earth. Kill me, and he'll have to find another ride, innit? It's the only thing that makes sense."

Ted took the last two steps, squeezing the hammer's handle. He lifted it over his head but stopped halfway. He let the hammer drop with a deflated sigh.

"Maybe there's no United Kingdom left, but before it fell, we were a nation that didn't execute its enemies. A tradition, I think, that should be retained. I won't kill you, Vamps, but I will take you prisoner. It will be up to the group to decide what to do with you. You killed their friend, and they deserve the right to judge you. If the Red Lord comes back, he'll be our prisoner too. Maybe we'll find a way to get him talking."

Vamps shook his head. "You'll regret it, man. Just kill me. Please!"

"I don't know you, Vamps, but I ain't gunna kill you. Maybe if the Red Lord pisses me off enough, then I'll change my mind, but right now I don't have it in me to kill you. Not if you're telling me you're not the one who killed Eric. No more death."

"But—"

"And if what you said is correct, we don't have time to stand around arguing about it. If you want us to keep the Red Lord from hurting anyone, let us keep you prisoner at the castle. It has plenty of space in the dungeon, and you'll have company."

Vamps frowned. "What do you mean?"

Ted motioned for Vamps to follow and marched into the cabin. He yanked open the door to the First Aid room and found Nathan sitting sullenly on the bed. The boy showed no emotion as he looked up at Ted, but he tilted his head curiously. "Hey."

"Come on," said Ted. "You're being moved to a different cell."

Nathan stood up. "Why?"

"Because tonight, this place is going to be swarming with demons. And I don't want you to die."

Ted took his two prisoners up the hill and into the castle. Then he shared the news that an attack was on its way. This time, nobody in the camp panicked. They were tired of waiting for a fight to come. It was time to get it over with.

39

DR KAMIYO

Through some bizarre twist of irony, Kamiyo's captors placed him and the others in the supermarket's pharmacy. It resembled a cell, but with a counter on one side instead of a wall. Someone always sat on a chair out front watching them.

"They have enough medicine here to keep us healthy for a year or more," said Kamiyo. "Not as many antibiotics as I'd like, but plenty of everything else. We need to make a deal with these people."

Philip pulled a face. "I don't think we have a strong bargaining position right now. And you say there's enough medicine here to keep our camp healthy for a year, but that would be at the expense of this group not having it for themselves. They would have to be mad to give it up. You can tell they know its value because of how organised everything is."

"I do not know what we have that they do not," said Aymun. "These people are afraid, and fear makes people clutch tight to what they have."

"So what would you do, Aymun?" Kamiyo had got to know the man a little over the last couple of days. At first, he was stunned to learn the man had once been part of an Islamic militant group, but then even more flabbergasted when he heard about the man's more recent exploits in Hell. He was a strange man, but always calm and never quick to anger. Kamiyo had started to enjoy the man's presence.

Aymun considered the question. "I would like to give you an answer, but human behaviour cannot be easily predicted. The only way to convince someone to consider an unfair exchange is to make them allies, not trade partners. Do not bargain with them when they are the ones with all the goods. We must implore them towards charity."

Philip huffed. "They're not going to just give us what we want."

Kamiyo didn't know what would happen, but he wished things would move along. All this waiting was driving him insane. He studied the shelves inside the pharmacy, noting how the boxes had been shuffled into matching groups. The people here were fastidious, working, rationing, exercising. They were no different to the people at the castle in many ways—and equally suspicious of newcomers.

Kamiyo was tired of always being a newcomer.

He moved away from the spot he'd been using to sleep. His captors hadn't provided blankets, so he had been using bundles of sealed bandages as a pillow and his coat for warmth. The only time he'd been out from behind the counter in the last two days was whenever he needed to go to the toilet. He was dutifully escorted and led immediately back. The only decent part of his imprisonment was the food. The stale biscuits they had given him with some boiled spaghetti had been sublime.

As always, there was a guard on the other side of the counter when Kamiyo approached. "Hey, I want to speak with Pritchard." Pritchard was the leader of this group, the bald thug who had assaulted Kamiyo and taken him prisoner. The man who carried around a toy gun painted black.

"Pritchard's a busy man," said the guard—an elderly gentleman, rendered weak by an apparent lifetime of smoking and drinking. Kamiyo knew he could overpower the sickly man, but the chances of getting out of the supermarket were slim. There were too many people—too many locked doors.

"I know he's busy, but so are we. We came from a camp just as large as this one. Let's work together. We can trade, protect each other."

The old man sighed, like he didn't have much of an opinion on the matter either way. "Pritchard will come see you when he's ready."

"That's not good enough! Our people are expecting us back. You've kept us here two days already."

"Tough luck. Pritchard's the gaffer, and he's otherwise occupied at the moment."

Kamiyo frowned. "What do you mean?"

"His old lady is about to drop a kiddie. She's not doing so well, and he needs to be with her. That's why he hasn't got round to dealing with you."

Philip rushed to the counter beside Kamiyo. "Chris is a maternity doctor! Dr Kamiyo, tell him."

The old man studied Kamiyo as though he were dressed like a clown at a business conference. "Uh-huh! You don't say."

"I *am* a doctor," stated Kamiyo. "I was a registrar at Manchester Hospital Maternity Ward. Let me help."

The old man huffed. "Women used to have babies just fine without doctors. We have a nurse in our group, and it's nurses what deliver sprogs, anyway."

Kamiyo nodded. "Yes, provided nothing goes wrong. You said it's not going well. The baby could be breech, entangled in the umbilical cord, or a hundred other things. You really want to take the risk that all will go smoothly while you have a trained doctor at your disposal?"

The old man swatted his hand at Kamiyo and groaned. "Fine. Fine. I'll go tell Pritchard you want to help. I'm sick of guarding you three, anyway."

The old man tottered off, leaving Kamiyo, Aymun, and Philip unattended. They looked at one another, all thinking the same thing: *should we run?*

While they were considering it, time ran out. Pritchard appeared, sweaty and breathless. Blood specked his unbuttoned white shirt. "Oliver told me you're a birth doctor, is that true? Is it true?"

Kamiyo nodded. "I was a doctor at a maternity ward. Is your wife okay?"

"She's not my wife, but..." He wiped sweat from his brow and began again. "Things aren't right."

"Take me to her right now."

Pritchard didn't even think about it. He nodded to the counter, encouraging Kamiyo to vault it. Once Kamiyo was on the other side, he waited to see if Philip and Aymun were allowed to follow. Pritchard didn't seem to object, so the other two men vaulted the counter as well.

Pritchard led them all through a staff-only door that led into a corridor. The small administration area that followed had several offices and a large staff room. It was from inside the staffroom that Kamiyo heard moaning.

The pregnant woman he'd spotted two days ago was lying on a sofa with her legs raised on the armrest. She was clearly in labour, but something wasn't right. Despite her moaning, she wasn't in enough pain. In fact, she appeared dozy.

"She's been like this for hours," said a young blonde lady in the room. "I don't know what to do. Shouldn't she be pushing by now?"

"Are you the nurse?" Kamiyo asked.

She nodded.

"What kind of nurse?"

"A general nurse. I worked at a GP's surgery. I'm Becky."

Kamiyo nodded. "Okay, Becky. I'm Dr Kamiyo. I need you to tell me everything. Have her waters broken?"

The girl nodded. Her wide eyes made her young age apparent. She'd probably been a nurse for all of two years. She clearly had no experience with delivery. "Yes," she said. "That's when we knew the baby was coming. We boiled water, got blankets, and gave her pain medicine."

Kamiyo nodded. With that information, he moved over to the labouring woman and examined her. He felt her tummy, and became relatively sure the baby was alive and not in distress. It was when he examined the woman's arms that he found his first clue as to what was wrong with her. "What are these patches on her arms?"

The nurse stuttered, so Pritchard spoke over her. "They're pain killers. The patches are slow-release, which we thought would be best."

"Why did you give her any pain relief at all?"

Pritchard looked confused. "Well, I thought—"

Kamiyo focused on the nurse. "What painkiller did you use?"

She turned toward the corner of the room. "Oh, I have the box over here somewhere. It's, um, bro... buppa..."

"*Buprenorphine*?" Kamiyo surmised.

Becky picked up a cardboard box and studied it. "Yes! That's the one."

Kamiyo shook his head. "You've given her morphine. A patch on both arms. She's in labour."

"Yes, well, I didn't want it to hurt," said Pritchard. "If she was to scream too loud, the demons might hear. The last attack almost finished us and—"

"She needs to push!" Kamiyo yelled at the man, who was a shadow of the combative brute that had put Kamiyo's lights out days earlier. "You've drugged her up to the eyeballs with morphine, and now she can barely stay awake. We need to rouse her and get her body working again."

Pritchard nodded. "I'm sorry. I'm so... Look, just tell me what I need to do."

Kamiyo ignored the man, and instead looked to Philip, standing by the door. "Philip, go back to the pharmacy. I need *Misoprostol*. I know they have it because I've seen it. It will help move things along." He reached down and pulled the patches off the labouring woman's arms. "Maybe look for some caffeine pills too. We need to get her heart rate up."

Philip raced off, colliding with Pritchard and knocking him aside. Becky stood in the middle of the room, fidgeting with her watch. Aymun patted her arm. "Easy child. This is not your fault."

Kamiyo took Pritchard to one side and made certain things clear to him. "There's a good chance both this woman and her child will die—not because of anything I am about to do, but because of the things you have already done. For future reference, when delivering a baby, less is more. Don't administer drugs you know nothing about just for the sake of it. Leave nature to take its course."

Pritchard had tears in his eyes. "Please, just help her."

"I will. Tell me her name."

"H-Holly. We've been together six years. We spent the last three trying to get pregnant, and when we finally do, the fucking world ends."

Kamiyo squeezed the man's shoulder. "These are less than ideal conditions. Let's try to salvage this situation, okay?"

Pritchard nodded, which prompted Kamiyo to get to work. He told Holly what he was doing as he examined her, but she was too out of it to respond. Her cervix was loose and dilated, but the surrounding muscles were lax. The baby was ready to come, but her body wasn't pushing. The morphine was stronger than her hormones.

He felt for the baby's head and found it. "Baby is in a good position, Holly. You've transitioned, and we're ready to get this little bundle out into the world. If you can hear me, I need you to push—almost like you're trying to do a poo, okay?"

Kamiyo still had his hands inside the woman, and he felt a slight flexing around his fingers. If it was Holly responding and trying to push, they might have a chance of pulling this off.

Philip came back with a shopping basket full of drugs. Kamiyo picked out the *Misoprostol* and weighed up whether to use it. "I think we're passed the point where this will help us. Did you find the caffeine pills?"

Philip nodded.

Truthfully, Kamiyo didn't know what he was doing. Labour complications were generally all mapped out, with protocols to follow for each occurrence and a team of staff ready to assist. A morphine overdose, however, was something he'd never encountered. He'd never seen an epidural over-administered even once. Holly was slipping towards a coma at worst, and an inappropriate high at best. The damage was done, and he couldn't reverse it. He could only halt its progression.

He looked for his nurse. "Becky, mix up the caffeine pills with water and try to get Holly to drink as much of it as you can. It's probably pointless, but if we give her even a slight boost, it might give us what we need to deliver this baby. We've just got to hope that Holly is still with us."

Everyone stood in a semi-circle around the sofa, the only

voices were Kamiyo's and Holly's. Holly's moaning had continued, which was a good sign. She still felt pain, which meant
she wasn't unconscious. Kamiyo soothed her as much as he
could, coaxing her to push. Her uterine muscles tightened
irregularly, but it was something. Becky got sips of caffeinated
water down her throat gently enough to keep from choking
her.

An hour passed before they knew it.

Kamiyo had the baby's head between his fingertips now,
and he pulled as gently as he could. His hands were slippery
with blood, and cramped, which made it slow going. He was
no longer sure if the baby was alive. If it was, it was dosed with
morphine. Becky and Philip, to both their credit were alert
and responsive to his every command. A good support team.
Aymun and Pritchard stayed out of the way.

"I can't stand this," said Pritchard after a while. "All the
death and suffering. I just... I thought if we could get this baby
out into the world... If we could just see a birth instead of
more death..." The man blubbered to himself, at a breaking
point.

"Ben, everything is fine. There's a picnic later."

Pritchard froze. "Holly?"

Holly smiled. "Where's Tony?"

"I don't know anyone called Tony. I don't think you do
either."

Becky gave Pritchard a sympathetic glance. "It's just the
morphine talking."

Kamiyo felt a twinge of hope. "No, this is good. Holly was
almost unconscious, and now she's chatting away. She's
moving in the right direction." He got firmer with the woman.
It was now or never. "Holly? I know you're confused, but you
need to push. Pretend you're on the toilet, and you need to
take the biggest shit in your life. Push it out!"

Holly giggled. "You sweared. Push shit out."

"Yes," said Kamiyo. "Push. Shit. Out." He looked at the others. Becky understood. She cleared her throat and repeated the mantra.

Philip twigged next. "Push. Shit. Out."

Pritchard joined in last.

Aymun remained silent and bemused.

Holly chanted with them, giggling. She had stopped moaning now, her pain receptors too dulled to fire, but she was awake. And she was pushing.

The feeling of her uterus writhing around Kamiyo's hands was amazing—like he was feeling life returning to dead flesh. It throbbed and clenched. The baby began to move. He pulled harder, decided that speed was now too much of a factor. His fingers moved higher and Holly pushed harder and harder.

The baby's head came down into the birth canal, held in place by the vaginal walls. Holly continued pushing while Kamiyo still had his hands inside of her. "That's it, Holly! Push! That's so good. It's almost out. Hard as you can now, sweetheart."

Holly screamed, her pain suddenly switching back on. She rose up on her hands and bore down, bellowing like an angry gorilla.

The baby slid out onto the sofa like a dead fish. It didn't move. A small pool of blood spread around it.

Kamiyo lifted the baby by the ankles and spanked it. Then he swooped a finger in its mouth to clear its airways. Still it made no sound.

But it stared into Kamiyo's eyes curiously and blinked. A sleepy newborn.

A baby high on morphine.

"The baby's alive, and it's a boy," he said with relief, "but he's suffering the effects of the morphine." With one hand, he parted Holly's shirt, and placed the baby down against her bare chest. Holly giggled, then went silent as she stared at the newborn on her chest. Pritchard ran over to her and kissed her head, completing the family picture.

For the moment, both mother and baby were alive. Kamiyo would cut the umbilical cord and check Holly wasn't hemorrhaging, but that was about all he could do. Nature would decide the rest.

Philip patted Kamiyo on the back. "That was pretty spectacular, Doctor. What should we do now?"

Kamiyo shrugged. "Now we try to make a deal."

40

HANNAH

The sun lingered majestically over the lake as though God wanted to make their last day special. From atop the castle walls, the forest below was an oil painting of mixed greens, oranges, and browns. The chirping of the birds and trill of insects, however, was absent. Did they know the demons were coming? Were the monsters already in the forest?

Hannah wished the sun would stay in place forever, never sinking behind the trees. She knew the death that the darkness would bring.

Their time was almost up.

She and Ted were in charge of... well, everything. The only other adults were Frank, Carol, and Steven, and they were keeping the kids accounted for. The last thing they needed was one of them getting caught playing outside the walls during an attack. Hannah had been unnerved when Ted had brought Nathan back inside the main camp, but even more shocked to witness the re-emergence of Vamps. Ted had encountered the man down at the cabin, and like Kamiyo, had been convinced that he was an innocent man.

Everyone in the camp wanted Vamps dealt with, but no one could agree on how. Murder was the most popular vote.

Hannah's rifle had seven rounds left, but she'd not held it since Nathan had used it to murder Jackie. It was stowed inside the pantry, but she retained the bolt carrier assembly in her pocket. The weapon was useless without it.

The dark ages had returned where people took refuge behind wooden stakes and stone walls. They would fight, not with tanks and grenades, but spears and bows. There would be no amnesty for women and children.

Ted had been working all afternoon to dig a ditch beyond the portcullis, making it even harder for the demons to assault the gate. He was still out there now and surrounded by all the male teenagers. What on Earth was he up to?

Hannah headed down the stone steps and ducked beneath the half-open portcullis. "What's going on, Ted? Why is everybody out here?"

Ted turned around with a slight grin on his face. "We're just taking a piss. Want to join us?"

Hannah frowned. "Huh? I don't understand. The latrine is on the other side of the camp."

To her amazement, the teens whipped their dicks out and started pissing on the ground right next to the ditch Ted had been working on. Ted seemed amused by her confusion, but he didn't explain what was going on. Instead, he put a hand on her back and moved her from the obscene scene. "How are we looking, Hannah?"

She chewed at her lip and shrugged. "As good as we're going to get. Frank has rigged up a load of plastic bottles and tin cans in the trees as a kind of alarm system. Was a good idea actually."

Ted chuckled. "He told you it was his idea? I told him to do that, the cheeky bugger."

"Oh…" Hannah chuckled too. "The sod. Well, we're all set. Just need to hunker down and get ready. Tonight is going to be the biggest night of our lives."

"I have a few more things to do first," said Ted. "The teenagers will need to fight, so I want to make sure they all know what to do. The attack will come at our front. Has to."

Hannah nodded. "The hill is steep on the other three sides, obviously, but if they come from the lake, they could try to make it through the sally-port. It's weaker."

"They'd be sitting ducks," said Ted. "They'd have no cover, and every time they lost their footing they'd tumble back down and have to start again. Vamps said the attack would come from the front, and it's the only strategy that makes sense."

"Okay, so if we're sure the attack will come from the front, we need to get the kids back ins—"

Ted waited for her to finish, and when she didn't, he frowned. "What is it? What's wrong?"

She shushed him. "Listen!"

Ted concentrated. There was a rattling sound—tin cans and plastic bottles.

Frank's rudimentary alarm system.

Terror seizing him, he turned towards the teens, now doing up their flies. "Lads! Get your pricks away and get your arses behind the walls. Now!"

41

DR KAMIYO

Kamiyo had to stop for two minutes to catch his breath. The shopping bags he carried weighed a tonne, and his backpack was so heavy it threatened to tip him backwards. Philip, older and less athletic, was struggling even worse, and had to use his spear to lean on. Aymun acted as though the pack on his shoulders was full of feathers.

"I'm wondering if I can make it back," said Philip, taking off his backpack to give his body a rest. He rotated his shoulders and winced. "Jesus."

"It is true," said Aymun. "I am a donkey lost in the desert, and I too must rest."

"You look like you could do this all week," said Philip incredulously.

"I know my body well, and it is ebbing."

Kamiyo sighed while prodding at the weeds with his poker. "We already wasted too much time as Pritchard's prisoners. We shouldn't rest for too long."

The other two men nodded their heads in agreement.

Holly and her newborn son had recovered from their ordeal with nothing worse than exhaustion. The labouring mother's failure to progress could have been fatal to them both, but now that it was over, they should recover well. Before leaving, Kamiyo had sorted out Folic acid and other supplements from the pharmacy to keep Holly and her baby healthy, and Pritchard had been so grateful, he'd told Kamiyo and Philip they could take whatever they could carry from both the supermarket and pharmacy. His people had seemed a little perturbed by that largesse, but no one argued. He found out from Becky that demons had attacked the group on several occasions, and that Pritchard's leadership was the only reason any of them were still alive. He had been a police officer before and had taken charge when things turned bad. Pritchard wasn't such a bad guy.

Kamiyo, Aymun, and Philip had filled their rucksacks full of rice, grains, and noodles; and stuffed pill packets into their pockets and half a dozen carrier bags. They even found seeds for tomato plants, mint, radishes, and cabbages. Even after that loss, the supermarket group still possessed a veritable bounty of supplies. In exchange for the supplies, Kamiyo had told Pritchard everything about their camp in the forest—how to get there and how protected it was. He told the man to bring his group and come join them. Together they would have everything they needed—supplies, protection, and manpower. Pritchard's group wouldn't have to worry about being defence-less anymore. Pritchard responded that he would think about it, and that they were free to leave with his thanks. There was no apology for the hostility of the last three days, but Kamiyo supposed it was water under the bridge.

Kamiyo estimated the castle would now have enough supplies to withhold a siege for several months—providing the walls took care of everything else. Having spent so long on the road alone, Kamiyo had seen enough of the demons to know their capabilities well. He couldn't imagine them bringing ladders and scaling the walls or constructing trebuchets and mangonels.

But he couldn't see them giving up either.

Philip heaved his backpack onto his shoulders again and puffed. "We should get moving again. The demons could attack any time. I'm sorry I'm dragging us down."

Kamiyo's own body was close to falling to pieces too, but he consoled himself by telling himself that once he made it behind the castle walls, he would collapse and take a rest. He just needed to push himself a little longer. "You're fitter than you give yourself credit for, Philip. I thought I was in good shape after being out on the road so long, but you're matching me step-for-step."

He smiled. "Used to do the London marathon every year. My wife had brain cancer, so I used to run to raise money."

"I'm sorry."

"Don't be. She beat it. Went through a year of hell, having to shave her head and puking all the time, but she never gave up. I suppose the marathons were a way for me to thank her for that—to suffer just a little of what she did. She could have given up and left me and Bray all alone, but she didn't. I always used to think of her cancer as a monster, eating her insides, but it was real-life monsters that eventually killed her. None of us had any idea, did we? If I had known what was coming..."

Kamiyo nodded. "You would have spent more time at home with your wife, with Bray? Anything but work your arse off for a future that didn't exist."

Philip looked at him, a glassy look in his eyes. He nodded.

"Me too," said Kamiyo. "I wish I'd experienced the taste of living before it all turned to ash and chalk. Philip, you had a wife, a child, businesses... I never got to have any of that. I envy you, Philip, even if I would never ever wish for the amount of pain you're in."

Philip stopped walking and seemed upset. His Adam's Apple bobbed up and down. Eventually, he put out his hand. "Thank you, Christopher. I'm sorry I gave you such a hard time. What you did back there to deliver that baby..." He sighed. "I know there was nothing else you could have done for Bray."

Kamiyo held the man's hand tightly and looked him in the eye. "We might have lost whatever chance of a life for ourselves, but there's a castle full of kids that still have a future. We just need to keep them safe."

"We will."

Aymun had stood by listening. Now he spoke. "Then we should make haste, brothers."

Kamiyo nodded and resumed walking. He yelped when something struck his face and then gave him a hefty bonk on the forehead. It didn't hurt, but as he stumbled in fright, he caused a racket—the sound of thin metal against metal.

Aymun slunk into the bushes, glancing around like a spooked leopard.

Philip steadied Kamiyo and glanced around warily. "What the heck? Who put these up?"

Kamiyo saw the strings hanging from the branches, each one adorned with cans, bottles, and other pieces of rubbish. "It's an alarm system," he said, then grinned. "It means we're nearly home."

"Thank God," said Philip. "Forget all that stuff I said about running marathons, because I'm going to puke if I don't sit down soon."

Kamiyo gave him a gentle shove. "Not long now. Let's keep moving."

42

TED

The castle courtyard was abuzz. Frank rang the bronze bell beside the well in case there was anyone caught outside. Steven dropped the portcullis.

The adults gathered around the campfire, the de facto lieutenants of the battle to come. Steven shook his head. "You told us the attack would come in the middle of the night. It's still daytime."

"I know," said Frank. "We can't worry about that now. Everything is set up. We're ready. Get your teams in place."

Frank glanced around. "Where's Steven?"

"He's down at the lake," said Hannah. "He hasn't brought today's catch up yet."

"Damn it!" Frank turned towards the rear courtyard. If Steven made it back soon, he would be fine. The attack would come from the front—according to Vamps.

But the young man had also claimed the demons would come during the middle of the night.

"Frank, get up on the front walls. I want to know what's coming out of the forest. Hannah, get up at the rear. I'm not so sure we can trust our Intel. And get Steven back inside these walls."

"Roger that, boss."

"What about me?"

Ted turned to see Carol. He had forgotten all about her. She'd been sickly for a long time after her Typhoid Fever and spent most of her time babysitting the kids. "Oh, Carol, yeah. I, um, need you to get the youngest children inside the castle. Take them to the upper floors and block the stairwell with whatever you can find."

She smiled a quivering smile, one prone to evaporate if she fell victim to panic. "W-Whatever you need, Ted."

Ted turned to the teenagers next, who had assembled themselves into a small regiment. They had spent the last weeks concentrating on nothing but this moment. Each was afraid, but their collective presence steeled them all individually. Teenage peer pressure existed even in this, and no one wanted to be the kid who ran away crying.

Ted addressed them all. "You know your jobs. Get up on those walls and prepare to rain hell."

The teenagers sprinted away, each heading to their own allocated post. Ted was proud of them. He prayed he got to tell them that.

If the demons were coming, did they have a hope of surviving? What if they fought the demons and won? Would that mean the entire area was safe? Would there be others nearby? Other demon armies in Northumberland?

Ted grabbed his hammer from where he'd left it and took some of the tools lying around. His hammer would only come in handy if the demons got inside the walls. It would be a last resort.

He started up the steps leading to the front battlements

and heard Frank calling out his name. "Ted!" he shouted. "Think yow better see this."

Ted picked up speed, taking the ancient stone steps two at a time. He moved up beside Frank, looking out over the edge of the wall.

Something emerged from the forest.

"Thank the stars!" Ted grinned, his tummy turning a somersault of relief.

Kamiyo waved at them from the bottom of the front approach. Philip and Aymun walked beside him. All three were encumbered with bags and bags of supplies.

"Hurry up, kidda!" Frank shouted down at them. "A lot's happened while yow been gone."

Kamiyo and the others started up the hill, about to pass through the gate. They looked tired and weary, and the weight on their backs was substantial.

Their return was just in time.

It appeared Vamps might still have been telling the truth. The demons hadn't attacked yet.

"OH NO!" A shout came from across the courtyard, all the way from the rear wall. "SHIT! HELP! HELP!"

Ted saw Hannah waving her arms to get his attention. She cried out hysterically.

Ted's stomach sank. Of all the people to over-react, Hannah was the least likely. He sprinted down the steps and raced across the courtyard, his hammer bashing against his jaw as he hefted it over his shoulder. The more he saw Hannah panic, the more he panicked himself.

He made it over to the rear steps and hurried up the battlements. Hannah grabbed him and shoved him up against the wall, making him look down the hill. Steven was down by the cabin.

Four-dozen demons chased him.

"No," said Ted. "No, no, no. They were supposed to come from the front. Everything is set up at the front."

"He ain't gunna make it," said Hannah gripping the edge of the wall. "Come on, Steven! Run!"

Steven was a picture of terror, arms pistoning, face like a bleached-white bedsheet. The demons shrieked at his back, enjoying the chase. Amongst their charred and blackened corpses, were leaping beasts and leering zombies. A full force had arrived.

Ted was silent, gripping the wall alongside Hannah and hoping his stomach didn't burst with the amount of acid swirling through it.

Steven was wailing now. Not calling out for help but wailing deep inside his soul. He started up the hill, slipping briefly but then regaining himself. The man was quick, if from terror or actual ability was impossible to tell, but he might just make it to safety if he kept up the pace.

"I need to get down to the sally port," said Ted, moving from the wall. I have to open it and let him in."

Hannah grabbed him. "What if you can't get it closed again?"

"You want me to lock him out?"

Hannah removed her hand and shook her head. Ted raced down the steps and around to the sally port. Already, he could see the top of Steven's head bobbing frantically. The demons were gaining on him. He still had a lead, but his limbs were struggling now. The speed and incline were too much to take in a sprint. The demons, however, seemed as energetic as ever as they savoured their kill.

Ted yelled out encouragement. "Come on, Steven! You're nearly here!"

Steven must have heard the words because he renewed his desperate effort. His hands became blades, cutting the air—

left-right-left-right-left. It was a gold-medal-worthy effort. He pulled away from his pursuers.

"He's gunna make it," Hannah called from above. "Shite, he's actually gunna make it."

Ted gritted his teeth, sure it was true. Steven had shaken off his pursuers, putting more and more space between them. He was going to make it through the sally port before the demons caught him. God bless the man.

Steven seemed to sense his victory. His wailing stopped, and a grim determination fell over him instead—the same focus Ted witnessed in Hannah so often. The man's fear had gone, and only his desire to survive remained.

Ted opened the sally port and threw an arm, ready to receive Steven and yank him to safety. Instinctively, despite still being ten metres out, Steven threw his own arm out in anticipation. He closed the distance quickly, sprinting in massive strides.

Five metres now.

Four.

Three.

"I got you," said Ted.

Steven reached out both hands, leaning forward.

He cried out.

A massive length of steel pierced Steven's thigh and pinned him to the ground. He bellowed in agony, stuck on his stomach and unable to get at the metal shaft running clean through his leg.

Ted stumbled forwards, needing to reach Steven and pull him to safety.

What had happened? He had been so close.

Hannah shouted at Ted to get back inside, but her words wouldn't make sense to him. He stepped towards Steven, writhing on the ground.

Something monstrous marched up the hill. Not a demon like the others. This was a huge and terrifying creature, three feet taller than any man, and more skeleton than flesh. Its dark eyes swirled with malice.

Ted froze. Hannah continued calling to him, her voice a distant echo somewhere behind him.

The giant abomination crested the hill and stomped towards Steven. Steven cried out for Ted to save him.

Ted couldn't move.

The massive demon clutched the metal spear jutting out of Steven's thigh and wrenched it free. With little interest, he casually rammed the spike into the back of the man's skull as he tried to crawl away. It came out of Steven's eye socket and pinned him to the ground again.

Then the creature turned its attention to Ted, and the open sally port behind him. Ted realised the threat marching towards him, yet he found himself unable to move a muscle. As numb as he may have become to the demons in this world, he had seen nothing so appallingly evil as this creature coming towards him.

I'm sorry Chloe. I can't do this anymore. Wait for me, please. I'm coming.

The vile creature roared, and a foul-smelling wind picked up.

"Wake the hell up, Ted." Hannah shouted in his ear as she wrapped her arms around his waist and yanked him backwards through the sally port. He stumbled backwards, still frozen, and could do nothing but watch as Hannah frantically slammed the gate closed just as the creature made it up to the walls. She dropped the thick steel bar across it barely in time, then reinforced it with several lengths of timber.

Ted felt his fingers move, and then more of his body came to life. Whatever soul-freezing terror had got hold of him began to fade away. He could no longer see that vile abomination, but only a single stone wall kept it at bay. He blinked a few times, then looked at Hannah. They shared a moment of mutual, 'oh fuck!'

"This is really happening, isn't it?" she said, face whiter than he'd ever seen it.

He nodded. "This might be the day we die. You ready?"

Hannah limped towards him, her ankle still sore. "Ready as I'll ever be."

"Me too. Good luck."

"Aye. Lead the way, pet."

"Follow me, luv."

They got to work.

43

DR KAMIYO

Kamiyo's heart lifted to see Ted and Frank waving from atop the wall. Part of him had feared returning to a castle overrun with demons, the bodies of his friends hanging from the walls. But they were alive and well.

Then there had been a hysterical yell, and Ted disappeared from view. Frank remained but was now waving a hand at them to hurry.

"That doesn't sound good," said Philip, heading towards the lower gatehouse as the yelling continued. Ahead, all along the inclined approach, wooden stakes had been driven into the ground. It also appeared that someone had dug a small ditch. It meant heading up the hill would be perilous.

"Should we go around to the sally port?" asked Kamiyo, raising his poker and looking around. "I don't want to end up impaled in a ditch."

Philip shook his head. "We need to get inside and find out what's happening. Just watch your step."

Aymun placed a hand on Kamiyo's shoulder. "Look at your toes as you walk. It is the same way one navigates a minefield."

Kamiyo didn't even want to know how Aymun knew that,

so he sighed and walked on. He navigated the first spike and instantly felt relief. Ted had arranged the stakes to prevent an army marching up the hill en masse, but as an individual, he could pass between them more easily than he'd anticipated.

Frank remained on the front walls as they climbed the hill, but then disappeared, hopefully to raise the portcullis.

"Shit!" Philip slipped and had to put a hand out.

Aymun hurried to gather the man back to his feet. "Go slow, my brother."

The portcullis raised and Kamiyo felt his heart lift. Then he heard distant screaming and feared the relief would be short-lived. It sounded like a man wailing. Kamiyo wanted to hurry, but the ground was muddy. One bad slip could put him on a spike.

Aymun and Philip were right behind him, and he waited for them to catch up. They were using one another to steady themselves, so it seemed like a good idea to stay together. He reached out to help Philip, but his hand froze in mid-air when he spotted something farther down the hill.

Movement.

It took a moment to register, but then Kamiyo's blood turned to ice in his veins. "Aymun, Philip. Run!"

Both men looked back to see what he was on about, and by the time they spotted the hunched-over demon loping up the hill behind them, a dozen more had burst forth from the tree line.

Kamiyo grabbed Philip and pulled him along. Aymun moved with them, until the three men moved in a clambering conga line, holding each other up while trying not to impale themselves on stakes.

The demons spilled through the lower gatehouse and clumped together, approaching fast.

"Where did they come from?" Philip cried.

"They must have been in the forest." Kamiyo scrambled on all fours, trying to keep his laden backpack from tipping him sideways. He dug his poker into the mud to keep himself anchored. "We must have just missed them."

"Words later," said Aymun. "We must hurry."

"No shit!" said Kamiyo.

They moved as quickly as they could, but it was perilous every step of the way. The stakes increased in number, assembled in loose walls now. Kamiyo had to pass through the gaps first, then pull the other men through after him.

The demons pursuing them shrieked and cackled.

Philip lost his cool and threw himself into a gap while Aymun was in the middle of passing through it. The collision unsteadied both men, and while Aymun fell forwards, Philip fell back. The weight of his backpack took over and dragged him down the slope. He let out a scream as he tumbled and rolled.

Aymun clambered up beside Kamiyo, then turned around. "We must go back."

"No, get inside."

"We cannot abandon our brother."

"I'll go!" Kamiyo shoved his backpack at Aymun and slid himself back through the gap before the man could argue. He was the one who had failed Philip's son. He would be the one to go back and save him.

Philip was a flipped over turtle, trying to roll onto his side so he could get up again.

The demons were already on him.

Philip screamed as the first demon leapt on him, a primate-like creature with razor-sharp talons. It slashed at his chest as he struggled to get free of his rucksack.

Blood sprayed the air.

Kamiyo hurtled down the hill, praying he didn't fall

forwards and land on a spike. Without his rucksack, he felt light, and he swung his iron poker with huge force. It struck the ape-like skull of the demon attacking Philip and sent it whirling backwards down the slope. It barrelled into a group of demons behind, which bought Kamiyo some more time.

The demon had slashed Philip's chest open, but it had also cut the strap of his rucksack. It allowed Kamiyo to free the man and pull him onto his knees.

"Come on, Philip. I need you to get up."

Philip was dazed, the wound painful enough to shock him. Blood poured from somewhere on his upper body. If he had any chance of not dying on this slope, he needed to get moving right now. Fortunately, he seemed to realise this, as he wrapped an arm around Kamiyo's shoulder and took a step with his support.

They made slow progress back up the hill.

The demons reorganised behind them.

Ted's spike walls were doing a good job of keeping the demons from swarming, and they were the only reason Philip and Kamiyo weren't dead yet.

That might change at any moment.

"Philip, come on! I need you to move faster, man."

Philip groaned and did his best to increase speed. Kamiyo glanced back and saw demons fast approaching—not just the ape-like creatures, but the blackened and burnt corpses. He also spotted the one he had struck with the poker. It was dead, skull caved-in and smouldering.

Like when he had struck the demon with the skillet in that kitchen almost a month ago.

Kamiyo realised they wouldn't make it. The demons were moving up the slope too fast. He shoved Philip towards the next stake wall and turned to face the first demons coming up the hill. He didn't have time to swing his poker, so he jabbed it outwards instead, stabbing a blackened monster right through the guts. The wound smoked and smouldered, and the demon's entire mid-section fell to ash. Kamiyo backed up the hill cautiously, swinging the poker back and forth in front of him, keeping the demons at bay. They seemed to be afraid, which was something he'd not seen before. It was like how Hannah had described the demon she'd seen in the village. These demons were showing fear, less relentless. More human. The fate of their fallen brother cowed them.

But not enough to stop them.

Kamiyo swung at another demon, and just missed crushing its jaw. It leapt back and blocked the other demons from moving up the hill. It bought Kamiyo another second, and he turned to shove Philip into the gap in the stake wall. Without his rucksack, the man slid through easily. Kamiyo was right behind him.

But as he passed through the gap, something tugged at his ankle. He looked back and spotted a demon lying on its front and clawing at his leg. It must have made a last-chance dive to keep Kamiyo from getting away. It had paid off.

Kamiyo tried to turn and use his poker, but he was too constricted halfway through the stake wall. There was no room to twist around. The demon continued pulling at his ankle while getting itself upright. Once on its feet, it would grab Kamiyo's throat and tear off his head.

"Get the hell off me, you damn dirty monster!"

Kamiyo fell backwards, dragged by his right arm. He thought, for a second, that Philip had recovered and was helping him, but when he looked around, he saw Aymun. The man had placed the rucksacks on the ground to come and help. He yanked Kamiyo through the stake wall. The demon came with him, still clutching his ankle, but now that Kamiyo was free, he swung his poker and took the top of its head off. It slumped to the ground, lifeless.

Kamiyo glanced at the poker in his hands and wondered why it was so lethal. Aymun saw his perplexed expression and gave him his answer. "Iron. It is anathema to the damned. Come, we must hurry."

Kamiyo and Aymun gathered Philip between them, and the two rucksacks, and clambered up the hill. Once again, it was slow going. The demons spilled through the stake wall behind them.

They reached the last stretch of ground before the portcullis, which was now raised several feet off the ground and awaiting their entrance. The demons were close behind them, which posed the risk of them rushing through the gate right behind the men. They would have to move fast to ensure that didn't happen.

"Drop the packs," said Kamiyo.

Aymun stared at him. "We need the supplies."

"They're slowing us down."

Aymun dropped the packs, and the three men picked up speed. The gate was right ahead. They could make it. Safety beckoned.

Kamiyo's feet slid out from beneath him, going in opposite directions. Aymun slid too, and Philip tumbled onto his hands and knees. They found themselves struggling in a sopping wet ditch.

Kamiyo smelt piss.

"What is this?" Philip asked wearily.

Kamiyo slid onto his knees. "The ground is soaked with piss. We'll have to crawl through it."

The three of them swam through the stinking mud, clawing their way towards dry land. The portcullis lay just ahead. It was almost close enough to reach out and grab.

Philip, wounded and losing blood, was the weak link once again. Aymun and Kamiyo had to pull the man between them.

The demons spilled into the space right behind them, but they too were taken by surprise at the suddenly perilous ground. One of the primate-demons crashed to the ground, then struggled to right itself as its limbs failed to find purchase in the piss-soaked mud. The demons behind it toppled, and a pile of writhing bodies grew.

"Keep moving!" Kamiyo cried.

"I'm trying," said Philip. "I'm hurt."

"I have got you, brother," said Aymun, pulling the man along.

The demons got their legs back under them, leaning against one another and treading over one another. The ground became a quagmire, but the demons swam through it.

"They're catching us up," said Kamiyo. "We need to go faster."

A demon reached out and grabbed Philip's trailing leg.

Kamiyo groaned. Would they ever make the short journey to safety? He didn't want to die here in a trench full of piss.

Philip kicked at the demon and shook it loose, but again it grabbed him. Two more demons made it up alongside and grabbed at him too. Kamiyo swung his poker at them but stopping to fight meant he was no longer moving towards safety.

A demon grabbed Philip by the shin. Kamiyo was about to strike at it, but before he made contact, an arrow pierced its flesh. Less than a second later, another arrow planted itself in the demon's skull. It released Philip's shin and collapsed face-first in the mud.

Aymun got a hand on dry land and started dragging himself clear of the trench. He turned back to help Kamiyo and Philip, offering a hand to each.

All three men made it to their feet, but they were

exhausted. They staggered towards the portcullis, ignoring the demons at their back for they had nothing left with which to fight. Arrows continued dropping from above. Kamiyo glanced up to see the camp's teenagers lining the walls.

The battle had begun. Shots had been fired.

Kamiyo shoved Aymun and Philip through the portcullis, then staggered in behind them. A growl caused him to turn back around. A primate demon made it out of the ditch and pounced at Kamiyo, razor-sharp claws ready to open his insides.

Kamiyo stumbled on tired legs. He wouldn't make it out of the way in time. So instead, he shouted, "Frank! Drop the gate."

The portcullis buried itself in the ground. The demon made it inside just in time—except for its lower half, which lay dissected on the other side of the thick iron spikes.

PART III

44

CALIGULA

Caligula cared not about the wooden door slammed shut in his face. He was not here for a quick victory. Too long a famine to feast on this blood too swiftly.

He looked down at the human corpse he'd impaled and removed the spike from its skull. Then, with one massive hand, he lifted the corpse into the air and tossed it over the walls. Let the humans keep their dead so they might wallow in what was to come.

Every soul inside the stone fort would perish before dawn. If it took a thousand troops to achieve it, no matter. Caligula had more than enough loyal creatures at his disposal. That was what had provided the luxury of attacking the fort from both sides. The humans might have high stone walls, but they lacked numbers. Most of them were children—he could sense their skittish heartbeats.

Their flesh would be a delicacy.

Caligula turned away from the castle and descended the steep slope. His troops clambered in the opposite direction, ready to assault the walls. They would do him proud this day, and he would savour their victory.

But there was something troubling Caligula, an ethereal beetle scuttling through the edges of his perception. He sensed a weakness in reality, a thinness to the air. An infernal gate existed nearby—a portal back to the Abyss. He didn't know where it was, but better it be left out of play.

A second presence also troubled him, a being not of this world. An ancient soul more ancient than his own. He did not know the being's identity, and variables were unwanted in war. Even if it were an ally, Caligula did not want their involvement. This victory would be his alone. A god did not share glory.

Caligula reached the wooden cabin at the bottom of the hill and assembled his Germanic Guard. "Torch this building," he told them. "Let the humans watch their tiny world burn. Tomorrow, this land will be reborn. I am Caligula, god of a new and everlasting empire. Go, make war and conquer."

"Yes, Imperator!"

45

HANNAH

Hannah watched the massive abomination retreat down the hill—although *retreat* was not the correct word. As the giant, skeletal creature marched away, a horde of demons threw themselves at the walls, and against the wooden sally port. Every thud made Hannah wince, but slowly, she gained confidence that the walls would not suddenly fall down. They were safe for the time being.

But they were besieged and surrounded.

The teens were impressive, lining the walls with their bows like a bunch of Elvish archers. They loosed arrows with a *pick-pick-pick*. Hannah could not see if their shots landed beyond the wall, but she could see the enemy amassing behind the portcullis, rattling it inside its alcove.

Ted climbed back up to the wall above the sally port, firing his nail gun she had retrieved for him at the demonic assemblage below.

"I need my rifle," she shouted up to him. "I stored it in the larder."

"Then go!"

Something flew over the wall and clattered into the courtyard. Hannah covered her mouth to keep from screaming when she saw it was Steven's mangled corpse. "Oh god..."

Ted saw it too, and looked sickened, but then he glared at Hannah. "Keep your head. Go get your rifle."

Hannah dragged her eyes away from Steven's corpse and sprinted across the courtyard. The pain in her ankle disappeared as adrenaline turned her body superhuman. She would have to make her remaining rounds count, but before she retrieved her rifle, she couldn't help but check on the other defensive line at the front of the castle.

Frank led the teenagers above the portcullis, barking commands and directing the fight. Hannah shouted up to him and asked if he had things under control.

He looked down at her. "Everything is bostin, kidda. The buggers are sliding around all over the place down there while we bury arrows in their skulls."

Hannah looked through the portcullis and watched the mass of demons. Some clawed at the gate, but beyond them was a pile of thrashing bodies. She understood now why Ted had instructed all the teenagers to piss down the side of a ditch. To attack the gate, the demons needed force, and it was very hard to apply force when you couldn't get your feet underneath you.

Satisfied that Frank was in charge, Hannah raced into the castle to retrieve her weapon. She had only seven rounds in the mag, but it would be seven guaranteed dead demons. She would make every shot count.

The Great Hall was empty, which made the fire blazing in the hearth oddly disquieting.

"Help me, please!"

Hannah halted. The voice was muffled, coming from beneath her. The dungeon.

"I need help. I'm hurt."

It sounded like Nathan and seeing how he was only one of two people being kept in the dungeon, she didn't see how she could be mistaken. The boy was a killer—possibly a psychopath—but he was also just a kid. If he was hurt, she couldn't ignore him.

She grunted in frustration and then headed for the castle's staircase and headed for the dungeon.

Nathan continued shouting. "He's crazy. Keep him away from me."

Shit! Vamps must have gotten loose. The prisoners were tethered to an iron hoop on the wall but, lacking handcuffs, they had been forced to use nylon rigging from one of the lake's sailboats. It was possible Vamps had got himself free.

She pulled the Ka-Bar from her belt, its weight immediately reassuring her. Nathan had gone quiet now, merely sobbing to himself.

The dungeon was dark, lit by a collection of candles in the centre of the room. Shadows flickered and danced on the walls and ceiling. Nathan huddled in the corner.

She went over to the boy.

"Nathan? What's happened?"

"Help me, I'm hurt!"

She hurried over to the boy. His forehead rested against the wall, and he was completely still. It felt odd. Wrong.

"Help me, help me, help me, help me."

"Nathan, stop! Just tell me what's—" She put a hand on the boy and turned him around to face her. His face was covered in blood, and he was unconscious.

So how had he been calling out for help?

Hannah sensed a presence to her right, and she turned just in time to see something slice through the shadows.

Vamps struck Hannah in the side of the head and sent her to the floor. She tried to get back up, but he kicked her ribs and sent the air rushing from her lungs. She clambered through the dark, trying to find safety, and then she realised she still held the Ka-Bar knife.

Vamps stalked her, but she flipped onto her back and sliced at the air. The tip of the large military knife caught Vamps under the knee, and he withdrew with a hiss before the shadows swallowed him up.

Hannah blinked and strained her eyes, trying to see in the dark. Vamps flickered in and out of view, but mostly he dissolved out of sight.

"Help me!" cried Nathan, although the voice came not from the boy who remained slumped in the corner. It was Vamps, using Nathan's voice in mockery. "Help me, please!"

"Fuck you, man. You're gunna die, I promise you."

"Death holds little meaning to that which is eternal. For you, it means endless suffering in the darkest corners of the Abyss."

"Sounds lovely. I need a holiday."

Vamps shifted in and out of the shadows, his eyes oily and his jaws full of wickedly sharp teeth. "Your petulance will fade with your screams. You think these walls will protect you? Even now, a gate opens in your midst, and my faithful Fallen shall crush you like ants."

The pain in Hannah's ribs became bearable, and she scrambled to her feet. She searched for Vamps in the dark, but he was nowhere. His presence strangulated the air itself, but all she saw were shadows.

What had he meant? A gate was opening? Did he mean the one beneath the lake?

And what of the Fallen?

Hannah took a step, wondering if Vamps had truly left, or if he was about to leap out at her. The dungeon was still, the shadows themselves seeming to freeze. The candles were the only thing moving, their tiny flames waving in an invisible breeze.

Then the candles blinked out.

"Oh shit!"

Hannah went for the stairs, but a white hot pain gripped her stomach. She gasped but struggled to make another sound after that. Her fingertips moved to her middle and sank into wetness. She was bleeding. Badly.

Vamps emerged from the darkness, his eyes shining like the surface of pennies. "Enjoy the darkness, for it shall last forever."

Hannah slumped to her knees, feeling her life slip away.

TED

The demons were everywhere, spilling out of the trees from all directions. The front approach was the castle's most secure front, with the stake walls and trench keeping the demons bunched up and helpless. Teenagers loosed arrows constantly, gaining confidence with every shot. Frank barked commands at them, keeping them all focused.

It was the rear approach that gave Ted concern. They had set up no fortifications there, and the wooden sally port was weaker than the iron portcullis on the opposite side. There was also that huge, skeletal monster. Ted would advise Hannah to locate the thing and bury whatever rounds she had left into its skull.

But where was Hannah?

She'd been gone too long. He rifle was stowed in the pantry which was right inside the castle. She should have returned before he'd even noticed she was gone.

Ted fired off the last brads he had left in his nail gun, then tossed the power tool aside. Several teenagers joined him at the wall and were burying arrows into the lines of demons hammering at the walls—but it wasn't enough. They would run out of arrows long before the enemy ran out of demons. They needed to do more damage.

Ted decided it was time to test his invention.

He ran down the steps, trying not to look at Steven's corpse, and headed for the children's rope swing. Its true purpose was far bloodier, and he got to work assembling the straps and carabiner clips into their proper locations. Finally, he picked up the pitchfork he had left there and shoved it in between a pair of entwined ropes. He wound the pitchfork around, using it as a large handle, tightening the ropes as they twisted round and round. As he did so, a small basket he had made from wood and a nylon tarp lowered. Once it was all the way down, Ted held the pitchfork in place with a hook and tie.

Here goes nothing.

He had designed the catapult to be maneuverable and light, and he had erected it using a trailer he'd found in the boat shed. It allowed him to wheel the weapon around and point it at the rear approach.

For ammunition, he'd cut blocks of wood from the heaviest trees—beech mostly—and piled them together into a stockpile. He grabbed the first one now and hefted it into the basket.

"Fire in the hole, you ugly shitbags."

Ted yanked the pitchfork from the ropes and stepped back. The tandem ropes untwisted rapidly, lifting the basket into the air faster and faster. At the top, the basket arm hit a crossbar and the block of wood launched into the air.

The catapult was less powerful than he'd hoped, and the block of wood didn't get much air. It sailed over the teenager's heads and only just cleared the wall. But the sound it made on the other side was gruesome, flesh and bone breaking. It had been a successful hit.

Ted wheeled the catapult closer and loaded it again. This time the wooden block sailed over the wall easily and resulted in that same glorious sound of demons being crushed and mutilated.

The teenagers turned back and grinned at him, revealing their delight at whatever they were seeing on the other side of the wall. He had brought them some breathing room. Now he needed to do the same for Frank.

Ted raced across the courtyard with his hammer but stopped at the old well. Kamiyo and Aymun were there, tending to a badly wounded Philip.

"Shite, is he going to make it?"

Kamiyo nodded, although he didn't seem convinced. "I stopped the bleeding."

"I'll be fine," said Philip batting the doctor away. "Just keep those monsters outside."

Ted chuckled. "I'll do my best. You got things here, Doc?"

"Yeah, we're good. Soon as Philip is stable, Aymun and I will be right on the walls beside you."

"Good man." Ted raced up the steps to join Frank on the front wall. The teenagers were like automatons, moving in rhythm—notch, pull, release, notch, pull, release.

Frank was sweating. "Ted," he said, a breathlessness to his voice. "This is really happening, ain't it?"

"Maybe there's still time for all of this to be a dream. I'm ready to wake up. How are things going at this end?"

"Take a butcher's yowself."

Ted looked over the wall and was shocked to see the ditch filled with demon corpses—a hundred or more. Arrows stuck out of them like porcupine quills."

"They die whenever they touch the gate," said Frank. "Just drop down dead."

Ted saw what Frank meant. Slumped against the portcullis

was a second, smaller pile of smouldering bodies. It was like they had been electrocuted by the iron.

"Well, that's a turn up for the books. Maybe this will all blow over in time for tea." But as Ted scanned the front approach, he wasn't so sure. There might be a hundred dead demons piled at the gate, but there were several hundred more on their way. The ditch was full of bodies, which meant the ground was once again solid.

Ted studied the piles of arrows at the teenager's disposal and estimated they would run out before the job was even halfway done. He put a hand on Frank's shoulder. "Time to light 'em up."

Frank nodded. "Alright, warriors, time to rain fire."

One teenager struck a match and ignited a small bowl of petrol. The other teenagers ceased grabbing their arrows from the main pile and pulled them instead from a smaller pile wrapped in moss and brambles. They dipped each fuzzy arrowhead into a canister of petrol and then lit them on the flaming bowl.

All at once, the teenagers leant over the wall and loosed their arrows, not at the demons, but at predesignated spots Ted had assigned them. The front approach had been soaked in petrol.

The grassy slope burst into flames, smothering a dozen demons in fire while trapping others between the stake walls. The wooden stakes caught fire too, and would reduce to cinders in time, but the loss was worth it.

Ted watched the demons burn with a grim smile on his face. Was this what war felt like—the only happiness was that of watching an enemy die?

With things under control, Ted needed to get back to the catapult. This siege would be a balancing act of trying to protect each side and letting neither fall. So far it was going well.

He hurried down the steps and back into the courtyard. Kamiyo and Aymun were on their feet now, with Philip resting against the well. All three men looked towards the castle—or rather at the person stumbling out of it.

Ted skidded in the dirt and stared in disbelief. "Nathan? W-What have you done?"

Nathan's face was a mask of blood, a wide gash above his left eyebrow. He looked lost, disorientated, but when he saw Ted standing there, he seemed to gain his senses. "S-She needs help," he muttered.

Ted was lost for words, so Kamiyo took over. "What? Who needs help, Nathan?"

But Ted already knew. He charged at the boy, hammer raised above his shoulder. "What the fuck did you do? Where's Hannah?"

Nathan didn't defend himself. He just stood there looking bewildered. "She's in the dungeon. She needs help."

Before Ted could crush the boy's skull, Aymun and Kamiyo bustled Nathan out of the way. Kamiyo put himself in harm's way and pointed to the castle.

"Go find her, Ted. I'll be right behind you, okay?"

Ted glared past the doctor at Nathan. "If I find out you did anything, boy. You'll be dead in the next ten minutes."

Nathan said nothing. It didn't even seem like he was listening.

Ted felt his heart beating against his ribcage as he raced through the castle to the stairs. The dungeon below was pitch black, not even lit by candlelight. Ted was about to call out to Hannah, but then decided he would just go down. He held onto the wall as he took the steps faster than he sensibly should have.

Hannah was too important to lose. She was too capable. Too brave.

She was his friend.

In the darkness of the dungeon, Ted's eyes saw nothing. But his nose smelt blood. He called out then, and his heart leapt when Hannah replied.

"Ted, is that... is that you?"

"Hannah, are you alright?"

"Just a flesh wound. My liver and bowels count as flesh, right?"

He found her in the darkness, having to rely on his fingertips to orientate himself. "What did Nathan do to you?"

"Not Nathan. Vamps."

Ted glanced around even though it was pointless trying to see. "Where is he?"

"Gone. He left me here to bleed to death."

"Well that ain't happening. Come on, get your arm around me."

"No, Ted, just forget about me. You need to defend this place."

"It's all going fine. Don't worry."

"No! Before he left me, Vamps—or the demon formerly known as the fucking Red Lord—told me there was a gate nearby, and that the Fallen were coming."

"What does that mean?" Ted wracked his brain. "You don't think..."

"Yeah, I do! Ted, I think... I think giant demons are going to come out of our lovely lake. It won't matter then how strong our walls are. They'll step..." She stopped to catch a pained breath. "...right over them."

Ted froze in the darkness, his throat turning to syrupy lead. He tasted metal in his mouth and realised it was the tang of Hannah's blood on his tongue.

He grabbed her under the arm and got her up. "You ain't dying in no sodding dungeon, luv. I need you around, you hear me?"

"I thought the only thing you ever wanted was to be left alone."

"Only because I thought there was no one left worth knowing. Now get your arse in gear and move."

With an agonised groan, Hannah limped through the darkness towards the stairs.

47

DR KAMIYO

Kamiyo met them at the top of stairs and helped Ted with Hannah. They carried her out into the courtyard where it was easier to see. The day was drawing late, and the sun gave off only a dull brown light. They sat Hannah down beside Philip, the well becoming an unplanned site for the injured.

Philip nodded to Hannah. "Slashed shoulder from demon claws, how 'bout you?"

"Disembowelled by a Hell God," she replied.

"Okay, you win."

Ted told them what had happened while Kamiyo got to work inspecting Hannah's injures. When he opened her shirt, he looked back at Ted with an awful expression.

"Don't look at me like that, Doc. Just fix it."

"He can't," said Hannah. "Man's not Jesus."

"Well, if Jesus wants to join the fight anytime now, that would be amazing." Ted was furious, that familiar feeling taking hold of him. Why were the demons doing this? What did they have to gain from wiping out a small group of humans? Was it pure evil, or was there a point to all this?

Of course there was.

He had heard all kinds of cosmic bullshit from both Aymun and Kamiyo—although Kamiyo had been regurgitating Vamps' words. The truth was, he didn't care. The demons had no right. This place was theirs.

He pointed at Hannah. "You don't die until I say you can, okay?"

Hannah nodded and smiled. Give 'em Hell, Ted."

"I'll give it back to them." He stormed back towards the front approach, needing to find out where to aim his catapult. Which side needed the back up most?

Then he heard the screams from inside the castle and realised it was neither. Carol and the children had taken refuge upstairs, just like he had told them, but they were screaming for help. The threat had somehow got inside the walls.

Vamps! It must be. After attacking Hannah, he hadn't come out of the castle. He had gone upstairs.

Ted raced inside the castle and over to the main stairwell, taking the cold stone steps two at a time. On the third floor, he encountered the first pieces of furniture. The stairs were blocked with chairs, armoires, and various other antique hardware from the castle's bedchambers. Carol had done a good job of barricading the entrance to the upper floor.

But somehow Vamps had got through.

The screaming stopped.

"Carol! Carol, are you up there?"

"...Ted? Is that you?"

"Carol, is everything okay?"

"Y-yes. What's going on? We heard screaming."

"What? I thought it was you. Are the children okay?"

"Yes, we're all fine."

"Damn it." Ted turned and sprinted back down the stairs.

He'd been tricked but didn't know why. All he knew was he'd been drawn away from the fight.

The courtyard wasn't suddenly full of demons when he got there, so Ted looked around to try to figure out the ruse before it was too late.

He spotted Vamps over by the portcullis—squatting down and grabbing it by the bottom crossbar. It weighed over a tonne, but somehow Vamps lifted it, raising the spikes out of their holes in the ground and raising the entire thing towards his head. Shrieking demons prepared to enter, salivating on the other side.

48

HANNAH

Hannah was in the worst pain she'd ever experienced, but she still had control of her limbs. It was hard to think clearly, but with only one thing to worry about, she didn't need all her faculties.

Ted seemed like he had everything in hand, so she took a moment to rest. "Can you strap me up, Doc?"

Kamiyo nodded. "Yes, I can try to reduce your pain. We found medical supplies, but..."

"We dropped our packs outside the gate," said Philip.

"That was stupid." She chuckled. "I could really do with some plasters."

Aymun appeared very sad. "It is never easy to watch a fellow warrior suffer."

"Hey, once, I had to stand guard duty in the freezing rain for eight hours while everyone else was watching England play in the World Cup. I know suffering, and this ain't nothing."

"You would have suffered more if you'd watched the game," mumbled Philip.

Hannah ignored the quip. "Doc, get me on my feet, okay? There's too much to do and too little time."

"What are you talking about? You're out of this fight, Hannha. I'm sorry."

"There's a gate nearby." Kamiyo didn't look shocked when she said it, which made it obvious he already knew. She gasped. "You've seen it? Where?"

"Beneath the lake. It's where Vamps came from. It's been inactive since the night I dragged him out of the water."

"Well, it's going to open back up, and when it does, one of those giant bastards will come through."

"Like the ones that attacked London in the early days?"

"Yeah. Those giant bastards."

"This is dire news," said Aymun. "I have faced the Fallen. They are invulnerable. They will slaughter us all."

Kamiyo groaned. "Thanks, Aymun."

Philip sniggered. "Gotta love a guy who tells it straight."

Hannah focused on Aymun. "There's a way to hurt them though, right? A way to hurt all the demons?"

Aymun frowned, but slowly nodded. "Yes. I have taken part in victories at both Syria and Portsmouth. The demons can be banished back to Hell if they are in the vicinity of a collapsing gate."

Hannah shivered as a gout of blood shot from her stomach. "Ugh, that felt weird. Aymun, how do you make a gate collapse?"

"You pass through it with a beating heart."

"Exactly! And my heart ain't done beating yet."

Kamiyo gasped. "No way, Hannah! It's suicide."

Hannah smirked. "How long do I got, Doc? Think I'll last the week?"

Kamiyo struggled to give an answer. All he could do was shake his head.

"It ain't suicide if I'm already dead. I'll be finished before the sun rises again, and you know it. If I'm gunna snuff it, then let's put my death to some use. Get me to the gate, and I'll sink my ass into that lake like a two-legged elephant."

"It's a good plan," said Philip. "My own odds aren't so great either. I'll be your back up. Maybe we can go down holding hands."

"You got it, buddy."

Kamiyo gave Philip a scalding look. "Philip, Hannah, you're both a little loopy from blood loss, so please refrain from making any monumentally stupid decisions."

"It's not stupid," said Aymun. "I have passed through one of these gates myself, and here I stand before you. Bravery does not always end in death."

"You see," said Hannah. "Maybe I'll be resurrected on the other side. I'm dead anyway if I do nothing."

Kamiyo sighed.

For a moment, it sounded like someone was screaming inside the castle, and they all turned toward the noise. Ted raced inside the castle in a panic. Hannah's instincts urged her to back him up with whatever crisis he was dealing with, but it would be a poor decision. She had a bigger target to focus on, and if she destroyed the gate in the lake, all other problems would eliminate themselves. It would be painful to abandon Ted, but she knew what she had to do.

She hoisted herself upright against the old stone well and then took some deep breaths. Kamiyo bound her torso with bandages, attempting to keep her guts inside. Her vision tilted back and forth like a plane in a storm, but so long as she focused in front of her feet, she was able to keep her balance.

"You sure you want to do this?" Kamiyo asked, looking hard into her eyes.

She nodded. "I should've died with my unit a long time

ago. They fought to the death, but I ran. I ran because I was afraid—because I was a coward." She realised she was crying and hated herself for it. She'd finally admitted out loud how she felt about herself, and it hurt far worse than her bleeding guts. "This is my chance to make things right. This time the demons won't fucking win."

Philip stood beside her, his face ashen from blood loss. "I was a lousy father," he said. "Hardly ever there for Bray, which is why it hurts so much that I lost him. I'll never get a chance to make it up to him, but there's still time for me to be here for these kids. I never sacrificed for Bray, but I will sacrifice for them."

Kamiyo shook his head. "This is insane."

Hannah put a hand on his shoulder. "Doc, this shit has been crazy since the moment those black stones appeared." He smiled at her, and they shared a moment. "You know, Doc, if I weren't a lesbian, I'd probably let you see my tits."

Kamiyo spluttered with laughter. "Oh, well, it's a shame things never worked out that way. So... how do you want to do this?"

"I need to get my rifle. Just get me to the sally port and I'll fight my way out. Philip, you sure you want to step out there with me?"

"Absolutely."

"Okay, then arm up, pet."

Aymun stood next to her. "I should accompany you. I have passed through a gate before."

Hannah shook her head. "Then you've already had your turn. No, Aymun, you need to defend this place. There's no point me closing the gate if everyone is dead by the time I do it."

Aymun sighed in defeat. "Then good luck to you, Hannah. May God see through the void and recognise your courage."

"Yeah. Okay. So, will someone please grab my rifle from the pantry?" She pulled the bolt carrier assembly from her bloody pocket. "It's time to make her whole again."

49

TED

Ted acted without thought, only anger and desperation controlling him. Knowing he couldn't cross the entire courtyard in time to stop Vamps from lifting the portcullis, he hefted his hammer into the air as hard as he could. The massive tool tumbled through the air, cutting an erratic arc. It was the only chance he had.

The heavy copper head struck the centre of Vamps' back, right between the shoulder blades, and dropped him like a lump of coal. The iron portcullis sank back into the earth, dissecting a demon that sought to crawl beneath it. Its body crackled and burned.

Ted closed the final distance between him and Vamps, just as the demon stumbled back to his feet. His left arm dangled from a shoulder six inches lower that it should be. Vamps grabbed it with his opposite hand and wrenched, popping the joint back into place. He did not wince or show any pain.

"You lied to me," said Ted. "You said the attack was coming tonight, and only from the front."

Vamps grinned, his tongue flicking in and out like a

snake's. "Truth and fallacy are human creations. Accept your fates or face further humiliation."

"Accept that this world doesn't belong to you, and I won't have to kick your arsehole into your throat."

Vamps hissed, then launched himself at Ted. Ted was not an agile man, so he only made it halfway out of danger. Vamps struck him in the chest and spun him around. He fell down in the dirt, then rolled aside and back up onto his knees in time to dodge a second attack. He needed to regain his hammer.

Vamps backhanded Ted and crushed his cheek. He fell down again, this time too dazed to get back up.

"Are you maggots the best your god could manage? Weak, flawed creatures that consider themselves superior to all? You are not superior. You are uninspired creations of an uninspired god. I shall replace you with beings so glorious that the sun itself will darken in their presence. Mine will be a universe of perfection."

Ted scrambled to his feet. "Perfection's boring. It's the screwed-up shit that makes life challenging."

"There is no challenge, only futility. You are a mere reflection of your creator's lack of imagination."

Ted grabbed a handful of dirt and threw it in Vamps' face, then used the distraction to scramble to his feet. "You see, that was challenging, but I pulled it off. Lots of things are challenging—like watching Man Utd play, or trying to get an erection after a night down the pub. Sex is one of those imperfect things you hate so much, but trust me, it's the messiness that makes it worth the effort."

Vamps rubbed at his eyes until they were clear of sand. "Then it is the first thing I shall erase."

Ted dashed for his hammer, and this time, when Vamps tried to attack him, he turned and threw himself into a tackle. He landed on top of Vamps and pounded at his face. The rage took hold of him, and he threw down his fists harder and harder, breaking bone and rupturing flesh. Blood went everywhere, and his mouth opened in an animalistic roar. Vamps might be a demon, but Ted was the true monster here.

He lost his mind to anger—but then suddenly realised it wasn't really anger that came over him when he fought the demons. It was grief.

Chloe called out to him from the shadows of his mind. The echoes of her screams rattled inside his skull, and he saw flashes of the balmy night they had torn her away from him. Demons had dragged his little girl from the flatbed of his truck while she slept beneath the blankets he placed on her. The entire under-construction housing estate had kept them safe for weeks, but that night the demons had finally come for them. Ted had been sat with the lads playing cards.

Chloe's screams were the last thing he remembered about her—her wailing voice fading into the darkness as demons carried her away. He should have stayed closer. She shouldn't have been sleeping alone.

All of that grief came out now, along with so much guilt he felt like he might grow wings made from it. His fists reigned down with so much anguish that Vamps' face turned to mush.

But as quickly as the grief came over Ted, it washed away. He fell away from Vamps, panting and sobbing to himself while clutching at the dirt and trying to pull the earth over himself. He wanted to be buried. This needed to be over.

Frank appeared at the bottom of the steps, and saw the emotional wreck that was Ted, but then he saw the bloody remains of Vamps and looked shocked. He looked back and forth, obviously confused, but then raced over to help Ted.

"Kidda, what the heck happened?"

Ted got ahold of himself. "Vamps set us up. H-He was opening the gate. I... I killed him."

"Yep, I'd say yow did that alright. Come on, kidda, let me help yow."

Ted took Frank's hand and got to his feet. He was about to say something when he saw movement in the corner of his eye.

The fight wasn't over.

Ted shoved Frank aside just as Vamps pounced, his face a ruin but slowly reconstructing. He had been aiming for Frank's back, but instead collided with Ted. He hissed and raised a clawed hand to cut through the air.

50

DR KAMIYO

"I have no idea how you expect to do this," said Kamiyo, as he removed the braces from the sally port. While it was a lovely and convenient solution in theory, it wasn't so easy as strolling down the hill and diving into the lake. There were maybe a thousand demons between Hannah and her destination.

And she was dying rapidly.

They were all dying.

Hannah shouted up at the teens on the wall and told them to clear a path outside the sally port. They nodded okay, calmed by their protected positions. The walls really had given them a chance, and not a single demon had got close to scaling the perimeter.

At least not yet.

Philip slumped up against the wall next to the sally port, holding a spear in his free hand. "I say we just walk out there casually, like we're conducting normal business. Maybe it will confuse them enough to buy us some time."

Kamiyo rolled his poker in his hands, hoping it was still magic. "Are you serious?"

"Got a better idea?"

Shouting erupted at the other end of the courtyard, and they turned to see Ted racing towards the portcullis. It was rising.

Kamiyo's blood ran cold. "Oh, no! Someone is opening the gate. If the demons get inside, we're done for."

Hannah shoved Aymun. "Go! Go help Ted. Philip, we need to do this now or it'll be too late. We stick close and smash anything that comes near. If we find open ground, we run. I only need to get to the lake alive. Don't matter if I'm in one piece."

Philip said he understood, which left Kamiyo with no other option but to open the door and let them actually do this. What if he opened the sally port and a stream of demons forced their way inside before he could close it again?

But if the portcullis opened, that would be a moot point. Hannah was right—they either did this or they were doomed. It was nuclear warfare or total annihilation.

"Okay, we need to do this." Kamiyo gripped his poker tightly, trying to will himself to move.

"Then stop standing there like a baby with a shitty nappy." Hannah shot him a pained look that indicated she would like to get going sooner rather than later.

Kamiyo shouted up at the teenagers. "Is it clear?"

They released a barrage of arrows, then shouted back down that things were as clear as they were going to be.

"Okay," said Kamiyo. "After fifteen, I'll open the door."

Hannah glared at him. "Are you joking?"

"Yes, I just thought the moment needed a little levity. After three, you ready? Three... Two... One!"

Kamiyo yanked the handle on the sally port and the heavy wooden door creaked open. It was like opening a gateway to Hell.

Demons spilled over each other like locusts, slashing at the air in the hope they might spill blood, and those at the walls scrabbled at the stone, trying to climb it. They made no progress in that regard, but Kamiyo saw, with horror, that a group of the ape-like monsters were raking at an area beneath the wall—like dogs digging for a bone. Dust and chips leapt into the air as the hole they were creating grew bigger. Each time a demon ran its claws to the nub, another would take its place. It would take them hours, but eventually, they would make it through to the other side. Hannah's mission had to be a success.

Kamiyo stood in the doorway as Philip and Hannah spilled out. Both were bloody and bruised, but each moved with purpose, as if the pain did not bother them. Their pain would have to wait.

Immediately, the demons were on them, a zombie hurrying towards them before the others. "Die," it shouted, somewhat humorously. At least it didn't shout 'brains.'

Hannah pumped a round into the zombie's face and killed it. Philip dispatched a burnt demon with his spear, sinking it into the creature's charred Adam's apple. Then he pulled it out and speared the next through the chest.

They had made a good start.

An area towards the far side of the steep slope was clear, so they started in that direction. They could throw themselves down it and be at the bottom in seconds. Then they would have a hundred metres to reach the lake.

Kamiyo studied the lake now and saw it glowing like it had the night he'd rescued Vamps. Something was preparing to emerge.

Hannah fired off another shot at a lunging ape, but the bullet hit its shoulder and didn't stop it. Philip leapt in front of Hannah and impaled it on his spear, which snapped as the creature fell down on it. Philip swore as he found himself defenceless.

A zombie sprinted at Philip, seeing him without a weapon, but Hannah took it down with another rifle shot. She had claimed to have seven rounds, so already she was down to five. They hadn't even made it to the slope yet.

Kamiyo remained in the doorway, not knowing what to do. He should close the sally port now and leave Hannah and Philip to their fate. Ted would need help with whatever was happening at the front.

And yet, he couldn't bring himself to abandon Hannah and Philip.

A demon spotted Kamiyo standing there, and the open sally port behind him, and sprinted towards him. If he didn't close the entryway in the next three seconds, the demon would spill into the courtyard, and it would all be over.

Philip and Hannah moved slowly, back to back, while trying to cut a path towards the slope. All Philip could do was kick out, and Hannah didn't have enough bullets to kill all the demons in front of her, so she had to resort to using her large knife.

"Damn it!" Kamiyo slammed the sally port closed. The crossbar kicked up and fell into place, locking it.

"Doctor? What the hell are you doing?" Hannah was looking at him in disbelief."

"I'm getting you to that lake," he shouted. He'd made a spur-of-the-moment decision, and now he had to commit to it. He swung his iron poker at the demon that had been hoping to get inside and knocked its head clean off, the iron slicing through its neck like cream cheese. He fought his way to Hannah and Philip and reached them in time to stab an ape about to leap at their backs.

Hannah was still staring at him, bug-eyed. "Doc, what the hell?"

"Just start moving."

They travelled in a loose triangle towards the slope, demons besetting them on all sides. Kamiyo took the brunt of the attacks, knowing his weapon was most effective. The poker carved through demon flesh with a symphonic delight.

Philip watched him in awe. "How are you doing that?"

"It's the iron," said Kamiyo. "Aymun told me demons have a lethal reaction to it."

Hannah frowned. "Then who was lifting the portcullis? That's made of iron too."

"It doesn't matter." Philip put a hand on both their backs and moved them towards the slope. "Let's go for a swim."

Just as they were about to descend the slope, the ground shook. It was a slight, almost imperceptible vibration beneath their feet, but it was enough to make them stop and look around. The demons along the walls and the ones attacking all stopped too. Some of them made a strange gesture of placing their right arms over their chest, like some kind of salute.

"Oh shit!" Hannah stumbled backwards, as something coming up the hill captured her attention.

Kamiyo turned and saw it too—a massive, flesh-patched skeleton the height of nearly two men. "W-What is that thing?"

"Bad news," said Philip.

Hannah grunted and spat a mouthful of blood, then she sneered with bloody lips. "You can just tell he's the kind of guy who borrows your biro and returns it with a chewed-up lid."

Kamiyo frowned at her.

She shrugged. "Just saying, he looks like a knob."

The massive demon stomped towards them. Hannah lifted

her rifle to shoot, but Philip pushed it down. "Save the bullets to get you to the lake. Both of you get moving."

Kamiyo grabbed Philip's hand and pulled at him. "We can all make it if we run."

"No, that thing walks faster than we can run. I'm finished. You two go do what you need to do to keep those kids safe."

"Philip, what are you...?"

Philip shoved Kamiyo away. He collided with Hannah, and in their weakened state, they slid backwards down the slope.

Philip was insane. Instead of running away, he strode right towards the massive monster. Other demons broke from their stupor and surrounded him until it was impossible to see past them.

Philip shouted from amongst the demons. "Kids! On me!"

Arrows rained down on the demons. They fell in droves, and the massive demon caught three or four shafts itself, but they bounced off its exposed bones without causing any damage. It towered over Philip, unperturbed.

Philip managed to see through the carnage to where Kamiyo was struggling to keep his balance on the slope. The man gave a small nod, and Kamiyo returned it.

Hannah pulled Kamiyo backwards down the slope. "Come on. We either die with him or make use of his sacrifice."

Reluctantly, Kamiyo allowed himself to turn his back on the horror, and they raced down the hill to the sound of Philip's agonised screams.

51

TED

Frank wheeled back as Vamps sliced a canyon of blood across his forearm. His small stature aided him, though, because Vamps second attack went sailing over his head.

Ted rushed in to protect Frank. He shoved the man away and turned to face Vamps.

Vamps slashed Ted's face.

Ted's vision turned red. He clutched his face, moaning as the worst, most sickening pain he had ever experienced washed over him.

Blood spewed from his left eye, which now felt foreign and strange as he fingered it—too squidgy. His vision curled inwards like it was being folded in half.

Frank appeared over him and tried to drag him back to his feet. "Jesus, kidda. You still with me?"

Unbelievably, he was. This was a fight for survival, so there was no question of throwing in the towel. He made it back up to his feet, and Frank thrust a spear into his hands.

The teenagers above turned their attention into the court-yard and started firing arrows at Vamps. Ted's bellows of pain must have captured their attention.

Vamps jarred and shook as shafts planted themselves in his body. The arrows jutted out of his thighs and torso, and one pierced the side of his neck. Blood squirted from him as though his body were a sprinkler.

But he didn't go down. Methodically, he yanked out each arrow and tossed them to the floor.

Ted staggered, not towards Vamps but towards his hammer. He finally got his hands on it and no longer needed the spear, so he launched it into the air and buried it in Vamps shoulder. That was enough to drop the demon to its knees.

A few more arrows sailed through the air, but then stopped. Ted glanced up at the walls and knew the teens had finally run out. Their stockpiles were depleted.

"You need to die," said Ted as he gripped his hammer and stalked Vamps. "This place is ours."

Vamps bled from his mouth, which made it a grizzly thing when he smiled. "Over is the sprawl of mankind, the most self-important of creatures. Finished are the ants who think themselves gods. Extinct is the species that thinks itself immortal."

Ted was weary, which was why he had very little to say as he lifted his hammer. "Shut up!"

He heaved the large copper mallet at Vamps' skull, but the demon reached up and grabbed it. He ripped the hammer from Ted's hands and snapped it in two like a twig. Ted crumbled as he watched the thing that had saved his life on several occasions fall to the ground in pieces.

Frank shouted. "Get back, Ted!"

But Ted was incensed. He bunched his fists and swung them like wrecking balls. Each blow landed, but Vamps absorbed them and then grabbed Ted by the throat. "Time to take your other eye."

Ted spat in Vamps' face.

Vamps roared.

Then there was another roar from somewhere close by. Aymun appeared wielding a chainsaw. "I hope you do not mind if I borrow this, Ted?"

Ted smiled. He had forgotten all about the two chainsaws he had brought up from the workshop.

Aymun whirled on Vamps and effortlessly sliced off a hand. Vamps actually cried out in agony and held up the stump of his left hand in panicked confusion.

"No!"

Ted broke free. Frank stood with him. Both men watched as Aymun and Vamps did battle. The demon was squealing and clutching his bleeding stump.

Aymun was quick, almost inhumanely so, and he managed to avoid every one of Vamps' retaliatory blows.

Frank was pulling Ted away, but Ted shook free. "What are you doing?"

"Moving yow to safety."

"There won't be any safety left unless we kill every demon here. I have to fight, even if I lose both eyes."

"Okay, kidda, then fight better because yow losing."

"Thanks for the advice. Now let me go."

Ted raced back to help Aymun, who had managed to avoid getting hit. Vamps' bloody stump was no longer bleeding, and in fact, his hand was regrowing where it had been missing. As much as they had wounded him, he was undefeated. His injuries healed within minutes of being inflicted. Even a severed hand.

The chainsaw was too cumbersome, so Aymun was forced to throw it down and fight bare-fisted. Ted no longer had his hammer, which meant he had to fight the same way. He started running, picking up as much speed as he could in a short distance, then shoulder-barged Vamps as hard as he could. It rocked the demon and gave Aymun an opening. The sprightly man punched the demon in the wind pipe and sent him backwards, choking.

"I fear he cannot be killed," said Aymun to Ted. "Yet we must keep him contained until Hannah completes her mission."

Ted looked at him with his one remaining eye. "What mission?"

"She is a brave warrior, our sister Hannah. She is going to pass through the gate beneath the lake. If she succeeds, we shall win this day. But we must survive long enough to see her victory."

Ted wanted to throw up, and he wasn't so sure it was from the throbbing agony in his ruined left eye. "That's insane. She can't do that! It's suicide."

Aymun shook his head. "It is not suicide. Merely a hastening of the inevitable. Your friend is mortally wounded."

Ted turned to face the courtyard. He was about to head for the sally port, to stop Hannah from being so reckless, but Aymun grabbed him before he could take off. Ted growled. "Get the fuck off of me."

"It is too late. She is already set upon her path."

Frank shouted out and alerted them. Vamps had cantered towards the small man and was about to tear into him. Frank threw himself forwards onto the ground and quickly scrambled between the confused demon's legs.

Ted and Aymun assaulted Vamps as he turned to face them. They grabbed the demon by the arms and attempted to restrain it. If they could just hold Vamps down long enough, even if it meant sitting on him, then perhaps they would give Hannah the time she needed.

If she isn't already dead.

What is she thinking?

She's trying to be a goddamn hero. Doesn't she already know she is one?

Hannah...

Ted growled and lost his temper. He let go of Vamps's arm so that he could pummell the demon's face. Even if he couldn't kill the demon, he wanted to make it hurt. Make them all hurt.

It was a mistake. With less arms holding him down, Vamps was able to snatch at Aymun's face and slice open his cheek. The sudden wound startled the man and made him let go as well. Now Vamps was free again. The demon struck Ted in the centre of his chest and launched him backwards. Aymun tried to grapple with him again, but Vamps pulled him by the arm and hefted him into the air head first. The man hit the ground painfully.

That left only Frank who, to his credit, did not hesitate. He barged into Vamps' hip and unbalanced the demon, but it was only a minor victory, and the demon quickly recovered. He backhanded Frank and knocked him unconscious.

Vamps marched towards the portcullis, which was utterly surrounded by demons now that the teens had run out of arrows. "Enough of this!" the demon roared. "I am no longer enjoying myself. It is time to end this. Enjoy your deaths, for you shall experience nothing after."

Vamps reached down and grabbed the portcullis. This time he was so enraged that he was able to lift the gate all the way up with one mighty heave. The demon held the giant gate over head as if it were made of tin. He glared at Ted with a predatory grin as his fellow demons spilled through the gap. The monster inside Vamps had won.

The demons were inside the castle.

52

HANNAH

Hannah couldn't believe Philip was dead—which was absurd because she'd witnessed the entire world die. Death should not be able to shock her anymore, but Philip's had been an ending on his own terms. That's what made it different.

He had bought them time.

Kamiyo was shocked too, for the doctor remained utterly silent as they slid down the hill on their butts, allowing gravity to pull them faster than they could run.

Once at the bottom, she asked him if he was okay.

"Just tired," he replied. "You still okay to continue?"

Hannah looked around. A group of nearby demons had already spotted them. "Don't think I have a choice." Her guts had gone icy cold, and she wondered how much longer she could stay upright. She raised her rifle and delivered two rapid headshots. "You got these?"

She meant the two remaining demons, still racing towards them after Hannah had just executed their mates. Kamiyo dispatched both with that deadly poker of his. The way it cut through demon flesh gave her the warm and fuzzies. It was a real-life *lightsaber*.

They lumbered towards the lake, Kamiyo having to help Hannah along. Philip had been her backup if she failed to make it into the lake, but now she didn't have the luxury of dying. She needed to stay alive and fight the lure of the beckoning darkness. Her vision swirled, and her lower legs grew gradually numb. Her steps got more and more uncoordinated. Kamiyo kept looking at her with concern. "I'm okay," she kept telling him. "I'm okay."

More demons tried to halt their progress, forcing Hannah to rattle off her last remaining rounds. It felt comforting to toss her rifle down for good, shedding the last memories of who she had been—a soldier in a war already lost. The time of guns and bullets had passed, and she didn't mourn it. If mankind did survive, she hoped it would regrow without the need to acquire such things ever again.

The cabin was an inferno, the entire outer structure was burning. The inside was smoking, and black waves billowed through the main entrance. Their idyllic hideaway had been razed. The loss was monumental, but all they needed was a foothold. A chance to carry on.

"Hey, Kamiyo," she said.

"Yeah?"

"If you survive this... Never stop being a nerd, okay? Be who you want to be."

He smiled drearily. "You have my word."

They were halfway to the lake now, almost past the fire pit out front of the blazing cabin. The heat from the flames grew immense, and they both sweated. The fire consumed the demons too, at least the ones too stupid to keep a safe distance. But there were hundreds more in perfect fighting shape. Most surged up the hill to assault the castle, but a sprinkling spotted Kamiyo and Hannah. They rushed towards them, screeching like birds. A pack of apes made up part of their numbers.

"Keep moving," said Kamiyo, pushing Hannah towards the lake.

"You can't take on all those apes alone. They're too fast."

He pushed her again. He looked handsome then in the flickering backdrop of the fire with his jet-black hair flopping over his face. She hoped he made it through this and found himself a tody piece one day. "I have no choice," he said, echoing her words from moment's ago. "Keep moving. I'll catch up."

"Kamiyo...."

"Move!"

Hannah stumbled away from Kamiyo, leaving him to face certain death. She had counted at least four apes and had previously witnessed a single one take down a dozen men. They were the most deadly of all.

The lake's edge lay only twenty metres away, and no demons barred her path. They amassed to her rear, flooding around Kamiyo.

Her numb legs wobbled, and she almost fell. Several times, her body just plain refused to move. She found herself willing her legs to take another step.

The demons surrounded Kamiyo, and he fought for his life. She wanted desperately to go back and help him, but it would achieve nothing. She couldn't fight anymore. All she had left was death.

And she intended to die after passing through the gate.

The lake had been glowing when they'd left the castle, but now it shone as if a giant torch hid beneath its waters. The surface frothed and roiled.

Something was happening.

Something was coming through.

She didn't have long.

Neither did Kamiyo. He took out the first ape with the first swing of his poker, but the second one dodged aside and took a swipe at him. He avoided the blow but proceeded to dance around desperately to stay alive. The apes were too quick and unpredictable for him to strike.

Hannah had to move quickly.

She focused everything she had left on making it to the lake's edge. She smelled the musty odour of the water and grinned. Might she actually manage to do this? It had been an insane plan, but her body was holding on.

The swans and ducks took flight from the churning waters, and the grey sky swallowed them up. Night was on its way, but Hannah would not live to see it. She was okay with that. Her death should have been beside her squad mates two months ago in Derby.

She was right at the water's edge now, passing by the boat shed Ted once slept in.

"Where are you slithering, little worm?"

Hannah halted, which didn't take much for she was barely moving. Before her stood the skeletal giant against which Philip had made his last stand. If there had been any doubt in her mind that Philip was dead, this was proof.

"Just leave me alone," she said, feeling like a petulant child, but having no other offence to offer.

The creature cackled. "Do you even know what stands before you, worm? I am the god, Caligula."

Hannah frowned, worried that her vision was darkening rapidly. "Don't have a clue what you're on about, pet."

"I am Gaius Julius Ceaser Augustus Germanicus, son of the great Germanicus, heir of the emperor Tiberius, and greatest of all rulers of Rome. I ascended to godhood upon my death, and now I am here to offer civilisation back to the world. Behold, my faithful guard."

A dozen large, muscular demons appeared from behind the boathouse, all clad in dirty sheets. She looked for an escape, but the only retreat was back to Kamiyo, who was as doomed as she was.

Hannah wobbled, her body begging to collapse. She couldn't take another step. "I-I don't care who you are, pet. You had your time, alright? You should have stayed dead."

"Kneel before me or find thine limbs torn asunder."

"This is England mate. Only person we kneel to is the Queen."

Caligula snarled, and with a flick of his bony wrist he summoned forth his bodyguards. As if he needed any.

The dozen muscular demons stalked towards her but were then distracted by something. A tiny demon appeared from the other side of the boathouse and launched a rock. The clump of stone sailed through the air and struck Caligula right in the face. The massive monster was absolutely stunned. So were his guard who froze in place, staring at the tiny demon who had assaulted their leader.

Caligula eventually spotted the demon too. "R-Rux? You earn yourself an eternity of torture, you fool! Guards, seize him!"

The tiny demon made an obscene gesture and shrieked. "Fuck you, Imperator!"

Caligula's jaw dropped in astonishment.

The tiny demon bolted with impressive speed, and Caligula's entire guard gave chase. That left just Hannah and the giant demon.

"I'm not quite sure what just happened, pet. You okay?"

Caligula was touching his cheek where the rock had hit, and for a moment, it seemed like he might actually walk away in complete despair. Then he seemed to shake himself back to task. He glared at Hannah. "You wish to break the seal beneath this lake, worm. Your plan is desperate and foolish, but you may see it out. Go on! Attempt to earn your glory. See if you can defeat a god."

Hannah couldn't make it to the water. She was finished. The horror was too much to bear. Unable to keep looking at the abomination in front of her, she looked away.

Kamiyo was holding on, but was bloody and battered. He had dropped his poker and was merely buying time now. Soon he would become too exhausted to dodge anymore, and the demons would tear him apart.

Hannah didn't know whether to watch her own death or the death of her friend, so she decided to close her eyes. But before she did, she saw one of the demons around Kamiyo fall.

But Kamiyo had been facing the other way.

Then another demon fell down, not dead, but badly hurt.

A *thud-thud-thud* sounded as rocks fell from the sky. Was it hailing? No, these rocks were too large. There were pieces of brick, too, and other chunks of masonry.

The demons were confused. Kamiyo gained some breathing room as they looked around, confused. He slumped to the ground, exhausted.

More rocks fell. Some struck the demons in the head and knocked them unconscious, others hit limbs and broke them.

What was going on?

A line of strangers broke from the tree-line—thirty or forty people at least.

Incredible.

The strangers each bore arms, some hurling rocks from large sacks, others chopping and hacking at demons with large knives and axes. They were methodical and uncowed, people who had faced demons before and learned how to shed their fear.

The demon army was taken completely by surprise. Their attackers delivered mortal wound after mortal wound, wasting no time in doing battle. It was chop-hack-move on. Demons fell by the hundreds.

And then something magnificent happened.

The demons started to run away.

In an increasing wave, the demons melted into the forest. Many screamed out garbled words that sounded like pleas. The demons were afraid. Their will had been broken.

Hannah turned to Caligula who was visibly concerned. But not by the sight of the demon army routing. He was, instead, staring off across the lake. The frothing waters had begun to violently churn.

A huge hand broke the surface of the water and clawed towards the darkening sky.

One of the Fallen had arrived.

It was all over.

Hannah collapsed onto her side, knowing her life was ticking down in minutes. She would have just long enough to see the slaughter of her friends. The giant demon would emerge and step over the castle walls. It didn't matter that the demon army was retreating, for one giant unkillable beast would be enough to eradicate every soul inside the castle. It had all been for nothing.

The huge creature continued rising from the lake.

Caligula was enraged, bellowing curses at the lake while petulantly stomping his feet. "No! No, this is *my* victory. Why are you here? Who summoned you? Who? Leave here at once!"

Caligula wanted no part of whatever was coming through the gate, and it had consumed his attention entirely. It bought

Hannah a modicum of pleasure in her final moments to know that the demons fought amongst themselves. Maybe they would be no different to humanity and would soon start killing each other.

Hannah's eyelids grew heavy, and she felt herself drifting away. She felt the same calm, determined focus she always felt in battle, but this time, it was peaceful and warm. Wherever she was going would be okay. It would be better than the horrors of this world.

At first, she thought she was seeing things, hallucinating as her brain shut down. Her darkening vision detected movement at the edge of the lake, moving among the reeds. It was Nathan. The boy was pushing a boat out onto the water. A rope encircled his neck, fastened at the other end to a large paint can.

What is the boy doing?

But she knew.

Hannah smiled and closed her eyes.

53

NATHAN

Nathan hadn't shot Jackie on purpose. Everyone thought he did it, but it wasn't true. It didn't mean he hadn't killed her though. Of that he was guilty, whether he had meant it or not.

When he'd fled the castle that night, it was with the intention to run away. He was afraid. The demons would come, and he wanted to survive when they did. Kamiyo, Ted, and Hannah were the only ones at the camp with any clue about how to stay alive. They had all made it out there on the road, and he needed to learn to do the same. That had been all he'd wanted that night.

But when he'd stumbled across Hannah's rifle, his plans changed. Suddenly, he asked himself the question of why he even wanted to survive so badly. Everyone hated him, not just now, but always. He'd never had any friends because he was so strange and morbid. He knew he was different. The bizarre and disturbing interested him more than it should have, but it wasn't intentional. Something about death and suffering just drew him in, made him yearn for answers that might be lurking there beneath the surface. Death fascinated him—but that didn't mean he wanted to be the cause of it. No way.

The only death he ever intended to cause that night was his own. Finding the rifle had seemed like a gift, a chance to make it all normal again. No more monsters or living in the woods with a bunch of people who hated him.

But it hadn't been as easy as he'd thought. When he tried to put the barrel against his forehead and pull the trigger, he found it difficult to do. The weapon was heavy and kept tipping away from him.

Then Jackie had leapt out of the shadows, barking his name. He had flinched. The rifle fell away, and his finger clenched around the trigger. To this day, he didn't understand how the freak-shot had occurred. The bullet could have gone in an infinite number of directions, but instead, it had struck Jackie right in the chest and killed her instantly.

Every night, he cried about what he had done.

Eventually, those tears had become too much.

Then came his latest miseries. Locked up by his camp mates, he had been left with nothing but silence and regret to keep him company. Then, today, Ted had moved him into the dungeon with that monster, Vamps. He was pretty sure the monster had killed Hannah. She'd been moaning on the ground when he'd awoke in the darkness. Vamps had almost killed him too, although he didn't remember how.

All he had wanted then was to get Hannah's help, but he was confused, feeling like his head was being held underwater. So he had groped his way to the steps to find an adult. An adult to please just make it all okay. He was tired of being afraid.

Ted had blamed Nathan of course, and almost flattened him with that hammer, but the doctor stepped in and saved him. After they pulled Hannah out into the courtyard, they completely lost interest in Nathan, which meant he was suddenly free to do as he pleased.

He had felt a burning desire to get away, to get away from these people who hated him, and who he had wronged so badly. If he was so different, then better he not be around 'normal' people anymore.

Part of him also wanted to leave before he was forced to watch them all die.

He had hung around for a while, thinking about what to do and where to go. Hannah—barely alive—and Dr Kamiyo started speaking about what was going on. He slunk around the side of the castle, deciding to listen to the adults talk while he summoned the courage to escape.

They said a gate was opening beneath the lake, and that a living person could close it by passing through, and that it would then explode like a bomb—a bomb that would only kill demons. The demons who had taken his sister, Sophie, and his mum. And almost everyone else. Suddenly, things had become very clear to him once more. Killing himself was the only answer that ever ended up making sense, but this way he could also do something good. He might never be normal, but it felt important to do the right thing before he died. Maybe his final act would make up for killing Jackie.

So he had slid out of the sally port right after Hannah, Philip, and Kamiyo did. As if through fate, he did so just as the demons around the walls became distracted by some massive creature marching up the hill. They were so enraptured by its presence that he'd been able to clamber down the slope and into the forest without any of them noticing.

He had chosen the forest side of the slope instead of the lake because he didn't want to be seen by Hannah or the others. They wouldn't trust him, and Hannah might even try to shoot him. If that happened, his chance of doing something

IAIN ROB WRIGHT

good would get snatched away from him. Then he wouldn't ever see Sophie again. She would be in the good place, and the only way he could join her was by saving everyone else.

When Nathan re-emerged from the forest behind the cabin, he had been set on immediately by monsters, and as he'd feared, he was completely unprepared. He had forgotten to bring his bow, or any other weapon, and all he could do as they approached him was scream. He wished his mum was there, holding him.

Then adults had appeared, spirits of the forest summoned by his terrified pleas. They leapt out of the trees and started throwing rocks and slashing at the demons with knives and axes. Within seconds, all the demons near Nathan were dead. A large bearded man with a bald head shook him by the shoulders.

"Where's Dr Kamiyo? He told us to come here. Shite, this is a fucking shitshow."

"I... I don't know."

"Damn it! This place is supposed to be safe."

Nathan didn't know what to say.

"Pritchard!" someone shouted. "I think I see the doctor. He's in trouble."

The big man cursed the air, then raced away with his small army. Once again, Nathan had found himself alone and ignored—just a weird kid that no one wanted to be around.

Next, Nahan went into the boat shed, avoiding detection of a dozen large demons that took off after a smaller demon. Inside the boat shed, he found rope and several industrial-sized paint cans. He picked the heaviest and attached it to his ankle via the rope. Then he wandered outside towards one of the row boats that sat along the water's edge. A warm, floaty feeling came over him, and the swishing he always felt in his tummy was gone. He felt calm. For the first time in his life, he wasn't doubting himself or wondering if what he was doing was wrong. It felt good to be sure about something.

Hannah and Kamiyo were both in danger, but he couldn't help them. If anything, their peril was helping him do what he needed. The demons were all distracted. The huge demon by the water's edge was the most distracted of all, staring at the frothing waters of the lake.

A giant hand broke from the water, followed by an arm and an elbow. Translucent skin shimmered over bulging muscles, and as the hand rose into the sky, a massive creature emerged beneath. It was the most beautiful thing Nathan had ever seen—a giant figure with golden wings and fair hair. An angel if ever there was one. Nathan wondered what would happen to it if it died. He hoped to find out.

While he was awed by what he was seeing, Nathan pushed the boat out onto the lake and got in. He bobbed about on the unsettled water, in danger of capsizing, so he picked up the boat's oars and rowed with all his strength.

The angel lifted a leg and waded through the lake. It sent up giant waves that tossed Nathan's boat into the air. His tummy flipped, and he remembered the time he and Sophie had gone on the pirate ship at the safari park. The echoes of her happy squeals put a smile on his face and made him even more eager to join her.

Tears fell down Nathan's cheeks as he thought about hugging her again, being her big brother. It was the only thing he had ever been good at. He might have been weird with no friends, but he had always been Sophie's big brother, and she had loved him. Proof that he was human and not a monster.

The angel spotted Nathan flailing about in his tiny boat, and a grin crossed its massive lips. All of a sudden, its beauty turned terrifying.

"No," Nathan cried, knowing he was so close. "No, you can't stop me. I'm going to do this!"

The massive creature raised its mighty fist into the air, ready to pound Nathan into oblivion.

"No! No, this is my victory. I am Lord of these lands. Why are you here? Who summoned you? Who? Leave here at once!"

The deep, sonorous voice came from the shore, and Nathan looked back to see the large, skeletal creature that had enraptured all the demons at the top of the castle's rear slope. It bellowed all sorts of obscenities—including ones not in English—and its words seemed to cause offence, because the colossal creature in the lake removed its focus from Nathan and glared at the smaller creature on the embankment.

Nathan rowed furiously, aiming for the centre of the lake, at the exact point that giant hand had first emerged. It must be where the gate was located. Beneath the frothing waters, a light shone, but it was fading. Closing.

He was going to be too late.

He rowed and rowed, as hard as he could, his arms burning. His stomach purged itself into his mouth, but he swallowed the burning vomit back down.

He would not give up. This was his only chance to be with Sophie, to make his soul worthy of whatever place now kept her.

Nathan reached the centre of the lake and stood up. The boat crashed up and down on the unsettled waters, but it wouldn't matter now if he tumbled over the side. He was right where he needed to be.

Nathan stooped and picked up the paint can and hoped it was heavy enough to speed his descent. If he drowned before passing through the gate, he wasn't sure what would happen. How deep was the lake?

He perched the paint can on the edge of the boat and took one last look towards the bank. Night had almost arrived, but there was enough remaining light, along with the glow from the burning cabin, to see the army of newcomers driving the demons into the forest. He saw the teenagers up on the castle walls, cheering in victory.

He saw Hannah lying on the ground and Kamiyo climbing to his feet a little beyond that. And he saw the skeletal monster and the massive angel continuing to argue, unaware that they were about to be blown to smithereens.

Nathan threw the paint can overboard and followed quickly after it. On the way down to the bottom, he pictured Sophie's smiling face, and at some point, before he blacked out, he was surrounded by a blinding yellow light. He wondered if it was Heaven.

54

TED

Demons spilled through the gate, and Vamps' burning glare of victory turned Ted's fury to ashes in his mouth. His temper had doomed them all. By lashing out and releasing Vamps' arm, he'd allowed the demon to break free, and then open the gate. Ted's actions had killed everyone.

The demons spread out everywhere, some heading up the steps to get at the screaming teenagers. Ted couldn't bear to see them ripped apart, and yet he deserved to suffer the consequences of his actions. He forced himself to keep his unruined eye open.

Frank and Aymun gathered beside Ted, ready to fight the impossible fight that would see them all dead. Ted would go down fighting, even if he had already failed. It was the only thing he could do.

Vamps was vulnerable while he held the portcullis over his head and seemed to realise it as Ted marched towards him with his fists clenched. A demon got in the way and tried to bite Ted, but Ted grabbed it in a headlock and snapped its neck. He continued towards Vamps, planning to tear the demon's arms off before he died. Even if they grew back, the agony he inflicted would be worth it.

Vamps had no choice but to let the portcullis drop to face the rampaging Ted. The iron spikes sliced two demons right in half and seared a half-dozen more that collided face-first with it.

Vamps threw his arms out to either side of him, and his claws extended. His face twisted into a ghoulish grin, and a nerve-rattling hiss escaped his jaws.

Ted charged, roaring like a viking.

An almighty earthquake knocked them both off their feet. The vibrating *BOOM!* had Ted covering his ears and screaming in pain. He had no idea what was happening.

The air whooshed, picking up leaves, dirt, and debris. Anyone still standing was now blown over or forced to anchor themselves.

A bright light suddenly consumed everything.

Ted's eyes were wide open, yet the light was not blinding. He stared right into it but felt no heat, or piercing stabs in his retinas. He wasn't sure how much time passed, but it might have been years. Tiredness crept into his muscles and he lay back, embracing the end of everything.

Frank's voice brought Ted back to reality. "Kidda, yow gotta open yow eyes and see this!"

Ted opened his eyes and saw stars with the one that still worked. Not stars in his vision but those hanging in the clear, inky-black sky. He sat up and looked around. Frank and Aymun were on their feet nearby, and the teenagers peered down from the walls.

The demons were gone. No sign existed that they had ever even been there besides the clutter of broken arrow shafts. The massive explosion, whatever it had been, had taken the monsters away.

Hannah, you did it, luv! You soddin' saved us all.

Ted grinned from ear to ear, proud of his friend, but already feeling her loss. He broke down in tears, losing control of himself completely. This time, his rage was all gone and all he felt was grief.

55

TED

DAYS LATER…

T ed moved to the front of the group, everyone looking to him to say something. In his previous life, he'd been a divorced builder with a daughter he loved. Now, he was the half-blind leader of a camp and a father to three-dozen children. It wasn't what he had ever planned to be, but it was a role he would never turn away from.

Buried in the ground at what had become the camp's graveyard were three new crosses. One was for Hannah, who had tried to save them all with her dying breaths. One was for Philip, who had given his life to make sure she succeeded. The third was for Nathan, a boy none of them had trusted, but had somehow turned out to be their savour. Kamiyo had witnessed the boy throw himself into the lake when all else had failed. If not for Nathan, everyone here would be dead.

Ted cleared his throat and began. "Before all this happened, I had a daughter. Her name was Chloe. I spent most my life building things, but she was my greatest achievement by far. Until she was born, I didn't know something could be so perfect." He smiled at the thought of her. It still hurt, but the memories also brought him joy. "Last Christmas,

I dressed up as Santa and asked her what she wanted. She told me she wanted to have a sleep over at the North Pole and help Santa deliver all the presents to the good children. She didn't ask for anything for herself, just to help spread joy to others. When the demons came, Chloe, in her innocence, kept telling me I needed to head to the North Pole to Santa's workshop. Santa had invited her to stay and would keep us safe. With all that was going on, I just humoured her with a laugh and a pat on the head. Then the monsters took her away from me, and I realised all of my mistakes at once, in a single moment. I should have spent Chloe's last days heading towards something, not staying still and waiting to die."

He wiped tears from his eyes before carrying on. He pulled the photograph of Chloe from his pocket and held it out to the assembled crowd. "After she died, I promised I would get her to the North Pole, if only in spirit. As long as I was alive, I would head north and drop her photograph, and myself, into the North Sea. Stupid, now that I think about it. The last thing Chloe would have wanted is for me to be alone." He looked at the faces in front of him—his new family. "I'm done trying to outrun my guilt. This is where I'm supposed to be, making Chloe proud by taking care of people and allowing people to take care of me." He wiped more tears from his eyes. "I'm just sorry that my new family is short so many members. Jackie, Hannah, Steven, Eric, Bray, Philip, Emily, and others who I barely even got to know. We will never forget them.

"Civilisation has restarted, and this is our graveyard to remember those who got us this second chance. Hannah and Philip died two nights ago trying to save us, and they did that through their actions. They courageously stepped out amongst the monsters and fought them, which allowed Nathan to slip by unnoticed and throw himself through the gate.

"None of us here understood Nathan. He was strange, and perhaps even dangerous, but he was brave too—perhaps braver than us all. He sacrificed his life to save us all. So I just want to say to Nathan, in case there's any chance he can hear me, that I'm sorry. I'm sorry I wasn't kinder to you Nathan, and I also want to say thank you. Thank you for showing us that we can do the right thing even when people don't deserve it. If Hannah is up there with you, tell her I want my sodding knife back. Cost me a monkey down the pub, that did."

The crowd chuckled.

"Anyway," Ted continued. "Today is a new beginning. The demons are gone because of the sacrifices of our old friends, and we welcome new ones in their place." He pointed to Pritchard and the newcomers from the supermarket. "We will spend the next weeks and months and years building a real community. We don't know what radius the gate cleansed for us, but for the time being at least, we can go scavenging in the surrounded towns with relative safety. Now is the time to gather supplies and find more survivors and reinforce ourselves here. I promise that the next time the demons face us, we will be an army like the one in Portsmouth. We'll push them back every time they dare to attack and show them what Hell truly is. Mankind is not something to be crushed, it is something to be feared."

The crowd cheered and whistled. The teenagers were already looking full grown—the events of the last few days had aged them. With Pritchard's group, they were now almost a hundred strong, and they had learned lessons from the siege that would see them more prepared than ever. Ted would set about reinforcing the walls further and creating a thousand arrows for the bows. He would build more cata-pults, and more spears. He would seek out every scrap of iron that existed. The demons would not be defeated with bullets and tanks, they would be beaten by stone walls and iron gates.

Demonkind was on the run. They had been routed like any other panicking enemy, and that fear, used so effectively against mankind at the beginning, would spread throughout their ranks. Their leaders were falling, and the promise of their paradise was being delayed again and again.

With his words all spoken, Ted moved to the side, next to the charred remnants of the log cabin.

Kamiyo came and joined him. "Can we put a new infirmary on your list of things to build?"

Ted laughed. "You got it, Doc. How are we set right this minute?"

"We salvaged half of what we dropped outside when the siege began, plus Pritchard brought everything we left in the Pharmacy, along with a whole lot of food. We're looking good, and with three groups ready to leave this afternoon, we should bring back more than enough to keep us going. I just can't believe we made it. We really survived, didn't we?"

Ted nodded, but then he sighed. "Not all of us."

"I'm sorry about Hannah. I know you two were close."

"Not as close as I should have allowed us to be. She saved me, Doc. As much as I fought her on it, she saved me. It should be me lying there in that grave."

Kamiyo shook his head. "Don't do that. Don't regret living. Hannah went out the way she wanted to." He took a moment and rubbed at his forehead and stubbly chin. "You still sure we shouldn't tell them?"

Ted grunted. "What? That a giant demon came out the gate and was still alive after the blast? You told me it was hurt. Maybe it ran into the forest and will never come back."

Kamiyo nodded. "It was mangled beyond all recognition after the gate exploded, but it was capable enough to escape into the forest. It feels wrong not letting people know about the danger they might be in."

"They know they're in danger. The specifics don't matter. You and I will ensure they're ready for whatever comes."

"And what about the Red Lord? Do you think he's dead? Aymun wasn't so sure. In fact, he left this morning to go search for him."

"The Red Lord was gone with all the other demons when I opened my eyes. No reason to believe he's any different from them."

Kamiyo didn't seem convinced. "But he was able to touch the iron gate and regenerate after injury. He's in a human body, not a demon one. Maybe the gate exploding didn't affect him like it did the rest."

Ted grunted. "Like I said, he was gone when I opened my eyes. The Red Lord is finished, I'm sure of it."

"I hope you're right, Ted. I hope you're right."

Ted headed for the castle. Whether the Red Lord was alive or dead, there was work to do.

56

VAMPS

Vamps woke up in the dirt, surrounded by trees. His face was wet, and he realised it was raining. The pitter-patter of the droplets on the leaves almost lulled him back to sleep, but then he sat bolt upright. "Where the hell am I?"

The last thing he remembered was being back at the cabin, helping Dr Kamiyo and his patients.

He got to his feet, which would have been fine, except for the fact he made no move to do so. He wrestled his legs back and forth, horrified by the resistance that seemed to come from his own brain. "What the...?"

"Do not defy me human!"

Vamps gasped. Words had come out of his mouth, but they weren't his. The Red Lord was still inside of him, but it wasn't the same as before. Vamps wasn't taking a backseat anymore. He was present.

"W-What's happening to me, man?"

"You are defying a god. Release your flesh to me and be a part of my glory. I am the Red Lord and I command you to obey."

"This... This don't feel the same, man. I... I can fight you."

Vamps's hand clenched into a fist, but he forced himself to open it again. "Ha! You my bitch now."

Vamps bit down on his tongue hard enough to make it bleed. "I am nobody's... *bitch*. You shall obey or die."

Vamps spat blood. "Do what you want, dawg, but I ain't letting you hurt no one else, you get me?"

"Silence!"

"Suck my big dick!"

"Argh! You will burn in a thousand hells for this."

"Look forward to it. Never been abroad before."

A presence emerged from the trees. The expression on the newcomer's face was a mixture of shock and fear, but also, perhaps, happiness? "Vamps, my friend? Is it you?"

Vamps gawped. "Aymun? What the hell are you doing here, man?"

"Is it you?"

"Yeah, it's me. The Red Lord is still here though, except..." His fist clenched again, and Vamps fought to open it once more. He succeeded, but this time he broke a sweat in doing so. "He's still in me, but it's like we're sharing a body now. We're both in control."

Aymun squinted for a moment, obviously thinking. Jeez, Vamps had missed the weird little dude. "I believe," said Aymun, tapping his chin with his index finger, "that the explosion at the gate weakened the Red Lord's hold on you. He can still manifest inside you, but no longer has the strength to cast you aside when doing so. I fear you shall not be in for a pleasant experience, my friend."

Vamps gouged his own cheek and drew blood. "Fuck man, it's like I got demon *Tourettes*. Can you help me with this?"

Aymun folded his hands together and looked very serious. "It is my duty to keep the Red Lord from doing harm, as it is your duty also. Together, the three of us will defy his will."

Vamps frowned. "The three of us?"

Aymun nodded. "I have been searching several days and nights to find you. Along the way, I gained a companion. David, it is okay. You may come out."

To Vamps' astonishment, a burnt, mangled demon loped out from behind the trees. His eyes seemed somehow human —afraid, compassionate... lost. In the most bizarre fashion, he gave Vamps a wide smile. "David help. David want to do good things."

"Traitor!" The Red Lord shouted from inside Vamps.

David shied away but didn't retreat. "David not traitor. David free to choose. David not choose monster. David choose happy."

Aymun grinned. "He is discovering more of himself every day, but from what I can gather, he died as a boy some time during the 14th Century in Wales. Or Scotland. This is not my part of the world, I am afraid."

Vamps shook his head, then forced the Red Lord aside in order to speak. "This is a bad idea, Aymun. You can't trust no demons."

Aymun waved a hand. "Hell's grip on demonkind is loosening. Many are returning to their former selves, which, I grant you, are mostly evil souls, but some—like our David here—are just misguided victims. David's mother was a witch and offered his soul to an archdemon in exchange for great power. His punishment was unjust. Many punishments are unjust. Hell is a place deserving of very few."

"Hell is a broken creation of a broken creator," Vamps spat, then shook himself and apologised. "That was him not me."

"I gathered."

"So, you said you were looking for me? What now?"

Aymun shrugged. "I do not know, my friend, but whatever happens, we shall face it as Heaven's warriors. We have won battles together, yes, but the war is not over. In fact, I fear it has only just begun."

"I shall gut you all and wear you as a cloak. I shall wash my feet in your blood. I shall..." Vamps rolled his eyes and groaned. "Sorry, that was him again."

"Once again," said Aymun, "I shall assume such words are not yours. Shall we begin our journey?"

"Where we going?"

"To Portsmouth. We must inform Major Wickstaff that there are people here in this forest. We must start working together to rid this world of evil, so to Portsmouth we shall go. Destiny leads us south."

Vamps smirked. "A reunion sounds sweet. Let's skiddaddle, bro."

And so they did.

57

TONY CROSS

Tony Cross didn't know why he'd been hailed by General Thomas, but he had a bad feeling about it. As a captain, he hadn't spoken with the General directly before, and he took most of his orders from Major Harvey who was a pompous prick at the best of times.

Most of the Sandhurst elite were dead, which was why Tony was now a Captain instead of a sergeant, and why he'd been deeply involved in the Middle East operations—jokingly labelled 'Operation Bring Back Gaddafi,' referring to the fact the dictator had been a far preferable enemy to the one they now faced.

After the human counter-offensive, Turkey had been liberated quickly, due mainly to its role as a forward-positioning base for western forces. The United States air base there had given humanity a massive advantage against the scattered demon forces. They had used the nation as a launchpad to liberate Syria, already full of armed locals, then Lebanon, Jordan, and Israel. Each country they reclaimed gave them more resources, more men, and more equipment. They took their time, but eventually they had reclaimed Iraq too, and then stomped a foothold into Iran. They were spreading out slowly and cautiously, closing gates and killing the Fallen as they went. They even had a regiment full of willing victims prepared to jump into the gates to close them. Many were locals, old or ill, but several more were devout Muslims who felt it was their calling to die for the sake of others. They were the bravest people Tony had ever met.

The demons were beginning to amass in Iran and Saudi Arabia, the smaller groups forming together and forming greater masses, like cancer cells beneath a microscope. There was much fighting still to be done, but mankind was strong and united. The contingent of the human resistance had left the Air Force base at *Incirlik*, relocating to what had used to be Camp Victory. It surrounded Baghdad airport and was the most secure area of the eastern front.

Tony had been instrumental in gaining that security.

So why did General Thomas want to see him?

General Thomas was a stoic, no-nonsense kind of man, and as such, he conducted business in a large tent outside rather than inside one of the many cement buildings.

Tony marched across the tarmac and approached the guard outside the tent. He didn't know the corporal, but then there were sixteen-thousand soldiers, of mixed nationality, currently working out of the base.

"Business?"

"Captain Cross reporting to General Thomas as requested."

The soldier nodded. "You're late."

"I'm five minutes early."

"That's late." The soldier pulled aside the flap so that Tony could enter.

The only things inside were a large desk and chairs, a laptop and radio, a cot bed, and General Thomas.

"You're late."

Tony saluted and stood to attention. "I apologise, sir."

The general had his hands behind his back, but he brought them forwards now and pulled out a chair. "No matter. Sit."

Tony took a seat on the other side of the desk. He began fidgeting, which annoyed him. The world had ended, and so had his contract of employment. He took orders from this man because he chose to, not because he had to. Yet, a general was still a general. "You wanted to see me, sir? How can I be of service?"

General Thomas pulled a pipe and tobacco from the desk draw. "Do you partake?"

"No thank you, sir."

"Do you mind if I do?"

"No."

"Good." He started to fill the pipe, but kept his eyes on Tony while he did it. "Now, let's get down to business, shall we?"

Tony shuffled in his seat, straitened up, and offered his full attention.

The general began. "Major Harvey is taking over operations in the desert. As of tomorrow, he will be *General* Harvey."

"Oh, that's excellent news, sir. Major Harvey is a good man." *And a pompous prick.*

"Indeed, indeed. That probably leaves you wondering what is going to happen to me, and why I have asked you here?"

"Well... yes, sir."

"Major Harvey isn't the only one getting a promotion. You're a good man, Captain Cross. In fact, you've done more good on the ground than anyone. The men speak highly of you, and your troops are the most lethal we have. Closing that first gate in Syria could even be described as the turning point of this entire resistance movement."

"Oh, well, thank you, sir. I'm just glad we managed to turn the tide here."

"Indeed, and turn the tide we have. Iraq is a brick wall that the enemy will struggle to climb, leaving all those behind it safe to fight on."

"And we'll reclaim Iran soon enough, sir, I'm sure of it."

There was a pause while the general took a drag on the end of his pipe. Once he'd breathed out the smoke, he shifted awkwardly. "Yes, well, that will indeed become a priority at some point, certainly. It's not the main focus right now, however."

Tony frowned. They had the enemy retreating. If they stopped pushing now they would lose momentum. Nothing makes men fight harder than recent victories. "I'm not sure I follow, sir."

"You and I are leaving this blasted desert. The human forces have the resources they need to secure the region, but there's little to be gained by pushing further into Iran. The Americans will remain and keep the line, but the rest of us are falling back to help liberate our own countries. We don't need to reclaim a bunch of desert. We need to win back our homes. Berlin, Paris, Madrid. London. There's no point defending the Middle East while our own interests fall to ruin."

"Our... own interests, sir? Surely our only interests are to survive as a species?"

The general grunted as if he didn't like what he was hearing. "The bigger picture has been secured. Here, at least. It's time to look within. Along with our forces still in Turkey, we are one of the largest remaining populations left on Earth. We have thirty-thousand armed men and women. How many people back home could we save with that number? Our countrymen need us. Britain needs us."

Tony nodded. He understood the sentiment, and would once have agreed. Yet, nations didn't seem to mean what they used to. He had the last months fighting alongside men and women from every nation on Earth. It had been a while since he'd thought of himself as 'British'. There was also something else to factor in. "Isn't there a force already liberating the UK?"

General Thomas took another drag on his pipe, and then blew the smoke into the air. "Yes, yes. General Wickstaff—self-appointed—has led a jolly good counter attack out of Portsmouth, but the lass can only do so much. We, however, can bring home ships, planes, helicopters, bombs, and, most importantly, manpower. We need to get home before the poor lass loses the gains she's made."

"With respect, sir, from what I've heard, General Wickstaff is an extremely capable leader."

"Yes, she's quite the marvel, but nonetheless, she has only made inroads. We need to get back and turn her counter-attack into a full blown offensive. Our home is an island, and there's a real chance we can rid the enemy completely. Once we have secured the British Isles, we will put our might behind the Americans. The United States are in dire straits by all account, and it will take a combined endeavour to get it under control. You shall be my second-in-command during our initial efforts at home."

Tony blanched. Second-in-command? What the hell was happening? A few months ago, he'd been an NCO. Now, he was being asked to serve directly beneath the general in charge of one of the largest armies left on the planet. "I don't know what to say, sir."

"You don't have to say anything, it's not a request. As much as I would love a pool of officers to choose from, I do not have them, so I must promote from within. You are a capable man, Captain Cross, respected by our troops and civilians alike. Our forces will be reluctant to leave this front, but they will gladly follow you home, I am sure of it."

Once again, Tony bristled at the man's authoritative tone. Tony could stick up his fingers and disappear into the desert if he felt like it, and probably take a thousand men with him. But much of what the general had said was true. The Middle Eastern front was secure. It might progress no further, for now, but nor was it in any danger of being pushed back. "Okay, sir. When do we move?"

"Three days. We hope to reach Portsmouth within three weeks. The Navy is assembled and waiting off the coast of Lebanon. We shall board there with everything we have and set sail home. By this time next year, we'll be Morris Dancing on the common."

"I'd rather be drinking a pint down the pub."

The general barked with laughter. "Yes! Quite. Okay, Major Cross, you're dismissed. Report back here at 0800 tomorrow and we shall discuss the logistics. I will attempt to get Major Wickstaff on the wire, too, so we can tell her the good news."

Tony cleared his throat. "That sounds good, sir. Could I ask something? What will General Wickstaff's role be once we arrive in Portsmouth?"

General Thomas frowned as if he didn't understand the question. "To continue to lead of course. She will operate as Colonel while you remain a Major at her disposal."

"But she's a general right now. You plan to demote her?"

"The woman appointed herself General. Colonel is still higher than her previous station. Do you have a problem with the proposed command structure, Captain, because I can get another junior office in here hungry for a promotion."

"No, sir, it's just... What if General Wickstaff refuses the demotion. She might claim equal authority to yourself."

The general sneered, not at Tony but at the thought. "If she behaves insubordinately, I'll have the woman tossed before a Court Martial. Anything else?"

Tony stood up and saluted. "No, sir. Of course, sir, a Court Martial, sir. I shall report back tomorrow as requested."

General Thomas waved a hand dismissively, so Tony exited the tent. As he marched across the tarmac he began shaking his head. *Court Martial? What bloody Court Martial?*

There was going to be another war, and this time it wouldn't involve demons.

58

DAMIEN BANKS

D amien looked out from the rooftop of the police station and steadied his nerves. This recent battle had been a tough one, and many of his allies had fallen. Nancy, the leader of the Hoosier Defence Force, stood beside him, studying the patchwork of dead demons and human corpses littering the courtyard below.

"They know we're here," said Nancy. "They won't stop coming."

Damien nodded. The woman was right. He didn't know who she had been in her previous life, but she was hardened by war and smart as a tack. "This last force was bigger than the others. The demons are reorganising, refocusing. Humanity isn't scattered throughout the planet anymore—it's groups like ours—and the way to wipe us out finally is to come at us in force."

Nancy placed down her AR-15 against the wall and leant over the safety pole, almost like she was in two minds about throwing herself over onto the tarmac. All at once she looked tired. "We can't survive many more attacks like this one. Every fight makes us weaker."

"Then we need to get stronger."

"How? Damien, you still haven't told me how exactly you came through a rip in reality two months ago. The men think you're a demon, one of them."

He huffed. "You know I'm not."

She sighed and seemed to think about it, which upset him. His hurt-pride was apparently obvious because she moved up against him, putting her warm body against his. "I've seen you kill enough demons to know you're on our side, but I also know you're not like the rest of us." She kissed his lips. "Not that that's a bad thing."

He kissed her back. Nancy was a good fifteen years older than he was, but she was attractive, and made slender by the constant battles. As he pulled away, he sighed. "I wish I knew what I am, but my powers never came with an instruction manual. The only thing I do know is that I'm stronger when Harry and Steph are with me, which is why I asked them to meet me up here."

She stepped back. "You're planning something."

He stared down at the dead men and women who had been alive just hours earlier. "I am."

Harry and Hannah arrived a short while later on the roof. Damien spent the wait cuddling Nancy, and enjoying the peace of being human and doing human things. The moments between attacks seemed to grow shorter and shorter.

The Hoosiers had already been holding their own when Damien, Harry, and Hannah had arrived, but they had gathered more survivors and more supplies before settling at this police station. Up until a few weeks ago, it had seemed like they would make it. But the first demon attack on the police station had lead to several more.

"Damien, you wanted us here?" said Harry, smiling as he

walked across the flat roof. The man had been holding up well during the weeks of constant fighting. He was a soldier by trade and past, and thus had found himself thrust into command where he was comfortable. Along with a US Marine Captain that was also part of their group, Harry was a leader amongst the fighting men.

Hannah was with him, and visibly hurt, bleeding from a bandage around her wrist. "One of them bit me," she explained. "Good thing they're not zombies, huh."

Damien moved towards her. "You're sure you're okay?"

"She's fine," said Nancy testily. "A flesh wound. We've all had worse."

Damien grunted at Nancy, wondering if it was jealousy he detected. Nothing had ever happened between him and Hannah. "I need to tell you both something."

Harry folded his arms. "Okay, what?"

"The three of us are special. We can... do things."

Hannah chuckled. "*You* can do things. We just tag along for the ride."

Damien shook his head. "No, I'm just aware of what I can do. You both have power as well. The three of us are totems."

Harry gave a lopsided grin, which he knew was the man struggling not to take the piss. "What's a totem when it's at home?"

"I'm not entirely sure, but a stranger visited me and told me what I was right before I opened the gate and got us out of that bad situation. He told me that there are other worlds, and they are under attack too. The worlds are all woven together in a kind of tapestry. People like us can move around the different strands."

Harry and Hannah were both looking at each other like they were wondering whether or not to restrain Damien and take him to whatever counted as the loony bin nowadays.

Surprisingly, the only one who seemed accepting of what he was saying was Nancy.

Damien was frustrated by his friend's incredulity, so he continued trying to convince them. "You've both seen enough to forget what you think is true, and accept that there's more. I'm telling you that we're—"

"Magicians," said Hannah with a chuckle. "Okay, you're right, Damien. I *have* seen enough to suspend my disbelief. So... what does it mean? What difference does it make?"

"That's what I want to find out. I think... I think we should join hands."

"I don't like where this is going," said Harry. "Are we going to sing?"

Hannah elbowed him. "Nothing wrong with a bit of peace and love. Don't you ever get sick of killing demons?"

"I never get sick of killing demons."

"Do you need me to stay?" Nancy asked, looking uncomfortable and moving away from the wall.

Damien immediately told her to stay. "You're the leader of the Hoosiers. The people here fight for you. Whatever happens, I want you to be involved."

Nancy reddened in the cheeks. She nodded and then settled back on the wall. She had spoken little of herself to Damien, and he only knew from other that she had been married twice before. Once to a Coast Guard captain, and once to a man who had died when the demons arrived. She also had two children, lost forever in England. Her pain was often obvious.

Damien stepped forwards into the centre of the roof. Harry and Hannah met him there, and the three of them joined hands.

"So how does this work?" asked Hannah.

"Last time, I just thought really hard that we needed to

escape." Damien licked at his dry lips. "This time I'm going to think really hard that we need help."

Harry and Hannah nodded. Without being asked, they closed their eyes. It seemed like the obvious thing to do, so Damien did the same.

He gripped each of their hands tightly and strained his thoughts until his brain ached. *Please send help. Whoever is out there, help us, please.*

There was a moment where it seemed like nothing was happening, but he'd experienced that before. He kept on concentrating, and waiting.

Nancy's voice piped up behind him. "Um, guys, I think you better open your eyes."

Damien opened his eyes last because Harry and Hannah were already staring over their shoulders when he looked at them. A gate had appeared on the rooftop, shimmering in the dusky twilight. They had done it.

"You sure that wasn't all you?" Hannah asked.

"I'm sure," said Damien. "I've tried to open a gate on my own before and it never worked. For weeks, I've been trying. It hasn't worked until now."

"Okay," said Harry. "We've opened another gate, but last time we needed one to escape. What's the point of it this time?"

"We asked for help," said Damien.

"Gates don't bring help, Damien. They bring demons."

As if insulted, the gate flickered and shimmered. A shadows formed in its centre, a figure wide and tall. Perhaps too tall to be human.

The thing that stepped out of the gate didn't look like help at all, and when its back exploded into a massive span of jet-black wings, Damien was sure they had made a grave mistake. This thing could not be there to help humanity.

"W-Who are you?" Damien asked, terrified to his core.

The creature stood tall, seven-foot at least. Its wings continued unfurling, casting a deep shadow over them all. It was naked, but for a loin cloth, and obviously male.

Its swirling black eyes peered at Damien, seeming to search out his soul so that it could be devoured. It spoke in a bone rattling baritone. "I am The Defiler. Exalted of demonkind." The creatures voice then rose towards a more human tone and a smile crossed its flawless face. "You may call me Sorrow." Those huge black wings suddenly retracted, as if they had never even been there, and in the newly revealed space stood a short, teenaged girl. "This is my ward, Scarlet."

The young girl grinned awkwardly and waved a hand. "Hi! We're here to help." She then bent slightly and clutched her midsection. "Urgh, do you have a toilet. I'm really bursting."

Damien looked back at Nancy who seemed as lost as he was. So this was what help looked like?

Damien shrugged. *I guess we'll take it.*

WANT FREE BOOKS?

Don't miss out on your FREE Iain Rob Wright horror starter pack. Five free bestselling horror novels sent straight to your inbox. No strings attached.

For more information just visit this page:
www.iainrobwright.com

Iain has more than a dozen novels available to purchase right now. To see full descriptions, visit the link below.

- Animal Kingdom
- AZ of Horror
- 2389
- Holes in the Ground (with J.A.Konrath)
- Sam
- ASBO
- The Final Winter
- The Housemates
- Sea Sick FREE!
- Ravage
- Savage
- The Picture Frame
- Wings of Sorrow
- The Gates
- Legion
- Extinction
- TAR
- House Beneath the Bridge
- The Peeling
- Blood on the bar

Sarah Stone Thriller Series

- Soft Target FREE!
- Hot Zone
- End Play

Iain Rob Wright is one of the UK's most successful horror and suspense writers, with novels including the critically acclaimed, THE FINAL WINTER; the disturbing bestseller, ASBO; and the wicked screamfest, THE HOUSEMATES.

His work is currently being adapted for graphic novels, audio books, and foreign audiences. He is an active member of the Horror Writer Association and a massive animal lover.

www.iainrobwright.com
FEAR ON EVERY PAGE

For more information
www.iainrobwright.com
author@iainrobwright.com

facebook.com/iainrobwright
twitter.com/iainrobwright

Made in the USA
Lexington, KY
23 December 2018